ADVANCE PRAISE FOR
THE CAIRO CODEX

The Cairo Codex is a riveting novel that portrays the unique bonds between two powerful women separated by millennia. Their relationship foreshadows a seismic shift in the Egyptian landscape. A splendidly researched and original historical novel that evokes the beautiful prose and exotic setting of *The Red Tent*.

—Jeffrey Small, Bestselling Author of
The Jericho Deception and *The Breath of God*

Lambert's life in Egypt was the stimulus for this multi-layered historical novel. *The Cairo Codex* combines the three great religions of the Middle East with modern and historical characters, suspense, and the challenges of life and politics in present day Egypt. This creates an altogether fascinating narrative that is hard to put down!

—Dr. Waguida El Bakary, former Associate Dean,
American University, Cairo

The most rewarding experience for any author is to *know* that you have written a great book and that perceptive readers will be able to share your story and enjoy your talent. Such is *The Cairo Codex*—a spell-binding novel of Egyptian history, religion, romance, and politics.

—David Appleby, composer, author of
Bravo Brazil! and *Music of Brazil*

I loved *The Cairo Codex*. After reading the Prologue, I was hooked and immediately felt propelled into Cairo. The writing is strong, as are the characters and story. Bravo! I'm looking forward to the next adventure of Justine Jenner.

—Paul Williams, archaeologist,
U.S. Department of Interior

The Cairo Codex takes us into two worlds, one of an ancient time when one notable woman began to influence history, and another when Dr. Justine Jenner discovers a connection between that world and her own. Readers gain insight into the world of archaeology—a world that, to the uninitiated, may seem a quiet, interesting and ordered world of discovery and scholars. Instead, we find the intrigue and thrill of a more sinister underworld where individuals will do almost anything to either steal the glory of a new discovery or hide a truth that may change the way we think forever. Is anyone right to trust anyone? *The Cairo Codex* can't be put down until the end of the last page and leaves you wanting more.

—Baroness Miranda Taxi,
Il Pero, Arezzo, Italy

The Cairo Codex merges the past and present into a brilliantly original story. Through an accident of fate, Justine finds herself with a stunning primeval text bound to disrupt the sensitive balance of religion, politics, and history. Lambert deftly weaves ancient and modern Egypt into a novel of intrigue, love, and adventure.

—Diane Zimmerman, author,
The Power of the Social Brain and
the forthcoming *Cognitive Capital*

In this compelling novel, the lives of two women, two thousand years apart, become intertwined when the ancient diary of one is found by the second, a young archaeologist, during a violent earthquake in a crypt in Old Cairo. Among the incendiary words contained in the lost diary is an indication of the impact of Buddhism on what would become Christianity and Islam. An original and splendidly researched work of fiction, *The Cairo Codex* encompasses religious and political intrigue in a riveting historical novel.

—Jacquelynn Baas, author,
Smile of the Buddha and
The Mind of the Buddha

THE
CAIRO
CODEX

Also by Linda Lambert:

The Constructivist Leader
Who Will Save Our Schools
Women's Ways of Leading
Building Leadership Capacity in Schools
Leadership Capacity for Lasting School Improvement

THE
CAIRO
CODEX

Linda Lambert

WEST
HILLS
PRESS

DEDICATION

—⚬⚬⚬—

This novel is dedicated to my son, Tod Taylor Green, whose creativity inspires me and loving spirit nourishes me. Tod's knowledge of introspection and meditation provided insight into the power of reflection informing the three major religions discussed in this novel.

I also dedicate *The Cairo Codex* to my mother, Lucretia (Lucrezia) Mae Lashmet, who is portrayed as living the life she had yearned for: imaginative, artistic, and free.

Tod and my daughter, April Smock, had a special relationship with my mother. Together, they shared many creative qualities and seemed to understand things about the world that escaped more ordinary mortals.

Lucretia died in August 2001.

PROLOGUE

Delhi is a great place—most bazaar storytellers in India make their villain hail from there; but when the agony and intrigue are piled highest and the tale halts till the very last breathless sprinkle of cowries has ceased to fall on his mat, why then, with wagging head and hooked forefinger, the storyteller goes on: "But there was a man from Cairo, an Egyptian of the Egyptians, who"—and all the crowd knows that a bit of real metropolitan devilry is coming.

—Rudyard Kipling, *Letters of Travel*

APRIL 8, 2007

THIRTEEN WORN STEPS DESCENDED to the uneven marble floor of the crypt. As Justine ducked into the cool air of the cave at the back of St. Sergius Church, she felt as though she were stepping back two thousand years. Nadia, her UNESCO host, had offered to give her a tour of Old Cairo, but she'd set off on her own this morning instead, eager to reacquaint herself with a city that held so many memories of her childhood visit.

Her boot bumped an electrical cord snaking up the stairs, sending two bare bulbs swinging from side to side, shadowing the crypt with patches of light and dark. She took each step with deliberate slowness, allowing her body to absorb the holy site where Mary, Joseph, and Jesus had supposedly made their home after their flight from Palestine. *Myth or fact . . . or something in between?*

The last time she was here, the crypt had been closed because of groundwater that had seeped in after the '92 earthquake. She and her mother had sat at the top of the marble steps, staring at the water below. "This is a story of history and magic . . ." her mother began, as she often did. While her mother had unraveled the tale of the goddess Isis, Justine had let her mind slip back to what might have been the ordinary lives of extraordinary people in this lonely place.

She could see now that at one time the crypt had served as a three-aisled chapel with an altar near the front wall. She ran her fingers across the smooth plastered walls surrounding four marble-crowned columns and supported by a roughly hewned wooden ceiling, almost feeling the pulse of stories untold. Shadows painted haunting images across the walls. *Perhaps ghosts or saints watch over this holy place.* While she wasn't a religious person, she could, like her mother, be swept up in the power of the historical moment.

She shivered. Somehow, despite the emptiness of the crypt, she was certain that it was here that she would find answers to the questions that drove her, questions that had been pushing against her mind since she was an adolescent.

So what was she seeking?

Nearly four hundred kilometers to the east of Cairo, the morning sun danced a crystalline ballet across the Gulf of Aqaba. Deep below the shimmering waters, the Arabian plate snuggled up against the African plate as it had for millennia. This morning, the earthen plates quivered—only slightly. But enough. Suppressed energy, like flexing muscles, reached the tipping point. The quiver snaked west across the African plate, under the Sinai landmass, beneath the Gulf of Suez, and into the eastern Sahara, creating a long ribbon of rupture. The quake hit Old Cairo some ninety seconds later.

Justine was still gazing at the arched ceiling when her feet began to move back and forth, her body swaying abruptly. *The crypt must be settling into the water table below.* Then a jolt ran up her spine and she was slammed against one of the stone pillars. The lights went out, plunging the crypt into blackness.

The shaking continued for what seemed like an eternity, although it must have been only seconds. Terror washed over her. Suddenly she was nine years old again, riding in the backseat of the family car as it approached the San Francisco Bay Bridge. It was 1989 and the Loma Prieta earthquake was about to rip a section of bridge away right in front of them. "Get out of the car!" her father had screamed. Hand in hand, they'd run east, back toward the city of Oakland. Justine turned around just in time to see their Toyota, and her new ballet shoes, teeter on the ragged edge of the torn bridge and then drop into the bay below.

She realized she was squeezing her eyes shut. Forcing herself to open them, she tried to peer through the darkness toward the direction of the exit. Cracking and crashing sounds deafened her as the crypt came alive. Grabbing onto one of the pillars to steady herself, she coughed as a cloud of fine sandstone dust entered her lungs. Then, to her horror, the pillar began to tilt toward her. She dove to the floor, throwing her arms up to protect her head. Plaster from the ceiling and walls rained down, covering her with a veil of dust. To her right, another of the large columns collapsed with a terrible roar.

Since no light entered the crypt, she knew that the stairwell was blocked. *Has the whole of St. Sergius collapsed on top of me?* Panic possessed her as the first aftershock hit, more ferocious than the initial quake. Huge chunks of plaster tumbled within inches of her face, trapping her in the hollow beneath the collapsed column, which had wedged against the wall of the crypt and held. She didn't move; she couldn't move. But she had to get out of here.

She began pulling pieces of plaster away from her with both hands, the jagged edges cutting her fingers and palms. The air was heavy and thick, sandstone dust crowding out precious oxygen. A thought seized her as she found it harder and harder to draw a breath: *I'm going to die here and no one knows where I am.*

The sound of her heart pounded in her ears. She had to act, to do something. Cautiously, she maneuvered herself into a crouch. The rumbling of the floor beneath her stopped; there hadn't been an aftershock for several seconds. She waited, relieved by the stillness. Careful not to press her back too forcefully against the column above her, she felt around her feet, finding a heel that had broken off her boot and her canvas bag. Then her fingers touched a surface of parched skin—the flaking edges of what felt like a small book. Something that had fallen out of her bag? She tried to remember if she'd been carrying a book, but quickly gave up and stuffed it into the bag with her other belongings.

She had just stuck her head out from beneath the column, searching for an exit, when the second aftershock hit with such fury that the encrusted ceiling collapsed around her, burying her alive.

SPRING, 2 CE

Sunlight skims across the WATER *beneath a pale lavender mist as I watch the Great River Nile come to life around me, warm sand rising between my toes. How long will these mornings be mine? For nearly eight summers I've been free to come to this river alone, to listen to my own thoughts. At home, Mother could never feel the warm waters touch her skin, never travel without a man at her side.*

I step into the river, embraced by the water rising around my ankles. Two white cranes, startled by the approaching light, take flight. Hundreds of birds ascend in harmony while a single pelican swoops into the water, finds its target, and emerges with a mouthful of squirming catfish. In the glassy waters below, blue and white lotuses with toothed leaves offer temporary homes to restless grasshoppers and water beetles. I try to still my worried thoughts. My husband moves slowly now and speaks of home. What will I say, what will I do, when the time comes to return to Palestine? Will I be listened to?

The waters part, two large protruding eyes and a gray leather mound surfacing into sunlight. I laugh as an indifferent purple gallinule spreads its wings and squats between the hippo's eyes. Colorful bursts of acacia, hyacinth, and oleander hug the towering palms around us. Inhaling the fragrant air, I feel a wave of exhilaration. What joy nature brings! Although melancholy is often my companion, I am grateful to God for these moments alone.

I kneel to catch some of the warm, clear water in my pot, and slip my sandy feet into leather sandals. Wet sand clings to the fringe on my tunic and I shake it to loosen the sand's tight hold. The cloth will dry quickly in this heat.

When I lean over the water, my thick blanket of hair divides by a peak at the center of my forehead and frames my oval face, tanned by the Egyptian sun. I see two dimples that deepen when I smile down at myself. I'm beginning to look like my mother.

Still holding on to memories of my youth, I shoulder the pot of water and start up the rise. The first thirst to be satisfied belongs to the sycamore tree near our home. This young sapling came with us from Palestine those many summers ago, the tender root wrapped in damp linen and kept in a small leather pouch at my side. Sometimes we could spare only a few drops of water to keep it alive. No one but I thought it could survive. The sapling is a piece of my life before marriage . . . when I was just me, no longer a child, not yet a wife or mother.

Beyond the sycamore, I water our small garden, tucking my long skirt into my girdle to cradle the vegetables and the figs. As I make my way up the short rise toward home, the sand gives way to patches of pale green grass followed by soil hardened by nature's neglect. Soon the tears of the goddess, the only source of moisture in the land of Egypt, will swell the waters of the Great River, bringing life to this parched land. Those welcome waters will push our families of Babylon to higher ground, but we'll return, and then we can plant the rich soil left by the floodwaters with golden grains for breads. Thankfully, the hungry waters will not come until after Passover.

At the crest of the rise, I turn back toward the Great River. In the distance, three giant pyramids stand north of the exalted city of Memphis, once the home of the pharaohs and capital of the greatest empire the world has ever known. My husband often travels across the waters to Memphis to watch Egyptian craftsmen at work and to buy cedar imported from Lebanon for making fine furniture. I have often gone along, comforted by those rare moments when we can be alone, when we can talk about our sons, our life together in this ancient land. As I gaze across the river, I see the remains of a tall stone pharaoh and giant white lion's head, gods protecting the magnificent golden city, and I spare a moment to pray that our God will protect us. The pot of water grows heavy, and I hurry up the rise to face the day of uncertainty and decision ahead.

℘

Ducking through the portal into our family home, a spacious cave carved into stone, I am surprised to find my husband sitting in shadow on a small chair near the far end of the table. Morning light reflects off the western wall and settles on the glass lantern set into a small niche in the sandstone. A miniature prism of multicolored light captures his attention. Deep in thought, he doesn't notice that I am here.

"Is anything wrong?" I ask, walking through the light into near darkness.

"I am just resting for a short while before I return to work," he says. "My body has lasted me these many summers, but I'm afraid my knees will forsake me while I still need them." Even in the subdued light, I can see his expression, an unfamiliar blend of youthful optimism and aged resignation.

"Are you sure that is all?" I ask, pulling forth a chair. Is this the moment when he will tell me we must return to our homeland? Is it possible that I could stay behind?

"I've many feelings about coming to Egypt, and they weigh on me. We had little choice but to leave when the place of Moses called to us." He pauses—then, seeming to notice something in my expression, asks, "Where are your thoughts?"

I am embarrassed that my own worries distract me. "I'm sorry, my husband . . . Moses called us?"

"Moses called us." He nods and continues, assured of my attention. "Herod was a madman, as are his sons. But I'm not sure we'll ever belong here. My end may be growing near, and our family is far away."

He has found steady work in Egypt—his fine furniture is sold at the weekly market and word of mouth brings farmers from miles around to purchase his yokes. Now that the Romans ask him to prepare the gates for the new fortifications, our family need not worry about our livelihood as before. At one time, such security was more than we could hope for, but my husband knows the Romans have no love of Jews, and he feels a sense of impending peril.

The morning light broadens its reach, reflecting on the sleeping pallets tucked into the shorter sides of the cave. I knew that marriage to a man of many years would be beset with difficulties, but I thought we could grow old together. Now he is growing old without me. I walk to him, taking his face in my hands. With my thumbs I gently smooth the leathery wrinkles around his soft brown eyes. As always, his eyes speak of both his love and acquaintance with sorrow. On either side of his thin mouth, small curved lines are drawn in memory of his frequent smiles. Gray hairs define his chin, eyebrows, and head. But the core of his character rests deep inside, where quiet courage meets humility.

As I hold his face, a tear warms my hand.

"You uncover my heart," he says, placing his rough hand on my cheek and touching my tears. He does not move to brush away his own.

For whom do I weep? "You have given me a life I cherish," I say, sitting close beside him.

"If we had not come to Egypt, we would not have lost her." The pain in Joseph's voice pulls at my heart.

"It was not your fault—not your fault," I insist. "It was God's will." God's will. How often have I said those familiar words, even when I am so unsure?

"Ho," Noha cries out, catching a whiff of simmering garlic. "What are you cooking, my friend? It smells like the feet of my donkey." She plunks a jug of wine down on the worktable near the entrance to the cave and settles onto one of the stools near the fire pit. Rachel, our family friend and midwife, who accompanied us to Egypt, does not turn around.

"Nothing so delicious," I answer. "Only a moonfish stew. Our eldest caught two large ones last night."

"Are you sure they are fresh?" demands Noha. "A terrible death comes to people who eat bad moonfish." I see a smile tug at the edges of Rachel's lips; both of us are used to Noha's scorn.

"Thank you for your concern, Noha," I manage to say politely. "I do believe they are fresh. We cleaned them last night and kept them in a cool place in the cave."

Noha scowls but says nothing in return. Scornful comments accompany Noha wherever she goes, though she saves the most cutting comments for her husband, Isaiah.

My youngest son waits for me inside the cave, where he has been listening to our conversation. "Why are you so kind to Noha, Mother? Her angry words make us all join in her misery." He sits halfway onto one of the wooden chairs, placing his elbow on the edge of the table.

"The more difficult it is to extend kindness, my son, the more we please God by offering it. Noha gives us all a chance to please God. But today I'm afraid I wasn't very successful in my heart." I pull eight clay cups from the wall.

My son grins and stands, taking the cups from my hands and placing them on the table. "But why is she so angry?"

"When we left Palestine, your father invited Isaiah and Noha to come with us. Noha opposed the journey, thinking it too dangerous and uncertain. She didn't want to leave her family. I understood. But Isaiah agreed to make the journey. Even before she arrived, Noha had made up her mind she would never be happy here." I take eight large wooden spoons from one of the niches carved into the cave wall and place them on the table below the cups.

"Will Noha ever be happy, Mother?"

"She may never be happy. God has not given her a happy heart." I reach out and tousle my son's dark auburn hair, pleased that he is still a child and welcomes my caresses. "What have you learned from the Rabbi today?"

A glint of mischief flickers through his deep brown eyes. "I find it most curious. The Rabbi quoted God's word, 'He will give rain to your land at the right season, the spring rains and the autumn rains.' But it doesn't rain here, Mother." He sits down again and places his chin in both palms.

"You are right to be curious. Sometimes I am confused as well, but I have noticed that when God does not send rain, He sends the Great River to overflow and make the land fertile. Listen for God's meaning and He will speak to you, my son." I notice an intense glimmer in my son's eyes when he wrestles with God's purposes.

He sits very still and gazes at me for a long time before nodding.

"I've heard more about Isis in the market," I say after the family sits down to our dinner of moonfish stew. There are eight of us at the long cedar table, including Rachel's husband, Samir, and Noha's husband, Isaiah. The late afternoon sun reflects off the eastern cave wall, holding the April warmth.

"Isn't she a pagan god?" asks Rachel, picking up the basket of warm bread and passing it to Noha.

"An Egyptian goddess of medicine and wisdom, Rachel. One worshiped by man," I say, my wooden spoon suspended over my bowl of stew. "Her husband, Osiris, lord of the underworld, was killed and cut into pieces by his jealous brother, Seth. From what I've heard in the market, Isis found the parts of Osiris scattered about the Great River, turned herself into a sparrow hawk and hovered over his body, fanning him back to life with her long wings." Feeling playful, I allow my spoon to become a bird and swoop through the air, landing on my young son's nose. It gives me pleasure when he giggles. "Isis became full with child," I continue, "and gave birth to a son, Horus, who became a powerful falcon god and avenged his father by slaying Seth."

"That is so," Samir rumbles in his deep voice. "Isis is a giver of life. The Greeks call her Theotokos, Mother of God." Although Samir converted to Judaism in order to marry Rachel, his heart belongs to the beliefs of his own people, and he takes pride in these stories. He reaches for the jug and looks around the table to find who is in need of more wine. Noha sets her cup down with a loud thud, signaling her disapproval of the story; she has expressed dissatisfaction before with my fascination with these Egyptian gods. She calls it childishness. Perhaps it is.

Samir refills her cup. Wine is a rarity in our household, reserved for days celebrating births and the Seder. Today is the day of Isaiah's birth.

My young son stops eating, his expression intent. "Is this true, mother? Can people come back to life?"

"If God wills it, my son. God is all-powerful." I feel unease with the sound of my own words and glance toward my husband.

He smiles at me and nods slightly before turning his attention to his older son. "What do you think of the power of other gods?" Our oldest son has been watching Noha's agitation and is startled by the question.

He pauses before answering. "I hear much talk of these Egyptian gods with magical powers at the canal," he replies, taking another piece of bread. "They do not know of the one true God. And I'm not about to tell them."

"Why, my boy? Why do you not share the word of God?" asks Isaiah, visibly disappointed. Without children, Isaiah considers our son as his own. I pity Isaiah sometimes, elderly now and cowed and bent by years of marriage to Noha.

"They would ridicule me," says our oldest. "I've heard it said that the Jews only need one God because we are a simple people."

I watch my husband closely as he stares at our son. Is he questioning his real motivation? I share his doubts.

My husband turns. "Isaiah, what is your thinking about these strange gods?

"I . . . I know there is but one God. It is not proper to talk of other gods." Isaiah is even more hesitant than usual, aware that Noha has turned away, upset about something he may or may not have done.

"Our Law also teaches tolerance and understanding. It is good to understand what others believe, is it not?" My husband says this with a gentleness he reserves for Isaiah and for me.

Isaiah lays down his spoon, preparing to speak, then changes his mind.

"Will our faith become weak if we talk of other gods?" our youngest asks, leaning forward, his elbow almost tipping his stew, his chair threatening to skid out from under him.

"Steady, my boy," cautions Isaiah, placing his calloused hand on the back of the boy's chair.

"Father . . . can it lead us astray?" he persists. "The Rabbi says, 'Beware of letting ourselves be fooled into swerving aside to the worship and homage of other gods.'"

"I see your curiosity must be satisfied, my son," says my husband. "God also tells us, 'If you cry to intelligence and call for knowledge, seeking her out as silver and searching for her like treasure, then you shall see what reverence for the Eternal is and find out what the knowledge of God means.' Knowledge makes us stronger. Ignorance makes us weak. If our faith is so weak that we can only keep it by shielding ourselves from knowledge, then we are not accepting the tests that God has set before us." My husband tears off a piece of warm bread and dips it in his stew. He pauses, waiting for our youngest to speak.

"But how are we to know what God wants of us?"

Silently, all of us gathered around the table tip our bowls to sip the last of the moonfish stew and pass the plate of figs.

CHAPTER 1

S HE WAS running.

Ahead of her, the yawing mouth of a cave reached deep into the flaking sandstone cliffs. Terror propelled her limbs. But what was she running from?

Moments ago, she'd been standing by a river, the sunlight skimming across the water, warm sand rising between her toes. She'd felt at peace, and yet beneath her contentment had lurked a darker worry, an omen of danger just out of sight.

Now, the blackness of the cave closed in on her. There was nowhere else to run. She couldn't breathe. She—

Justine jolted awake with a gasp, her forehead pressed against the cold aircraft window. Overhead, the seatbelt sign pinged—they'd be landing soon.

She forced her racing pulse to slow and shook her head to dislodge the last remnants of the dream. Outside the window, the sapphire Mediterranean came into view, and the unsettled feeling left by the dream was replaced by excitement. Leaning forward, she placed her palm on the window as though she could reach out and take hold of Africa, the country that had beckoned to her since she'd visited with her parents as a teenager. At twenty-six she was returning to Egypt, free to discover it with her own eyes.

The plane passed over sparkling beaches; the new Alexandria Library rested near the shore like a giant disc, a spaceship with hundreds of Oriental eyes.

Continuing its descent, the Lufthansa 747 aimed south across the verdant Nile crescent, emerging atop a landscape of tawny desert stretching as far as Justine's eye could see. The sight ahead was nearly indecipherable: a tan, leathery blanket covering the city of nearly eighteen million, a few skyscrapers protruding above its smothering shield. She smiled as she recalled a comparable sight: two deep ochre towers extending above a white fluffy mantle of fog—the Golden Gate Bridge.

As they made their approach into Cairo International Airport, the runway met the plane with jolting intimacy. Reaching for her briefcase and purse, Justine stood up precariously and wormed her way back into a lightweight blue suit jacket. She was both exhilarated and apprehensive about what lay ahead. The Community Schools for Girls project would give her insight into today's Egyptian girls, as well as help her to understand her own confusing roots. *How am I to understand myself as a modern Egyptian woman? Am I an heir of Isis or of today's Islamic women cloaked in hijabs?* These were the questions on her mind.

She stared out the windows as she waited to exit with the other passengers crowding into the aisles. No longer the glorious view of Alexandria and the delta—leathery brown smog blocked her vision now. Heat rushed in from the open doors and the familiar chime signaled that everyone was free to go. Free to go. What an unfamiliar, though exhilarating, notion.

She had never really felt "free to go." Raised by an Egyptian mother and a Berkeley professor father, she was often caught in the cultural crosscurrents of two stalwart individuals, both with immutable ideas about how to raise their headstrong daughter.

Justine's Egyptian mother, Lucrezia, deliberately sought to marry an American, assuming she'd enjoy a more emancipated marriage than she could have had with one of her own countrymen. She was wrong. Morgan Jenner, with his roots in the American Midwest, was more than moderately protective of his exotic wife and young daughter. Each having disappointed the other, her parents divorced shortly after Justine moved to Chicago for graduate school.

Chicago had not been the liberating solution she had hoped. The endless demands of graduate work felt like a form of voluntary servitude. But here she was, for the first time, free of her father's control . . . free of school . . . doctorate in hand . . . assuming her first professional position . . . free to go.

It seemed like a lifetime since she'd last walked through these corridors. When she was fourteen, her father, a renowned archeologist, had accepted a two-year assignment on a dig near the Serapeum at Saqqara, and her mother had come planning to take classes at the Cairo Modern Art Museum. Lucrezia, speaking rapid Arabic, had insisted on a customs line that didn't exist, since the Egyptian custom was to cluster and push until you reached the desired window. Morgan had tensed against the press of bodies and held tightly to both his wife and daughter, juggling his briefcase and computer over his broad shoulders.

Justine remembered her mother reprimanding him sharply, "This is my home, Morgan. I can take care of myself." Without answering, he had loosened his grip on her, but not his daughter. *No, not his daughter.* She'd been the last among her friends to date, and even then he'd insisted that a parent or another couple accompany her.

The Cairo airport was not what Justine remembered. The walkways were still a drab off-white, made even duller by dim fluorescent lighting. But there were quasi-lines this time, and an almost orderly check of passports and visas. On the periphery, young men in unfashionable suits and worn briefcases jockeyed for a place in line while a few women fully covered in black burqas milled around with small children in tow. Male family members steered them toward passport windows.

Justine offered her passport to the customs officer and smiled as he cheerfully said, "Welcome to Egypt . . .Welcome back to Egypt, Miss," noting the earlier Egyptian stamps that she had retained in her passport despite having obtaining a new one.

"*Shukran*, thank you," she replied, surprised that her Arabic returned quickly, as though she had put on an old record, one her mother had played for her as a child. She eased back into the crowd, surveying the people ahead, looking for her host. As she scanned the group of greeters just beyond the rope, she spotted the sign—DR. JUSTINE JENNER written in large block print. A middle-aged woman with a head of wild, graying hair held the sign with both hands, a bulky leather purse dangling over her right shoulder. Wide-set black eyes and shaggy brows crowned a deeply tan face with small lips. Sensible black shoes protruded from under a dark blue skirt. *Just as I had imagined her.*

"Nadia. Nadia Mansour," Justine cried out, waving her free hand. The two women had been in touch by e-mail and by phone on several occasions after Justine applied for the position with UNESCO, but this was the first time they'd met in person. Nadia was the Director of the Community Schools for Girls project and a part-time professor at the American University of Cairo. She would be Justine's supervisor. Her gregarious personality had seeped through their earlier communications.

"*Inshallah*, you're still in one piece," Nadia observed.

Justine laughed as she reached for Nadia's outstretched hand. "Dr. Mansour, I'm delighted to finally meet you!" she said, struggling to keep her carry-ons from sliding off her shoulder.

Nadia gripped her arm, steering her toward the luggage area. "You have a reservation at the Shepheard and your Garden City apartment will be ready when Allah sees fit," she said. "But first, we'll tackle the luggage."

They stood and watched as an avalanche of motley bags tumbled out from behind a black leather curtain, some tied with ropes, others merely taped-up boxes filled with T-shirts, baby clothes, and plastic shoes intended for sale in the street markets of Cairo.

"See those bags?" Nadia pointed to the ragged assortment of containers. "A metaphor for modern Egypt: tied together haphazardly, containing Western goods brought in by eager entrepreneurs, products for all ages, all sneaking out from behind a black curtain. Our primitive economy."

Justine laughed at the honest observation. She attempted to respond over the cacophony of voices, but when she realized she couldn't be heard without shouting, she simply stepped forward and pulled her new luggage and cardboard boxes from the carousel.

Nadia picked up one of the suitcases and handed it to a waiting porter in old sandals and a flowing kaftan. "My car is just across the street!" she shouted, leading the way. The porter followed them across two lanes of traffic, pushing a squealing cart that carried Justine's luggage and two boxes of books wrapped and tied neatly with dark green cords. "Taxis are no longer allowed directly into the airport, so traffic here has improved," Nadia said, pointing toward her car. "My air conditioning doesn't work. Sorry."

Justine attempted to open the car door. The handle swung loose in her hand. "I'll get that," Nadia grinned, reaching across the passenger seat and opening the door from inside. "Better take off that cute jacket."

Justine obediently removed her blue linen jacket and laid it neatly in the backseat. "How long into town?" she asked. *I hope I can survive this heat. I didn't realize it would be quite so smoldering in April.*

"Everything you remember about Cairo . . . traffic, size, pollution . . . just double it," said Nadia, settling into her ancient Renault. "Today it could take a couple of hours to get downtown. Five million more people since you were here last, and I swear, they all have a car!" She handed Justine a bottle of warm Evian.

Justine couldn't help smiling at Nadia's capacity to be tolerant and exasperated at the same time. "Where does the British accent come from?" she asked.

"I attended a British school as a child. Even though the revolution was ten years old, my mother insisted: 'You can never tell when those British colonists will come back and reclaim our land. Be prepared.' That was 1962."

"Prepare for all eventualities. Sounds like my parents, although each of them had their own notions of preparedness. My father is American and my mother's Egyptian. Turned out to be an unworkable combination."

"Your parents are celebrities of a sort here. Your father's digs are as notorious as your mother's beauty." Nadia stopped at a booth to pay the airport fee, then jammed the Renault into gear, causing it to lurch forward.

Justine reached down for a seat belt that wasn't there. "Notorious? That sounds romantic, but a bit ominous."

"Well, some of your father's discoveries have been controversial—like the dig at Darshur. I understand that a few questions remain within the Ministry of Antiquities and among the expats. I believe I was working with the Education Ministry at the time." Nadia paid close attention to the traffic, her head swiveling back and forth, as she turned out of the airport and onto Sharia Al Uruba Boulevard, a street lined with symmetrical, towering palms.

"What have you heard? About Darshur." Justine leaned forward and reached back to pull her damp silk blouse loose from her skin. Suburban Cairo gave way to the City of the Sun, Heliopolis. Polished chrome storefronts housed glitzy shoe stores and boutiques facing east toward giant hotels.

"I really don't know the details, but it's rumored that the Darshur find may have challenged exactly how the biblical exodus happened. As you can imagine, anti-Semitism is still strong enough here that some people savor any suggestion of fraud around the Jews' favorite story. It raised quite a row for a while."

"Dad told me the evidence wasn't strong enough to claim validity. He likes to make sure everything is on the up-and-up. Personally, I think it's a non-story."

Nadia tilted her head slightly and pursed her thin lips. Justine couldn't tell whether she believed her or not. She suspected not. "And my mother? What made her notorious?"

"Her beauty. Her flamboyance. Her ability to gather fascinating people around her. Your mother's parties attracted royalty and important government officials. I gather that your father would have preferred to stay out of the limelight."

"Sounds like Dad. He doesn't like to mix business and pleasure. And he doesn't consider himself socially suave—but I think he's wrong there. Women seem to find him dashing. But how could you possibly know so much about my parents?"

"Cairo's a small town. Nearly eighteen million souls and yet we all know each other's business, especially English-speaking professionals. Sort of a class by ourselves, huddling together for reassurance and inspiration and gossip. We love gossip." Nadia was still grinning when her cell phone rang. "Okay. *Shukran.* This afternoon across from the Shepheard." She hung up and slipped the phone back into her skirt pocket.

Justine was mulling over Nadia's notions about her parents and Cairo culture when she noticed the Baron's Palace set back a few hundred yards from the street. "I vividly remember the night of the ambassador's ball at that palace," she said, pointing toward the ornate, Gaudí-like building. "I was only ten, but they let me tag along in my long blue dress. I was awestruck. But now you can hardly make out the elaborate exterior of Buddhas, elephants. Serpents too, I think."

"It may return to its former glory soon. It's being renovated. But don't be too impressed by any of the façades along this boulevard. Go a block in either direction and the city is still the same."

Nothing is ever quite as it seems, or as it is written, in Egypt. "Tell me about the schools." Justine understood Egyptian protocol: never move into business straightaway, ease into it like a warm bath.

"We're really pleased with the project so far! The girls are learning so fast, as though they were born ready and waiting. Well . . . I suppose they were," Nadia said. "And you, how did you find out about us?"

"My dad suggested I check out the State Department website and that's when I found out about your new UNESCO project. To work with such a pioneering effort in girls' education, and in Cairo, no less—it's exciting to return here with my own job."

"Good fatherly advice." Nadia swerved to avoid an aggressive bus. "We're excited to get you. With your training in anthropology, interest in women's studies, and knowledge of Arabic, you were made for the job." Beads of perspiration glowed around Nadia's tiny mouth. They were both reluctant to open the windows to the onslaught of exhaust and noise, so the car was a virtual oven.

"I imagine that hiring an anthropologist for an education project isn't the norm . . ." Justine let the words linger in the suffocating air.

"No, it isn't. I had to do some fast talking. Tradition can be as firmly rooted in the U.N. as it is in the countries they serve. And in this case, we have to consider both UNESCO and the Egyptian ministries. But we can talk in more detail in the morning, when you're rested—and we're both cooler."

I wonder what kind of opposition I'll face, particularly among those who resisted hiring me? "Fine with me. My mind and questions will be clearer after a rest." She took a packet of Kleenex from her purse, handed one to Nadia, and pressed another to her perspiring forehead and upper lip. *What I would give for a bottle of cold water,* she thought, sipping the warm water Nadia had given her.

As she leaned back, she noticed how little green could be seen, even surrounding the palm trees. Abandoned by the rich floodwaters of the Nile more than half a century ago, when the Aswan Dam was built, ancient fields of green had been replaced by a vast coverlet of concrete. The car descended the flyover onto Sharia Ramses and Ramses Square, and Justine quickly recognized the ornate blue and white train station, a sign that they were getting close to the center of Cairo.

"Tahrir Square is coming up," announced Nadia. Within moments, they approached the world-famous Egyptian Museum on their right and merged into the Square, the center of the Cairo beehive. People moved every which way, weaving in and out of traffic; horns and the ancient engines of cars bought in the '70s and somehow kept alive buzzed nonstop.

Fanning out to their left was the massive downtown leading to Islamic Cairo. Further ahead sat the notorious Egyptian administrative center lovingly known as the Mogamma, a citadel to brittle British bureaucracy. Veering right, they could see the Nile and Garden City just ahead. All familiar now.

"Tahrir Square is known as the busiest intersection in the world," said Nadia by way of warning. "In order to cross these crowded lanes, you either take your life in your own hands and move offensively, or look for a friendly traffic cop to stop the traffic."

"I've never driven here. At least not yet."

"Better wait a while before you try it. Watch the rhythm of the traffic and you'll get the hang of it. Notice the women." Justine watched as a family with three children wove like ducklings through the traffic ahead of them.

Women everywhere were wearing the hijab, the headscarf; a few were fully covered with the niqab. "The headscarf is everywhere. I didn't realize things had changed so much."

"Fundamentalism is raising its head . . . and covering it. More than ninety percent of the population is Muslim now, and almost all of the women are wearing the hijab, at least in public. Otherwise they get hassled on the street. The daring few who don't wear the scarf are of the upper classes or work for Western companies. And then, of course, there are the Coptic Christians, who stand out more than ever."

"You're Muslim, aren't you?"

"If your question is why don't I wear the hijab, I guess there are a number of reasons," said Nadia, adjusting the scarf she wore loosely around her neck.

Justine blushed slightly. "I'm being too inquisitive," she said.

"Not at all. You see this bushy, wiry hair of mine? It's hard to tame. But that's not the real reason. I'll admit: I'm a bit of a renegade. I like to think of myself as a modern Muslim. As far as I'm concerned, the headscarf takes away a woman's individuality. We all begin to look alike. And besides, it's just too hot."

Justine looked directly at the scarf laying on Nadia's shoulders and grinned.

Nadia pulled at the fabric. "Just in case." She smiled. The traffic opened slightly as they merged from the square onto a side street. The Shepheard Hotel appeared on the left. The Nile glistened silver and turquoise just ahead, a cement railing separating the river from the waterfront promenade known as the Corniche. Two men dressed like palace guards appeared at the car window.

"Will you both be staying with us, my lady?" inquired the older of the two guards.

"Only my friend. *Shukran*," Nadia replied.

Justine gazed up at the towering façade and memories of the original Shepheard crowded her mind. The memories were older than she was, and they didn't belong to her but rather to her grandmother Laurence, who had spent many afternoons having tea on the sweeping terrace with her parents.

She remembered hearing stories of the great hotel as the playground of adventurers and travelers from all over the world. The shaded terrace where her grandmother must have sat in deep wicker chairs held a commanding view of Ibrahim Pasha Street. The grand entrance encircled a spiral staircase leading to the Moorish Hall, deliciously cool and dimly lit by rays coming through a huge dome of colored glass. Laurence had described plump, embroidered chairs set around little octagonal tables. Intimacy with discretion had been the watchwords of its glamorous clientele: Churchill, Lawrence of Arabia, Roosevelt, princes, sheiks, queens, and great authors. The original Shepheard, like the glory days of Cairo, had been consumed by fire some fifty-five years ago.

"If you're up to it, I've asked a few friends to join us on a felucca this evening," Nadia said. "I think you will enjoy meeting them. I'll bring a light dinner and we'll have a relaxing sail. That would give you about three hours to rest."

"I would love to." As the cool air of the lobby enveloped them, she and Nadia gave a sigh of relief nearly in unison, then went to check in.

The suite that was to be Justine's home for the next few weeks opened into a sitting room that led to a small balcony overlooking the Nile. Narrow spiral steps wound upward to a bedroom with an even more superb view. "This is extraordinary. I may never want to leave."

"You'll get tired of hotel food soon enough," Nadia assured her. The hotel porter deposited the luggage in the bedroom, and Justine handed him a ten-pound note from the cache Nadia had loaned her. Both women sought a cold bottle of Evian from the room's refrigerator.

"See you in the lobby at seven, then," Nadia said, after drinking nearly half of the bottle in one swig.

After she left, Justine removed her damp blouse and skirt and fell spread-eagle across the bed. She was asleep within moments.

CHAPTER 2

———⚮———

B Y 6:45, JUSTINE HAD TAKEN a nap and shower and changed into a light green sweater, gray linen slacks, and flats. Damp chestnut ringlets surrounded her face. With a small purse and jacket in hand, she descended the stairs to the lobby, exchanged money at the desk, and turned toward the restaurant known as The Caravan. The old Shepheard did not have a monopoly on ornate beauty, she realized. Chandeliers of amber glass reflected on richly carved wood known as mashrabaya, accented with lines of exquisite arabesque lettering. Gothic arches and flourishing palms towered over marble floors, and lamps shaped like lotuses lit the room. Above, a marble balcony circled the eastern side of the room, serving as counterpoint to the huge windows overlooking the Corniche and the Nile to the west.

"Feeling better?" Nadia asked, walking up behind her.

"Much, yes. Thank you," she replied, turning toward the older woman, who was loaded down with a covered basket and satchel heavy with food and bottled juices.

Nadia stood several inches shorter than Justine's 5'8", so her bundles nearly touched the ground. Justine took the heavier one and followed her toward the entrance.

"Impossible to park close by," said Nadia. "But the felucca is directly across the Corniche." A policeman volunteered to escort them across the busy street and onto the wide sidewalk that lined the river for miles in either direction. "This is one of the main meeting places for Cairenes at night. It's exquisite in the early evening when cool breezes blow in from the northwest."

Justine could feel the welcome breeze against her face, slightly ruffling her long hair, drying the ringlets in place. Several couples strolled by hand-in-hand while young girls wove through the crowd selling garlands of jasmine. Justine handed two Egyptian pounds to one of them and bent down while the girl of six or seven placed a garland around her neck. She handed a second garland to Nadia. "*Gameel, Gameel awee, very beautiful*," said Justine, touching the child's ivory cheek. The sweet smell of jasmine merged into the tantalizing aroma of corn roasting on a homemade grill built into half of a tin barrel, split lengthwise and balanced on wheels.

"Hello there!" Nadia cried, waving as the two women descended the steps from the Corniche to the shore of the river and the moored feluccas. The odor of dead fish momentarily entered Justine's nostrils, but was quickly masked by the fragrance of gardenias growing at the bases of towering date palms. "Justine, meet Magda Shehata and Amir El Shabry."

With their dark good looks, Magda and Amir could have been sister and brother. Magda was striking: lustrous black shoulder-length hair, eyelashes like little Chinese fans, and an eagerly warm demeanor. A classic Egyptian beauty. She took Justine's hand and pulled her toward her, kissing her on both cheeks.

Amir was handsome in that mysterious Arab way, although with a distracted expression and cool eyes. His handshake was limp, a little clammy. He clearly didn't want to be here. *Then why is he here? A favor to Nadia?*

Nadia finalized arrangements with the manager of the small fleet, then stepped adroitly across the wide bow of one felucca and into their assigned vessel. She nodded to Amir to follow. Amir stood, one foot on each rocking boat, and gripped the forearms of Magda and Justine in turn as they navigated the unsteady course.

The felucca was just as Justine remembered: a large, worn wooden boat with padded benches encircling a table in the middle. On the bow, a large mast was wrapped tight with the furled sail. An elderly man in kaftan and turban squatted on the bow talking to a young man in Western dress. The cherry-tinted sun dropped behind the western skyline as lights around the river and on the island of Zamalek released the glow of evening.

Justine felt the warmth of bygone pleasures. The last time she'd been on a felucca was with her parents. *We were still a family then, or at least I was young enough to believe in the myth of family solidarity.*

"This charming lad is Mohammed Shalaby from Naser City," said Nadia, introducing the man who'd been waiting on the boat. Mohammed was short, with graying sideburns. He blushed and extended his hand, which Justine grasped. Amir stepped forward and shook hands with Mohammed, as well as with the ancient pilot beginning to maneuver the boat into the river. A smaller motorboat nudged them along, the three boisterous youth aboard it blasting Arabic rock music from a hand-held boom box. After the felucca caught the wind, the smaller boat would return to shore.

Nadia busied herself laying out a light supper of hibiscus juice, falafel, and pita sandwiches.

"Do you and Nadia work together?" Justine asked Magda. Soft purple waves licked the side of the boat, while in the middle of the river the fountain near the Ghezira Sheraton began to spout multi-colored water.

"I don't work with the schools. Nadia and I met through mutual friends. And I just love her. She's like my older sister. My job is with Coca-Cola International. Unfortunately, the demands of my job mean that my two daughters are being raised by my mother. Perhaps that's a good thing. I'm not always so patient."

At that very moment, the felucca's giant sail unfurled with a boom, revealing a large Pepsi Cola insignia. They all laughed at the uncanny timing. "So much for romance," Justine observed. "Western capitalism rises."

"So much for business!" Magda exclaimed. "We're in fierce competition with Pepsi here." She glanced around the boat, catching the eyes of each of her friends. "Don't let me hear of any of you frequenting a place serving that forbidden drink!" Hands were raised spontaneously in solemn vow. "Good!" she exclaimed. Turning to Justine, she added, "They put in extra sugar—deadly for a country with a diabetes epidemic!"

Mohammed was standing at the table, holding a pita sandwich. "I am Egyptian like Magda," he shyly told Justine, "although my mother is Jordanian." He spoke in heavily accented English. The front of his sweatshirt boldly announced, I LOVE MY APPLE. "I have a small computer sales and repair shop in Naser City."

Justine would never have taken Mohammed for a computer salesman. His appearance was rough, and yet he had a proper way of presenting himself. *A cross between a camel driver and a member of Parliament*, she thought.

"Mohammed had a thriving business in Baghdad before the first Gulf War," Nadia added. "Where's Lulu tonight?" she asked, attempting to coax Mohammed through his social unease.

"Business was a little easier in Iraq, I understand. Right, Mohammed?" said Amir. "Our tariffs here can squelch any fledgling venture." Sarcasm tinged his voice.

"You are correct, my friend. Import taxes in Egypt on all types of machines, including cars, make them too expensive for most customers." As Mohammed relaxed into the conversation, his shoulders eased and he sat down. He held his sandwich in both hands, and balanced a glass of hibiscus juice between his knees. "We wouldn't have come back from Iraq if it hadn't been for the first Gulf War. Egyptians were forced out when Mubarak supported the war." He paused to take a drink. "Lulu couldn't be with me tonight. She has a meeting at the Modern Art Museum. We have two sons at Ain Shams University. That's my story."

I'm sure that's not all his story, Justine thought, smiling and nodding as they watched the museum come into full view. She'd spent many hours there with her mother. The nearby Cairo Needle loomed tall, in full command of the evening skyline.

"I met Mohammed and his wife years ago when I was working with his mother on a project with the women of Bulaq," said Nadia. "That was before the community schools. Unfortunately, I see her less often now. A wonderful, generous woman. She was handing out microloans before it was fashionable."

"And, what do you do, Amir?" Justine asked, almost reluctantly. He, alone among the group, did not seem to be in a festive mood.

Amir hesitated as all eyes turned toward him. He was tall, even for an Egyptian, she noted—and she had little doubt that he was Egyptian. *Where else do men wear woolen scarves on a warm evening?*

Amir explained that he worked at the Egyptian Museum as curator of the Ptolemy exhibition, and occasionally lectured at the American University of Cairo. "Nadia and I see each other often in the faculty room at AUC. And, like Mohammed, we're family friends."

"You're an archaeologist, then?" Justine lifted her hair with both hands to collect the soft breeze.

"By training, but I don't get into the field as much as I'd like." He stood, feet apart, at the table, pouring himself a glass of juice. "I was involved in a few digs in Alex when the new library was being built."

"I understand you're trying to redesign the Ptolemaic section," said Magda. "It's one of the worst parts of the museum. Few artifacts and no written descriptions. The last time I took my daughters there, we skipped that part."

"You're going to see quite a difference soon." He smiled warmly, clearly taking no offense. "When you and your girls come back, let me know and you'll be my guests. I'm negotiating with the new library in Alexandria and the British Museum to return several artifacts as well."

"I hear that getting the West to return artifacts can be frustrating," said Justine. The breeze billowed her light sweater and she felt a welcoming coolness.

Amir brushed a curly lock of hair from his eyes. "I'm banking on a new international agreement developed by the Arab League. We'll see. I'm not going to let myself get too optimistic. I'm not much of an optimist anyway." His friends laughed.

Certainly not an optimist, Justine thought wryly. She detected a definite streak of arrogance.

"And why are you here, Justine?" His tone was challenging, edgy.

"I'm here for a few reasons, really." She met Amir's gaze. *There is something in his eyes, something he's not saying.* Suddenly, she had the odd sensation that they'd met before. She shook it off and turned toward the others. "My mother is Egyptian and my father American, a complicated mixture—at least it was when I was young. As you heard from Nadia, I'll be working with her on the Community Schools for Girls project, visiting classrooms and teacher training sessions. As an anthropologist, I'll be observing how children interact when they are learning—how they interact with teachers." The felucca began a rhythmic rocking, responding to the wake of a good-sized motor craft.

"I'm also interested in visiting St. Sergius again. I understand the ground waters from the last earthquake have been cleaned up. My mother used to tell me amazing stories about Isis and the Virgin Mary when I was a girl. That the Holy Family lived in Egypt much longer than Christians think."

"We Muslims think so. They were here about seven years," Mohammed said without reservation. "As an Abrahamic religion, Islam honors both the old and new Christian testaments. Yet we have our own ideas about the Holy Family and Egypt since they traveled here for so long."

Justine nodded. "I'll bet my mother learned some of her stories from Muslim friends."

"Childhood stories are among our most powerful influences," said Amir, his voice distracted. "Is there another reason you came?"

The question startled her, though she wasn't sure why. "Well, yes. To meet some old friends of the family, particularly my father's former teacher, Dr. Ibrahim El Shabry. Dad tells me that he may be long retired, but he's still engrossed in his research."

Amir looked surprised, but something about his expression struck Justine as disingenuous. "Ibrahim is my grandfather," he said. "My mother's father. He's retired, but keeps his office at the Rare Books Library near AUC."

Justine's eyes widened. "El Shabry. Of course. I should have made the connection. Amazing. Nadia, did you know that?" She turned.

"No, I didn't," said Nadia, arching an eyebrow, equally surprised.

"Curious," said Justine, hanging on to one of the roof slats covering the table as she moved closer to Amir.

"Curious? Why curious?" Amir's voice was sharp.

"I was resisting saying 'small world,'" admitted Justine.

"I can see why. Typical American phrase, 'small world,' meant to simplify the complexities of this world. Western anthropologists"—he nodded slightly toward Nadia to include her in his declaration—"tend to reduce what they see here to its bare bones, then suppose they understand Egyptians."

Nadia smiled gently, clearly tolerant of Amir's occasional sarcastic remarks.

Justine laughed lightly. "Well, 'small world' would have been rather Disneyesque," she confessed. "Western anthropologists have been known to be overbearing. Among other things."

Amir flushed slightly. "If I'm wrong, I apologize," he said. "I'm afraid that my experience with Westerners has often been disappointing." He held her gaze, returning her grin. "Perhaps you'll prove me wrong."

"Can we meet around ten in the morning to talk about the project?" Nadia asked, as she and Justine made their way back to the hotel. It was dark now, but the hotels provided ample lighting as they traversed the busy boulevard.

"Perfect." Justine hesitated. "Interesting man, Amir."

Nadia frowned. "He's not usually so edgy. You see, his brother has disappeared. He really didn't want to be here tonight."

"I'm sorry to hear about his brother."

"Zachariah was radicalized while he was volunteering in Imbaba, one of the poorest areas of Cairo. When he was in secondary school, he saw poverty, suffering, lack of services and medical attention, especially among the elderly. He listened to those who attributed the decline in people's lives to Westernized capitalism and the current regime's pandering to the West." Nadia paused just outside the entrance to the Shepheard. "Last year he joined the Muslim Brotherhood but found it too moderate for his tastes. Three months ago he left for Afghanistan."

"Al Qaeda?" Justine shivered as she thought of September 11th. Her cousin Patricia had been at her desk on the 98th floor of the World Trade Center's north tower that day. Pat had been Justine's age, and even though they hadn't seen each other frequently, Justine missed her terribly. Involuntarily, her mind careened to scenes of Pat trying to escape her tragic fate that morning.

"Al Qaeda could be involved. We just don't know," said Nadia, touching Justine's arm as though to bring her back—to bring them both back—from somewhere. "But I hope that tonight was pleasurable for you in the balance." She smiled. "See you in the morning?"

"At ten. And Nadia, thank you."

CHAPTER 3

S TEPPING OUT OF THE SHOWER, Justine grabbed a towel and caught the phone on the fourth ring. *Probably Nadia changing our appointment.*

"Hello, Justine?"

"This is Justine." She sat on the edge of the bed, facing west, peering over the bedroom's balcony and through the top of the two-story window. The breadth of the Nile lay before her.

"This is Amir." When she didn't react, he continued, "I wanted to apologize for my behavior last night. It was inexcusable, perhaps unforgivable."

She thought about what Nadia had said, the stress of missing his brother. "Please don't give it another thought," she said, drying her hair vigorously with the towel. "Actually, your honesty was refreshing."

"You said you wanted to see my grandfather. I thought I could walk you over to his office this afternoon."

"That would be great. I have a meeting with Nadia later this morning, but I'm free this afternoon." She was curious to observe this man in the context of his family.

"Shall I meet you in the lobby of your hotel around four?"

"Four would be fine." They hung up at the same time and Justine sat for a moment, gazing out at the rose colored fog on the Nile. *It's very early,* she realized. *Too early for anyone not suffering from jet lag. He must have been truly bothered by his behavior last evening.*

She reached for her green Lycra running suit and shoes, worn into shape by almost daily use. *Several hours till I meet with Nadia. Time for a run, another shower, and a third reading of the proposal.*

When she stepped out onto the sidewalk in front of the Shepheard, the streets were quiet except for a few donkey carts hauling garbage. It was 7:00 a.m. in Cairo, and ten hours earlier in California. At the corner, she ran in place for a few moments then moved cautiously across the Corniche, stepping onto the high curb and turning south. To her right floated the stationary, gleaming white Shepheard dinner boat, framed by soaring palms; the walkway to the boat, now chained closed, was lined with trimmed bushes and hyacinths.

Unused to sidewalks cracked and raised by roots of banyan trees bulging through the cement, Justine almost tripped twice within the first few minutes. Once, she barely caught herself by reaching for a limb over her head and swinging across the defacement. Soon, though, she found the sidewalk pattern: smooth, then cracked and rising, smooth, then . . . *Everything has a pattern*, she thought. *But they're not always so discernable.*

As she found her stride, her breath fell into its familiar pattern and she tried to absorb the city around her. She moved past Garden City and the Four Seasons on her left. Floating restaurants, colorful islands of nighttime gaiety, lined the shore to her right. Out of the center of the Nile arose Roda Island and its grand Manial Palace, built for King Farouk's uncle, Prince Mohammed Ali Tawfiq. He was a man who couldn't make up his mind, so he'd built his palace in all the popular styles of the day: Ottoman, Moorish, Persian, and European rococo.

By the time she reached the Roman aqueduct, cutting east through the city, the town was waking up. Bean pots on rollers moved into the side streets; bakers raised their storefronts, displaying layers of Egyptian baladi bread, which resembled pita. Young men on bicycles took to the streets.

About a mile from the hotel, she stopped. In this part of the city, new and maintenance construction gave way to houses and stores scarred by vehicle exhaust and crumbling around the edges, pressed together like crowded children scrambling for a ball.

Turning away from the Nile, Justine stood for a moment to get her bearings, bending over, hands on her thighs, stretching her back. A hand, not her own, reached under her from behind, firmly stroking between her legs then withdrawing as quickly as it had arrived. A wave of terror shot through her stomach and chest. For a moment, she couldn't believe what she'd felt. She swung around to see a stooped man in a gray kaftan and woolen scarf limping swiftly away.

She could have caught him easily, but what would she say? What would she do? Would the authorities pay her any mind? Not in Egypt. She turned and ran back to the hotel, stumbling occasionally, shaken by the violation.

Justine was still jittery when she entered the hotel's coffee shop to meet Nadia at 10:00. The story of her morning run poured out. "I did a very stupid thing this morning. I went out running in a tight Lycra suit. An invitation."

Nadia listened quietly, reaching across the wide table to take her hands. "Believe me, it's so rare. In spite of your attire, I find myself disturbed . . . you should be able to expect safety."

"Let's forget about it. I should have known better." The last time Justine was in Cairo, she'd been a scrawny kid, hardly a target for sexual advances, but that was no excuse for forgetting cultural codes. More than anything, she was embarrassed. After all, she was a professional anthropologist now. A Ph.D., for goodness' sake. She stared out the window for several moments. The Nile was now a sheet of glass, the tan sky tipped with pale blue. "Amir called this morning. To apologize. He was very gracious and offered to take me to see his grandfather this afternoon."

Nadia smiled. "I'm pleased to hear he called. Amir is a proud man, so it's difficult for him to apologize. I hope you found it in your heart to accept his apology." She signaled to the waiter for tea.

"Of course I accepted his apology." Justine paused. "Do you think he'll tell me about Zachariah?"

Nadia shook her head. "Probably not. At least not until he gets to know you better. I know Amir fairly well. His mother and I were close friends—we went to school together in Alexandria—so I've watched him grow up. Are you going with him this afternoon?"

"We'll meet at four and walk to his grandfather's office. I look forward to reconnecting with his grandfather. Besides, I'm willing to trust that there is more to admire in Amir than I've discovered so far."

"I appreciate your willingness to keep an open mind." Nadia smiled. "Amir means a lot to me, and I was afraid that last night would have closed the door for you." She tilted her head. "Some people would have walked away."

"I'll admit, I sometimes make quick judgments unless there is a good reason to do otherwise. I take pride in reading people and drawing conclusions on little information. It's one of my talents—and probably one of my weaknesses."

Nadia laughed softly. Her mass of thick hair moved like gray Jell-O. "I tend to trust too quickly and am sometimes disappointed."

The tea arrived then. Justine added a little honey to hers and stirred it slowly.

Nadia picked up the hot china cup and blew on the rich brown surface. After a few sips, she shifted the direction of the conversation. "Have you had an opportunity to read the proposal and think it through?" The proposal for the UNESCO Community Schools for Girls project described several rural schools built primarily outside of Cairo. In small villages, there were not enough girls to make up schools with separate grade levels, and parents often forbade their daughters from walking to larger, nearby villages. Attending school with boys was not considered an option in rural areas, but ungraded all-girls schools were proving workable.

"I've read it several times, most recently this morning. It's impressive and ambitious. Ungraded instruction, parental governance, community commitment. Tell me something I didn't read in the proposal."

Nadia smiled, then said, "Gratitude. I hadn't thought much about what gratitude looked like in children. Eagerness, aliveness glowing in their eyes. But there is something more. A yearning beginning to be fulfilled, a longing they had no reason to expect would ever be met. Some days I leave a school and find myself teary with unexpected happiness."

Justine felt her eyes well up. "You surprise me, Nadia. I guess I expected something else. Longing would seem a rather adult emotion. I'm not sure I've seen it in children."

"Perhaps there are other words to explain what I'm seeing. But you said I surprised you. What did you think I would say?"

She sipped her tea before speaking. "Some kind of education-talk, I suppose. Reading and math and tests and achievement. I'm becoming jaded by the direction U.S. schools are taking. It's as though the human side of children is being exchanged for a technological view of life and learning. You know, children as objects, as robots."

"I know what you mean. As women, we've all had that experience."

"I'm afraid so. I'm enchanted to think about children, especially young girls, brimming with emotions and longing. I can hardly wait to get into the schools and see how all the pieces come together." She paused, holding Nadia's gaze. "What are you hoping to learn from me?"

Nadia nodded as though she'd been pondering this next question. "Well . . . we're hoping that an anthropologist with your background can show us some things our eyes can't see."

Some things our eyes can't see, Justine mused, glancing at young women in hijabs passing on the sidewalk below. *I wonder what yearnings these young women have?* "A lovely invitation," she said.

"We want to understand how the girls relate to each other and how they're learning. Most importantly, we want these girls to have the confidence and the ability to make choices that will bring them more freedom later on. Such freedom is rare in our world." The conversation paused for a moment while the waiter replenished the hot water for their tea.

"Such freedom is rare in any world," Justine said once he'd departed. "And as you've indicated, a critical element of freedom is choice. We may want to ask ourselves: How do these girls choose? Are they generating their own measuring sticks for choice? Mimicking peers? Trying to please adults? Remaining silent as a form of non-choice?"

Nadia's lips expanded into a grin. "Exactly. We've thought that what passes for choice is often just imitating others, but we've not been able to observe keenly enough to know how to intervene. You can understand all that? Just by *watching*?"

"Well . . . there's a little more to it than that," Justine admitted, energized by Nadia's enthusiasm. "I think we can observe those things. As soon as the girls trust me I can code behaviors within learning circles, questions, silences. Then we'll know how to intervene."

The waiter returned with two menus, as though waiting for them to realize they were hungry. Nadia suggested some traditional Egyptian fare for sharing: kofta, tabbouleh, and babaghanoush with baladi bread.

"I'd like for you to visit some schools first. We have two new ones in the area. One in the City of the Dead, a unique community in the middle of urban sprawl, and the other in Birqash, a small village about thirty-five kilometers northwest of town that hosts the camel market. What if we start with the school in Birqash on Monday morning? Then you can help me get ready for a dinner party that evening. Do you have any plans for tomorrow?"

By 3:45, Justine was reclining in one of the brocaded chairs in the lobby, her ankle-length skirt almost touching her sturdy walking shoes. She stared at the ceiling, allowing herself to be mesmerized once again by the huge amber glass chandelier overhead.

"Beautiful, isn't it?" asked Amir, standing behind her, his eyes following hers. "I wish I'd seen the original. My grandmother said it was a vision to behold."

Justine smiled as she stood and turned to face him. "My grandmother also told me about the glory days of the original Shepheard. She stayed there often as a young girl." She paused to shake Amir's hand; she observed that he was clean-shaven and more relaxed than he'd been the day before. "Thanks for meeting me today."

"You're quite welcome. Shall we go? We'll be walking across Tahrir Square, and several blocks east of American University. Do you have your passport? You'll need it for identification."

"I do," she said, thinking that they probably made a striking pair. Both were tall, and their coloring contrasted dramatically. Her with caramel-toned hair and matching eyes; Amir quite dark, with ebony hair and deep brown eyes. They walked swiftly toward the square.

"Tell me, Justine, what is an anthropologist? At least from the perspective of your work here?" They walked close to each other, but observers would have little doubt that they were strangers.

She laughed at what seemed like such a basic question from a man whose museum work surely put him in contact with anthropologists on a frequent basis. "One of my professors used to say that no one can agree on what an anthropologist actually is. The field is quite fragmented, including several forms of anthropology, archeology, linguistics, even paleontology. As a cultural anthropologist here, I'll be observing students, teachers, and parents in order to understand the behavior patterns among them and whether they are learning in the ways envisioned by the project."

Amir kept his eyes straight ahead, but she thought she could see puzzlement in his face. "I see. I guess I associate anthropologists with observing primitive cultures during colonial times. A rather paternal, or maternal, profession."

"Ah, the arrival of the white colonial mother. Let me tell you about my last job," she said, being careful not to trip on the uneven sidewalk.

Before she could say anything further, Amir took a firm hold of her arm. As they stepped into Kasr Al Aini traffic, he alternately held up his hand to alert drivers they were coming through and touched the hoods of cars to cause them to slow down or stop.

It was a fascinating dance—both the drivers and the pedestrians seemed to be taking responsibility for each other. *Perhaps this is what Nadia meant by reciprocity.* Justine willingly relinquished responsibility for her life to Amir and enjoyed the crossing.

As they stepped up on the high sidewalk near the main entrance to American University, Amir gave a small bow. "Please continue. I'm sorry we were interrupted."

Justine straightened her blouse, trying to ignore the feeling of heat where his hand had lingered. "My recent work. I was hired by IBM to sit in on team and board meetings and try to figure out how their culture was being recreated with new staff on board. Quite fun. And primitive."

Amir chuckled. "My naiveté often gets me into trouble. I seem to like to blow on the yogurt."

"Blow on the yogurt?"

"An old Egyptian proverb. If hot soup burns you, you learn to blow on it before you eat it the next time. After a while, you may get so careful that you start blowing on your yogurt as well."

"A useful proverb! May I steal it?" Justine wondered when Amir had been burned . . . and by whom.

"Be my guest." He steered her across another small intersection. Sitting on the corner was an old colonial mansion with white shutters and ornate French cornices carved with the label "Rare Books Library."

Friendly guards asked for identification before allowing them to enter a carefully groomed garden exploding with blossoms of yellow and blue, potted palms, and rattan furniture. Inside the library, two flights of circular stairs surrounded the stairwell. On the top floor, Amir knocked gently on the door to room 305.

A deep, gravelly voice cried out, "Come in!"

From behind a cedar desk that was almost as large as he was stepped Professor Ibrahim El Shabry. Justine recognized the playful eyes from her childhood, but little else. The years had taken their toll.

"Justine, my child, how wonderful to see you again." He stepped toward her, looking up. "You've grown quite tall. Like your dad. But then, you know the bones of an old man shrivel. Before the mind does, if we are fortunate. But how could I forget those dimples and amber eyes?"

Justine reached out to clasp his hands. "Wonderful to see you again, Dr. Ibrahim. I believe the last time was more than ten years ago. I remember a party at your home. On the big lawn. Dad sends his greetings and a message about staying out of trouble." She was struck by how much the professor's body had aged. His white hair and beard framed a deeply wrinkled face. His piercing black eyes, though, were at once young and timeless.

"Ha! Just like Morgan. Lecturing me about his own follies!"

Justine laughed lightly, realizing that it was serenity, not age, that she primarily felt in Ibrahim's presence. He motioned her and Amir toward three chairs clustered in front of a wall of books. Against another wall, Justine was surprised to see a computer.

"Your dad's a fine fellow—like a son to me. As you know, we worked together for years. Met him when I lectured at Berkeley a hundred years ago," Ibrahim said, motioning toward a chair. "I hear he's in Peru looking for hidden treasures. Tell him he owes this old man a letter."

"I will, sir. I'll tell him you're well and feisty. He calls frequently. He often forgets I'm no longer a little girl." She grinned, not so unlike a little girl.

"Feisty, at least. These old knees don't let me get into the field anymore. Of course, I remember your beautiful mother, Lucrezia. Black hair. Green eyes. We called her Creta the Cat. It's been too long, too long," he said nostalgically. He turned toward his grandson. "Amir, my boy, how good of you to bring Justine to see me. I don't see you often enough. Do you think she's changed much?"

Justine turned, wide-eyed, toward Amir, who looked quite sheepish. "You knew me as a child?" He continued to catch her off-guard.

"I knew you," he said, helping his grandfather into one of the chairs. "Yes, Grandfather, I believe she has changed a great deal." He turned back to Justine. "My father was working in a United Emirates bank when you were here last, so we were out of country. I haven't seen you since you were quite young, and I didn't realize that Nadia was bringing you last night. It wasn't quite the place to reminisce." His explanation was matter-of-fact, but she sensed again that with Amir, much more was left unsaid than was spoken.

Ignoring, or perhaps not noticing, the tension between them, Ibrahim continued cheerfully: "The two of you used to play together as children at the Ghezira Club. Quite competitive." He paused, searching for the next words. "How is your younger brother, Amir? I haven't heard from Zachariah for a long while."

"I haven't heard from him recently myself, but I'm sure that he is doing well. He has a new job in Kuwait," said Amir, wincing almost imperceptibly.

Justine hid her surprise at his quick fabrication—he'd lied to her by omission the night before, and outright just now to his grandfather. *Who is this man?*

"Tell him to call me, will you? I worry." A flicker of sadness traveled through Ibrahim's expressive eyes.

"I will, Grandfather. And I will leave you now so you can visit," offered Amir, starting to rise from his chair.

"Nonsense, my boy. Stay." Ibrahim patted his knee. "We can have tea, talk awhile, and then you can take me home."

"As you wish, Grandfather. I'll see to the tea."

As Amir walked out of the room, Ibrahim turned to Justine. "The two boys are terribly close. Always were. Amir is the oldest and he would do anything for Zachariah. Zach has had some problems. Gets depressed, angry. But he's really a good boy."

"I'm sure he is, sir." Justine patted his hand, watching his eyes well up.

Amir returned, followed by an elderly man shaped like a question mark, who carefully balanced three cups of tea on a tray.

Justine watched the crippled man gently place the tea on Ibrahim's cedar desk. He appeared to be about the same age as Ibrahim, in his mid-eighties. *How invisible he is*, she thought, *as though he isn't even here*. "Thank you," she said to the anonymous man.

Ibrahim nodded faintly to the servant, then proceeded to add three cubes of sugar to his cup. Catching Justine's eye, he smiled and said, "The one indulgence left at my age. So, what brings you back to Cairo, my dear?"

She explained her work with the community schools in simple detail. The female students, teachers, her observations. "They're called 'community' schools because each small community must provide the space and governance, though the project provides the teachers, curriculum, evaluation, and training."

Ibrahim's eyes lit up like a small boy's. "Wonderful idea! Much needed. You are providing a great service to Egypt, my dear."

Justine flushed. "Thank you. This project was a wonderful opportunity to return to Egypt. Ever since mother took me to Old Cairo as a child, I've been intrigued by the travels of the Holy Family here, especially Mary of Nazareth."

Ibrahim nodded thoughtfully. "There is little in the Bible about Mary. But there is more to be found about her in the Koran. I've always found that amazing," he said.

Amir was watching Justine with uncharacteristic approval—perhaps to acknowledge the respect and care with which she spoke to his grandfather? She sensed a deep affection between the men.

She tucked her hair behind her ear, feeling how the waning afternoon sun touched her skin. "Father reminded me that you and my mother are both Coptic Christian . . ." It was an invitation.

"I was raised a Copt and the beliefs are an important part of me. Jesus, Mary, sacrifice, fasting, worship. 'Copt' stems from the original name for Egypt, *Misr*. We give more attention to Mary than Protestants do—we're more like Catholics and Greek Orthodox. We even have our own Pope here in Cairo. So yes, I am still a Copt." He nodded. "However, about twenty years ago, I set out to explore and understand other religious traditions. I've been in search of the essence, the common center—the heart, if you will—of religious thought."

"Have you been successful in your pursuit of the essence of religion, Grandfather?" asked Amir, sipping his sweet tea, one leg crossed over the other.

"I've found some success, my boy, although the road stretches out for a lifetime. May God give me enough time to discover more of the Tao."

"The Tao?" asked Justine.

"Each religious tradition has a Tao, a Way, by which we are to live our lives," he said. "Each religion seeks to enrich the soul, to find Truth. My dear friend Rabbi Yitzhak Kaduri, a Kabbalist, said, 'Love thy neighbor. All else is commentary.' Yitzhak died last year at the good age of 106. May God grant me such longevity." He paused in remembrance, and a deep, long sigh escaped him.

Ibrahim turned slowly toward Justine. "Egyptian proverbs engraved on our tombs before the time of Abraham implore us to 'Know ourselves and love our neighbors.' The great men Jesus and Mohammed asked the same of us. 'Hurt no one so that no one may hurt you,' said Mohammed in his last sermon. Shared virtues show us the way. But it is easier to understand them than to live our lives by the Tao." A little breathless again, Ibrahim stopped and combed his gnarled hand through his beard.

"And what are those virtues, Grandfather? How do we find the Way?" Amir leaned in, his elbows resting on both knees like a young boy.

"The virtues are well known to you, my boy, but we humans have great difficulty living them. We are continually tested. Among the great virtues, we find first and foremost compassion, then love, humility, forgiveness, tolerance, truth-telling, and mercy. Jesus was exceptionally clear about these virtues. To him they were more important than the letter of the Law. The Tao says that courage comes from mercy."

"Courage comes from mercy?" Justine puzzled. "I'm not sure I understand."

"Mercy means compassion, kindness, forgiveness toward those who have offended us." She could see why her father had often spoken of the influence of Ibrahim's enthusiasm; his eyes radiated passion as he spoke. "Think of the reconciliation trials in South Africa. The South Africans have moved past their pain and their history of suffering by overcoming their fear of each other and practicing forgiveness. Bishop Tutu says that forgiveness requires us to relinquish our right to revenge. That takes courage."

"But how do we live the Tao, Dr. Ibrahim? It would seem that many of us attempt the good life, but so often stumble on our egos." She glanced briefly at Amir.

"The ego is indeed a big stumbling block. The Buddhists and Kabbalists suggest that if we can stand back, listen, and give up the temptation to react, our egos may flow away into the silence, into the Great River of Life. Each tradition—the Jews, Buddhists, Copts, Muslims, Essenes—offers us tasks to prepare us for the Way: sacrifice, poverty, fasting, prayer, giving, forgiving. The Tao says he who is gentle and yielding is the disciple of life. I think this may be what Mohammed meant by 'submission.'" Ibrahim raised his glasses and rubbed his nose. "Enough of my philosophizing for today, my children. Can you take me home now, Amir?"

༄

A few minutes later, Amir returned, and the taxi pulled out into the busy traffic alongside the Roman aqueduct. Gazing out the window, he said, "Grandfather has lived here all of his life, and although the building is falling down around him, he refuses to move."

"This life may make the Tao easier," Justine suggested. They both smiled.

Amir suddenly leaned forward and told the driver, "*El ahramaat, Sawe Taks*." The driver made a U-turn and headed west toward Roda Island.

"The pyramids?" She was surprised. "I thought you were taking me back to the Shepheard."

"You haven't been to the pyramids yet, right?" His dark eyes sparkled playfully.

"I just arrived yesterday, so you know I haven't been there on this trip. I'm not fond of being abducted," she said lightly.

"Ah, but it's the right time of day. The sunset is almost upon us." With that, Amir took out his phone and checked for texts. As he read one, Justine thought she could see anguish wash across his face, and he remained on his phone for the rest of the drive.

As they rode in silence, she allowed herself to relax, gazing at the miles of new development east of the Nile and recalling the conversation with Ibrahim.

After a few minutes, she leaned forward and addressed the driver. "Hassan," she said, reading the nametag hanging from the dash. "Are you from Cairo?" she asked in Arabic.

"No, miss," he said over his shoulder. "From Aswan. To the south."

"Aswan is so beautiful. You must miss it."

"*Iwa*, I miss my mother, my brothers. But no work in Aswan. Few tourists since 9/11."

"I understand. It was a tragedy for all of us. Do you have family here?"

"Good family, but sad for me. For my daughter, Adara. When she was six, she pulled boiling water off stove. Scar her body. Horrible, Miss. Horrible! Now she sixteen in year three secondary school. She depressed, isolates herself. She says she won't marry—no one will want her."

In the rearview mirror, Justine watched Hassan's eyes moisten; she turned to see if Amir was listening. His fingers had stilled on the keys of his phone, and without looking up, he nodded solemnly. Health coverage didn't exist in Egypt, at least not for families like Hassan's. "Let me talk with our agency doctor," she told the driver. "I'm not sure if anything can be done, but give me your phone number."

"Thank you, Miss," he said, handing her his card and falling quiet.

As the pyramids began to rise above the glitzy shops of Giza, Justine's attention was drawn to a black canvas-sided army truck in front of them. Four young soldiers dangled their feet from the back, kicking the air, laughing, and smoking. Soon the truck turned north onto the desert road, providing the young men with a clear view of the pyramids. None of them looked up.

"They didn't even look," exclaimed Justine. "One of the great wonders of the world in their line of sight and they didn't look up!"

Amir smiled wryly. "We Egyptians cherish our history, but sometimes the youth pay no attention. Without history, the pyramids are just a pile of rocks."

She turned toward him to see if he was kidding. He shrugged.

The taxi entered a gate alongside the Sphinx, where Amir showed his government pass. "Taxis are usually not allowed on this road," he explained, "but we're headed for the desert plateau about half a mile to the west." The taxi drove forward onto the road, weaving between the largest two of the three pyramids.

The dark, towering walls of the Great Pyramid Cheops and his brother Chephren blotted out the sky. At no other place on the massive Giza plateau could Justine have felt the same eerie powers of the unexplainable. She trembled. Ahead, the slanting walls of the pyramids blended sand and sky into a golden V. The taxi wound into the Sahara sands and parked atop a plateau crowded with Bedouins, complete with turbans and camels. Dusty maroon cloths stretched out on the ground, displaying the wares of local traders: small alabaster jars, daggers, silver jewelry, and striped camel blankets with long black tassels.

One of the Bedouin leaders, holding the reins of a camel in one hand, gestured invitingly toward Justine as she stepped from the car. She took several steps toward him.

Two hands grabbed her firmly by the waist. She turned, eyes flashing with indignation. "What do you think you're doing?" she demanded.

Amir raised his hands in pacification, amusement written on his face. "If you walk up to the camel, you'll be lifted on top to have your picture taken. He'll expect generous baksheesh. There'll be no turning back." Now quite serious, he warned, "Bedouins don't like to be disappointed."

She laughed softly. "*Mafeesh mushkilla*, no problem . . . I didn't even bring my camera." She turned around as the now displeasured Bedouin moved toward Amir with his camel whip raised in the air.

"Perhaps we should leave," he said, his voice tensing. "Quickly."

OLD CAIRO, 2 CE

My young son holds tight to my hand and the basket used for our purchases. Across the Great River to the west, giant pyramids loom above the landscape.

His eyes are wide, his mouth slightly open as he looks at the golden saffron from India, purple saffron from Persia, and green mint from the Sinai, all pressed together in canvas bags surrounding a one-eyed man in a turban.

The local market, nestled in the center of our small, but expanding, village is always busy in the days before Passover. Double flutes and sistrums, rattles with soft metallic sounds to soothe the gods, are but breezes blowing through papyrus reeds, while the thundering voices of passionate speakers of all persuasions throb in the air. A cacophony of tongues and a distinctive mix of facial features and dress attest to varied countries of origin . . . many from the East have trekked across the desert from the Red Sea and will go north on the Great River to Alexandria, Crete, and Rome. Purple-skinned Nubians who have herded camels from the South now tether them at the edge of the village. Still others are the color of olive oil from The Fayoum.

"Mother, where do all the people come from?" My son's eyes are excited, sparked by the exotic peoples and products.

"They come from many places—the East, Persia, Nubia, and villages in the desert. They meet here for today's market. Tomorrow they may go on to Heliopolis or Memphis."

We walk among overflowing bags of oranges, lemons, and small bananas arranged together with local garlic, onions, and lentils. Tunics, prayer cloths, and tablecloths embellished with gold and silver threads are displayed on a large spread of fabric under the shade of a blue canvas awning.

"What have we come for today, Mother?" he asks without taking his eyes off the flying, snake-shaped stick being thrown about by a group of small children.

"To find some saffron for our fish stews, some olive oil from The Fayoum, a few pieces of papyrus, and a small gift for your father—that is, if merchants will accept a few coins and some buds of garlic." Not unlike other families in the village, our family grows food, fishes, and makes most of our own clothes and furnishings. Barter is the usual medium of exchange, although the Romans have given my husband a small number of dinars for his work on the gates, and our eldest earns a few more from his work on the canal. Recently, we purchased a new donkey.

I stop beside a seated man who is unbothered by the swirling fury around him. The scribe, surrounded by his papyrus, pallets, pens, and ink, sits in the middle of the market, ready to take dictation from travelers eager to send letters to their families. I ask for three pieces of papyrus.

"Why the papyrus?" my son asks. "For writing to our family in Palestine?"

"Yes, my son. Our family members are hungry for news from us. They ask about how you and your brother are growing up and what it is like to live in this land. They miss us. And your father misses his family." I take a few clusters of garlic from my pocket to hand to the scribe.

My son hesitates before asking the question I know has been pressing on his young mind. "I have noticed that Rachel and Noha do not write. Can only some women write?"

"All women can write if they are taught how. Just as you were taught to read and write."

The scribe, a neighbor to the north, holds up his hand and gently refuses the garlic. "I do not need any garlic today. Why don't you have your son bring me radishes tomorrow?"

"It will be so," I say. I direct us toward a large stone near the side of the market. As we sit down, a young boy appears and asks if we would have tea. I agree and he scampers off.

"How did you learn to write, Mother?" my son asks, balancing on the edge of the rock and folding his tunic between his tanned legs.

"It is unusual for women to learn to write. You have observed well. I was fortunate. My grandmother taught me when I was but a girl. She thought it important for women to be able to do many of the same things men do. Grandmother considered inequality the source of all evil. I wish you could have known her."

"What did she mean by 'inequality is the source of all evil'?" he puzzles.

The tea arrives in two chipped, mismatched cups. I hand the boy a cluster of garlic. My son has an inquiring mind, much like I did as a child. "What do you think she might have meant?"

"I don't know. To me, most people seem unequal: Noha is not like Rachel, Isaiah is not like Samir."

"I see the same things. But Grandmother also talked of inequality between the rich and poor, men and women, the educated and uneducated, the old and the young, Jews and pagans, Romans and Israelites. These inequalities lead to misery, hatred, and wars, which are evil. Her family came from Mt. Carmel and had many strong ideas about how life should be lived. Many of these ideas I carry with me."

"But why did God make us unequal if He wanted us to be equal? I don't understand."

"I'm not so sure God made us so. Perhaps we did that to ourselves. It is we who choose to obey the powerful and deprive others of their rights. Perhaps God gave us these choices to test our compassion."

We sit silently for a while, sipping the strong tea to which the boy has generously added a little honey. As he always does when he is struggling with an idea, my son sits very still, as though hypnotized by some distant object. I try to follow his eyes, but they seem to rest in the air over the market. We finish our tea and set the cups on a small tray left nearby.

No longer holding my hand, my son occasionally stops to look at displays of tools and musical instruments. Two Egyptians display amulets, ankhs, and djed pillars.

"These adornments are tucked into the long wrappings of mummies for their trip to the afterworld," I explain. "The Egyptians believe that when people die they go to a land far beyond the sunset and will have need of many tools and foods."

At the far side of the market square, narrow alleys lead to temporary living quarters for traders and other visitors. "Do you believe there is a land beyond the sun?" my son asks as he bends down to smell the bread baking in a public oven. Smells of the freshly baked bread, jasmine and mint, and human waste escaping from the alleyways blend into their own odor, neither repugnant nor fragrant.

"I would be grateful if God prepares a place for us to be with Him after we die. But our people do not savor the idea as others do . . ." I let my words trail off as my son is distracted by a small child of about three who runs in front of us, almost knocking into me. The beautiful child has the face of an angel—curly golden hair, long lashes, and a mouth the color of pomegranate. She throws herself into the lap of a woman sitting among a few prayer cloths offered for sale. The woman's black, uncovered hair glistens, and her unusual eyes are black with golden flecks.

I cannot comprehend whether her eyes tell of contentment or resignation. Her tunic is old and frayed with broken threads, as though the garment has been washed with a rough stone. As the child cuddles deeply into her lap, the fabric draws back to reveal rough, uneven stubs ending just below her knees. With an air of dignity, she quickly shifts her position and lowers her tunic.

"Good morning, my lady." She addresses me with a confident air as my son clasps my hand and holds tight.

"Good morning, my friend." I return her smile. "These are beautiful prayer cloths. Did you make them?" I kneel to examine the fine needlework.

"The Goddess has given me the gift of needlework. This is how I spend my days." She beams with the pleasure of pride.

"And how much do you want for such beautiful work?" I inquire.

"Mother," whispers my son, gently pulling on my sleeve, "don't we have enough prayer cloths? Will we have enough dinars left?"

"One can never have too many prayer cloths," I assure him, keeping my eyes on the woman and handing her enough dinars for two cloths. My son and I exchange glances, and his furrowed brow changes to an expression of understanding. I realize I have not witnessed this gaze of wisdom from him before. He is beginning to comprehend. I am pleased.

As we walk away, I say to my son, "The woman has great pride and dignity. It is better to be charitable by buying her needlework than to give her alms. The giving of alms will only bring her shame."

He nods as if sharing an important secret with me. "Perhaps the men from the East will exchange some saffron for garlic."

"And the olive oil can wait for another day, although Noha will not be happy." We both grin at the thought.

The golden saffron glows among the more subdued spices of coriander, cumin, pepper, mint, dark paprika, and teas. Copper jewelry glistens beside ornate vests. The merchant, or rather the son of the merchant, must be about my son's age, perhaps a few summers older. We stop in front of the colorful array of treasures.

"Welcome, my Egyptian friends, how can I take your dinars today?" asks the young man in Aramaic. With his black curly hair and fetching smile, he could be Samir's son.

"We have something better than money," my son quickly replies. "We bring you jewels of garlic."

"Ah, so. I have met my match! Next, you will offer me some rounded stones. What is your name?" His baggy pants, sash, and adorned vest give him the air of a youthful sultan.

My son introduces both of us.

"I am glad to meet you," he replies, bowing from the waist and moving his right arm in a flowing movement up over his head. "My name is Ravi. I am here with my father. We have traveled from India. A long way from here."

"We live nearby," offers my son. "I was born in Palestine and we traveled here to Egypt when I was a baby in my mother's arms." The two boys recognize something familiar in each other. A radiant curiosity?

"We can always use some garlic, my father and I. I can offer you a small pinch of saffron for one stew, my lady." The clever boy picks up a large sycamore leaf from a small collection he keeps under the display cloth and fills it with a generous pinch of saffron. He hands it to my son, who carefully folds the leaf over the saffron and places it in the basket, nestled beneath the prayer cloths.

"We thank you, Ravi," we both say, almost at the same time. My son moves on reluctantly as we bow and take our leave.

"Perhaps Ravi and his father would like to try the fish stew made with the saffron," I suggest. "Would you like to invite them to come to dinner tonight?"

"Could we, Mother? May I invite them?"

"As you wish, my son." He turns and hurries back to the spice quarter while I slowly study other wares. I am glad to see my son's confidence growing each day. He often reminds me of myself. I remember the day my mother told me that I would marry an older man. "He is a good man. He will take care of you," she said.

"I don't need a protector," I had insisted. Yet my husband is more than a protector. He is my friend. What will I do when he is no longer with us?

My son quickly catches up with me. "Ravi was much pleased, Mother. He said he was tired of his father's cooking. He will ask his father and let us know soon. I told him how to get to our home."

"That is good, my son. I'm sure the others will not mind. Your father is interested in new people and their ideas," I assure him, feeling somewhat rash for not consulting my husband first.

With the papyrus on top of the basket, we start home. "What about a gift for father?"

"A prayer cloth?"

"I'm sure he will appreciate a new prayer cloth." My son gently takes my hand again, this time to help me over the rough terrain between the marketplace and home.

CHAPTER 4

———⟨⟩———

J USTINE AWOKE DREAMING OF A FIERY sunset and walls closing in on her, suffocating her. Startled, she sat up shivering and forced herself to take a deep
breath. She picked up the remote and turned on the television. She needed
another voice in the room.

"Hamas, a splinter group of Egypt's Muslim Brotherhood, was established
in 1987. Since its victory in Palestine in January of 2006, it has shown no inter-
est in changing its charter provision, that calls for the destruction of Israel. Mr.
Netanyahu, how are Israel and the international community working with
Palestine under these conditions?" asked Wolf Blitzer on the late edition of
CNN news.

"There can be no work with Palestine until Hamas agrees to—"

Hardly comforting, she thought, turning off the familiar, strident voice of
Bebe Netanyahu. She stretched and padded down the stairs to take a shower.
The trip to the pyramids with Amir had been majestic, and today she felt the
pull of Old Cairo, St. Sergius Church, and her past.

As she sat at her dressing table, methodically packing her camera, notebook, and water into a canvas bag, she wondered, *How long will Cairo be safe?*
Americans were already hesitant to travel to the Middle East, most of them
limiting their visits to Egypt to cumbersome group tours. Islamic extremism
was reaching epic proportions. The Egypt that she'd known as a young girl
was rapidly disappearing, politically and religiously tearing itself into separate
camps. The Cairo street called out for a hero who would stand up to the West,

and Iran's President Ahmadinejad was looking quite good to many who wanted a spokesman for anti-Westernism.

Outside, though, it was a beautiful Sunday morning seemingly unmarred by political concerns. Justine headed to Tahrir Square, walked down the stairs into Sadat station, and purchased a ticket to Mars Girgius. The Metro, built by the French in the 1980s, was a spinal cord running underground through Cairo, with ribs branching across the Nile to Mohandeseen and Giza. The Metro was considered efficient, clean, and safe—qualities that would make New Yorkers envious.

The ride south to Old Cairo—Babylon—took only fifteen minutes, a trip that would have taken an hour by car. On a good day. In spite of the growing anti-Westernism among Cairenes, this morning the people in the Metro seemed friendly toward Justine. Yet before that thought could fade, she sensed a critical stare from three young men standing toward the back of the car. She pulled her scarf up over her long hair and turned away.

Stepping out of the Metro at Mars Girgius, she descended the stairs alongside Roman fortifications and the Coptic Museum courtyard. Massive round sandstone fortifications formed huge labyrinths that circled inside each other. Two thousand years ago, the Nile had lapped up against these shores, and the delta—which now began north of Cairo—had fanned out to Alexandria. For four hundred years, the Romans had found it important to build where they could keep an eye on the river and desert trade routes.

The last time Justine had visited Old Cairo, her mother had explained to her why so many religious groups considered this ground sacred. Legend had it that the Holy Family had stayed here during their flight from Palestine. It was believed that this was where baby Moses had been found in the reed basket, and where he later collected the Children of Israel to begin the fateful march to the Red Sea. It was also rumored, although with less confidence, that St. George of dragon fame had been tortured in the catacombs below the Ben Ezre Synagogue before being sent back to Palestine for his beheading.

Bypassing the Hanging Church built atop one of the Roman forts, where a small group of tourists listened to a German guide, Justine continued east on Mars Girgius. Stepping down onto the flight of stairs leading under the towering clay arch in the wall surrounding Old Cairo, she proceeded along a narrow cobblestone corridor past the St. George nunnery and a large antiquities shop, closed on Sunday. A few locals brushed shoulders with her as she walked. Muslims on their way to work; Copts readying for church. The narrowness of the alleys felt claustrophobic, their shadows cloaking the occasional beggar crouched silently in a corner. After several turns, she spied St. Sergius just ahead. Ducking under a low-hanging wall, she entered an even narrower passageway that was filthy with debris. Would she ever stop being surprised by such neglect of historic places?

Five more steps and she entered the sanctuary of the fifth-century St. Sergius Church, supposedly named after one of two martyred Roman soldiers, Sergius and Bacchus. Justine, however, preferred to think that the church was named for Pope Sergius I. It was he who, determined to stir the faith of the people of Rome, had initiated all-night candlelit processions through the city for the Virgin Mary on feast days.

Her thoughts raced back to her earlier visit here with her mother—the day she'd become captivated by the life of Mary. Her mother had suggested it was the Egyptian goddess Isis—Theotokos, the Mother of God—who had created the context in which Mary and Jesus could be so easily accepted, worshiped. The magical qualities Isis possessed had spread throughout the Greek and Roman world. People were drawn to her tenacity in saving and resurrecting her husband, her ethereal qualities, and her devotion to her son, Horus. At that time, any god worth his or her salt was born of a virgin mother, Lucrezia had explained. Although powerful and all-knowing, Isis was most often depicted as holding and nursing her son. Her maternal tenderness, coupled with such strength, was irresistible. Thus the scene had been set for Mary and Jesus to come along.

"Isis and Mary were even portrayed alike—long, ringleted hair falling luxuriantly, a crown of flowers, a mirror emitting a divine light. It was easy for many to transfer their loyalties, especially in Egypt," her mother had said, sitting on these very steps and pointing toward the paintings. Where had her father been? Justine tried to remember. Off on his dig at Saqqara, probably. They'd been so caught up in her mother's stories that it had grown dark by the time they left St. Sergius and returned to the hotel. She remembered opening the door and seeing the fury on her father's face, the loud argument between her parents that night. And then Justine had been shuttled off to stay with her mother's sister for the rest of their time in Egypt.

Such thoughts crowded her mind as she stepped into the narthex of St. Sergius, a long hall on the side of the church reserved for those who were new to the church and needed instructions, those who had confessed to sins and were seeking penitence, and for women—considered sinners ever since Eve corrupted the Garden. Christian leaders and historians once feared that if the myths of Isis and Mary as virgin mothers were broken, somehow the religion would be broken as well. It must have seemed reasonable at the time. But today?

Ahead of her, a large basin, formerly used for blessings during the Epiphany, was now boarded over. At the end of this long hall was the baptistery. The nave, or center of the church, was separated from the side aisles by marble pillars with arches and columns that supported the timber roof. In the pews, two elderly women kneeled in prayer.

Justine noticed with disappointment that figures once carved in detail on the columns were only barely discernable now. Adorning the right wall were icons of religious subjects dating to medieval times, including Christ's birth, miracles, baptism, and resurrection. During a recent renovation of the church, a carving of the Last Supper had been added showing Jesus sitting with his disciples at an ancient Egyptian offering table.

She slid into an empty pew near the center of the church. Ahead of her, an elevated marble pulpit embossed with ebony and ivory rested on ten columns. The sanctuary screen was decorated with large crosses and delicately chiseled with scrollwork. At the entrance, she'd picked up a small booklet written by the resident priest that described the art scenes throughout St. Sergius. Two-by-fours rested loosely on the rafters, most likely used for cleaning paintings in the dome. Justine looked up to admire the panel engraving known as "The Flight into Egypt." The now-famous painting illustrated Mary on a mule, wearing a crown and holding Jesus, followed by Joseph and a woman reported in the booklet to be Mary of Magdalene. A strange depiction, she noted, as it was generally accepted that Mary of Magdalene was a contemporary of Jesus.

This impressive edifice would not have existed 2000 years ago. She imagined Mary sitting as she herself sat today . . . right here beside her. *What was it like then?* What would she have been thinking about? Was she concerned about her children, her marriage, the health of her family? What about the Romans? And Herod's army? Were they a real threat? Or were her thoughts more mundane . . . like what to serve for dinner? At the time Mary had lived in the cave below this church, the Great River Nile had been close by, and in the far distance had been the hills known as Muqattum. Would there have been a bench here? A fire pit? *What was it like to live in a foreign land and try to carve out a life for your family?*

Like the other churches, the synagogue, and the mosque in Babylon, St. Sergius was an active place of worship. Only a few scattered people sat here now, but in less than an hour hundreds of parishioners would crowd into the church to receive absolution from their priest; women with covered heads would file into the western narthex. While the Prophet Mohammed was blamed for making the headscarf a modern-day habit, it was in fact an ancient tribal custom that preceded even the Christians. Older Christian women still wore headscarves to church. *What is it about hair?*

Justine decided she would join the congregation after her visit to the crypt, the entrance to which was behind the altar area, beneath the choir room. As she entered the crypt area, she found a young docent who introduced himself as Michael. *A good Christian name.* He was lean, with a restrained air and a long-sleeved plaid shirt buttoned to the top; within the stone walls of the church, the air was cool.

"I understand the Holy Family lived here," Justine said, running a hand along the banister at the top of the crypt stairwell.

"You have found it," responded Michael with a delight that made her suspect she was his first visitor of the day. "The Holy Family came here from Palestine. Their last stop before coming to Babylon was Mataria, which is now in Shoubra. They stayed here for six months and then traveled south. They took a boat downriver at the Church of the Blessed Virgin Mary in Maadi." He spoke with the cadence of someone reading a prepared script. "It is known that they traveled to Assuit from Maadi."

When he took a short breath, Justine said kindly, "Thank you. I appreciate the information." In fact, she knew that since the Nile had not been far from this church two thousand years ago—certainly not more than a few hundred feet—the port at Maadi, being a mile or so west, would have been underwater then. She chose not to say so. Much like the painting of The Flight into Egypt, there were nebulous areas where challenge would not be welcome here. "Are you a volunteer here? Do you live nearby?"

"I volunteer every Sunday, Miss. And grew up just over there," he said, pointing to the east.

"The church must appreciate your work. Tell me, how long was the Holy Family in Egypt?"

An expression of pride flickered across the docent's face. "They journeyed in Egypt for three and a half years. Then the Angel Gabriel appeared to Joseph in a dream and said, 'Take your son and go home, go out of Egypt. The man who would kill your son is now dead.'" By quoting Matthew, Michael had provided the definitive answer.

Justine nodded. "I have heard that the Muslims tell another story. They think the Holy Family stayed in Egypt for a longer time. What do you think?"

"This is what our church teaches, my lady." Michael's voice tightened with impatience. "Oral history is important here. Many churches and monasteries have been built on the sites where the family stopped and stayed for short visits. The Roman soldiers were chasing them because they'd fled with the Messiah. This history was confirmed when the Virgin Mary appeared to the Patriarch Theophilus, Bishop of Alexandria, in the fourth century." His confidence grew as he picked up the momentum of his story. "Our Lady told the bishop about the journey of the Holy Family and where they had stopped along the way. Our priest says the bishop had the good sense to find out many things from the Virgin."

"He did indeed. I have not heard the story of the Patriarch before. You are very fortunate to have this history," she acknowledged with a smile. "May I go in now?"

"Certainly, my lady." His performance over, he stepped out of her way, and she descended the thirteen worn steps to the marble floor of the crypt below, thinking, *What happened two thousand years ago in this anointed cave?*

As the cool crypt air brushed against her warm neck, she imagined the day ahead. It was particularly beautiful outside. The Nile had glistened like scattered diamonds as she'd stepped out of the Metro and glanced to the west. What would she do with the rest of her day? Perhaps a stroll at the Ghezira Club, followed by a frosty hibiscus near the pool? A visit to the new Cairo Opera House?

✑

The earthquake hit with such force that its memory would stay with Justine for decades to come, inhabiting her dreams like an unwelcome stranger. Nearly crushed by falling debris, smothered in darkness and sandstone dust, her consciousness clung to those last moments before her adrenaline caused her to fight back, to prevent herself from being buried alive in the crypt . . .

When the second aftershock passed and the ground stilled, she forced herself to sit up. Thankfully, the columns had held. A searing pain in her head made her wince. Something wet dripped into her left eye, trickling into the corner of her mouth. Tasting the salt of blood, she lifted her fingers to her head and discovered a jagged gash. Her hair was growing wet with the blood. Was there a possibility she would pass out? She had to get out of here before that happened.

She dug ferociously, then crawled gingerly through the new opening she'd created in the plaster pilings. Had she lost something? She turned back and reached for the canvas bag that held her camera and—

A sharp sensation seared her right leg. She shuddered. *I've been cut badly, but I'm not feeling much pain now. It will come.* A groan sounded above her, and she forced herself to focus, moving on her knees toward where she thought the entrance was—or, at least, had been. She had to reach the stairs before the beam above her collapsed.

Fallen plaster was layered like crackers around sections of caved-in Corinthian cornices. Ahead of her, a welcome stream of fresh air entered her nostrils, along with the musty smell of mildew. Finally, her right hand touched the bottom of a step, and she nearly cried out with relief. She slowly eased herself upward, ignoring the shooting pain in her ribcage. A small beam of light began to dance sporadically around the crypt. On the sixth step, several two-by-fours secured by fallen plaster and bricks blocked her way.

"Are you there, my lady?" a man's voice yelled down. "Are you all right?" The flicker of light grew stronger, illuminating the steps above.

"I'm here! Help me, Michael," she screamed back. As she watched, Michael began to unwedge the two-by-fours, a flashlight balanced in one hand. In short order he'd cleared enough space to provide a narrow passage out of the crypt. He took her hand and pulled her toward him. Justine held on tightly to steady herself, fighting back the dizziness, her foot seeking the top step.

"I think we can get out this way," he said, his voice trembling as he took in the gash on her head, her hands, the blood running onto her ankle. He led her into the well of the church. Shattered amber chandeliers and panels from the dome lay across smashed pews. One of the Corinthian columns leaned against another. Plaster and dust were beginning to settle and filter the meager light coming in from outside. In one of the untouched corners of a pew, an elderly woman in a scarf and long, dark paisley dress sat frozen in place, sobbing and praying aloud. Her wrinkled features moved closer together until her eyes were but small slits, reminding Justine of an apple doll she'd had as a child.

"Please, let's go, ma'am. The church may collapse any minute," Michael begged in Arabic. The old woman turned toward Michael and reluctantly nodded, slowly standing. He and Justine each took hold of an arm, gently ushering the old woman toward the door. Thank God the full church service had not yet begun.

As they stepped out into the narrow passageway, made narrower by fallen debris, Justine asked, "Where are the others?"

"Many ran when the building began to shake. Our people are afraid of God's wrath," he said.

"And you came back for me?" Justine was as astounded as she was grateful. He nodded. "Thank you," she said simply. A wave of nausea momentarily moved through her and she fell silent, her leg and head throbbing. The elderly lady was nearly white, her skin matching the whites of her wide-open eyes. They all ducked under the remaining archway and proceeded down the cobblestone alleyway. Collapsed walls of sandstone and layers of plaster and glass made their progress slow. The huge window on the antiquities shop had shattered into the passageway; life-sized statutes of the Egyptian gods Anubis and Horus had tumbled out into the walkway. The gods loomed large before them, as though chastening them for centuries of neglect. As they passed the statues, the old woman cried out in renewed terror.

Several minutes later, the three of them emerged into the chaos of Mars Girgius Street. A few tour buses were still sitting in the usual places. People screamed and ran as a smaller aftershock jarred the street. A part of the outer wall of Old Cairo had caved in upon itself, as had many of the buildings that lined the north side of the street. Two small cafés were no longer visible. Screaming sirens filled the air. Above, an innocent blue sky with powder-puff clouds seemed unaware that the earth was collapsing.

Justine suggested to Michael that he stay with the older woman. "I will find my way back," she said, although she had no idea how she would. Certainly the Metro was no longer an option.

"No, my lady, we must stay together. You are hurt and it's not safe," Michael insisted, holding tightly to both women's arms.

"I thank you for saving me, Michael. I don't know what I would have done without you, but I will go now." She touched him gently on the cheek. She was not sure why she needed to separate herself from the pair, but she found herself almost as unnerved by the old woman's hysteria as by the threat of another aftershock. She turned east and hobbled toward the cluster of black-and-white taxis. There were no drivers in sight. Cars sped frantically along Mars Girgius.

"You're hurt," shouted a voice from across the busy street. Justine turned to see a man racing toward her from Amr Ibn al-As Mosque. "Justine, it's Mohammed!" the man exclaimed.

Mohammed. Mohammed, she repeated to herself. With a start, she recognized Nadia's Mohammed from the felucca. The Apple T-shirt. Their meeting seemed so long ago.

Examining her torn skirt, cut leg, and bleeding hands, as well as the blood matting her hair, Mohammed took hold of both of Justine's shoulders. "I'm taking you back to the hotel. It's right on my way home. I live in Mohandeseen, and fortunately Lulu and the kids are at her mother's in Alex."

His obvious concern was comforting. Relief flooded through Justine, and she began to cry softly.

"I'm not sure which streets are open, but we'll give it a try," Mohammed said, the timidity of two nights before now gone. Justine slipped into the passenger seat of his waiting Fiat. The engine responded on the first try and Mohammed slowly pulled into the panic-stricken traffic.

"Were you in Babylon this morning?"

She nodded, then winced. *Not a good idea.* "I went to see the crypt under St. Sergius. I was there when the earthquake hit."

Mohammed's jaw was set, eyes straight ahead. Both hands tightly gripped the wheel. "That must have been frightening, and you're quite bloody. We need to get help for your head . . . I was in the mosque across from Old Cairo. Fortunately, the mosque has been newly restored, so it withstood the quake. Allah's punishment was not as severe this time."

Justine forced herself to talk, to keep herself distracted. Her head and leg throbbed with each beat of her heart. "Egyptians already seem devout to me. What more do you think Allah wants from you?"

"We masquerade devoutness to fool our gods. Our women wear the veil with tight jeans. We listen to Western music, see your violent movies, and yearn for an easy life of self-indulgence. We hardly object when America occupies a Muslim country. American politicians wear hunting jackets, and we fit neatly into their big pockets. What have we come to?" He asked the question vehemently, as though speaking to Allah.

"Yet there are scientific explanations for earthquakes, are there not? You're a man of modern technologies and science," she pressed. She was starting to feel clammy; she wondered if shock might be setting in.

"Allah has created the science of earthquakes, but He reserves the 'when' and the 'where' to send His message about how we live." They drove along the aqueduct and turned onto Kasr el Aini, moving away from the Corniche, a one-way street going in the wrong direction. The giant hotels circling the Nile could be seen as they turned. They appeared untouched. *Perhaps things aren't as bad as they seemed in Old Cairo.*

Qasr al-Ainy Street told a different story. Random destruction was everywhere. Deeply cracked buildings seemed to lean on each other for support. Some houses had collapsed inward while others remained standing. *Is this God's selectivity?* Two Red Crescent trucks raced by, on their way to dispatch aid. In the distance, the minaret on Ibn Tulun Mosque had toppled into the courtyard below.

Mohammed looked devastated by the destruction outside the car. "We have no building codes—at least none we abide by," he explained. "The plaster is watered down, foundations are not secured, and beams are left out of critical support areas. The '92 earthquake was only a 5.9 and yet we lost over five hundred lives and more than ten thousand buildings. Worst of all, we panicked. More than forty school children in Shoubra district were trampled. We're a careless people." He shook his head in dismay.

Ahead, Tahrir Square was closed. "We'll turn here and park near the British Embassy." Mohammed glanced over at her. "We'll need to walk, but it's only a few blocks to the Shepheard. Do you think you can make it?"

Justine assured him that she could.

On foot, they made their way along the Corniche, which was strewn with rubble from cement blocks, plaster, glass, and uprooted sidewalks. Contrary to Egyptian custom demanding that unrelated men and women should not touch in public, Mohammed held Justine's arm and carried her bag.

To her great relief, the Shepheard stood tall and firm. It would take more than an earthquake to destroy the Shepheard a second time. Solicitous staff illuminated the dark corners of the lobby with candles.

"Dr. Jenner!" the manager exclaimed. "You're hurt. A doctor will come soon. Very soon. One guest had a heart attack; another stuck in the elevator. The ambulances cannot get through. We will do what we can," he promised.

"If you can manage, Justine, I will see to my home now," Mohammed said, rapidly dialing a number on his cell phone. Anxiety flickered across his strong features. "I haven't been able to reach anyone by phone, even in Alex, and I have a handicapped neighbor. He'll need my help."

"I'll be fine." *I've been consumed with my own experience . . . and distancing myself from the tragedy,* she thought numbly. "I don't know what I would have done without you," she said, taking both of his hands in her own and holding them briefly. Mohammed squeezed her hands in return, then turned toward the door as a young female staff member took Justine's arm, reached for a master key and candle, and guided her up the dark stairwell.

CHAPTER 5

―❦―

SCATTERED GLASS LAY ACROSS THE FLOOR of the room like small pools of water after a spring rain, catching the deep pinks and gold of the late afternoon. With its jagged edges, the broken window gaped open like the giant mouth of a shark, filling the full height of the two-story room. Justine sat on her bed and gazed at it for several moments, mesmerized by this Salvador Dalí-like image.

Without taking her eyes off the scene of beauty wrought from disaster, she picked up the ringing cell phone beside her bed. The cuts on her leg and forehead were held together by a series of butterfly bandages, and the doctor had left a box of painkillers and antibiotics on the night table.

"Justine?"

"Mother?" she replied in a flat tone, still disoriented.

"Are you all right? I just heard about the earthquake."

An image of Lucrezia in her white, flowing kaftan, sitting on her terrace in Fiesole, Italy, flashed into her mind. "I'm fine, Mother. Would you hold on a moment? Someone's at the door." She slipped her feet into flip-flops and hobbled down the steps to the living room. Reaching for the door, she motioned Nadia in. "Watch out for the broken glass," she warned.

"You're hurt!" exclaimed Nadia as she followed Justine back up to the bedroom. Justine quickly held her finger to her closed lips.

"What did she say? You're hurt, aren't you? Tell me what happened," her mother demanded.

"Just a few scratches. A couple of stitches. A few butterfly bandages. I was lucky." As calmly as she could, Justine explained what had happened in Old Cairo. The damage she'd witnessed. Nadia sat on the edge of the bed and listened. Justine drew her legs up to her chin and examined the long cut on her calf as she talked into the phone.

"How frightening. I'm so sorry." Lucrezia's warm voice trembled. It made Justine wish her mother were here, but she knew it was neither possible nor wise. "I'm coming over. I'll get a plane tonight."

"Please don't try, Mom. No one can move around the city. The road from the airport is closed, and things are just too chaotic. I'll call every day—we'll stay in touch. I'll let you know when it is safe to travel. And Mom . . ."

"Yes?"

"Thanks for calling. I really appreciate it. You remember the woman I told you about? Nadia? Well, she just arrived, and the hotel doctor has been here."

"I'm so relieved that you have help . . . but are you sure? You're only a few hours from Florence."

"I'm sure, Mom. I appreciate your offer. By the way, what does the news say—how strong was the earthquake? No electricity here as yet."

"The report on BBC says 6.4. Not big by universal standards, but somewhat larger than the '92 quake. And I know buildings in Cairo can fall down by themselves. Is the Shepheard intact?"

"The Shepheard's in fairly good condition. A few broken windows. Have you heard from Dad?"

"He's still in Peru, but I'm sure he will be calling one of us whenever he can get through. I'll talk with you tomorrow."

"You're not as courageous as you sound," Nadia said gently when Justine had ended the call, her eyes welling up.

Tears began to form in Justine's eyes—at first, little droplets of moisture. "No . . . no . . ." Then emotion bubbled up from deep inside and turned to convulsive sobs.

Nadia moved to her side and took her in her arms, patting her softly on the back. "Cry it out, honey. Take your time."

They sat together for several minutes until Justine slowly pulled back, drying her eyes on the sheet. "I'm sorry," she said. "I didn't mean to . . . I rarely cry . . ."

"It's good for you. We all need a good cry from time to time, and you've been through a lot." Nadia settled in on the end of the bed, folding her chubby legs together. "How did you escape and get back to the hotel?"

"The docent moved the boards blocking the way and pulled me up the stairs. I have to admit, I was terrified . . . then Mohammed found me stumbling along the street when he came out of the new mosque—it remained standing—and he had a car. We were able to work our way back to the hotel. I was never so glad to see anyone in my life! He says the earthquake is the wrath of Allah."

"Probably right," Nadia said with a weak grin. "Mohammed is a good man. He can always be trusted to do the right thing. Hopefully another incident won't test that rule, but I'm extremely grateful to him for helping you. We could have lost you . . ." Nadia had a way of fidgeting when she was nervous or upset: her eyes moved back and forth between the bed, the window, and Justine; her hands smoothed her skirt and the flowered blue comforter.

"Is your family all right?" Justine asked. "Have you heard from the schools?"

"My family's fine. I only have a few scattered nieces left. My husband died a few years ago. I've received calls from three of the schools. I'm concerned about the one in Birqash. No word of any kind, and I can't reach anyone."

"What will you do? Should we go out there?"

"Tomorrow. I'll go tomorrow. I was planning to go anyway."

"I'm going with you."

Nadia examined Justine's leg, forehead, and hands and shook her head. "I don't think so. You need to take care of yourself."

"Please, Nadia. I'd like to go," Justine insisted.

"Let's see how you feel in the morning. Okay?"

As Justine nodded, both women were startled by a fierce pounding on the door, which was accompanied by—or precipitated by—a horrible roar as the jagged remains of the room's two-story window gave way and came crashing into the living room.

"Open up! Open up!" Amir's panicked voice was not distinguishable until the sound of falling glass subsided.

Nadia slipped on her shoes and made her way to the door. "That sound was the window giving way!" Nadia yelled. "We're okay!" She opened the door and stared at a disheveled Amir. His shoes were muddy, his jacket and shirt torn, as if he had just crawled out of a war zone. "Come upstairs," she said, and they picked their way across the glass and up the stairs.

"The sound was horrible," Amir said uneasily. "I thought you were both in danger . . . Oh, my god, you are hurt!" he exclaimed, catching sight of Justine. "You look terrible."

"Thanks a lot," she said, managing a weak grin.

Ignoring her slight indignation, he inspected her wounds, disregarding the cultural boundaries that would have normally prevented his examination of her leg, arms, and face.

"Only a few cuts. I was lucky. What's the report on your family, your grandfather?" she asked, moved by Amir's unguarded concern, his tender gaze. Turning her head, she wiped the last of the tears from her cheeks.

"I went directly to my grandfather's house. You'll remember how dilapidated his home was already."

Justine nodded.

"He was sitting on the floor in the middle of his house. Two walls had fallen against one another. He looked like a patient Bedouin contemplating his fate. It's a miracle he was unharmed, yet he resisted when I told him he would have to go home with me. I said I'd carry him if I had to. Heliopolis has suffered little harm, although sections of both Coptic and Islamic Cairo are severely damaged."

"Sounds like your grandfather. It's a good thing you insisted," Nadia said. "And now you need rest, young lady. You won't be able to get services for a while, so I brought some fruit and water to tide you over. I'm told that the electricity should be back on sometime tonight. If you still want to go tomorrow, I'll call you first thing in the morning." Nadia nodded at Amir that it was time to go.

"*Iwa*," Amir said absently. "I'm on my way to Islamic Cairo to look for survivors . . ."

"I'm going with you," Nadia said, bending over to tie her shoes and find her purse.

"Thank you both for checking on me. I appreciate it so much," Justine said, yawning. "Amir, please tell your grandfather that I said to stop being so stubborn. And, Nadia, I do want to go with you in the morning. I'll expect your call."

✑

The electricity came back on suddenly at 4:30 a.m., waking Justine in a cold sweat, dreams rushing by like a frightening kaleidoscope. She gasped. In her terrifying nightmare, all the air had been sucked out of the crypt, and yet beneath it there'd been something else—the gentle undulation of the Nile, a bustling spice market, and some sense of unnamed worry, that same tension that had been tugging on her ever since she landed in Egypt. A cool breeze came in through the gaping window. The events of the previous day tumbled through her mind in random order, as though waiting to be rearranged. It didn't make sense yet. She fell back into a fitful sleep.

When she awoke again, it was 8:00 a.m. and the lights were still on. Slipping into her unlaced sneakers to climb over the layers of broken glass, she went down the stairs and into the bathroom, where she looked in the mirror. *My god! My head is swollen and purple—I look like hell!* She touched her head and flinched. After a long pause, she carefully stepped into the shower, struggling to keep her wounded leg and head out of the direct flow of the tepid water.

The intensity of her fear in the crypt bothered her. Was it justified? Could the same reactions have been expected of anyone in those circumstances? *I kept my wits about me. I took cover, found my belongings, and worked my way up the stairs. I didn't freeze up. Maybe that's the best I could have hoped for.* She shut off the water, refreshed her bandages, and decided to be kinder to herself, at least for the time being.

Standing before the empty window, she watched the now-quiet city, the silence disrupted only by distant sirens. People moved about with boards and rolls of duct tape as if in a silent movie. Far to her right, Justine could see that the massive glass front of the Semiramis Hotel had collapsed into the driveway. A row of soldiers stood guard. The river and sky looked as indifferent as they had the day before.

The phone rang. "Do you still insist on going?" asked Nadia.

"Absolutely. Where will I meet you?"

They decided that Nadia would pull up on the river side of the Corniche in thirty minutes. Sitting on the side of her bed, Justine pulled on her brown leather boots, a khaki skirt, and a long-sleeved blouse. She found a hat with a modest brim and pulled it down over her bruised forehead. No telling what conditions they would encounter today. "Ready!" she declared, observing herself in the mirror as if she were a stranger.

She reached into her canvas bag and extracted her small bottle of warm water, her notebook, and her scarf. Where was her new camera? She was disturbed by its loss, but her attention was quickly diverted when her fingers brushed against an unfamiliar surface. She grasped the item and pulled it from her bag.

A little book of worn leather with a shiny patina stared back at her. A faint memory floated into her consciousness . . . something small and unfamiliar at her feet when she crouched under the pillar during the earthquake. An earlier visitor must have dropped it. *But this is no modern notebook.* A slight, momentary dizziness caused her vision to blur, then refocus.

Her skin tingled as she carefully opened the stiff leather cover, which looked vaguely like that of her grandmother's bible. One line of words appeared on the first page, which was followed by fewer than a hundred fragile and discolored pages, all of them inserted as full sheets and tied together along the rib of the book. She turned the pages cautiously to keep from crumbling them into crusty flakes. The language looked vaguely familiar, although—except for a few Greek words distributed sparsely throughout—she couldn't read it.

Someone's Bible? A Koran? A Rabbi's prayer book? Might it have been dropped by Michael or the priest? When she held it, the images from her dream came back to her—the dark cave, the warm water.

She felt it somehow—this was the missing piece to a puzzle, but what puzzle she didn't yet know. When she glanced up, her eyes caught the clock: she was running late to meet Nadia. She gently wrapped the treasure with her best silk blouse and placed it under a stack of underwear in the dresser.

∽

Nadia and Justine drove out of the city to the north, crossing the July 27th Bridge. Several buttresses were cracked down to the water line. They wove through Bulaq on a poorly paved road that turned to dirt not long into the thirty-five kilometers to Birqash. The city gave way to fields of beans, mango trees, and community gardens on the left, while the right shoulder of the road hugged one of the canals branching northwest from the Nile to form the Delta. Clusters of red rhododendron, yellow oleander, and acacia growing at the base of sycamores and willows hosted an occasional hoopoe bird and miniature crane. Garbage-filled ditches gaped between the flowering roadside and the canal. Every few miles, a small village embraced the potholed road. Driving was necessarily slow. Justine wondered whether the Renault could make it.

She watched the contrasting colors and primitive villages as they flowed by, but her mind was on the book in her drawer. *Any book that old must hold great significance . . . perhaps it is as old as the time of the Mamluks, or even medieval times. The 1500s were radiant in Cairo, as they were elsewhere . . . literacy abounded, and books were traded like saffron.* The more she thought about it, the more her excitement grew.

As the car bounced in and out of a particularly deep pothole, she was shaken out of her private thoughts.

"What is your greatest fear about what we are going to find?" she asked Nadia.

"My greatest fear?" Nadia paused, pressing her lips together. "I guess the safety of the children and their families. I'm praying that the quake left them unharmed. But returning my calls wouldn't be at the top of their list . . . I'm sure everything's okay," she reassured herself. "We're not seeing a lot of damage as we drive, are we? Birqash might have been out of range of the quake."

"Who would have called you? The teacher? A parent?" They were passing villages thrown together with aluminum, plaster, and clay bricks around small stores selling boxed milk, tissue paper, bread, a few canned goods, bottled water, and soft drinks. Miniature refrigerator cases offered lunchmeats, cheeses, and yogurt. Some sold plasticware as well: brightly colored bowls, bottles, and floppy sandals. A few were open; most were not.

"Layla should have called me. She's the teacher. Then Om Mahmoud, the mother of two of the students and the community leader of the school council. I surely would have heard from her if anything had happened." The road was a continual stream of small villages now, with tiny cafés and clothing shops that looked like mini Walmarts, devoid of anything made of Egyptian cotton, which was exported for the high price it brought in Western markets. "It's nearly impossible to know if anything has happened. The men will drink their tea and smoke their water pipes under any conditions." She shook her head as she glanced at another café brimming with local men huddled in conversation over a scattered array of cups and small plates.

"Is it unusual for a woman to lead the school council?" asked Justine, seeking to distract Nadia from the increasingly disturbing scenes around them. People were milling around a few collapsed buildings. As in Cairo, the effects of the quake here were erratic—seeming to have no pattern, no rhyme or reason.

"It's not unusual for a woman to lead the council in our project," Nadia managed. "We actively recruit women leaders as role models. Right now, four out of the six council leaders are women." She glanced at Justine, "I'm glad you came along today. I'm more anxious than I thought. It steadies me to talk."

Justine nodded, careful not to jar her throbbing head. She'd taken a couple of Tylenol before leaving the hotel, but they weren't helping much. *Perhaps this headache accounts for my strange reaction to that little book.* Staring at the dead camels strewn along the side of the road, she asked uneasily, "Is this a result of the quake?"

"I'm afraid it isn't. We're nearing the camel market. When camels die from the strain of the trip from the Sudan, or other ailments, they are just thrown along the side of the road. A common practice."

Memories of the old camel market rushed back. "My dad took me to the market in Bulaq when I was a kid. Drivers and herders in flowing robes and white turbans, romantic characters holding hands in a circle until a deal was struck. Camels were sold for transport, and for food, as I recall." Scenes of unnecessary cruelty were vivid in her mind: camels beaten with long sticks while they stood still, unable to figure out what was wanted of them. "I was outraged to see the camels beaten and told my dad I wanted to do something about it, anything. I was disappointed when he said, 'No, Justine, it is their way.'"

"He was right. It is their way."

As the car approached the next village, they could hear the wailing of women before they could see them—the piercing sound of sorrow, an eerie trilling of the tongue signaling life's most dramatic moments. It sounded like death. A large crowd was gathered in a circle, the wailing women on one side, men on the other. By the size of the small coffins, three children lay dead.

Nadia's eyes were welling up as she parked the car just beyond the crowd, near to the school. Two sides of the aging, white-plastered building had collapsed inward. Wooden tables and benches, books, and papers were scattered across the now-visible floor. As Nadia headed toward the crowd of mourners, Justine stood back, surveying the damage. She understood that families were particularly sensitive at times like these and might not welcome a stranger in their midst, so she joined a small, helpless crowd standing nearby. The women were weeping. Justine entered a nearly collapsed store and grabbed several bottles of water, leaving a few pounds on the counter, and returned to the bystanders to hand out the bottles.

Seeing that one woman was simply holding one of the water bottles, leaving it unopened, Justine took the bottle from her, opened it, and offered her a drink. The woman lifted her eyes and met Justine's, and the story of the quake poured out of her. After two more conversations, Justine was able to piece together the story of the catastrophe and heartbreak.

She and Nadia found each other shortly after the service, faces pale from watching the villagers' agony. "These children died when the school collapsed—while sitting in a learning center," said Nadia. "One of the girls was six, the others two and seven. Other children have been injured. The six-year-old was Om Mahmoud's daughter Nora." She and Justine reached for each other and held on in a tight hug.

Justine said quietly, "I talked with some of the neighbors. There was the quake, then two strong aftershocks. Small aftershocks during the night. At the first aftershock, the school collapsed, and a couple of the neighbors were injured trying to find their children. They were also in the school when the last aftershock hit."

Nadia held Justine at arm's length. "How are you?"

"A little shaken, but I'll be okay. Did you find the teacher?"

"She left and no one can find her. They think she was unharmed. She should have called me, but she may have been too traumatized."

"Let's find her," Justine said, her leg and head throbbing anew.

"*Iwa*, we'll leave the families with their grief and return when they're ready to think about rebuilding the school." Nadia snapped into action and walked toward her car. "I'll call Om Mahmoud in a couple of days," she said over her shoulder. "Today is not a time to talk about the future."

Since the passenger door was nearly impossible to open, Justine slid into the Renault through the driver's seat, hugging two bottles of Evian and wincing as her leg rubbed against the frayed seat cover. "Was the school built by UNESCO?" she asked as Nadia started the car on the second try.

"No, the building was an old storage area that the community converted into a school," Nadia answered once they were back on the road. "In our project, each community provides its own space. But I still feel responsible. I never questioned its safety, never asked about whether it met building codes. Those questions are just not asked."

"Mohammed told me that building codes here are either not known or not followed. It's not as though you neglected to follow good practice."

"I understand that, but my guilt is hungry. I feed it with what I have before me."

Justine grew quiet as she considered Nadia's confession. She hadn't thought of guilt as hungry, but understood that it could be. She could feel the dampness of tears on her own cheeks, and she turned to gaze at Nadia's tearful eyes. How awful to think of three young girls lying in homemade coffins and the grief of family members who had sent them to school so that they might have better lives. *How will Allah's actions be interpreted here? Will it feed old doubts about Allah's plans for girls?*

"Do you know where Layla lives?" Justine knew how difficult it was to find teachers for rural schools. They needed to find this one.

"In Shoubra, one of the oldest and most fragile parts of Cairo. I doubt if much is still standing. But it's so far from Birqash. Surely she couldn't be home."

"Let's give it a try," Justine pressed.

"At least her family might know where she is."

As they approached the Nile north of the city, Nadia turned onto the damaged bridge leading into Shoubra. She had predicted accurately. The destruction here was much more pronounced than in downtown Cairo. They wove their way through the debris to a small apartment behind a closed butcher shop. People were inside, even though one wall of the building was leaning inward. Justine and Nadia stepped through the rubble to the front of the apartment.

"Layla! Layla!" Nadia called from the street. "Are you there?"

An older man came out of a second-floor opening. "She's here, Miss Nadia, but terribly upset. Do you need to see her now?"

"We just came from Birqash and want to offer our condolences and prayers for the loss of her students and her school."

A slight young woman in her early twenties appeared at the opening and stood near her father. She was disheveled and distraught; dried blood was caked on her forehead and right forearm. "Miss Nadia," Layla said timidly.

"We are so glad you're okay. Please, let us talk to you," Nadia persisted. The young woman reluctantly made her way down the slanted stairwell and into the alleyway. Her plastic shoes and the sash of her cotton dress were ripped. Nadia held her while she sobbed.

"How did you get back?" Nadia finally asked.

"I walked most of the night, then got a ride." Between sobs she continued, "I should have helped the children. I didn't save them. I couldn't save them." She collapsed into Nadia's arms again.

"There was nothing you could have done," Justine said. "The building was old and in poor condition." She emphasized her words with an expression that she hoped was calm, tender.

"Layla, this is Dr. Justine. She will be working with us. None of us had any warning that the quake was coming. An act of Allah."

Layla stopped shaking and nodded toward Justine, her eyes traveling to the purple edges of the gash visible on her forehead. She turned back to Nadia. "I feel so sorry for their families. I should have stayed and helped out, but I was so afraid for my father. He's been sick and his legs are crippled." Her father remained on the balcony, an eagle protecting its young.

Justine wondered if Nadia's relationships with all the teachers were so caring and maternal. She had already been the subject of Nadia's care and concern herself. *We need each other; we all need each other.*

"Don't give it another thought. I understand that you needed to get home. Please, help your family and take care of yourself. I'll come back soon, *Inshallah*, and we can talk about how to put the school back together."

Justine held Layla's hand and spoke gently. "Like you and the children, I was caught in the earthquake and was very frightened. It is okay to be afraid. All we can do now is make the future of your students better—give them a life to be proud of."

CHAPTER 6

⋘

SUNLIGHT STREAMED ACROSS JUSTINE'S pillow, waking her up. It was Tuesday and she had slept for nearly twelve hours. When she'd returned to the room the night before, much was unchanged—the broken window gaped open, her bed was unmade, and dirty towels lay on the bathroom floor—though, thankfully, the shattered glass had been swept up. This morning she was feeling refreshed, yet shaken, as she lay in bed and recalled the days leading up to this moment—the earthquake, her injuries, the school.

She shuddered and squeezed her eyes tight, forcing the images to go away. But they didn't; her mind refused to let go. She also had unfinished business: the little book wrapped in her silk blouse in the drawer across the room. *What is it?*

She propped her head on her folded arm and stared at the dresser as though she expected it to speak. Then she picked up her cell phone.

"Amir?" she asked. "This is Justine."

"Justine. How are you? I've been busy . . . the Museum isn't open, it needs a lot of cleanup . . . not sure we have everyone out as yet . . . but then you called . . ."

In the background, she could hear hammering and what she thought might be a small bulldozer. "I'm so sorry to bother you. How terrible that there may still be bodies under the rubble."

"I'm joining another team around noon. What can I do for you?"

"I assume your grandfather's still with you in Heliopolis . . . and I think I've found something that might be of interest to both of you." She paused.

"Of interest? What?"

"A little book, a codex, really, that I found in the crypt during the earth-quake. I think it's very old, at least hundreds of years."

Amir was quiet for a surprisingly long time. "I'm coming right over," he said and hung up.

∽

"You're right on two counts," observed Amir just a few minutes after he ar-rived. "This is a codex rather than a book, and it is very old. No one could have dropped it. It's not the sort of thing you carry around." He held the codex in both hands like it was a newborn.

The sky was nearly white, interrupted only by two white cranes flying par-allel to the river. In the light, the codex looked even more battered, more entic-ing, and Justine felt again as though there was some reason she had found it. "I'd like to show it to your grandfather—he's still at your home, right?"

He raised a brow. "You know you won't be able keep it. Our laws are very clear in that regard, requiring that any such find be taken directly to the Supreme Council of Antiquities office. In fact, any antiquity must be left in place, *in situ.*"

"I know that provenance is a major issue, but it's a little late for that, don't you think? I didn't know what I had." Her voice grew impatient.

Amir smiled. "You're right, of course. If it had been directly uncovered dur-ing an approved search by a certified archaeologist, it would be more credible. Unprovenanced artifacts are more subject to claims of forgery. But it is a little late to worry about that now."

Justine allowed herself to relax. "I do know archaeology is quite ruthless when it comes to discoveries—my father taught me that. Archaeologists want to know about the world and what's in it, but they don't want it found by anyone else. A malady suffered by most scientists, I'm afraid." She took the small book from Amir, wrapped it in a towel, and placed it in her canvas bag. Swinging her purse over her shoulder and carrying the bag level in both hands, she headed for the door. "Shall we go?"

They drove most of the way to Heliopolis in companionable silence. "My father told me that when an artifact is turned over to the Supreme Council, it might not be seen for years. Do you find that to be true?" she asked. "I'd just like to know the possibilities here before giving it up." She watched Amir's profile, sketched darkly against the morning sunlight, noticing barely discernable fine, tight muscles near his mouth and eyes.

"There's a lot of truth there. The Ministry—and my renowned boss, Omar Mostafa—are notorious for burying finds that don't fit with their narrative. That is, unless political pressure or a great deal of money is involved, which could be one and the same." He continued to pay close attention to the traffic, his features almost lost in the shadows of the car.

She smiled wryly. "Ah, it hadn't occurred to me that the Great Mostafa was your supervisor. I should have known."

"You know him?"

"Everyone knows him. I've seen him several times on National Geographic and the Discovery channel. Once on Charlie Rose."

"And . . ."

"He's certainly blustery, full of himself. I'm not that certain of his expertise."

Amir laughed fully. He had a fine laugh, genuine, engaging, and Justine found herself glad that she'd called him.

In the old section of Heliopolis, they found a narrow parking space in front of an apartment building topped with Doric crowns, one section of a full block of indistinguishable structures built by the British. "My parents will be at work, but grandfather will be here. I'll warn you—he's irritable. I didn't give him much choice about leaving his apartment. He's a puzzling man: he savors new discoveries and ideas but abhors personal change." Amir turned off the engine and pulled the keys out of the ignition.

"My father's like that. Perhaps that's why they got along so well. An 'adventurous conservative,' I call him. The contradiction was even more confusing to my mother, who expected an American archaeologist to provide her with a daring life."

"And that's not what she found?"

"Not at all. He may have been daring in his professional life, but as a husband and father, he was quite protective."

Amir nodded. "We men shield women too much. I'm not sure what we're afraid of, but I suppose it's the ancient fear that wild women bring shame on the family. You probably know that tribal families that were shamed or humiliated were cast out into the desert to die?" He leaned across her lap to open the door from the inside, close enough that she could smell his musky warmth. "The handle doesn't work from the outside," he explained.

A common malady with Egyptian cars, Justine mused, feeling her heart quicken.

✧

"Where have you been, Amir? I thought you were going to take me to work today," demanded his grandfather, appearing quite small in an overstuffed divan surrounded by large, ornate chests. Photos of Cairo in its glory days adorned the walls. A walnut coffee table held glass candy dishes and several copies of *Cairo Today*—a typical middle-class Egyptian family's living room.

"You needed a little rest. You remember Justine?"

"Oh, yes. Hello, my dear." Ibrahim's voice softened as he noticed her. "You look like you've been in a fight with a camel driver."

Justine laughed. "I was beaten up by a collapsing church. The St. Sergius, to be exact. I didn't take it personally."

A grin expanded Ibrahim's sagging jaw, but was quickly overtaken by the concern in his eyes. "The St. Sergius? Collapsed? The home of the Holy Family?" He seemed to sink further into the couch.

Justine glanced at Amir, quickly realizing that to a devout Copt, such destruction would be devastating. "I overstated it, Dr. Ibrahim. A column and a few two-by-fours fell on my head—the church will be fine. Really."

"I was hoping to return to my office today," he said. "I work better there."

"I can understand needing your own space, sir. If you could just take a moment. I found a little book in the crypt at St. Sergius." Amir nodded at her to continue, then left to fetch tea while Justine described Sunday's experiences. She folded back the towel and laid the little book in Ibrahim's frail, veined hands.

For a long time, he cradled the volume as though it were his first grandchild. "St. Sergius," he said, delicately lifting the cover to examine the first page. "Could the book have survived from the days of the Romans? The Turks?

The Syrians? The Arab invasion? Surely no earlier than the days of the Syrian Islamic leaders . . . when was that? About nine hundred years into the current era?" He was talking aloud, but to himself.

Several minutes passed as Ibrahim ruminated on the endless possibilities. He ignored Amir's return and the tea. Justine tried to read the professor: his expression, his movements, his mind. The elderly man revealed little except for a flushed face and small patches of white around his temples.

What does that mean? Exasperation? Excitement? Fatigue?

Amir remained respectfully silent, allowing his grandfather his private thoughts. Finally, he spoke: "Most of the writing appears to be Aramaic. Astounding. Grandfather, you realize that this codex is very ancient."

Ibrahim turned to Justine as though he hadn't heard. "You must write everything down. Exactly where you found it, when, what time. Who else was with you. The information must be exact. Unfortunately, this is now an unprovenanced find, which complicates matters."

Justine and Amir glanced at each other.

"You will write everything down?" Ibrahim persisted.

"Of course, I will write everything in great detail." She paused. "What do you think it is, sir?" She kept her voice steady. Patient.

"What you have here is an ancient codex, the ancestor of the book. Think of the evolution of writing as the scroll, the codex, and then the book. You see how the codex opens naturally in the middle?"

Amir added, "Each sheet is a whole piece of papyrus, with a spine created by tying the pages together. You can see that these pages have been forcibly folded for a very long time, causing them to crumble finely along the spine. This cover must be made of sheep or calf leather reinforced by glued layers of papyrus."

Ibrahim looked up from the codex. "As to who may have written it . . . there are many tests to run and people to consult. Be careful whom you trust," he warned. "May I keep it for a while?"

"I was hoping that you would want to spend more time with the book—the codex," Justine said. She forced herself to tamp down her excitement. "But why do you say to be careful whom I trust? Surely I'm not in danger."

Ibrahim's expression darkened. "Many of the major finds of the last decades have religious implications. Dangerous territory," he said.

"Grandfather's right," Amir acknowledged.

"Understandable, I guess," she said, shrugging slightly, though she wasn't sure she did understand. "What are our next steps?"

Her shrug had not escaped the now-alert professor. "My dear, don't dismiss the possibility of danger once you're in possession of a provocative artifact. As to the next steps, we will need to hand it over to the Supreme Council of Antiquities at some point. That's why I have asked you to carefully document the find. These notes will accompany the artifact when we formally make the transfer. Fortunately, I have enough credibility with the Council that they may not question my decision to do some initial tests. In fact, it will be helpful to them." He stared down at the codex again, his glasses slipping to the end of his long nose.

Amir glanced at Justine, his eyes revealing a flicker of disappointment at his grandfather's willingness to delay the transfer to the Supreme Council. She hoped his respect for his grandfather would trump his feeling of obligation to his boss. "What kinds of tests are you referring to, sir?" she asked. "Of course, I'm aware of carbon-14 dating. What others do you have in mind?" She reached for the teapot and refilled each cup.

"Carbon-14 dating of the leather and papyrus is the starting point," offered Amir. "Translation by experts in Aramaic script, the primary language of the book, will help to identify the language patterns and forms used during the period in question. The contents will provide us with context clues—who wrote it, his habits, behaviors. As you can see, a patina or chemical buildup has formed on the cover." Justine could see that Amir was becoming equally intrigued by the mystery.

Ibrahim nodded at his grandson, his right hand trembling as he laid it lightly on the ancient codex, his crippled fingers pointing to the glossy part of the surface. "And if you can find the place from which the codex came, the patina on the crypt's sandstone can be tested as well."

"Then neither of you think someone might have dropped it in the crypt before I arrived?" Justine asked.

"Unlikely," said Ibrahim, rubbing his nose underneath his glasses. "An old codex like this, not something to be carrying around."

Justine nodded and, noting Ibrahim's exhaustion, reminded herself that he, too, had been through a harrowing experience in the last couple of days. "Perhaps we should be going," she suggested. Amir quickly agreed. She picked up her purse and canvas bag.

As Amir reached for the doorknob, Ibrahim added, "Andrea LeMartin, the prominent Aramaic script translator from the Sorbonne, is a visiting professor this semester at AUC. We may be able to consult with her."

As Justine turned back around, she noticed that Ibrahim's eyes now beamed with the playfulness of a young boy. "Will you take me to my office tomorrow, my boy?" he asked.

"I'll pick you up at nine in the morning. Now get some rest."

"I was impressed with how clear your grandfather's mind is. After all he's been through," Justine said on the drive back to the Shepheard.

"He hasn't had such a rare find in his hands for many years, perhaps since he worked with your father. I just hung around as a kid, but your dad treated me like a son."

Justine felt a sharp pang in her chest. "The son he never had," she murmured, but Amir heard her.

He chuckled. "Hardly. But I think I know how you feel. Zachariah was always grandfather's favorite." He glanced at her. "Tell me about what happened yesterday."

Justine swallowed hard and gazed at Amir with affection. She told him of her trip with Nadia to Birqash, the children and their families, the school.

"And three children died in the collapse? Tragic." He remained quiet for a while, his eyes glistening. "Zachariah was involved in a tragic incident once. He was volunteering at a school in Bulaq and the school bus stalled on a train track."

"The train couldn't stop?" Justine shivered as she visualized the impending accident.

Amir shook his head. "Zachariah was with the kids in the back. Six were killed, yet he survived . . . it was hard for him to forgive himself. It's called survivor's guilt, I think . . ." He stopped as though there was so much more to say. "I must call Nadia. See what I can do. And I'm due in Shoubra in an hour."

"The teacher lives in Shoubra. It's pretty damaged." Justine watched his profile— his throbbing temples, his reddened eyes. "Just let me off near the train station up ahead. I can walk from there."

"Thanks," he said. He pulled up to the curb behind a line of buses and leaned over to open the door. Drawing back, he met her eyes and said, "I understand from Nadia that your apartment will be ready soon. If I can help, let me know."

"I will," she said.

It was Wednesday, the third day after the earthquake—a lifetime ago. Nadia would soon be by to pick up Justine for their visit to the school in the City of the Dead. Justine's cuts were healing nicely, but her bruises continued to spread beyond her bandages into pools of yellow and lavender. She managed to mask the evidence of injury with a long denim skirt and a blouse with wrist cuffs—except for her face, to which she applied more makeup.

Her internal clock was still crazy: she was waking too early and sleeping at odd hours, her dreams filled with strange images. This morning she'd set off at sunrise for a run—her first since the quake—then showered and dressed for a modest breakfast in The Caravan. Now, searching the seams of the magnificent room for earthquake damage, she noticed a vertical crack in the low-hanging balcony, damage that, no doubt, rendered it unsafe. Settling into a window seat, she was astonished once again by the chameleon nature of the Nile, its changing moods and colors—the pinks of morning among her favorites. Fashionable young Muslim women with matching scarves, purses, and shoes passed by on the sidewalk below. "We masquerade devoutness to fool our gods," Mohammed had said. *I'm sure he meant God. Allah.*

"Justine Jenner? Dr. Jenner?"

She glanced up from her morning tea and met the eyes of a man of about average height, not classically handsome, but somehow strangely sensuous. "I'm Justine Jenner. And you are?"

"Nasser Khalid," he said. "I heard you were in town." He placed his hands on the back of the chair across the table and leaned forward.

She raised an eyebrow and stared at him. "In a city of eighteen million, you heard I was in town?" The events of the past week had placed her on guard.

"Ah." He smiled disarmingly. "You could use an explanation. Well, I teach part-time at AUC and your name was being bandied around in the faculty room. So I started asking questions."

"Very resourceful," she said. "But how did you know who I was?"

"The clerk at the desk told me you were having breakfast in here. And unless you had changed gender, taken to the veil, or aged thirty years, you were my only choice. Truthfully, I also saw you walk across campus with your dad once. I was a student of your father's at Berkeley."

Justine relaxed. "Cross-examination over. Please join me. I'm always delighted to meet a student of my father's." She closed the flap of the school project in front of her and moved it to one side.

"Durrell?" he asked as he sat down.

Justine was puzzled only momentarily before she realized he was making reference to Lawrence Durrell's *Alexandria Quartet*, set in World War II Alexandria. Durrell was legendary in Egypt, making "Justine," the title of the first book in the series, a popular name. Other than Nobel Prize–winner Naigub Maufouz, he was the most notable writer of the Egyptian scene.

"Two sources, really," she replied. "My mother thought Durrell's *Quartet* the best novels ever written, and my grandmother was smitten with D.H. Lawrence. Her name was Laurence. As is the custom in Egypt, her name was spelled with a U instead of a W."

"You're fortunate, it might have been 'Balthazar,'" he said, referring to another title in the series. He gave her a crooked Harrison Ford grin.

"And you? Named after President Nasser, I assume."

"Guilty as charged. My mother was hopelessly in love with him." He paused and poured her another cup of tea from her own pot. "What brings you to Cairo?"

The grin stole her train of thought. *What brings me to Cairo?* she asked herself, embarrassedly aware that Nasser was watching her labor over an ordinary question. "I'm working with the UNESCO Community Schools for Girls project," she finally said. "And you?"

"A unique agenda. Schools for girls. As for me, I'm Egyptian, and this is my home. After I finished at Berkeley, I searched for work with several archaeology teams here, but when that didn't happen, I accepted a part-time teaching position at AUC. A couple of archaeology classes and one on ancient history. 101 stuff." He shrugged.

"Do you enjoy teaching?" Suddenly self-conscious about the injury on her forehead, Justine touched her fingers to the discolored area and shook her head slightly so that a lock of hair flowed forward.

"I enjoy teaching, but would rather be digging." He flashed that grin again.

"How long were you at Berkeley?"

"I finished in '04. My first two years were on a scholarship at the University of Dayton in Ohio. Then I moved back to Cairo in the fall of '04 and started at AUC the next spring."

"What was it like being a student of my father's?"

"Difficult sometimes," he said, rubbing the ridge of his nose. "Your father is exceptionally knowledgeable and demanding, but also personable and supportive . . . But enough about me." He nodded toward her forehead. "How did you survive the quake? I can't help but notice that nasty bruise."

"I was trapped in a crypt in Old Cairo. It collapsed around me. Scared me out of my wits," she admitted. "Fortunate to have escaped at all, and with only a few cuts." She briefly explained about the church, the darkness, and her escape with the help of the young docent.

"What an ordeal! Are you all right now?"

"Physically, yes, but on Monday we found that three children had been killed in one of our schools in Birqash. It has been quite a week so far." She found herself staring at the table as a wave of sadness washed over her. She shook her head, forcing a smile. "Shall we order more tea?"

Nasser's expression conveyed both empathy and charm. *How does he manage that?* "No tea for me now, thanks," he said. "A horrible few days, but you seem to have survived well. Has it dampened your resolve?" His dark blue eyes matched his turtleneck sweater.

"If anything, it has strengthened my resolve. Witnessing the community of mourners and meeting the teacher face to face—seeing Nadia's pains and hopes—I am drawn in deeply. Nadia is the woman I work with. These experiences make me feel honored to be a part of it all. But even so, I'm still trying to make sense of these three short days."

"I almost envy you. Intensity speeds up life and makes it more meaningful," Nasser said.

Justine found the observation disconcerting, yet intriguing. "Right now I don't have enough distance to be analytical, but I'll give it some thought."

"Are you going to be in town long?"

"For several months. Perhaps more than a year."

"Will you be living at the Shepheard?" Those dark eyes held hers.

She shook her head. "I'm moving into an apartment in Garden City later this week or early next. Not far from here, almost around the corner from the Four Seasons."

"I would like to see you again. Would you be so kind as to give me your cell number?" He patted his pocket as if in search of a business card.

"I would like that," she said, smiling and writing her number on a small notepad with "Shepheard Hotel" printed across the top.

CHAPTER 7

———— ❦ ————

THE CITY OF THE DEAD: A PLACE where nearly a million of the living joined the thousands buried in Cairo's notorious cemetery, an area nearly as large as Venice. Small tombs that looked like dollhouses had become home to families who subsisted without basic plumbing and water services. For years the government had sought to dispel this encroachment upon holy ground, but it had finally given up. Now small shops and an occasional water faucet made life there somewhat more bearable.

Justine felt as though she were still observing the scene with the uncomprehending eyes of the teen she'd been when her father had brought her there. Flies crowded around the eyes and mouth of the small girl of about five who stood in front of her. Her curly hair, the same color as her skin, looked as though it had never been combed. She wore a faded pink cotton dress with a sash that had come loose on one side; the long sash, decorated with a bow in the middle, touched the dirt near her bare feet. The young girl stared intently at a dead donkey lying in the middle of the street. Across the back legs of the donkey lay a dog; both were surrounded by flies.

Justine couldn't take her eyes off the girl. She wanted to hold her, to comb her hair, to chase away the flies, to sew her sash. Such a beautiful child. *What does it mean to care?* Her Western notions connected caring with cleanliness and order and combed hair . . . and battling flies.

As though on cue, a somewhat older girl emerged from the doorway beside the child. The older girl was wearing a clean blue and white school uniform and carrying a backpack. The contrast between the two girls was disconcerting.

"The school is at the end of the street," Nadia said, her voice sounding far away. "Justine?" she said. "We'll walk from here."

Nadia started down the street, watching carefully where she stepped. Justine caught up with her and Nadia instinctively reached for her hand. They greeted children on both sides of the street, some of them well dressed and carrying backpacks. Still holding on to Justine, Nadia turned toward the school and up the six steps leading into a white-plastered building that mercifully had withstood the quake.

Children were laughing and playing. The two women entered an intimate classroom untouched by the streets below. Nadia had explained that, while it was unusual to have a community school in the middle of the city, the only other school in the City of the Dead was co-ed and situated about a half-kilometer away, in the remodeled part of the complex. Parents were reluctant to let their daughters walk the distance and attend school with boys. As in the smaller rural villages, families here were exceedingly traditional in their notions about males and females, intent on keeping them apart.

Nadia introduced Justine to the teacher, a lovely young woman named Samira, perhaps eighteen years of age. While universities in Egypt certified teachers, high school completion was considered adequate preparation in cases where positions were difficult to fill. Samira wore a long dress of soft green with a matching hijab. She smiled, reached for Justine's hand, and turned to introduce her to the students in her limited English.

"Good morning, Dr. Jenner," said the children in unison.

Justine found a chair in the back of the simple room, furnished with the same type of wooden benches and stools that had been present in the collapsed school in Birqash. Pale orange walls surrounded a green-trimmed blackboard hanging behind the teacher's desk. On either side, children's art displays were taped to the wall: watercolors of community gardens, stick figures of families, a dog with sorrowful eyes, a funeral crypt labeled "my home." Learning centers were organized into each corner near built-in cabinets of blocks, mimeographed work sheets, and crayons. Two long shelves partially filled with ragged paperback books stretched out below large, paneless windows.

Thirteen girls with expressions of joyful expectation wore the matching uniforms Justine had noticed earlier. As they opened their small backpacks to take out today's homework, it gave her a warm, pleasurable shudder to realize that she would be working with this endearing group of young girls. *What influence will I have? Will these girls trust to me? Will they think we have anything in common? Anything to share?*

Samira drew symbols for several different kinds of activities on the board: learning circles, silent reading, a small group art project, and a math game with blocks. Small books lined the wall shelf. Justine tried to put the codex from her mind, but she was undeniably curious about it, eager to find out whether Ibrahim had learned anything yet.

The children quietly moved into the four learning circles, taking out activity trays with reading games, and Samira pointed out one of the circles for Justine to join. The group of girls appeared shy and reluctant to initiate, leaving decisions to each other that were slowly and painfully made. *When they learn to trust me, they'll be more relaxed and responsive to each other—I hope.*

"What do you think she's looking at?" asked Madiha, the tallest of the three girls. Assuming that Justine could not understand Arabic, Madiha focused the conversation on Justine without turning in her direction.

"I don't know," said Nita, stealing a sideways glance at Justine.

"She doesn't look scary to me," said Assma. "I think she's pretty. Look at her shoes."

"They can fool you. They make all nice—" began Madiha, only to be interrupted.

"Are you finished with the lesson?" Justine asked in Arabic, knowing that the longer she let this conversation proceed without revealing herself, the more they would feel manipulated, deceived.

Startled, the girls looked at each other. Assma and Nita blushed and looked down. Madiha spoke first. "We didn't think you could understand us."

"I didn't mean to mislead you. I'm sorry. I learned to speak Arabic as a child. You see, my mother is Egyptian," Justine explained.

"I think you're pretty," repeated Assma as though she hadn't been heard before.

Justine smiled. "Thank you," she said.

"Can I touch your hair?" asked Nita, tentatively reaching out.

"Of course. Can I touch yours?" She reached for the child's silken black hair.

"My brother said we should be afraid of Americans. You seem like an American to me," declared Madiha defiantly. "What do you want?"

"I'm here to see how you girls are learning so we can be better teachers. So we can make better materials for you," said Justine. "You are partly right, Madiha. My father is American, but he has worked in Egypt often. I grew up in California and Egypt."

"Miss Samira is already a good teacher," insisted Madiha.

"I'm sure she is. I'm observing you girls more than I'm observing your teacher. But I promise to tell you what I learn." Justine smiled gently.

Still unpersuaded, Madiha broke eye contact and turned toward her classmates.

That one will take time. "Shall we start again?" Justine asked.

"Well, what did you think?" Nadia asked as they ordered lunch at Abu Bakr restaurant on Qasr al-Ainy.

Justine ordered her favorites: tabbouleh, babaghanoush, and pita with a Diet Coke. "I was impressed that such a joyful island exists in the middle of this unusual community," she began. "Samira has a helpful and warm manner with the children, and they seem to trust her. I found the girls to be quiet and shy at first, hesitant; but I realize they can't be expected to trust me as yet. They began to talk about me in Arabic, not realizing that I understood. That was my fault. I should have spoken Arabic from the very beginning. Madiha said her brother told her to be afraid of Americans."

"Afraid? Did she tell you why?"

"No, but I told them that my mother was Egyptian and that I had learned to speak Arabic as a child. Assma and Nita were fine with that explanation, but Madiha was still distant, mildly hostile."

"The City of the Dead has several radical quarters where Westerners are despised, the Muslim Brotherhood revered. I'm afraid Madiha must have been warned at home. I'm sorry you had to experience such hostility today." Nadia lowered her head in apology. "What a week you've had!"

Justine waved her hand dismissively. "I'm just grateful that the girls were honest with me. What do you hear from Birqash?"

Nadia's eyes teared up. "I haven't heard from Om Mahmoud, but I did get a call from the mayor saying that the fathers in the community, many of them at least, will start repairing the school next week."

"That's very encouraging, don't you think? I was afraid that they would be so overwhelmed by the deaths that they'd give up. That the villagers would see the earthquake as a sign that girls shouldn't be educated."

"Some do hold that opinion. According to the mayor, the conflict has been fierce. A few fathers pointed out that the boys' school, less than a quarter-kilometer away, was undamaged. It wouldn't be difficult to draw the conclusion that Allah doesn't approve of educating girls. I wouldn't be surprised if some families take their daughters out of school."

"Surely that would be its own tragedy. Those young women will long for something they only knew for a moment. They'll feel empty and not know why happiness doesn't come their way. I wonder if some of them may start to regret even beginning an education, or dreaming of how their lives might have been different from their mothers'. It's that same old question, isn't it? And one I've never settled for myself. Is it better to have loved and lost or never to have loved at all?"

"In this case, I almost think it would have been better not to have known what was possible. As you say, girls who have known learning and had it withdrawn will never feel satisfied with their lives." Nadia stared across the restaurant, her attention drawn by two young sisters chattering noisily at another table. "Have you ever loved and lost, Justine?"

Justine nodded. "In that instant, I learned more about what I really wanted in life. Losing that love was not a tragedy, though. It was in grad school. Lasted over a year, but it wouldn't have worked out. And you? Loved and lost?"

"I lost my husband. He died six years ago of complications from diabetes. But we loved one another for twenty-six years. It was a good marriage. I miss him every day."

"I'm so sorry." Justine reached across the table and took Nadia's hands in hers. *I used the phrase carelessly and opened up her pain.*

"I don't speak of it often, but it's an important thing to understand about me. Part of who I am. I would have told you eventually," said Nadia, squeezing Justine's hands. "We also had a child, a son. One child. It was a difficult birth. He only lived for three days. That I regret as much as losing Ahmed."

Justine's eyes welled up. "I can't imagine the pain of losing a child," she said. *Nasser called my life "intense." I don't even know what intensity is. For Nadia, the mothers in Birqash, and the children in the school today, life is more difficult than I could have imagined. Would I be able to handle such a loss?*

OLD CAIRO 2 CE

With a crockery bowl of bread dough huddled under her arm, Rachel walks in from the east, near the ancient cemetery, where she and her new husband Samir make their home. "Good day, my friend," I say, always joyful to see Rachel. Perhaps ten summers older than me, she has a welcome smile and jovial face, round and pleasing. Her black eyes smile with her. She prides herself on her needlework, and her tunics are the envy of women in the village. Since she is a midwife of considerable skill, we felt safer when she agreed to accompany us from Palestine.

"How go you? Has your day started well?" Rachel asks.

"It has been a good day, thanks be to God." I gently stack charcoal from a small box in the middle of the oven and light the fire.

Rachel reaches into her pocket for a handful of cornmeal and scatters it generously on the worktable, then turns to the task of rolling the dough into small mounds. "I delivered a baby last night. A precious little girl. God gave her a difficult birth." Her hands move with added intensity.

I carefully push the charcoal into a circle and place a flat piece of pottery in the center. "What happened? How are the child and mother?" The fire pit has a steady blaze, licking the earthen pot of water. Waiting for Rachel's story, I dip my hand into the small jar of salt and take a pinch of black cumin and a few pieces of garlic, adding the spices to the simmering water before I wipe my hands on my tunic and sit down to listen.

"The family is Egyptian," Rachel begins as she sits down on a small stool facing me. "They live on the other side of the village. The woman's husband objected violently to a midwife from Palestine, so he refused to call for my help. Finally, a neighbor came for me, and her husband forced the screaming man outside. The woman—her name was Jasmine—was in terrible, terrible pain. The baby was coming out feet first, so I didn't think Jasmine or the baby would live. But as you know, I have learned some ways to bring children into this world when others give up hope."

"It is God's gift."

Rachel nods solemnly. "I held my knife to the fire to purify it, then cut her body enough so that I could reach in and pull the little girl out. The child had started to turn blue, but soon she began to cry. I think she will survive." Rachel pauses and gives an exhausted sigh, wiping away a tear with her scarf. "This was one of the most difficult births I've witnessed."

"And . . . the mother? Did she survive?"

"I always carry a little silk thread in my pocket, so I was able to sew up the opening I had made large. I soaked sycamore leaves in balsam and placed them on the wound. She was very brave, and when I laid the little girl on her breast, she smiled at both of us. I think she will live, thanks be to God."

"You are a wonder, Rachel." I throw my arms around her.

"Will we ever be accepted here?" Rachel whispers into the nape of my neck. As I hold her close, I remember my own loss. Tears fall for Jasmine, for Rachel, and for myself. I am still holding her when Noha can be heard coming up the rise near the corral. Rachel and I let go of each other, dry our eyes, and pretend to return to work.

CHAPTER 8

⸺⊗⊗⊗⸺

PROFESSOR IBRAHIM APPEARED QUITE DAPPER as he carefully lowered himself onto the fringed Bedouin pillow next to Justine. The Tabullah Restaurant might have been a stage set for *One Thousand and One Nights*, the carved Arabesque brass tables, lounging seats with red recessed lamps, ancient Oriental artifacts, cozy corners, and ornate pipes giving off an air of timeless mystery. Customers from the nearby British and Canadian embassies joined with exotic locals here to make this one of the more popular Lebanese restaurants in Cairo.

Ibrahim had called shortly after Justine and Nadia had finished their visit to the City of the Dead. He was excited to report that Andrea LeMartin was interested in exploring working together on the translation of the codex, and that this evening he would introduce her to the French linguist.

"Will you order the wine, Andrea?" Ibrahim asked the woman seated on the other side of him. Justine couldn't help notice the way Amir smiled at his grandfather's flirtatious manner. Tonight, Ibrahim seemed decades younger than when she'd last seen him.

"Ah, *mon ami*, you reveal my snobbishness. Shame on you," Andrea said, then turned to the attentive waiter. "I will ask for your best Egyptian wine," she ordered in French. "We shall have two bottles of Grand Marquis cabernet."

Unpretentious yet elegant, Andrea LeMartin was a striking woman in her late forties, although it was difficult to surmise the exact age of this French beauty. A simple deep green silk dress enfolded her voluptuous body, complementing her violet eyes and almost burgundy hair. Her sense of presence made her appear taller than she was. Tiny gold hoop earrings and a single gold wrist chain were her only adornments. Justine glanced at her own nails and shoes, smiling at the realization that Andrea made her feel self-conscious. *She looks more Egyptian than I do.*

"And for salads," Amir said, "some labna, kofta, babaghanoush, and the house tabbouleh?" Relaxed in his role as co-host of this dinner, he smiled expansively. He turned a warm gaze first on Andrea, then Justine, as though to draw them into his radius.

Justine felt herself being absorbed by his obsidian eyes as his gaze lingered on her. Extricating herself with a deep breath, she turned to Andrea. "Tell us about your interest in Aramaic script."

"My favorite topic." Andrea's wide-set eyes sparkled as she began to talk about the ancient language. "You may realize that Aramaic is the best and longest attested Semitic language, in use for over three thousand years in Palestine, Syria, and Mesopotamia. At one time, like my beloved French, Aramaic was the primary language of life and diplomacy. That period—more than a thousand years in length—was the formative period of Christianity and the foundation of Islam. Greek and Hebrew—and later Latin—derived many of their original meanings from Aramaic. I find it historically humbling." She paused to curl a miniature triangle of pita and dip it in the labna topped with olive oil.

"I find it particularly fascinating how much the language evolved over those many years," she continued. "There were great changes in grammar, the lexical collection and usage, allowing us to identify periods based on time and place. Language development is a living process, you realize, with great power to help us understand what we find."

She glanced at Justine as though to ask, "Is that what you wanted to know?" Justine smiled back at her. *If the codex is written primarily in Aramaic, surely Andrea is the one to unlock its secrets—whatever they are.*

"Give us an example of such a period, if you please," urged Ibrahim, obviously enthralled, though Justine was certain it was information that he already knew well.

"Well, let's take the Dead Sea Scrolls, *chéri*. Documents with which we are all familiar. They represent an extensive set of Aramaic scripts dated within the first hundred years of the current era, probably written by the Essenes and thankfully stored in the dry caves of Qumran around the Dead Sea. The pattern and form of these words, so carefully drawn, represent a standard through which others of the period can be interpreted."

"Tell me, Andrea, the finds at Nag Hammadi, written in Coptic—could those have originally been translated from Aramaic?" asked Justine. Discovered in clay jars near the village of Nag Hammadi in Upper Egypt in 1945, the codices contained more than fifty Gnostic texts.

"Indeed. Most of them," replied Andrea, slowly sipping her cabernet. She turned to Ibrahim. "Is that not so, Professor? Ibrahim may be too modest to tell you that he was also involved in the translation of the Nag Hammadi Codex." She gave him an encouraging smile.

Ibrahim blushed almost imperceptibly. "The codices included many things, new texts such as the Gospels of Thomas, Philip, and Truth, and Eastern manuscripts, such as sections of lost texts from Zoroastrianism. Most of the papyri appear to have been translated from ancient and middle Aramaic. I was pleased to find that the blending of beliefs, or religious traditions, was much more fluid then."

"As it should be today," Justine said, recalling the professor's pursuit of the Tao. Ibrahim looked at her with appreciation and nodded.

"Translation was an important art during those days when Alexandria and Hellenization were at their zenith," offered Amir. "The entire known world responded to the culture and style of Greece, a love affair that didn't end with the Romans. Two thousand years ago, the Hebrew Scriptures—the origin of all of the religions of the book—were translated into Greek in the Alexandria library. And, of course, the gospels of the New Testament were written in Greek as well."

"A fact that has led some of us to believe that Christianity developed among the Diaspora, rather than in Palestine itself," observed Ibrahim. "No earlier copies of those original gospels exist in Aramaic."

"That's a debatable observation, my dear professor," observed Andrea. "Just because Aramaic gospels have not been found doesn't mean they don't exist." She placed her hand on his, the gold chain on her wrist resting across his forearm.

Clearly this debate is not a new one, Justine mused, surveying her dinner partners. *It's like I'm observing an Oscar Wilde play. Into what role am I cast? Do I cast myself?*

"Granted, most mysteries in human history are still to be unraveled," admitted the professor, bowing his head slightly, "but the learned Greek used in writing the gospel texts lead many of us to assume that such work may have been done in the strongholds of Greek culture throughout the region, regions where Jews had immigrated during the Diaspora. Most probably in Alexandria. Isn't that right, Amir?"

Amir nodded gallantly, an amused grin on his face.

"You Egyptians," goaded Andrea. "You want to claim credit for everything of value—the beginning of civilization, Moses and the Exodus, Jesus and his family, the transfer of Hebrew texts to the world, the beginning of Christianity."

"Couldn't you manage to find the birthplace of Mohammed somewhere along the Nile?" asked Justine.

"Don't think we haven't tried," laughed Amir. "In fact, I'm thinking of a new dig . . . starting near Aswan."

"May I join you?" offered Justine, winking at him and laughing lightly. "I've always thought we might find Mohammed here. Why not? He conquered Egypt eventually."

"You may join me on the hunt," Amir said enthusiastically. "Bring shovels, gloves, and a few dozen eager students." Laughter moved around the table, followed by their arriving food. Chicken, aubergine fattah, kofta, and rice joined their generous, unfinished salads. Several minutes passed as they ate in silence.

"You *are* Lucrezia Jenner's daughter, aren't you? You have her sense of humor and grace," Andrea said appreciatively.

"I am. And thank you," Justine said, genuinely surprised. "You know my mother?"

"I have known and respected your mother for many years. She's a scholar, a poet, and a bit of a raconteur. We used to hold a few salons together in Florence and Paris, depending on where we were at the time." It was obvious that Andrea recalled those days with fondness. "How is she?"

"Quite well, and enjoying life. I've talked with her a couple of times this week. As you might imagine, she's been concerned about the effects of the earthquake."

"Of course she would be. Please give her my regards."

"I will . . . Andrea, has Ibrahim talked with you about the codex I found in St. Sergius?"

"He has," Andrea whispered, glancing around them to assure herself that no one was listening.

Ibrahim reached for the uncontested check. Justine lowered her voice and asked: "Do you think it might be of any significance? Might you be interested in working with us?"

Andrea waved her hand dismissively. "I don't think it's anything of importance."

The evening concluded as pleasantly as it began, although Justine was deeply disappointed. She'd hoped . . . *What?* she asked herself. *That Andrea would be as excited about the codex as I am? Surely she is wrong about its importance.* For several moments she was lost in thought. When she looked up, Amir stood by her shoulder.

"Ready?" he asked.

She smiled up at him, stood, and allowed him to escort her out of the restaurant.

∽

Justine entered Groppi's through its front door, which was framed by blue mosaic and situated on a corner of Midan Talaat Harb Square in downtown Cairo. The looming statue of Mr. Harb, founder of the National Bank, in his tarboosh stood watch over the entrance. At one time, Groppi's had been second only to the Shepheard as the gathering place for writers, adventurers, self-appointed celebrities, and pashas, but it now failed to dazzle. Life had leaked out of Groppi's like perfume from a broken vial and left only a colorful shop full of candies and cookies behind—but the fragrance of warm cookies still issued forth a friendly invitation.

Andrea had called soon after Justine arrived back at the Shepheard last night and suggested this morning meeting. *I wonder what she has in mind?*

Perhaps she's changed her mind about the codex. Or has questions. She's late, she observed, glancing at her watch. Having grown up with her father's compulsive regard for time and her mother's exasperating lateness, she'd chosen to follow her father's punctuality while avoiding some of his more infuriating qualities.

Reminding herself again that punctuality was far from a universal habit, she busied herself, fondly observing the place where her father had once brought her for tea and cookies. Ochre-tiled floors, fresh fica, potted palms, and paneled windows crosshatched with wood still offered a promise of elegance, though it was quickly compromised by the fading beige walls and poor lighting. Three men who might have been pashas in another age wore shiny rayon suits and horn-rimmed glasses, yet retained a dignity that spoke of pride and confidence. All four women in the room wore hijabs. No one laughed, especially the sad waitress.

"Groppi's still reminds me of a Paris patisserie. But rough around the edges," Andrea said as she slid into the seat across from Justine. "I'm sorry I brushed you off last night. I was being cautious. A touch of French paranoia."

"Then you think the codex *is* important?" Justine asked excitedly, letting go of her annoyance about the night before.

"I've only taken a cursory look at it, but the Aramaic seems to be well formed, readable at least. I thought we might visit for a while and then walk over to Ibrahim's office. Do you need to go to a school this morning?"

"Not today. We're going to The Fayoum tomorrow." Justine leaned forward. "I'm pleased that you think this codex might be important. Last night I was certainly having second thoughts." As much as she wanted to ask her a flurry of questions about the codex, she sensed that Andrea preferred to wait until they were with Ibrahim.

"I apologize. I should have explained myself when I called your room. Please forgive me. And I do look forward to working with Lucrezia's daughter. She's told me so much about you over the years that I almost feel you could be my own daughter." Andrea appeared sincere, if not apologetic, and Justine suspected she was a woman who did her own thing in her own time, including the gradual release of prized information.

"I'm flattered," said Justine. "You must know some of my darkest secrets!"

Andrea winked conspiratorially. Tea arrived with a small plate of chocolate cookies Andrea had ordered in the front of the shop, wrinkled little things with miniature mounds of white frosting and delicate red cherries. "I fancy these cookies," she admitted. "I'm a chocolate addict."

"Another thing that we have in common," Justine confessed. "And you're not the first person to suggest caution with regard to the codex. I'm afraid I'm pretty naïve about the need to protect information."

"I'll share some of my experiences with you one of these days—times when my innocence got me in trouble. Now tell me, how have you found your reception in Cairo?"

"The people have been as warm as ever, even more welcoming than I had expected. Amir is not an easy man to get to know. But last night he was quite warm."

"He's always wary at first, withholding a part of himself. But I can tell he likes you. I've known Amir for as many years as I've known Ibrahim. And since he's some fifteen years my junior, I've watched him grow up. He is a man of pride and shame—a dangerous combination: deep pride in Egypt, its history, and its people, yet he's ashamed that Egypt couldn't make the revolution succeed."

"What do you mean, 'dangerous'?"

"Shame can make him lash out, respond to imagined offenses. And, of course, pride brings arrogance, a cover for his . . ."

". . . shame." Justine finished Andrea's thought.

"Believe me, neither is the real Amir. When you get to know him, you'll find he can be sensitive as well as sensible. And forgiving. But in many ways, he is France after World War II. *Comprendez-vous*? We are prickly, overly sensitive, quick to anger. Unfortunately, others feel the brunt of our confusion until we learn to trust, which doesn't come quickly. And some people don't stay around to find out."

"That's helpful, and I think we may have moved pass the suspicious stage. He is being charming, and is terribly excited about the codex."

"That's good to hear. Patience has its own rewards—not that I have any, you understand." She laughed.

"You seem to have escaped the French predicament yourself. How so?"

"If you mean our prickliness? I think I've escaped it for the most part, although I require that you worship everything French." She smiled again. "I was born after World War II, so I didn't experience the Vichy shame directly. And I've tried to cultivate a sense of humor. Being a woman helps. Empathy is expected."

"So true. I have yet to fully realize that power. Of being a woman, I mean."

"You're an accomplished and beautiful woman. Be patient and forgiving with yourself." Andrea paused to finish her second cookie. "Speaking of exceptional women, I've always wondered why your parents separated. They're both adventurous and seemed well suited for each other."

"I think it had less to do with my father, although he was overly protective, than with my mother. She passionately wanted to be free. She didn't want to become a line dancer."

"A line dancer?"

Justine grinned. "That's the metaphor she uses for a woman who waits until her husband dies to do what she wants, then takes up line dancing and dances as fast as she can."

"A useful metaphor!" Andrea laughed, reaching for the last cookie. "Now, let's go talk to Ibrahim about this codex of yours."

"This may be a significant find," began Ibrahim, settling into the chair behind his cedar desk, a cane nearby. "Andrea and I think we'll need to bring in team members with different areas of expertise. We don't have the means here to do many of the dating processes. I will discuss our needs with Omar Mostafa, Director-General of the Supreme Council of Antiquities, but this is a delicate transaction, since Omar is a man of theatre; he fashions himself a star. That is not to say he isn't fully competent and qualified, just that he also demands the limelight. And he may demand the codex, especially when he hears that an American is involved."

Justine raised a brow and opened her mouth to speak.

"At any rate," Andrea interrupted, "he'll take the credit. But Ibrahim believes that if he and I offer to lead the team, Mostafa may welcome our participation and make available the full resources of the Council offices at the Egyptian Museum. We have a few other team members in mind, but we wanted to consult you first."

Is there anyone who doesn't know Mostafa? And what is this about an American's involvement? Justine decided to take a different tack. She was already beginning to understand the mixed feelings about her father here. "Are there disadvantages in bringing others in? My father often suggested that things can get bogged down with too many spoons in the stew."

"Good question. One critical issue is that the codex will sometimes be out of our hands—and we won't be able to control the release of information," Andrea replied, stretching her arms over her head and narrowing her eyes. "Things can get stretched out, but I think we can expedite things. At least, I would hope so, since I'm just at AUC for the spring and summer sessions." She paused, then added, "Perhaps I could extend my leave if this gets really juicy."

Justine laughed. "I'm finding this really juicy already. How about you, sir?"

"I'll tell my good friend Mostafa I haven't long for this world, so I need to proceed with all reasonable haste," said Ibrahim, grinning and pulling at his beard.

Andrea winked at Justine, and both women assured him that he would be around for a good long while. Ibrahim waved them off. "There is one other issue," he added soberly, "that I've encountered before. If the findings are too provocative, there could be problems."

Justine frowned. "You both have warned me now. What kind of problems do you have in mind?"

"Let me tell you a story," said Ibrahim. "It was about twenty-five years ago, and I was in my full stride and fervor as an archaeologist. Dashing, I would say. At any rate, I was working with your father, Justine. He was still wet behind the ears, a little cocky. We uncovered a tablet near Darshur."

Her heart sped up. *Here it comes, the story I've been waiting for.* The one her father had refused to speak about.

"At first I was greatly excited. It could have been another Rosetta Stone—about a hundred years too late. It appeared to have inscriptions in more than one language. As you can imagine, we were thrilled, and we sat up at night debating our options." Ibrahim pulled his tea toward him and contemplated a small glass paperweight on his desk for several moments before continuing. "Our first take on the tablet—it was maybe three hands high—was that it was in hieroglyphics, Greek, and Coptic." He carefully placed his gnarled hands one above the other, measuring the tablet in the air. "It turned out that the Greek and Coptic were interwoven and there was a fourth language: ancient Hebrew. We decided to keep it hidden in our work area near Darshur, and we worked on it in the evenings. But the languages weren't the issue."

"Why not?" pressed Andrea.

"Yes! Why not?" echoed Justine, almost holding her breath.

"The true find may have been in the message, my dear young women. The message was the jewel. At least, the message as we thought we understood it. It told about the promise of the Pharaoh to Moses and his wife Zipporah. The Pharaoh offered to let Moses lead the Children of Israel out of Egypt if he would leave Zipporah behind. She agreed, but Moses resisted. 'Better to leave me behind than to cause firstborn Egyptian sons to perish,' argued Zipporah. The story on the tablet claimed that Moses had finally agreed. We even inferred that the Passover never happened. That is, the part of the story of the Exodus where God kills the firstborn sons of Egyptians but 'passes over' the houses of the Children of Israel. The central story confirming that the Hebrews are God's chosen people." He paused, permitting the weightiness of his last statement sink in. "But we never got that far. The tablet disappeared."

"Didn't you have enough information to bring the inscription to light?" urged Justine. "Couldn't you have done something?"

"We'd made a few sketchings, but had no photos. We had no tablet. No hard evidence. But there was something else that haunted us: Did we want this information to come to light? Is all knowledge superior to faith?" Ibrahim's eyes suggested that he had slipped back in time, reliving those moments.

"But surely you've answered that question for yourself, Ibrahim," said a startled Andrea. "You're a scholar and archaeologist. Your profession demands that evidence supersedes faith."

"Absolutely," said another voice. They turned to find Amir leaning against the doorframe. "Are you three plotting without me?" He grinned, but his eyes were steely.

"Hi, my boy," said Ibrahim. "I was just explaining that it hasn't always been so clear to me that knowledge trumps faith. Living one's life in the Middle East has its consequences," he said defensively, staring downward as though he were ashamed to have his grandson hear his doubts.

Amir's full eyebrows drew together. He appeared momentarily stunned. Then he strode across the room and pulled up a chair. "Surely you're speaking theoretically," he said.

Ibrahim nodded gratefully, his Adam's apple pulsing only slightly.

Justine glanced at Amir, then Ibrahim, amazed that there was a time when the elder El Shabry had been tempted to suppress evidence. *And what does this say about my father?* "Truth trumps tradition every time," she said decisively, sounding more confident that she felt. Her stomach tightened, a signal that something was wrong, something was missing. "There are rumors, Dr. Ibrahim. Rumors that have darkened my father's credibility." Her voice tight, she drew a deep breath.

"What kind of rumors, my dear?" asked Ibrahim.

I have trouble believing he hasn't heard them too. "That the evidence *was* withheld to protect Judaism. I can see how such a rumor would spread in an Arab country. But are the rumors true?" she asked, although she wasn't sure she wanted to hear the answer.

"I know the rumors . . . and they are just that," insisted Ibrahim. "I'm not sure even your father and I know what might have happened. When the tablet was stolen and never recovered—and as far as I know, it didn't show up in the antiquities market—we moved on. 'Best to let sleeping dogs lie,' your father said."

Justine's face flushed as she heard one of her father's familiar homilies. Was he as conservative in his work as at home? Not apt to challenge tradition or overturn prevailing "truths"? That possibility had never entered her mind before, and she couldn't accept it now. *He's a scholar, a scientist above all.* She glanced at Amir, who met her eyes with remarkable tenderness.

"Trust your father," was all he said.

She swallowed and regained her focus. "Let me ask you, Andrea, and you, Ibrahim"—she turned from one to the other—"why do you think this find is significant? What do you know that I don't know?"

"Andrea," said Ibrahim, nodding in her direction, his head bobbing up and down.

Andrea stalled by taking a long sip of her tea. "Perhaps for three reasons," she began. "First, it was found in the cave thought to have once been inhabited by the Holy Family. Of course, this story is most likely myth, and there is no telling how many people have lived in that cave over the generations. We need the carbon-14 dating to situate the possible author or authors. However, the language is very familiar to me, not only as Aramaic, but as similar in phrasing, pacing, to certain renowned documents—I'm still examining that premise. From the small phrases I'm able to translate now, I can say it is written in first person."

First person?

Ibrahim swayed in his seat. Amir raised an eyebrow, glanced at Justine, and stepped alongside her, lightly brushing her shoulder.

Justine blinked; her face flushed again, this time with excitement. She jumped up and paced the room, taking immense strides. "When can we get a team together?"

CHAPTER 9

L ESS THAN A WEEK LATER, JUSTINE STEPPED out of a taxi and onto the high curb at number ten Aisha al-Taimuriyya, the address of her new sixth-floor apartment. A narrow but popular artery traversing Garden City, the street began near the Four Seasons Hotel on the Corniche, curved east past the Indonesian Embassy and police station, and emerged near the Blue Nile grocery on Qasr al-Ainy. The elderly Nubian boab, or doorman, his skin the glistening color of eggplant, hurried to take several of her bundles.

Shortly, Nadia, Amir, and Mohammed would be there to help her move in. She'd had two messages from Nasser. It looked as though he wouldn't make it this morning.

Nestled entirely between the Corniche on the Nile and Qasr al-Ainy, Garden City, like Cairo itself, was the home of secret gardens. Hidden behind stone, brick, or wrought iron walls and gates, and shielded from the omnipresent swirling dust, lay recurring images of the Garden of Eden. Burgeoning flowers and palms, willows and sycamores, green lawns sprouting fountains, and perfumed air all held the secrets of this glorious city. Such beauty was more and more rare here; secrets, more precious still.

At one time, these gardens had not been so secret. Flowing from palatial villas down to the Nile, colorful carpets of grass and flowers had hosted grand parties and welcomed Cairo's elite. Sumptuous villas had been home to Egypt's wealthy businessmen, foreign diplomats, and rich scoundrels. Such grandeur grew from the dark side of colonization—wealth at the expense of the many—yet Justine remembered her excitement whenever her family had received invitations to these splendid events.

Carrying her buckskin suitcases and followed by the overloaded boab, she took the wrought iron elevator to the sixth floor and entered her new home. She motioned to the boab to set everything just inside the door beside her luggage. After thanking him for his assistance, she walked from room to room, elated to have a place she could finally call her own, even if it belonged to someone else. The furnished apartment was large and full of sunlight. Overgrown cabinets of Islamic design almost brushed the high ceilings. A large living-dining area, a small office, and two bedrooms led to a terrace running the length of the apartment. The European-style kitchen, while small, was fully equipped. Every window opened onto a view of buildings turned brown by smog and neglect, lines full of clothes, unkempt rooftops covered with TV satellite dishes and an occasional pigeon cage. *What happened to the glory of Garden City?* How was it that its residents had grown accustomed to such deterioration? She knew the answers to her own questions: servants could no longer be used like slave labor; thankfully, power had been more democratically dispersed in the fledging republic.

Within the hour, her friends arrived with arms full of falafel, foul, and pita, towels, glasses, sheets, and lilies. By early afternoon, having unpacked Justine's few personal belongings and dozens of books, the moving party was sitting down to pita sandwiches and tea.

"One of your most important relationships here," Nadia said between bites, "will be with the boab. You said his name was Kamala?"

Justine nodded.

"The boab can be your protector, your mother, your father, your eyes, and your ears. Little goes on in a Cairo apartment house without the notice of the boab."

"Never get on the wrong side of that man," Amir said as he flopped into an armchair nearby to check his texts. "Kamala may sleep on a cot in the back of the garage, but his dignity demands respect."

"While I don't need another parent, I can use extra eyes and ears," grinned Justine. "Thanks for the advice."

Mohammed stood by the table methodically cutting into a falafel and placing both halves into a hummus-lined pita. "How did you survive the earthquake, Justine? A traumatic beginning to your life here. I was concerned when I left you at the hotel that it might be too much excitement too soon."

"Thanks to you, Mohammed, I survived it well—physically, at least. But I've found the deaths of the children in Birqash and the damage to the poorer areas of Cairo rather devastating," she said, tucking both hands into her blue jeans and hunching her shoulders. "It made me feel rather helpless." She looked at Nadia, whose eyes still welled up at the reminder of the children and their families.

"People who suffer in Egypt don't have any kind of insurance," said Amir. Justine noticed the muscles on either side of his mouth tighten and then relax again. "It's not like the U.S., where even the Hurricane Katrina victims expected substantial help." The room was growing warmer as sunlight insistently seeped through the French doors.

"Expected is the operative word there," said Justine. "It wasn't necessarily forthcoming." She paused. "Amir, you'll remember the story of the taxi driver and his daughter, the horribly scarred young woman I referred to our agency doctor . . ."

"What happened to her?" asked Mohammed.

"Dr. Bakry just said, 'Send her to me,' and when he saw the girl he referred her on to the head of plastic surgery at Cairo University, who will perform corrective plastic surgery on her. No cost. No fuss." Justine was still astonished by the selfless action, executed so casually.

"I'm not surprised," said Nadia. "Egyptians turn to one another. For medical care, small loans to help with family weddings, bean pots, sewing machines . . . it's our way."

Mohammed stood silent, pensive, his plate in one hand, juice in the other. "I recognize and appreciate how we help each other, yet, unfortunately, much of the help here now—in Shoubra and Bulaq particularly, as well as in old Islamic Cairo—is coming from the Muslim Brotherhood. They're doling out money for food, clothing, and rebuilding." A hint of sarcasm permeated his voice as he spoke of the proud and patriotic group that had originated in Egypt in the '20s during the struggle against British occupation and King Farouk's oppressive rule. Presidents Nasser and Sadat had both been part of this group, but had separated themselves from the Brotherhood's influence as the social changes the two presidents advocated for confronted a sharpening fundamentalist agenda. An agenda that had been suppressed for the last thirty years.

"I've seen their charities at work," Nadia added. "When your mother and I used to visit families who had taken out microloans, Mohammed, I saw young men from the Brotherhood going into damaged houses—that was after the '92 earthquake—and handing out money." She absentmindedly fingered her wedding band. Justine had observed Nadia in at least a dozen black blouses made of every kind of material. In the Muslim world, mourning a spouse was a lifelong occupation.

"The Brotherhood originated direct family help and taught it to fledgling groups like Hamas and Hezbollah. I've got to admit, it works well," Mohammed said. "Bastards," he added caustically.

"If someone showed up with money or to take me to the doctor or make sure my son had a school uniform," said Justine, "I'd support him and his group as well. Wouldn't you?"

"Aren't you ever tempted to support the Brotherhood?" provoked Amir. "The MB Bureau guide claims to support moderation and democracy."

Justine noticed dark circles under Amir's eyes and saw in him a sense of pervasive melancholy. She watched him closely, acutely aware that he worried about his brother Zach's radicalization in the Brotherhood. Perhaps even Al Qaeda.

"The price is too high. You know that!" exclaimed Mohammed. "To the Brotherhood, there is only one way to think. Their real intention is to change the constitution to Shariah law. What is their war cry? 'Islam is the solution.' You think we have it tough now—Shariah would take us back a thousand years!" Mohammed's voice rose as he slammed down his plate.

Amir nodded. "I agree. But their support is broadening. Professionals, syndicates, fellaheen . . . many are choosing to believe them when they talk about democratic reforms and moderation. They could well come to power."

"Not peacefully. Not with Mubarak in office. In spite of his crimes, he keeps a lid on extremism," said Mohammed darkly.

Justine listened in fascination to the provocative discussion. She found herself thinking back to Ibrahim's warnings about the possible dangers inherent in the codex discovery, and to stories she'd heard about people just disappearing. Anything could be used to provoke violence. *Even an innocent artifact?*

Nadia glared at the two seething men and attempted to redirect the conversation. "Remember, we're here to celebrate Justine's new apartment . . ."

Mohammed shook his head, ignoring Nadia. "The foxes are in the henhouse now. As long as our economy is crippled, if a vacuum should occur—if Mubarak died—the foxes would have their run of the place."

Nadia placed her hand on Mohammed's forearm and spoke to Justine. "Women could lose all the progress we've made. Shariah is highly punitive; even stoning is permitted for small transgressions. Women could not travel without their husbands' permission. In Iran, the marriage age for girls has been lowered to nine years old. We could be fully covered with black burqas. Imagine. There wouldn't be a free press. Not that there is now . . ."

In spite of the heat, Justine felt chilled. "It seems to me that if the government would offer the people a few safety nets, the Brotherhood wouldn't have such fertile ground for securing an advantage."

"Where the government fails, the Brotherhood prospers," said Nadia, stacking the dishes and handing them to Amir.

"Democracy is more than a safety net, although that would help. We need the rule of law, an open press, fair elections," said Amir, follow by a low sigh.

"Yet didn't the Brotherhood, masquerading as Independents, just pick up eighty-eight seats in the fall election?" asked Justine, portioning out coconut cake. "Haven't they become unstoppable?"

"If the economy doesn't pick up, they may become unstoppable," said Mohammed. "U.S. policy in Iraq and with Israel and Iran just plays into their hands. The U.S. is even better at recruiting Islamists than the Brotherhood." He stood and put on his jacket. "I'd better head out before my blood pressure goes through the roof."

As though on cue, Nadia gathered up her belongings, kissed Justine on either cheek and headed for the door. "Goodbye, dear friends. I'll see you tomorrow, Justine."

Amir stayed behind, casually puttering with the dishes and chairs as though he was leaving, just not right away. Justine wondered if he would open up to her about his brother now. When Nadia and Mohammed closed the door behind them, he asked with uncharacteristic shyness: "Would you join me for a drink at the Four Seasons? It's just a short walk."

"Not like this," she laughed, surprised, motioning to her soiled T-shirt. "Give me just a minute." She went into the bedroom to find a clean white silk blouse and a pair of simple gold hoop earrings, slipped on a pair of black flats and brushed her hair.

Three blocks to the west along Aisha el Taimuriyya stood the Four Seasons Hotel. The exquisite lobby was awash with long-stemmed bird of paradise flowers, chrysanthemums, roses, and lilies all placed high in tall, clear vases and tilted at a precarious angle. The effect was stunning. Justine momentarily stood in awe of the opulence.

"I'm sorry to bring you here, but it's the closest place to your apartment," Amir said with some embarrassment as they sauntered toward the elevators.

"It's breathtaking," said Justine, still staring at the unique flower arrangements as she followed him into the alcove and a gleaming brass elevator. "Why are you sorry?"

"The Four Seasons is Cairo's most exclusive hotel, representing the ultimate in consumption in a country that can't afford to feed its poor. Millions will change hands in this room tonight," he said, stepping from the elevator and pointing toward The Bar.

A corner table was vacant and provided a fine view of the entire room. They slid into the angled booth on opposite sides. Justine soon understood Amir's observation. The Egyptian house wine was listed at sixteen dollars a glass and the room was crowded with international businessmen—Arabs, sub-Saharan Africans, Brits, Asians, and Americans—all in expensive suits and dangling cigarettes or small cigars. Multiple jeweled rings adorned well-manicured hands. Three elegantly dressed women wearing veils and being ignored by their table partners huddled in their own intense conversation. Mammoth alabaster chandeliers and gold-framed mirrors reflected amber light from the Nile below onto the embossed wallpaper.

"What kinds of transactions are going on here?" Justine asked. "What are they buying and selling?" *I should never have worn jeans to a place this elegant. Although they're not as poor a choice as my Lycra running suit would have been.*

"Oil, sugar, cotton, wheat, rice . . . you name it. We actually import 75 percent of our wheat and mix it with our own poor-quality grain. This year is the 40th anniversary of the '77 bread riots and not much has changed, although in many cases we now export products formerly made available to our own people through subsidies. Like sugar. Cotton. The IMF put a stop to that," Amir said flatly, motioning to the waiter.

"Why?"

"Capitalism demands that we make available more products for international trade. Making such products accessible to our citizens at low prices interferes with that requirement. IMF's requirement."

"The price of gasoline is quite low here. Isn't it subsidized?" She tilted her head and pushed her hair behind an ear. Her golden hoop earring caught the amber light.

"It's the one subsidy that keeps this city on wheels. If we had to pay European prices for oil, Egypt would come to a standstill. Even with the necessity of gas, the IMF is hardly tolerant. But enough about our economy." He turned to the approaching waiter and ordered two glasses of cabernet. Justine was intrigued by his contempt for this grand lifestyle, one in which he himself had been raised. She knew that his salary at the museum must be exceedingly low, as was true with all government agencies, and he would need a family source of income or to take on multiple jobs. From what she knew, both El Shabry brothers were absorbed by a desire for social justice.

Amir softened his voice, seeking a more ordinary conversation. "I noticed today that the Blue Nile sells this cabernet, but I have to warn you, it won't be the same. What they sell to the big hotels and what they sell at retail is quite different. Nothing is quite as it seems." His words could apply to any number of situations in Egypt, but his usually serious features relaxed. "Don't be too swayed by our cheerful demeanor."

"I wouldn't have accused you of having a cheerful demeanor." She grinned.

He released a totally disarming smile and nodded without taking his eyes from hers.

"How were we as children?" she asked. "What do you remember?" Whenever Amir shifted into his charming self, her equilibrium became deliciously disturbed and she found herself breathless. "Since your grandfather reminded me that we played together, I've been trying to recall those days. They're somewhat blurry, although I remember parties in a beautiful garden."

"There was a garden. It belonged to my mother's parents," Amir said, coaxing out his own memories. "Grandfather Saad was a diplomat, and the family owned one of these villas in Garden City where the garden flowed down to the Nile, through the area now owned by Shell Oil. We'd gather there on holidays, and the guest list often included your parents, who I assume had been introduced to my parents by grandfather. They added flair to any gathering, especially your mother. I remember her stunning dresses."

"Her dresses?" Justine teased. The wine and several miniature appetizers appeared before them on the carved ebony table, which was adorned with a single lily.

"Your mother always wore long, flowing, white gowns and dramatic silver jewelry. And your dresses were made of some shiny material, perhaps taffeta or satin, and were quite colorful. The skirts bounced and crackled a bit when you walked." Amir laughed. "This proud little girl named Justine marched around the garden as though she owned it. You were quite stubborn, as I recall, insisting we play hide and seek. You stayed hidden for the longest time."

Justine was both flattered and embarrassed by his keen memory of her. "I'm still stubborn," she admitted, "but I don't wear taffeta anymore. Whatever happened to that house?"

"The house is still there, but when part of the land was confiscated by the government for new development along the Corniche, my grandparents moved to Zamalek. That was several years ago. We can walk by the house on our way back to your apartment."

"I'd like that. They must miss the house, those times. Life seemed more hopeful then. Or perhaps it was just that I understood less about the world."

"Perhaps some of each. The population in Cairo has changed rapidly; it's now nearly eighteen million. Too many people devouring the air, the space, the resources. Before the revolution, people were extremely poor. They are still poor, but for different reasons. Do you realize that there are about the same number of people in Cairo as in all of Australia?"

"That's astounding. Difficult to grasp. Yet I see little effort to address the issues, except for an explosion of incomplete apartment buildings on the out-skirts of town."

Amir shook his head and stared out at the Nile for several moments. The lights reflecting in his eyes revealed a deep sadness. He turned back toward her, changing the subject. "How is your mother, Justine? I haven't heard about her in years."

"Mother is doing quite well. She loves Fiesole and the Italian culture—and her art and poetry have flourished, become rather exceptional. The most fas-cinating artists and writers attend salons at her home. A stimulating life. I hope I can say that at her age."

"Enticing indeed. I've always wanted to ask where the name 'Lucrezia' came from." Amir's left hand slowly turned the vase holding the lily, first facing it toward Justine, then himself.

"Mom often claims she was named for Lucrezia Borgia, the flamboyant daughter of one of the popes, but actually it was for another famous Latin, the poet and philosopher Lucretius. My Italian grandmother's family members were followers of Epicureanism. I've flirted with the philosophy myself."

"Epicureanism." He raised a teasing brow. "Isn't that the pursuit of plea-sure?"

"A popular misunderstanding," Justine corrected, but grinned. "Pleasure was defined differently by the original Epicureans. For instance, Lucretius's most famous poem teaches that pleasure is about equilibrium while pain means that the universe is out of balance. I find the notion intriguing."

Amir held her eyes over his wine glass. "That's a novel concept to me. Per-sonal pain being connected with the balance of the universe."

"The Epicureans say there are two fears that must be dealt with: the fear that the gods will capriciously interfere with your life, and the fear of death. These are very old fears; I don't know if things have changed much. At that time in history, the Romans, like the Greeks and the Etruscans before them, believed in many gods—gods who were capricious, self-centered, and often immoral. The Jewish concept of one god with a moral purpose was not part of their thinking as yet.

"Epicureanism tried to provide that moral compass," Justine continued. "Pleasure was understood as truth, justice, freedom, and it assumed that we all had the free will to choose wisely. The highest pleasure was acquiring the knowledge to set us free from pain."

"I'd like to think that religions have evolved since the time Lucretius described the fear of death," Amir said, his hand brushing against hers as he reached for a tiny crackers. "Isn't the offer of heaven or paradise rather appealing?" His eyes widened as though he were offering a reserved ticket to the hereafter.

"Perhaps . . ." She searched for the right words. "But what about hell? A little off-putting, don't you think?" She tilted her head. "I'd prefer to imagine that I had the freedom to monitor my own life. I suspect that my attraction to anthropology, which involves a high reliance on intuition and the senses, may be a result of my affinity for Lucretius's philosophy." She surprised herself by considering a connection she hadn't observed before. She paused for several moments, staring at the lights reflecting in the Nile. "Amir, I'm obsessed with this codex. I dream about it, I'm distracted during the day. Could it have anything to do with the Holy Family? Might Joseph have written it? The midwife?"

Amir was pensive, but not dismissive. "Possibly Joseph. Not the midwife. Women weren't literate then. Maybe James."

"James?"

"Joseph's first son. There is a great deal more to James than we know. After all, he became the leader of the movement after Jesus died."

"Then what about Jesus himself? Could he have written it?"

Amir chuckled. "Hardly. He couldn't have been more than two and a half or three when the family was in Egypt."

"It's fascinating to speculate." She smiled. "I'll try to be a little more patient." Then she paused once again, realizing that such patience was not possible. "Amir, I've noticed a sadness, a concern in your eyes. You often seem distracted. Are you worried about your brother? Nadia said you knew she had told me about his disappearance."

Amir stiffened. "I wish she hadn't said anything. But your observations are perceptive. I'm fearful that his behavior will lead to disaster for him and our family."

"Do you feel comfortable telling me more?"

Amir gazed at her until she was almost convinced that he wasn't ready to confide in her. "Not only did Zachariah leave for a training camp in Afghanistan, but I think he may have converted to Islam," he said. He was tense, all signs of playfulness gone. "Our family have been Copts for more generations than we can remember, probably since St. Mark came to Alexandria in the first century."

"Such a conversion would be a dramatic move," agreed Justine. A dark curtain had fallen over his demeanor; his shoulders slumped forward. "Had anyone in your family anticipated such a move?"

"We never thought he would go that far. He started asking hard questions when he was fifteen or sixteen and spent most weekends working with the poor—getting them groceries, talking with the children, taking care of the sick. It was hard for him to understand such suffering. It's hard for any of us to understand."

"This is when you started to suspect?"

"We admired his compassion, but when he forced us into heated arguments about Western capitalism and Christianity, we feared the changes coming. I worry that some morning I'll open a newspaper and find his face there."

"I'm so sorry. Hopefully, you'll be able to find him soon, let him know how much you care," Justine said softly.

"We were never close, but now I don't know him at all—what he is capable of," Amir said in a sad whisper.

"We were never close?" But Ibrahim said they were very close. Which is it? Why the different points of view? And if one of them is lying . . . why?

CHAPTER 10

JUSTINE FELL INTO THE COMFORT OF HER own bed and was asleep long before she finished thinking about the evening and Amir. Zachariah and Ibrahim.

Her first wakeup call came from the covey of pigeons caged on the roof of an adjoining building, her second from her ringing cell phone. *Cooing certainly beats an alarm*, she thought as she reached for her phone.

"Are you all moved in?" asked Nasser. "Sorry I couldn't make it to your housewarming yesterday. I got tied up with some of my students. How about dinner tonight to celebrate—and to apologize?"

"Not a problem. I'd love dinner. I'm going to a school today, but I'll be back in the late afternoon." Justine imagined his dark blue eyes and sensuous grin and wondered where he was, what he was doing right now.

"Eight o'clock? I'll come by your apartment. Ten Aisha El Taimuriyya?"

"Apartment sixty-two." Just the sound of his voice made her heart quicken, her toes grow warm. *How easy am I?* she mused. *Can I be swept up by a captivating grin?* "Perfect," she said. They had met once in The Caravan and talked on the phone a couple of times about her new apartment, but she really knew very little about this man, except that he had once been a student of her father's.

She took her time deliberating about what to wear that night when she got home from her day with Nadia. She finally settled on a dark blue cocktail dress—to match his eyes—and simple gold earrings. She left her hair full and flared out at the sides, noticing with amusement the amount of attention she was giving to her appearance. She straightened the lilies on the dining room table, shut the French doors, and sat down to catch up on BBC news.

The knock on the door occurred a couple of minutes before eight. "How did you time that so well?" she asked as she invited Nasser in. "Parking is impossible here."

He paused and blushed a bit. "To tell the truth, I got here a little early in order to find a place to park. I read the paper in the car."

"How early?" she teased as she reached for her shawl.

"About half an hour." He grinned sheepishly. "I know Americans like to be on time."

"I'm flattered," she said. "My confession is that I changed my dress three times." She scrunched her shoulders as though to say, "There it is."

They both laughed in that light, lilting way that sounds like music. "Nothing like starting off a relationship with honesty," Nasser declared, taking Justine's shawl from her hand and wrapping it around her before leading her out the door.

The Arabesque, a quiet little restaurant off Tahrir Square, reminded Justine of the Tabullah, with the added intimacy of a sheikh's tent—round brass tables, Arabesque trim around the ceiling, and amber lamps. Justine and Nasser sat on huge, fringed, golden pillows.

"Tell me, who is the real Justine Jenner?" he asked, flashing his irresistible grin.

She laughed. "That's a tougher question than you would think. I seem to be a woman in transition . . . from a daughter and student to an independent person and anthropologist . . . from an American to an Egyptian . . . and I'm known to be stubborn at times," she added.

"I find stubbornness seductive," he said, sitting back on his pillow, eyeing her with amusement.

"Oh? How is that?" She folded her arms across her chest.

"Take right now," he observed. "You have a challenging sparkle in your amber eyes, and your body tells me you are ready to take me on. I find that captivating. Mysterious."

Justine felt a warm flush of embarrassment and desire move across her face. She unfolded her arms and rearranged her skirt, thankful that it was not taffeta. "Well," she grinned, "I love old movies and good books, particularly romantic ones. I would say I'm spiritual but not religious. I trust my senses and use them in my work. Enough for now?"

"Enough for now," he nodded, as though this were only the first install-ment. "What do you mean by 'spiritual but not religious'?" A young Sudanese waiter decked out in a gold-trimmed vest, pantaloon pants, and a tarboosh set wine, bottled water, and salads on their brass table.

"By spiritual, I mean I'm conscious of a greater purpose in life. I believe that we should leave the world a little better than we found it. I'd say I have an intense desire for truth and a deep reverence for nature," Justine said. *What is this religious talk with both Amir and Nasser? A litmus test?*

"Does God fit into your picture?" he asked casually, as though it held little importance. The corner of his mouth curled slightly.

"Not necessarily. I'm not sure a god is essential to my worldview—although I don't dismiss the possibility," she assured him, deciding not to go down this road again tonight. "And what about you? Who is the real Nasser Khalid?"

Nasser rebalanced his weight on the pillow and released a low, comfortable sigh. "Perhaps I'm in transition too. I'm not sure I'm cut out for the teaching business. I'm looking for a way into the world of archaeology. I've got three sisters, all younger, and a traditional father. I admire my mother but would like to see her stand up for herself more often. I like to play football and read philosophy. Philo is my favorite. I'm a Christian of sorts." Nasser paused and held her eyes, his gaze a combination of altar boy and prince.

"Tell me about your sisters," she asked, trying unsuccessfully to ignore his seductive expression. *A man of many faces.* He had a way of disconcerting her that she relished, yet which somehow made her uncomfortable.

"They're a lot like you," Nasser said. "Independent, rather bold. They're each pursuing a career. Nura tells me you can't trust a man to always take care of you."

"I would have to agree with Nura. How old is she?"

"Twenty-one next month. She's in the faculty of law at Cairo University and can argue anyone under the table." He grinned. "Maha is 18 and will be entering the faculty of medicine next year. Leila is just 16 and still in secondary school."

"You're proud of your sisters," she offered. Each reached for the bottle of water to refill the glasses, and their fingers touched. Justine felt a slight tremor move through her body. *I wonder if Nasser felt the same.* She glanced at his face for clues.

After a brief pause and a slight look of surprise, he responded, "I am proud of them, I admit, even though they can be a nuisance. 'Take me here, take me there,' 'Why can't I come?'" he mimicked playfully.

"They sound like young women everywhere." She laughed. "You said that you weren't sure you were made for teaching. What are your options?"

"The university pays very little, and the assignment is semester to semester. I keep holding out for an archeology assignment, but I may have to get into business. Maybe the oil business."

"I can understand the need for more lucrative work—but the oil business is quite an environmental offender."

Nasser's expression became grave, the sparkle in his eyes replaced by dark, gunmetal gray. "That's business, Justine. It doesn't compare to what the Chinese are doing in Africa or are permitting to happen in the Sudan."

"I suppose not," she said, tempted to add: *But is that the standard you want to go by?* She sensed she was crossing some invisible line.

Nasser was quiet for several moments, slowly eating his shwarma. When he looked up, he readjusted his expression once more. "You have a point. But I'm a realist, not a crusader. I may have to go where the work is."

"I've never been sure what it means to be a realist, but I hope you find work with an archaeology team. We're all better off if we can follow our passions, don't you think?" She forked the shwarma onto her plate and topped the pulled beef with a dollop of labna.

"Oh sure, sure. A realist, in my book, is someone who accepts what he can't change. Now as for passions, they can take many forms." The words hung in the air between them. "Do you play the piano?"

Justine was suddenly conscious of Nasser's gaze on her lips moving silently to the music, her fingers searching for invisible keys. "I did as a child . . . why?"

"I love to watch your hands when you talk. They're the graceful hands of a piano player or dancer," he observed.

"I do love music, but my talking style can be credited to my Italian grand-mother." She unconsciously crossed her hands in her lap. *Like with Amir, I have this strong sense that Nasser has many secrets, yet he touches something in me that I haven't felt since my first love . . . God, I've got to be careful. I'm not ready for this . . .*

"Dr. Jenner?" the waiter asked, handing Justine a note. She sat forward, startled. *Who could possibly know that I'm here?* She read the note from An-drea, refolded it, and placed it in her purse. She checked her cell phone. It was turned off.

She looked up at Nasser's quizzical face, tamping down the excitement she felt after reading Andrea's note. She raised her glass of wine. *Time for that to-morrow. Tonight I'm just going to enjoy this attractive man.*

"Sorry for the interruption last night, *chérie.* I was so excited about the codex that I came by your apartment. Apparently, your cell phone was turned off, but the boab had overheard the two of you discussing the restaurant."

"I'm glad you were able to reach me," Justine said simply. "How are you this morning, Dr. Ibrahim?" She had just walked over to his office in the Rare Books Library.

Ibrahim was gazing at the bougainvillea climbing up the wall below his window, his bushy eyebrows drawn close together. "Fine, my dear, fine," he said, pulling up a chair for her. "I called a photographer friend in Geneva. Ancient parchments are his specialty. He'll be here soon to photograph the codex. I'm quite pleased."

"Good, Ibrahim. Good," said Andrea, looking eager to get on with her own revelations. "I know it's nearly impossible, but I have to believe what I've seen. I've only examined random portions of the codex, but the writing is very close to that of the Dead Sea Scrolls."

"What does that mean, exactly?" Justine asked, a strange chill running through her. She vigorously rubbed her arms through the thin silk fabric of her blouse as her two colleagues stared hungrily at the little book.

"These delicate little formations are written in the Jewish book-hand style, although most of it is in Aramaic. The script is carefully drawn with delicate flourishes . . . see this line?" Andrea drew her close, holding her forearm and pointing. "The hieroglyphs are less than an eighth of an inch high, and some letters, or I should say words, or phrases, are virtually the same as those in the Scrolls. And there are little drawings along the sides of some pages—flowers, birds. See here . . ."

Justine examined the miniscule letters, which looked much like the algebraic sign for pi or some form of shorthand. She'd seen writings from the Levant to Egypt from the same period as the Dead Sea Scrolls, although, frankly, they all appeared almost the same to her. She squinted and drew closer.

"Here," Ibrahim said. "Try this." He handed her a magnifying glass.

"This form of writing was perfected during the Herodian period and was usually written on calfskin—I think the cover may well be calfskin," he said. "Remember, the Dead Sea Scrolls were buried in several caves twelve hundred feet below sea level, so they were protected by the dryness. Hundreds of fragments.

"The author could be an Essene—highly unlikely, but I wouldn't rule it out," he added, excited as a young boy.

"Did you both come to the same conclusion?" Justine glanced from Andrea to Ibrahim and back again.

"I can read Aramaic, but I am not a paleographer. I can't distinguish between fine differences," said Ibrahim, vigorously rubbing his right knee. The stairs were causing him problems these days. "I'm not finely attuned to the differences in the shape and form of the letters like Andrea is. I think it may be time to consult my colleague Amal Al Rasul, the director at the new Centre for Writing and Calligraphy at the Alexandria Bibliotheca. Amal was at Cairo University with me before he recently founded the Centre. His specialty is paleography. When could you two go to Alexandria?"

"Ibrahim is right, perhaps the two of us should make the trip," affirmed Andrea, giving Justine a conspiratorial wink. "I want confirmation by an expert in ancient Middle Eastern languages."

Justine grinned. "Let's do it! I'll work it out with Nadia."

As the two women walked out into the lush garden of palms, willows, and bougainvillea surrounding the library, Justine said, "Receiving the note last night was a bit disconcerting. I'll have to be more careful. Especially if I want to keep my love life private."

"From now on, you may indeed need to be more careful," Andrea said seriously. "Religious and political forces managed to keep the Dead Sea Scrolls secret for nearly fifty years after they were discovered in the 1940s. You'd be amazed how people of like minds can conspire. And those caught in the middle do not fare well."

Justine stared at her in amazement. If this little codex was of the same origin as the scrolls . . . *What am I getting myself into?*

OLD CAIRO 2 CE

As my youngest son and I stroll through the market once more, he is careful to stay within the length of two donkeys. "I must be able to see you," I tell him. The souk, the market, is a fascinating cauldron of colors, sounds, and motion. Aromas of roasting pigeons and breads fill our nostrils. Turbans adorn the men of the East, while white robes signify travelers from Arabia. Melons and lemons, almonds and camel livers, snakes and silver, silks and spices, baskets and painted amphora . . . wonders to be sold and bartered for line tables and fill baskets.

A sistrum flute plays sweetly from one of the alleyways leading away from the open market, luring my son away. For a moment I lose sight of him in the dark caverns of the village. Turning right into a narrow passageway, he moves toward the song of the flute. Mud brick houses hover close to each other, blocking out the sunlight and clutching into their womb the odors of human sweat and sizzling fish that permeate the air of the nomadic quarter. Shadowy figures move silently along the path, carrying heavy bundles that bump him as he passes.

I watch as he turns his attention away from the burdened traders and peers into an opening in the wall where a man is grabbing the hair of a woman who kneels at his feet while a frightened child looks on. Below the window, a lone woman of perhaps eighteen summers sits playing the sistrum. My son stands mesmerized by the melancholy melody and the tortured scene. A single tear moves down his cheek.

From nearby, a beggar calls to him, "Alms, my boy, alms." The beggar takes hold of his arm, pulling him. My son can surely smell his rancid breath, see the bloodshot eyes and rotting skin tucked into a long woolen scarf.

"I am sorry, sir, I have no alms. But how can I be of service?" he asks, undisturbed by the wretchedness of the man who holds his arm. The beggar loosens his grip. His face sheds the lines of menace made more noticeable by ruined teeth and poxed skin. His hideous face becomes smooth, his expression almost beatific. His eyes fill with wonder.

"Has God sent you?" he asks without guile.

My son lightly touches the man's matted hair, smiles, and quietly turns away.

"My son, where are you?" I call from the entry to the alley.

"I'm here, Mother," he says and hurries toward my voice.

CHAPTER 11

⸺✎⸺

THERE WERE MANY GREAT SOUKS, OR MARKETS, in the world—Fez and Tangiers in Morocco, Tunis, and Istanbul among them. Khan El Khalili in Islamic Cairo was one of the most ancient. Miles of narrow alleyways snaked sinuously through the fourteenth-century structures. Anything could be found there, from leather and gold to stuffed miniature camels, Turkish furniture, tents, hashish, spices, and even false teeth. Sexual desires could be satisfied, business negotiated. The Khan came to life at night, shop lights and the voices of merchants circling the high walls of mashrabaya portals and carved arches. Incense and pipe smoke mingled with the smell of overrun sewers and debris. The diminished tourist trade had made the salesmen bolder, but not offensively so.

Justine had not been to the Khan since returning to Egypt and was pleased when Nadia asked to meet her there. They settled on 7:00 p.m. at the edge of the souk.

She stepped out of the taxi across the street from Khan el Khalili, in front of Al Azhar University. Built in 970 CE, Al Azhar was the oldest continuously operating university in the world, still known for preparing Arabists and Imams. The university drew Muslims from as far away as Timbuktu, Europe, and Indonesia, and was further distinguished as one of the only fully operating Islamic universities in Egypt, others having fallen into disarray or been turned into modern faculties of law. The university's magnetism was as much a product of its sheikh as its antiquity. The Sheikh of Al Azhar was the highest theological authority for Egyptian Muslims. Between the extensive complex that formed Al Azhar and the sacred Sayyidna al Hussein Mosque across the street, this was the bustling center of medieval Islamic Cairo.

Justine descended the stairs into the dark tunnel running underneath Al-Muizz Li-Din Street and emerged near a row of outdoor restaurants. The mosque ahead was the burial place for one of the Prophet Mohammed's grandsons, and therefore out of bounds to non-Muslims. The square, known as Midan Hussein, formed the eastern border of the souk. Ragamuffin child beggars darted across the small strip of grass in front of the mosque. Three of them closed in on Justine, blocking her path to Nadia, who was standing at the corner of one of the restaurants. She patted them on the heads and said, "*Mish Mumpkin*—not possible." She knew if she opened her wallet for the children, fifty more would follow.

Nadia was dressed in her usual attire, black with gold jewelry, comfortable loafers. Even though they'd been together earlier in the day, she warmly opened her arms in welcome.

"I thought we might shop for a while, then get something to eat. Does that suit you?" she asked, taking Justine's hand and walking toward the main entrance of the souk. Brass amphorae and vases formed a border to the small café on their left, and rows of silver shops lined the right side.

"It does. I could use a few things yet for my apartment. I need candlesticks, a tablecloth, napkins . . . and a few other items that I'll know when I see them. Perhaps some spices. Definitely earrings."

"I need a cartouche for my niece's sixteenth birthday, and I'd ask that you hold off on the tablecloth and napkins. The women of Bulaq do beautiful needlework and they're holding a bazaar at the Anglican Church next week."

"A bazaar sounds great . . . and so does the chance to meet some of the women you've worked with in the past." As they moved into the Khan, Justine's senses were bombarded with layers of odors—pesticides, frying fish and grilling meats, sizzling donuts, and human sweat.

"Come in, my ladies, look at my shop." The young proprietor touched both of her own eyes, then gently placed her hand on Justine's elbow. Justine and Nadia stepped inside, clearing their nostrils with the sweet scent of perfume.

Within an hour, the two women had made many of their purchases and woven back through the alleyways to Fishawi's Coffeehouse, the long-time haunt of the Egyptian writer Naguib Mahfouz. Huge, gilded mirrors encircled a crowded room of small tables filled with elderly men leaning in toward one another mysteriously, cigarettes poised in long, thin fingers. Brass sheeshas stood nearby while roaming hawkers tried unsuccessfully to interrupt conversations. Dark in spite of the mirrors, Fishawi's was nestled in the middle of the Khan, avoiding all direct light. For more than two hundred years, this coffeehouse had been a center of Cairo gossip and literary exchange.

A boy of about nine moved gracefully among the tables balancing a silver tray of clear glass teacups. His bearing revealed the delicacy of innocence mixed with the premature sophistication granted to those who overhear forbidden conversations.

"Tell me about the women of Bulaq," Justine asked as soon as they had placed their order with the young boy. The tables were crowded; the whirling smoke formed an eerie mesh through which they spoke. "The comments you made a few days ago about women and the Brotherhood were chilling. Why don't women fight back now, demand more rights, get enraged? Would women actually vote for the Brotherhood? Support them?"

Nadia stared at the cigarette burns on the table. Justine waited.

"Did you know that the U.N. estimates that 90 percent of women in Egypt have been circumcised?"

"The clitorectomy? The cutting of female genitals, often involving the removal of the clitoris? I know it's a common Islamic practice in much of Africa, but I find that nearly impossible to believe." Justine nodded at the boy for their tea as a second, even younger, boy appeared with a tray of rice-stuffed vegetables called *mahshy*, two grilled pigeons, and labna.

"Genital mutilation steals intense sexual and psychic energy from women. Makes them more passive. It takes education and support for women to develop a self-directing consciousness. To find some fire in their bellies. We . . ."

Justine's eyes narrowed. "We . . . You, Nadia? No."

"Yes." Tears formed in both women's eyes. "When I was five my grandmother, my beloved grandmother, and my mother held me down and robbed me of my clitoris. It took me years to come to terms with that betrayal—that women I loved would diminish my capacity to love."

Justine was shocked, not only at the vast numbers of women involved, but that Nadia, the woman she cared for, worked for, was telling her this traumatic story. Justine spooned the *mahshy* onto her plate, topped it with a bit of labna, and set the pigeon to the side. "You are telling me that the fire of resistance has been stolen from most Egyptian women."

Nadia nodded, turning to grasp her pigeon like an ice cream cone. "But not all. Not the middle and upper classes. Educated women have found a way to overcome this physical handicap. Women are still the future of Egypt, Justine, but they must be legitimately empowered. There is legislation in Parliament to outlaw female circumcision, and I expect it to pass. And real empowerment is what our schools are about."

"Empowerment comes from within, both within the individual and within the culture. We can only help create the conditions in which this can happen. And that's what we'll do," Justine said with revolutionary resolve. She wrapped her small napkin around her roasted pigeon and began to eat it as Nadia did. "I hear you can eat these whole things, bones and all."

"Do you recognize the man at the table to your far left?" whispered Nadia. "No, no . . . don't turn around. He's wearing a green plaid shirt and smoking one of those new cigarettes. His face scares the daylights out of me. I noticed him a couple of times while we were shopping."

Justine shifted her position so she could see him. "He's familiar. I have seen him. Perhaps it is just a coincidence."

"Perhaps, but I've noticed him watching you closely. He's too serious for my taste. I think he may be following you."

Justine shivered. Was this what she's been warned about? Was she in real danger? Could word of the codex have leaked already? "Let's find out," she said, laying down her unfinished pigeon. "I'm going to finish my shopping and I'll meet you at the entrance in an hour."

Nadia was silent for several moments, then she picked up the bill and placed ten pounds on the table. Justine followed suit. "Don't try to be brave, Justine. That could be dangerous. I have no idea what this could be about, but be cautious. Promise?"

"I promise," Justine said, patting Nadia's hand. "Don't worry, I won't confront him." She picked up her purse and shopping bags, walked out of the restaurant, and stepped back into the alley, careful to avoid the sewer water standing in front of the Khan El Khalili restaurant, then wove through numerous leather shops and turned right toward the spice market, an alley brimming with burlap bags of saffron, cumin, cardamom, ginger, cloves, and hibiscus. She turned back toward the main part of the Khan, entered and exited an antique shop, and re-entered one of the leather shops. While eyeing a small bag, she caught a glimpse of a green shirt across the narrow alleyway and saw the man watching her reflection in the window. Her heart beat rapidly, her hands clammy with perspiration.

"*Masa a nur*, good evening," she said, walking directly toward the man in question. "Haven't we met before?" She smiled disarmingly, feeling a fine burst of adrenaline.

"*La, la*. We do not know each other," he stammered in street Arabic. "I just shop. If you will excuse me." He quickly walked on. The face was memorable: small scars along his upper lip told of a lisp awkwardly corrected in childhood, and his black eyes, too close together, gave him a look of permanent exclamation.

She followed him. He walked faster. *What am I doing?* But she couldn't seem to help herself; it was as though she was chasing a piece to a puzzle. *What puzzle?* she asked herself, not for the first time.

The scarred man was walking faster. Justine began to run, splashing some sewer drainage on her linen slacks. *Damn.* As she turned the corner between two leather shops, she slammed into a tall, striking man dressed informally in a sweatshirt and jeans.

"Amir!"

"Oh, hello Justine," he said averting his eyes, his shoulders stiff.

"What brings you here?" she asked, instantly deciding not to tell him about the stranger she was chasing.

"Nothing important. A few things to pick up. If you'll excuse me, I need to be going." And he was gone, disappearing among the crowd of shoppers and hawkers.

Justine turned into a less busy alley and pressed herself against the cement wall. *What is Amir doing here? He was so evasive . . . Can I trust him? Is there a connection between him and the man with the scarred face?*

In the middle of her thought, the man in the green shirt appeared in front of her, his ugly face only a few inches from hers. Justine shrieked. He braced one hand on the wall behind her and pressed a brass Arabian dagger flat against her chest with the other.

"Don't follow me." He glared at her, his eyes so penetrating she felt as though they could bore right through her.

Justine started to shiver. Terrified, she managed to ask, "Why are *you* following *me*?"

A crooked grin revealed deteriorating yellow teeth. He shoved her hard against the wall and walked away.

Justine felt dizzy, nauseated; she stood there several more minutes to get her bearings. She was still shaking and fighting tears when she met up with Nadia.

"Are you crazy?" Nadia demanded. "I saw you talking to that man. He might have pulled a knife and killed you right there!"

Justine looked sheepish. "He did pull a knife, one of those daggers right out of some dumb movie. He doubled back and confronted me. All he said was 'don't follow me' and then he pushed me hard."

"You're in danger. Perhaps it has something to do with your father. Or just that you're an American . . . but that doesn't make sense . . ." She paused and stared at Justine.

"Did you see Amir? I bumped into him and he was so cagey, elusive. What would bring him here? Could he be hunting for Zachariah?"

"Amir? No, I didn't see him. I didn't think Zachariah was back in Cairo. They're not close, you know, although Amir carries his family's anguish. Zachariah is actually Ibrahim's favorite, the old man would do anything for the boy. But Amir has just about washed his hands of his younger brother."

There's that disconnect again. Who is close to whom? "Amir is a responsible man. Wouldn't he help the family find his brother?"

Nadia stared off into the market. "Yes. Amir is a responsible man," she declared flatly.

✑

When Justine walked into her apartment, the house phone was ringing.

"Nasser? I'm so glad you called!" she said, and without a pause, she continued: "I was followed tonight in the Khan." She had seriously considered calling Amir, but after tonight she just wasn't sure . . .

"Are you sure?" he exclaimed.

"I'm positive. We—Nadia and I were shopping and she noticed him, then I spoke to him and he threatened me."

"Threatened you? How?"

"He confronted me with a dagger to my chest, then pushed me against the wall. All he said was 'don't follow me.'" Justine could hardly believe what she'd just said. *This sounds like a third-rate movie.*

"This is serious, Justine. No accident. Do you know any reason why you might be followed?" asked Nasser, tension mounting in his voice.

A moment of silence followed.

"Justine?"

"No, no, I can't . . ." Her mind raced. "I found something special in Old Cairo during the quake. I . . ."

"Don't say another word. I'm coming over." He hung up before she could respond.

Within the hour, Nasser was at the door. Justine had busied herself by changing into a cotton kaftan and making tea. *Can I trust Nasser? Should I tell him about the codex?* By the time he arrived, she had made her decision.

Nasser held her for a few moments, then settled into the overstuffed chair across from her. "You must have been very frightened."

She nodded and explained what had happened during the evening and the events surrounding the codex, although she wasn't entirely forthcoming. She didn't reveal any of her conversations with Ibrahim. Andrea. Amir. Or any of their primitive speculations. Although she did say that the codex was in safe-keeping with Ibrahim.

Nasser had let her talk without interruption. "You've found an ancient codex in the crypt where the Holy Family lived, and your colleagues speculate that it might be important?" He sat forward, gazing at her intently.

"I—I'm not sure yet," she said, beginning to have second thoughts about her careless revelation. "We may have to hand it over to Omar Mostafa at the Ministry of Antiquities."

"Has Ibrahim shown it to Mostafa yet?"

"I don't think so. No, I'm sure not. What do you know of Mostafa?"

"Everyone knows the Great Mostafa and understands that he likes to be in on things from the beginning. He'll take credit for whatever comes of it."

"That's what I've heard." Justine smiled for the first time this evening. "But Ibrahim has assured me that I'll be part of the decisions regarding the findings. That is, if anyone can make such assurances."

"Don't be surprised if that agreement doesn't hold. You said you were going to Alexandria? I can drive you."

"Thanks for the offer, but Andrea is driving. We leave at the end of the week." Justine kicked off her shoes and folded her feet under her.

"Be careful," said Nasser. "After what happened tonight, don't take any chances. I want you to call me before you leave."

"I'll call you. And thanks, Nasser. For everything." She felt tears welling up. *Now what is this? Relief, gratitude . . . some other emotion?*

He placed his hand on her shoulder. "Would you like for me to stay tonight?" he asked.

"I'll be fine," she said, staring into his deep blue eyes. "I need to think, and I have a deadbolt lock on the door. I feel better now. Thank you so much."

As they said goodnight, Nasser kissed her hands, then moved his lips from cheek to cheek, brushing her mouth lightly. She felt a warm current of desire.

It was after midnight, but she was unable to sleep, so chose to sit in the living room attempting to read. So much had happened tonight, she couldn't sort it all out. Exhilaration followed by waning confidence, fear and desire, anticipation and relief. A roller coaster of emotions.

The ancient wrought iron elevator came to a stop on Justine's floor. Her heart quickened, for she had heard the only other occupants on this floor come home an hour earlier. As she listened, heavy feet stepped from the elevator and moved toward her door. She waited for the knock that didn't come. The footsteps and elevator remained quiet. She sat watching, frozen in place, mesmerized by the shadows of large shoes flush to the front door. After what seemed like an eternity, a piece of paper was pushed under the door. When the waiting elevator descended several floors, carrying the man in large shoes, she walked to her door and picked up the note.

In large block letters it read: *IF YOUR RIGHT EYE OFFENDS YOU, PLUCK IT OUT.*

CHAPTER 12

⎯⎯❦⎯⎯

THE MORNING LIGHT AND PERSISTENT COO of pigeons soaked through the tall French doors and awakened Justine once again. Not having slept until the early hours of the morning, she felt groggy and disoriented. Her stomach tightened as memories of the previous evening began to crowd into her muddled mind. Being followed in the Khan, the cryptic note slipped under her door . . . combined with the earthquake and deaths of the week before, it was more than she felt ready to handle. Talking with Nadia and Nasser had been comforting, but she needed someone who might be able to help figure out what was going on. She reached for the phone and called Ibrahim and Andrea.

She arrived at Groppi's around nine and found a back table in the still-quiet coffeehouse. Two veiled women stood in the candy shop; two young men in Western dress claimed a table on the opposite side of the room. The radiant morning sun made dark silhouettes of Andrea, Ibrahim, and Amir as they walked toward her. She hadn't called Amir, nor was she expecting him. After the encounter with him in the Khan, she felt uncertain of his motives.

The three of them sat quietly while Justine explained the events of the night before. She omitted her brief encounter with Amir as well as her conversation with Nasser. Amir appeared appreciative of the omission, yet uncomfortable in her presence. Justine handed the note to Ibrahim, which he read and passed on to Andrea and Amir. The waitress came to their table twice, but couldn't attract their attention.

"What could it mean?" Justine quietly demanded, hoping that someone would understand. She waited for her answer while the demure waitress reappeared and took their order. Andrea ordered tea all around, three croissants, and her favorite miniature chocolate cookies. *Nothing ruffles her*, mused Justine. "Even for breakfast?" she said to Andrea.

"The quote is from the Gospel of Matthew, 5:29," said Ibrahim gravely. "It's a teaching in Jesus' Sermon on the Mount. If I remember correctly, the entire section goes like this:

> '*If your right eye is a hindrance to you,*
> *Pluck it out and throw it away;*
> *Better for you to lose one of your members than to have*
> *All your body thrown into Gehenna.*
> *If your right hand is a hindrance to you,*
> *Cut it off and throw it away;*
> *Better for you to lose one of your members*
> *Than to have all your body thrown into Gehenna.*'

"Of course, most of us understand it allegorically, as a metaphor," he concluded. His voice was hoarse.

"Gehenna?" asked Justine.

"Hell," said Amir, without making eye contact.

"Your 'right eye' may refer to the codex. It would need to be something that could offend you or others, violate beliefs. The codex could do that—eventually," Andrea said. "Is there anything else it might refer to?"

"Seems like a bit of a stretch, but I can't think of anything else," admitted Justine. "My actions in Cairo should not be offensive to anyone . . . I wouldn't think." She remembered the humiliating morning when she went for a run in skintight Lycra. "And the incident with my father and you, Ibrahim, was such a long time ago."

Ibrahim pursed his lips and waved it off.

"If the note does refer to the codex, someone thinks its contents are dangerous," offered Andrea, devouring her second cookie. "But how would they know? *We* don't even know."

"What do we know?" asked Amir, still avoiding direct communication with Justine. "Let's enumerate. First, we know it is an ancient codex and where it was found."

"And that it lacks provenance," Ibrahim added.

"That it appears to be written in the hand of the Dead Sea Scrolls and in first person," Andrea interjected with pride.

"That is a great deal," Justine realized. "Have any of you sat around together and wondered aloud . . . speculated on its source, meaning?"

Ibrahim looked sheepish. "A little fun, my dear, no certainty at all. Andrea and I brainstormed possible sources. But we don't know the dates as yet and there are no dates in the codex."

"A little fun? Like the Holy Family? After all, where it was found . . ." *Why does no one look surprised? They're not keeping me in the loop.*

"Not impossible," confessed Ibrahim. "Although hundreds of people could have lived in that cave over the generations. We won't really know anything until we have the material dated."

"What else do you recall about the Sermon, Ibrahim?" said Andrea, diverting the conversation. She placed both hands around her teacup as though to heat them, even though the morning was already becoming quite warm.

"The Sermon suggests how to live, how to relate to others. In that day, some of Jesus' suggestions were quite radical, even contradictory," Ibrahim said admiringly. "He said blessed are the poor, the persecuted, the peacemakers . . . He explicitly challenged the Old Testament admonition of 'An eye for an eye, a tooth for a tooth' by suggesting that his followers turn the other cheek and love their neighbors—and their enemies. The Sermon tells us to be humble, to forego public praise, to give alms, and to pray in private. What puzzles me is that some of his teachings in the Sermon are hallmarks of tolerance and love, while others are harsh and judgmental. The same dual nature is revealed by the teachings of Mohammed in the Koran. I'm convinced that many of the teachings attributed to both men were never spoken by them. Whoever chose the phrase in the note did not intend to represent Jesus' more gentle and loving nature—of that we can be sure."

"It's a warning," Amir murmured coldly. "The person who followed you in the Khan probably left the note." The others turned to him; his tone and demeanor implied that, more than a warning, the note was an omen of evil.

"But how would anyone know about the codex at all?" asked Justine. "We haven't told anyone." *Except.*

"There's no explanation that's not sinister," said Andrea. "I'm as puzzled as you, *chérie*. And if they knew anything, why wouldn't they make the warning more direct?" She paused. "Amir, what are you thinking?"

"Egyptians are given to mystery. We believe that the more mystical and obscure a warning is, the more frightening and effective it is. That is undoubtedly true. I don't know why you were given the warning, but I intend to find out. But be careful, very careful."

Justine examined his face, his flashing black eyes. *Why is he so angry? Because of me—or some plan gone awry? Be careful, Justine. I do need to be very careful. But of whom?* Out of all of them, Amir was the one who'd initially been reluctant to keep the codex. Her eyes moved from person to person, then caught something through the window. "I see Nadia's car outside," she said, picking up her purse and briefcase.

As she stepped around the table, Andrea said quietly, "I'll come to your apartment around three o'clock tomorrow and we'll drive to Alexandria. I'll have the codex with me."

Justine nodded and silently vowed to put the codex out of her mind for the rest of the day. But as she and Nadia drove away from the café, a black Mercedes sedan pulled away from the curb and followed at some distance.

CHAPTER 13

———— ⟨∞⟩ ————

"FOR ME, ALEXANDRIA IS ONE OF THE TRULY great cities." It was Thursday afternoon, and Andrea continued her enthusiastic travelogue as they drove past the Masr train station and turned right, heading north toward Alexandria's newly remodeled Corniche. "Alexandrians invented the notion of the 'mouseion'—the museum—nearly 2,400 years ago. If you listen, Alexandrians whisper poetic words from their terraces."

"So far, I'm not impressed." Justine's last visit to this city was when she was fourteen, but the beaches had consumed her then. Adolescents had different priorities. Boys and beaches; beaches and boys.

"Ah, you're not far from wrong." Andrea smiled with the charm perfected by the French. "The glory days of Alexandria are history. Lawrence Durrell called her the 'Capital of Memory,' for she lives in memory, not in reality. But when E.M. Forster was fresh from *Howard's End* and still working on *Passage to India*, he took the time to write a little guide about Alexandria—my point being that he was so captivated with the romance of Alexandria that he couldn't keep her out of his mind. The new mayor seems to have jolted the city back into history with the new Bibliotheca and a Corniche worthy of its legend. The city may be coming back to its glory days," said Andrea. "We'll see."

"Durrell and his perspective on Alexandria have been something of a family legend. My mother gave me *The Alexandria Quartet* when I was nine. I recently reread it and understood it a little differently this time." Justine smiled wryly at the gross understatement.

"I would imagine. *The Quartet* is a sensual and confusing experience. Yet to find Alexandria's true greatness, we must go back to before the Islamic invasion. When the Muslims invaded, they decided that Cairo was the only city of merit in Egypt. But once upon a time, as they say, Alexandria was the center of learning for the entire world. I know you know the history, Justine, but I enjoy telling the story of Alexander, the precocious and daring young student of Aristotle's and son of the King of Macedonia, who came to Egypt and found a pristine shoreline that he claimed as Alexandria. He must have been a fascinating man." She paused and looked at Justine, inviting her to continue with another part of the story.

Justine grinned and took her cue. "I understand that the ancient library had the largest collection of scrolls in the world. It's here that the Jewish scrolls of the Old Testament were translated into Greek. And it was here that St. Mark founded the Christian church." The streets were wider than in Cairo now, opening up to the coastline beyond. As they drove over a rise in the avenue, an immense fort on a small, protruding peninsula came into view.

"And then the scourges of man and God began to attack the City," Andrea continued. "The library was burned in three fires and an earthquake swallowed the great lighthouse. By the fourth century, Romans were firmly ensconced in Christianity and no longer adored all that was Greek."

"Most people seem to think that Julius Caesar burned the library in its most final destruction. But I have a different theory," Justine said. "I think the Patriarch Theophilus is the culprit. The same Theophilus who had the vision of the Virgin Mary and asked her where the Holy Family had journeyed in Egypt."

"Well, he was intent on getting rid of pagan documents, and the library was full of them: the papers of Socrates, Plato, and Aristotle, as well as the teachings of the great Eastern scholars," Andrea agreed. "During the heyday of the library, scrolls were confiscated from ships entering the harbor. Thousands of scrolls could be found there."

"The desire to destroy pagan documents may not be over," observed Justine.

Andrea nodded as she turned onto Saad Zaghloul Street. "We're staying at the Metropole just ahead. At one time we might have stayed at the historic Cecil, across the square, but it's now overpriced by the Sofitel Corporation and has lost some of its character."

Although grandly situated on the square in the Eastern Harbor, the entrance of the Metropole faced south, away from the square. A doorman in a smart red palace guard uniform carried their luggage into a high-ceilinged lobby with sumptuous Italian décor.

"You are now standing on the very spot where Cleopatra lived in her grand villa," the enthusiastic clerk explained. "The Cleopatra obelisk, found beside the villa, is now in Central Park in New York." While he was correct about the obelisk, Andrea later explained that the ruins of the villa had actually been found farther out in the bay. "But why spoil a good story?"

A flamboyant winding staircase encircled an ornamental wrought iron elevator of black and gold. Past the elevator, an intimate tearoom boasted red velvet chairs and small ebony tables standing near draped windows. An elderly man no more than four feet tall opened the elevator door. Justine thought him to be about a hundred years old.

As they turned toward their individual rooms, Andrea suggested dinner around 8:00 p.m. "I want to introduce you to my favorite restaurant," she said. "I have another story to tell."

Justine's tall, narrow room had been part of a grand ballroom at one time; sliced off like a piece of wedding cake, it retained the decorative frosting around the ceiling. An Italian period desk and chair snuggled close to the large bed, which nearly filled the room. A small balcony overlooked the narrow alley below. Compared to the room, the black and white–tiled bathroom was surprisingly spacious. Justine sat on the edge of the bed and peered straight across the alley and into an open window, where a young man painted papyrus. She leaned back on a mound of pillows and opened a copy of Mahfouz's *Miramar*. John Fowles' introduction was an eloquent critique of the city Mahfouz had loved, describing her as "languorous, subtle, perverse, eternally *fin de siècle*; failure haunts it, yet a failure of such richness that it is a kind of victory . . ."

Fin de siècle . . . Eternally in the nineteenth century . . . couldn't this describe most of Egypt? What is its appeal for me? Perhaps it's in my genes or my desire to romanticize decadence. Is Alex more perverse than Cairo? I doubt it, but I do seem to be in the midst of a perversity I don't quite understand. Laying the open book across her chest, she watched the changing cloud formations through her window until it was time to get ready to meet Andrea.

∞

"San Giovanni is an Alexandrian tradition," said Andrea as they left the car with the valet. Situated on the Corniche about five kilometers east of the hotel, the towering alabaster restaurant and lodge had none of the external elegance Justine had expected. "When they were rebuilding the Corniche and erecting the short bridge across this arm of the bay, they built around rather than through this property. The bridge looks as though they took the top off the pink and white Montazah palace nearby and made it into a series of hats, doesn't it? Such an unnecessary shortcut across the bay. But it is pretty."

"It certainly is," agreed Justine, enchanted by the small bridge highlighted with torches. The restaurant matched the formality of the doorman and maître d'—old world class, ivory linen tablecloths, and a grand piano. The two women were seated at a window overlooking the bridge and the roiling water below. *A world gone by . . . all but forgotten*, she thought as she noted the presence of only one other couple in the room. "I know so little about you, Andrea. Tell me about the significance of this restaurant, this city."

"I will tell you the story of my lost love," replied Andrea, turning to the waiter to order her favorite French burgundy, Clos Vougeot.

"Perhaps you'd rather not talk about it." Justine noticed sadness seeping into her eyes.

"I want you to know. It is an important part of who I am. My first—and my last—dinner here was with Francois. We were to be married. That was more than twenty years ago."

"Did you marry?"

"We didn't get the chance. He was killed in Algeria a month later. You are too young to remember the Algerian uprising."

Justine nodded.

"He was in the French Foreign Legion. Their barracks near Algiers were raided in the early morning, four of the Legion soldiers kidnapped. Francois was among them. He was found a few days later—bound, tortured, and shot execution-style. His mother called me that night." Andrea's voice was raspy as she focused on the reflections of the bridge lamps in the sea below, light illuminating the moisture in her eyes.

"I'm so sorry, Andrea." Unsure of how to give comfort in the face of such profound tragedy, Justine sat quietly, smoothing her napkin and watching her.

"It was a grand passion, *chérie*. You know what a romantic I am. The idea of the French Foreign Legion intrigued me. And I thought, 'The colonial wars are over . . . he will be safe.' I was wrong."

"How did you meet?"

"We met through a family friend when Francois was on leave from India. He had that certain *savoir-faire* that swept me off my feet—an American expression, I think. Physically he resembled Amir, but he was more transparent, more accessible. He would notice the things that escaped others . . . a child about to lose her strawberry ice cream cone, an elderly man watching a beautiful girl. The world was full of wonders for Francois. And through him, for me. That was 1982. Since then, I've had lovers, but I've never found another grand passion." She drew back from the window and met Justine's eyes, searching her face for signs of the understanding two women can find in each other.

"I would imagine that such a man comes along only once in a lifetime," said Justine. *Will I ever find such a grand passion? Will I recognize it if it comes my way?*

"If at all. Shall we order?" Andrea turned to the elderly waiter and asked for the house specialty for both of them: a mound of rice stuffed with seafood and a salad with a slightly sweetened vinaigrette. "I'm sure I recognize that waiter. This restaurant is exceedingly loyal—they keep their staff for life." She watched as he walked slowly away, a slight limp on his right side. "Have you found your grand passion, Justine?"

"Not yet—at least, I don't think so. No, not yet. I dated a few men in graduate school, but none I couldn't leave when I came to Cairo."

"Ah, I hear a secret." Andrea's slight smile betrayed the relish every French woman cultivates for details of *les affaires de coeur*.

"I've met an attractive man here in Cairo," Justine admitted. "Turns out he was a student of my father's. I hardly know him, but I'm intrigued."

"What intrigues you?"

"He's definitely attractive, with a Harrison Ford grin. Yet that's not what intrigues me . . . no, it's his empathy, the way he can cut through to the meaning of things—or the danger, like what it means to live life intensely."

"He does sound exceptional. How will you know if he's the one for you?"

"I wish I knew. I've never been in love. Not actually. I guess I think something inside will signal me. Mother used to say, 'You'll know it when it happens.'"

Andrea laughed. "Like a bell going off?"

Justine grinned. "Something like that." She paused and concentrated on her rice. "We do have a great deal in common. He's an archaeologist, but teaching part-time at Cairo University. Unhappily, I think. When I called him about being followed the other night, he came right over." She put down her fork and stared at Andrea, suddenly aware that she had revealed something she'd intended to keep private.

Andrea was silent for a moment, her expression changing almost imperceptibly. "Did you tell him about the codex?"

"Not much. I'm sure I can trust him," she hastened to say, but Andrea's sense of disquiet invaded her.

"I'm just cautious. I'm sure it's all right, but my policy is to hold such finds close to my chest. And, of course, we know there's been a leak already. I'll not worry about it. I would love to meet this charming man." Andrea sighed as though releasing tension.

"Can I trust you with this charming man?" Justine teased.

"Ah, with a French woman, in matters of the heart, you can never know for sure," Andrea smiled. "Would you like to talk about tomorrow?"

"I would. What can we expect from the director?"

"Amal Al Rasul is a scholar and professor emeritus from Cairo University. A powerful man, from what I understand. Opinionated and well connected. Skeptical. Friends in high places. Ibrahim asked him to take a look at an old book we were bringing. Just that," explained Andrea. "He'll make a decision as to whether the Centre might get involved."

"Will he be able to tell anything in just a couple of days?"

"Certainly. He'll examine a random number of phrases in as many pages. Just a preliminary assessment, but he'll be able to get a sense of its importance. Still, I wouldn't expect a final verdict yet. About the Centre's involvement, I mean."

That night, Justine's dreams were peopled by shadowy villains, unsolved mysteries, and impossible choices. Such images had haunted her since she'd arrived in Cairo, then intensified after the night in the Khan. She awoke at three in the morning in a cold sweat. Was it the mystery or the danger that bothered her the most?

By nine on Friday morning, Andrea and Justine were driving the short distance to the Bibliotheca. They parked on the street in front of the University of Alexandria. A modern incarnation of the ancient center of learning, the new Alexandria Bibliotheca was designed to revive Egyptian science and scholarship.

As they walked toward the back of the commanding structure, Justine saw that it was shaped like a giant, low-slung disc that sloped toward the Corniche, although the perspective from the ground was quite different than her view from the plane had been when she'd arrived in Egypt. From the air it looked flatter. A reflecting pool accompanied the library, buttressed by a running wall embossed with hieroglyphs. The building sat to the north of an enormous courtyard decorated discerningly with sculptures. To the southwest, a theater and planetarium faced the Corniche beyond. The complex formed a horseshoe enclosure finished with a tall building of classrooms and meeting halls directly across the courtyard to the west. On the exterior second floor, a long walkway connected the Bibliotheca with the planetarium, creating the illusion that it emptied into the sea beyond. Another second-floor walkway ran south across the street, joining the university to the library complex.

They had been told to enter through the second door to the right of the main entrance of the Bibliotheca. As they walked into a lobby of glass, tile, and steel not unlike the new De Young Museum in San Francisco, Dr. Al Rasul came toward them with a jaunty gait. "Dr. Andrea, I presume." He bowed, shook her hand, and turned toward Justine. "And you must be Dr. Justine. I knew your father. A great man. How is Dr. Jenner?"

Before she could respond, Al Rasul led them into his office and introduced Mahmoud Hassan, a Jordanian paleographer. "Please forgive me," the director said. "You were going to tell me about your father." He waved the two women toward chairs near the desk.

"Yes. My father is in Peru at the moment, working just below Machu Picchu. He has reason to believe that there were developments—like suburbs—surrounding the main complex, which might contain a library."

"A library! That old dog. Into the most fascinating ventures. As always, I envy him," said Al Rasul resoundingly.

Justine laughed. "He does have a nose for intriguing finds. How do you know my father?"

The director turned to draw the others into the conversation. "Justine's father has an uncanny way of discovering significant artifacts. A sixth sense. We worked together in the Valley of the Kings, and he uncovered a woman's jaw that revealed evidence of early dental surgery. We also worked together for a short time at Saqqara. This was about ten years ago. Ah, but I've been remiss. Let me introduce my colleague properly. Dr. Mahmoud Hassan, renowned paleographer, will be with us for a year." The young Jordanian sat quietly while the director continued to describe his credentials.

Hassan's appearance was as unimpressive as his credentials were impressive. Of medium height and build, he wore a conservative suit of dark gray with a gray tie. His eyes were gray also, yet with an intense, searching expression that demanded a second glance. *Unremarkable, yet intriguing*, Justine thought. *I wonder why he would bury such inviting intensity in a mass of gray tones?*

"We'll order tea," said Al Rasul as they took their places at the elegant ebony table.

"I've been here three months," Dr. Hassan began by way of explaining himself. "Dr. Al Rasul has generously asked me to serve in residence. It may surprise you, but there are still a few fragments from the Nag Hammadi find that have defied identification. It is a joint project with Claremont College in

California and the Coptic Museum. Being a part of this magnificent biblio-theca is an honor."

"So, my lovely Cairene colleagues," Al Rasul said, "tell us about this codex you found. Ibrahim told me very little. He was rather mysterious."

Andrea turned to Justine. "Why don't you start?"

"Perhaps I should begin with the day of the recent earthquake, April 12th. I'd been in Cairo for a couple of days when I decided to visit the old crypt under St. Sergius in Old Cairo."

"The crypt where the Holy Family is supposed to have lived?" Al Rasul in-terrupted.

"The very one," Justine said. "I've been fascinated by the crypt since my mother took me there many years ago. At any rate, I was in the crypt during the earthquake. The columns and many of the walls collapsed, the electricity went out, two-by-fours and plaster fell into the stairwell . . . I was trapped." She strained to keep her voice steady as she shivered.

"That must have been terrifying," said Dr. Hassan, his gray eyes softening.

Justine glanced at him with appreciation. "It was," she said. "Thank you for your concern. As I began to crawl out of the crypt, I picked up the things that had fallen out of my bag. Although I didn't know it at the time, I also picked up a small book that didn't belong to me. I didn't even realize I had it until the next day."

"You found the codex in the crypt?" asked Al Rasul, eyes narrowing. He and Hassan glanced at each other, exchanging a knowing expression. "May we see it?"

Andrea unlocked her brown leather briefcase and handed the treasure, wrapped in fine linen, to Dr. Al Rasul. He began, almost in a whisper, "Ah . . . it is a codex. Indeed. What steps have you taken to find out what you have here?" He stroked the leather cover and handed it to Hassan.

Andrea explained, "Ibrahim El Shabry and I have begun to translate a few passages."

"Any conclusions so far?" asked Al Rasul.

"The entries seem to be some kind of personal notes," said Andrea. "It's written in first person. The Egyptian museum staff has agreed to arrange for the carbon-14 and patina dating. Amir El Shabry intends to locate the area in the crypt where the codex may have been lodged."

"Of course," Justine added, "it may not have even come from the crypt."

Al Rasul sipped his tea. "True. But for now, you want a paleographer to assess the codex. I believe you said you could leave it with us until Sunday, but such a short time will only serve to tantalize."

"Tantalize enough for you to decide to work with us, perhaps." Andrea tilted her head seductively.

"Fair enough," agreed Al Rasul. "Hassan and I will remain in possession of the codex until Sunday, when you will return." It was a statement rather than a question. "Now, a private guided tour of the Bibliotheca is in order."

A young female guide led the two women into the great library. Within moments, their eyes were drawn to the interior of the breathtaking Alexandria Bibliotheca, eight layers of reading rooms cascading down the inside of the giant structure, which, from the outside, had the appearance of a flattened pyramid. The windows, designed like the huge almond eyes of an Egyptian princess, were slanted so that light was everywhere but never direct.

"The collection is already as big as the original one," said the young guide in flawless English, "and we have an astounding goal of eight million documents. The composition of rich woods, glass, stainless steel, and marble were chosen to suggest the most elegant of international institutions without losing the sense of being truly Egyptian." She tilted her chin slightly upward, her eyes embracing her guests and the vastness of the room.

The main reading rooms led outward through numerous hallways at the side of each floor. "This room, known as the Media Centre, contains thousands of films and videos. Here we have a little theater and listening rooms for smaller groups. Name any film and we can probably find it." She smiled proudly, revealing perfect teeth, flattering her high cheekbones.

As the three women headed toward the ancient manuscript room, Andrea spoke to Justine in French. "I think that Al Rasul and Hassan will agree to help us, don't you?"

"They're obviously intrigued. They'll work with us, unless they think the codex is too recent or forged."

"I'm optimistic. And there's another reason . . ." taunted Andrea.

Justine stared at Andrea, then turned to thank the young guide for the tour.

"What 'other reason'?" demanded Justine as they walked toward the entrance.

"The Bibliotheca is new, and Al Rasul is fresh in his position; a major find could draw international attention to the library. That is, if he thinks it credible," she said. "But for now I know a lovely beach with cabanas on the grounds of the Montazah palace."

The weekend sped by, the two women taking delight in the past and present of Alexandria. Visits to the Catacombs and Fort Qaitbey, built on the tongue of land that once housed the Pharos Lighthouse, were punctuated by long walks along the Corniche, meals at the Fish Market, and morning coffees at the nearby Brazilian Coffee Store. Unlike the intimate souks of Cairo, the souks of Alex spread out along streets and alleys. Here they found loose blouses and colorful sandals.

On Sunday morning, Andrea and Justine made their way to Lawrence Durrell's house at number 13 Sharia Maamoun. A disappointing, dilapidated building. Al Rasul called for a second time, asking to move back the time for their second meeting; with the morning free, they found time to savor the history of the great poet Constantine Cavafy, his home now a museum. Built on the edge of the Greek Diaspora and nestled between the red light district of Attarin, the Greek Orthodox Patriarchate, and a Greek hospital, Cavafy's home was situated among what he had characterized as "Temples of the Flesh, the Soul, and the Body." As they moved through the alleyways and shops of Alex, they explored each other's lives, yet said little about the codex. Metaphorically, they held their breaths in anticipation of that afternoon's consultation.

It was nearly 4 p.m. when Justine and Andrea re-entered the Centre. Both Amir and Nasser had called to remind them to get back to Cairo before dark.

"The desert road is not safe after dark," Amir had told Justine before they left, and the two women had promised to return to Cairo before sunset—but that wasn't going to happen.

"Please sit down," Dr. Al Rasul said solemnly when they entered his office. "We have much to talk about." For over an hour, Dr. Hassan explained exactly how they had examined the codex, describing the patterns and forms of letters compared to different historical contexts, as well as the internal consistency among segments of the codex. "Such a cursory look tells us there are great similarities to the Dead Sea Scrolls and some of the Nag Hammadi papyri," he said excitedly, although it was hardly his style to appear excited. "The internal consistency seems quite uniform, although the entries were clearly made over an extended period of time."

"Like a personal journal." Andrea smiled encouragingly.

The exchange of words around Justine faded into the background. *A personal journal*, she mused. *About the Holy Family? Yet there is no reason to believe that. The cave and the crypt have been used by every revealed religion for hundreds of years.*

"I'm prepared to work with you in Cairo," Al Rasul said, forcing Justine back into the conversation. He added cryptically, "That is, if we can solve the other mystery . . ."

"Another mystery?" Justine frowned. "Your voice suggests a discovery that may not be welcome."

"A few pages are missing. Perhaps the first four or five. And there isn't a title page. Of course, the author may have just begun writing without such a page. While we're tempted to report that the pages could have been removed by the author, who, becoming dissatisfied with something he had written, decided to remove them, we don't think so. The removal is skillful—and, we think, recent. Since it is a codex, the attached papyrus leaves have come loose, nearly falling out." Al Rasul's jaw firmed in dismay.

Andrea and Justine stared at each other in shocked silence. "We had no idea," said Andrea, both astonished and embarrassed. "May I see the codex?" She handled it delicately. Examining only the first few pages, she placed the book back on the table, as though it had become overly warm to her skin. In spite of her newly acquired tan, her face was ashen. "Are you sure that the re-movals are recent?"

"If the pages had been removed long ago, the edges would have turned dark. As it is, the papyrus tone is unchanged. It's a mystery that must be solved. But for the moment, it doesn't diminish the promise of this find. It could be several thousand years old, but we'll need to wait for the carbon-14 dating to confirm that. I'll call Ibrahim and make the arrangements."

The sky was crimson by the time Andrea's dark blue Kia left the city limits and entered the desert road south to Cairo. "The delta is beautiful this time of evening," Andrea observed. "We will not please Amir, however, because we can't get back to Cairo before dark."

"Nasser will be anxious too," added Justine.

"Mmm . . . I find it delightful that two handsome men worry about us. *N'est pas, chérie?*" They laughed uneasily, both stinging from the revelation of the missing pages. For Andrea, the humiliation had sprung from a failure to discover the deletion herself; for Justine, it had not challenged her expertise, which was slim at best, but fed a simmering fear that she had stumbled into something more complex and dangerous than she was prepared for.

"What did you notice when you looked at the codex, Andrea?" she finally asked.

"The title page is gone, as well as a few of the following pages. Just as Al Rasul reported. They had to have disappeared in the last few days. I didn't check it when I placed it in the briefcase just before we left Cairo."

"What do you think happened?"

"Bear with me while I just think aloud. There aren't many times when pages could have been removed. They could have been taken from Ibrahim's office, or Amir's family home. Since someone is following and threatening you, we can assume there are people who want the codex either taken or destroyed. But the fact is: the pages had to have been removed since the last time I examined the codex less than two days before we left for Alexandria!" Andrea paused.

"Then we should assume that the missing pages may reveal an unthinkable, unrevealable truth," said Justine, thrilled by her own pronouncement.

"The thief would have to know exactly what he or she was doing, which pages to take out. There are extraordinary scholars at Al Azhar, many of whom are interested in suppressing any information counter to accepted belief, but how would they have gotten access to the codex?" Andrea kept her eyes on the busy road as she reached down to fiddle with the broken heater.

Justine pulled their jackets from the backseat, surprised by how sharply the temperature had fallen as night swept over the Sahara. To her right, the shadows of three galloping camels moved across the darkening desert sands like sailboats on an open sea. Several moments passed before she asked distractedly, "Where was the codex during those days? With Ibrahim?"

Andrea nodded. "With Ibrahim. He keeps it in a small safe under his desk. But he isn't in the office all of the time, and security is never that good. There are guards at the gate, yet the garden walls seem fragile. I'm anxious to tell Ibrahim and see where it leads. There's little we can conclude for now." The muscles around her lips contracted.

They sped along in silence for some time. The twilight deepened to purple, and a fuchsia ribbon formed along the horizon. Andrea said evenly, "Headlights from a large black car have kept a steady distance behind us for some time. It doesn't seem to draw closer or fall further behind. Not the typical Egyptian driver."

"Do you think we're being followed?" Justine turned around to see the car, but it was nearly impossible in the twilight.

"A good possibility. I'm going to speed up and find out if they keep pace with us. The Wadi Natrun rest house is just a few miles ahead."

Justine couldn't keep her eyes off the headlights shining in the rearview mirror. Andrea varied her speed. Each time, the driver of the car behind them adjusted his speed, keeping the same distance between them. It was as though the pursuing car was attached to their bumper by a long metal rod.

Andrea pulled into the parking lot of the rest house. The Mercedes slowly drove on.

Inside, they sat at a table. Coffee was about all they could handle at the moment.

"No chocolate cookies?" Justine asked somberly.

"I didn't see any," replied Andrea, distracted. "Perhaps I should call Amir and ask him to call the desert police, a special patrol in these parts of the open road."

"Do you think we should get back on the road?" She glanced at the door each time it opened. She knew she would recognize the unforgettable face of the man from the Khan if she saw it.

"We have little choice. This place will close up soon and we'll be sitting ducks."

They drank the rest of the bitter coffee in silence. When they pulled back onto the road, they were driving for less than a kilometer before the familiar headlights reappeared. "There's no doubt now that we're being followed. I'm only hoping they just want to scare us. I called Amir while you were in the restroom."

"And? What did you tell him?" *What would I want to tell him? He's tried to distance himself from Zachariah, yet Ibrahim says they're very close. In the Khan, he was suspicious, evasive. Why was he there? Then, the next morning at Groppi's—he refused to make eye contact. It wouldn't surprise me at all if he took the missing pages. He certainly has access.*

"I told him we were being followed and to call the desert police."

"Fine," Justine said irritably, reluctant to share her suspiciousness of Amir until she was more sure. "Fine! The police aren't likely to show up very quickly, are they? We could be dead by then."

"Or worse. They could steal the codex," Andrea said grimly.

The Mercedes' headlights drew closer. Andrea pushed the accelerator to the floor. The speedometer read 95 kilometers when the intruders pulled along-side them as though the Kia were standing still and began nudging the car toward the ditch running parallel with the highway. Andrea slowed down; the Mercedes slowed in concert.

The right wheels, then the left wheels, of the Kia began to vibrate as it hit the soft sand on the shoulder of the road. Fenders screeched as the two cars collided. Andrea could no longer control the car. Justine placed her hand on Andrea's shoulder, squeezed tight, and closed her eyes. Panic rippled through her body as Andrea cried out, "Here we go!" The Mercedes turned back onto the shoulder at the last moment as the Kia spun off the edge and stopped violently in the ditch below. Justine was thrown forward, hitting her head on the dashboard. Andrea's body stopped short of plummeting into the steering wheel, restrained by the only seatbelt in the car.

The pursuing car parked not more than five meters from their left bumper. The Kia's headlights sprayed eerily across the desert beyond.

For several moments the two women sat still. Justine put her hand to her forehead, feeling the pain throbbing in her recent stitches. Haunting images were sketched by the strangely dispersed light. Remnants of the ancient sea of Tethys formed the outlines of shallow lakes, while spongy wetlands of open water harbored what appeared like paper cutouts of ducks and cranes.

"Are you okay, Justine?" Andrea finally asked, reaching for the briefcase and shoving it under her seat.

"Nothing seems to be broken, but I hit my head," answered Justine, attempting to examine her arms and legs, trembling all over. "You?"

Two figures emerged from the Mercedes and headed toward the Kia. One slipped on the loose sand and nearly slid into the door on the driver's side. Justine watched the second man through the rear view mirror. Neither she nor Andrea moved. The man to Andrea's left stood up and seemed to wait for the other man as he placed his hand on the left fender of their car and lowered himself into the ditch. Justine snapped on the interior light, causing the man with the misshapen lip to cover his eyes.

Just then, the larger man grabbed the arm of the man from the Khan, pointed in the direction of the desert, and motioned him away. They turned and quickly raced back to the car, speeding into the distance. Another car slowed as though preparing to stop, then continued on toward Cairo. The two women stared at each other in disbelief and opened their doors, stepping out into the soft, still-warm sand.

As they gazed into the dimly lit desert, they saw two figures looming in the darkness. In the far distance, three rounded forms and a steeple crowned with miniature crosses broke through the afterglow of the evening.

As the figures in deep brown robes approached the car, Justine called out, "Did Mary send you?"

"Mary is always with us," smiled the shorter of the two monks.

CHAPTER 14

⬥⬥⬥

"YOU SAID WHAT?" EXCLAIMED NADIA, GAZING at Justine with amusement. "Since when did Mary become your guardian angel?" After a day in the community school in the City of the Dead, the two women were attempting to relax in Justine's overly warm apartment.

"I don't understand it either. I was feeling panicky. After all, I did hit my head. Again. I'm beginning to feel like a punching bag. When the ghostly figures came out of the desert, everything became surreal," she said, perspiring from the heat that tenaciously held on to the long afternoon. She handed Nadia a cold bottle of Evian and took a long drink from her own.

"I see a new bruise. What's this all about, Justine?" Nadia held the cool bottle to her forehead. The slowly rotating ceiling fan moved the warm air without cooling it. "It's not routine that people who come to Cairo get chased and threatened."

"My dreams have been so vivid since the earthquake. Reality seems to be blending with illusion. Do you think I'm losing my mind?" She looked at Nadia with wide, moist eyes, recalling Joan Didion's notion of the "shallowness of sanity." Had she dipped below that shallow patina?

"Perhaps." Nadia smiled warmly. "But I think I have a right to know: what is going on?"

"You do have a right to know," Justine admitted.

"Let's start with last night. Who were your saviors?" Nadia left sanity to sort itself out.

"Two monks from the Wadi Natrun Monastery who were walking toward the rest house. They noticed the commotion and headed toward us. While we were talking, the desert police pulled up. Then Amir." Justine relaxed into the details of the story.

"Amir?"

"Andrea had called him from the rest house." She left it at that.

Nadia was pensive, but held firm: "Why, Justine? Why is all of this happening?"

Justine took a deep breath and imagined Andrea there beside her. "Don't tell anyone," she would say. She shook her head to clear it, sighed, and began: "During the earthquake I found an old book in the crypt." She paused to take off her shoes; Nadia removed her loafers. "We took it to the Alexandria Bibliotheca to have it analyzed. Partially, at least. I'm sure the men were after the book, called a codex. But why, I don't know. They couldn't know its value; my god, we don't even know what it is. All we know is that it's very old and some sort of personal journal." She trusted Nadia, and trust was not a nebulous concept to Justine.

"Why would they want it?" pressed Nadia. "To destroy it, suppress it?"

"Search me. For some reason they think they know more than we do." Justine left the complication of the missing pages to another time.

"Egypt has very exacting rules with the United Nations, Non-Governmental Organizations, and Western countries," Nadia said darkly. "If you're a guest here, best to stay away from political and religious conflict." She smiled belatedly, but it didn't do much to soften her words.

Justine blinked. *Now she tells me!*

༄

"I don't drive in Cairo anymore," explained Ibrahim as Justine slid into the taxi beside him on the following day. "I'm afraid I'll kill someone."

"Very wise," she assured him. "I haven't attempted driving here yet, but I'm planning to get an old car as soon as I can figure out how to maneuver through the streets." Just arrived back from a school, she'd barely had time to put on a fresh blouse and wash her face before Ibrahim had called to say he was waiting downstairs. She observed the professor closely; he was relaxed and playful, although she was sure that Andrea had talked to him about the missing pages.

"Good luck," Ibrahim laughed. "The Ministry of Transportation hired a German team of traffic experts a few years ago to tell us how to improve the situation. After many months, they realized that we Egyptians were not going to stop at red lights, so they recommended this crazy system of one-way streets where you have to make U-turns to go in the other direction." Ibrahim adjusted his French tam, a present from Andrea. "Driving here is a dance. That's the secret," he revealed, as though it was an insight that could only be gained by years of struggle.

Justine laughed. "A bit like the square dance we did in middle school, only not as organized. I'm surprised that a German team could make sense of it all."

"They couldn't. They had a Turkish Muslim engineer with them," Ibrahim said proudly. "Culture is everything, Justine."

"Everything, Professor?"

"Well, just about . . . We're nearing the St. Barbara Church grounds in Old Cairo, and I haven't said much about Father Zein Hakeem. Zein and I have been friends since our college days. Not only is he knowledgeable about the Coptic religion and the history of St. Sergius, but he's also a good storyteller and knows a particular tale I want you to hear. I think you'll like him."

A story I need to hear? Ah, the plot thickens. "I'm sure I will, professor. Have you told him about the codex?"

"Not yet. Andrea won't let me," Ibrahim said with a devilish grin as their taxi turned into one of Cairo's many secret gardens and stopped near a three-story office building of aging white stucco. Sycamore branches and ivy covered the seating area nearby where three priests leaned toward each other, absorbed in conversation. A towering stone wall left by the peripatetic Romans formed the western boundary of the vast property, revealing layers of civilizations that blended effortlessly in the ancient world.

Justine could have picked Father Zein out of any crowd. He looked just as she'd imagined. Embracing Ibrahim, his graying hair and flowing gown completely enveloped the shorter professor. Laugh lines were etched into his aging face; his eyes were saucy. He turned toward Justine and squeezed her extended hand gently.

"Follow me, my dear," he said. Slowly, Father Zein led them up winding stairs to an imposing office, where he waved them toward two velvet-upholstered chairs in front of a massive desk. He released his own considerable weight into a large chair situated between his desk and a window opening to the lush garden below.

For several moments, he absently arranged the items on his cluttered desk, giving himself time to regain his breath. "Before 1981, St. Barbara Church was a church of the dead. Now it is a church of the living. We have five priests here—two more were just ordained—a school for English, and technological training. We're an active, alive institution."

A timid, elderly man entered the room, knelt, and kissed the hand of the priest before quietly receiving the order for tea. *Such worship must be routine,* thought Justine, *for there are no signs of discomfort on Zein's part.*

"Professor Ibrahim and I have known each other for a hundred years or more. Isn't that so, my friend?" Zein asked playfully. "Where did you get that God-awful hat?"

"Dashing, don't you think?" Ibrahim's shaking hands delicately touched his black and green plaid tam on all sides. Turning to reveal his pleasing patrician profile, he replied, "We've known each other for at least that long. But you're not going to talk me out of my hat."

Father Zein smiled and waved his hand dismissively. "We met in New York, where we were both students of philosophy at City College. I was dating a beautiful young woman and Ibrahim was jealous. He tried to steal her away, but she recognized the better man." As Zein talked, Ibrahim was clearly enjoying himself. "Rebecca now lives in New York near our children. I've one daughter in Cairo. My wife's not fond of Cairo, and I've grown weary of New York."

"You see, my dear," Ibrahim explained to Justine, "in the Coptic Church, priests can marry, but only before they're ordained. Father Zein wasn't ordained until 1981, when he came to St. Barbara."

"I see," she smiled. "That must cause quite a last-minute run on weddings."

"Ha! You are so right, my dear." Father Zein laughed, placing both hands on his stomach. "I just reserve the church for a month before ordination." He cleared his throat. "I understand from my friend here that you have some questions for me. I am happy to oblige." He shifted his weight in his oversized chair and pulled at his beard with a ring-adorned hand. Even Spielberg would have trouble topping this man as a character in a period movie.

"Let me start with an easy one," said Justine. "How do Copts and Muslims get along today in Egypt?"

"If that's an easy question, I may not be able to answer the hard ones." Father Zein paused. "I would say we tolerate each other quite well. You may know that before the Muslim invasion in the seventh century, Coptic Christianity was the religion of Egypt. In fact, Christianity began in Egypt, established in Alexandria by St. Mark. Even the idea of monasteries started right here in the Eastern desert. Egyptians took to Christianity like ducks take to water. Ah, perhaps even better."

"Better than ducks, Father? That's quite a claim."

"Well founded, I'd say. Keep in mind that the Holy Family came to us. Our land was the safe haven when Herod ordered all of the male babies under the age of two killed to make sure the Messiah did not live. We were honored by the visit of Mary and her new son."

"Further," added Ibrahim, "the worship of the goddess Isis was the primary religion in Egypt and much of the Roman world at that time. Egyptians were wholly committed to a mother figure who had resurrected her husband and devoted herself to her divine son. She was considered the giver of life and the mother of God. We realize this tale is a little heretical. But there you have it."

Zein shook his head in disagreement, but distributed the tea. "Sugar? Milk?"

"I remember hearing about Isis from my mother. Why heretical?" asked Justine. "Transferring the worship of one woman and son to another would seem to be quite natural, as well as rational."

Father Zein scoffed. "To think that the path to worshiping Mary and her divine son came through paganism is unthinkable, my dear. We prefer to believe that coming to Jesus Christ occurs through divine epiphany."

"I see," said Justine, who understood it at one irrational level. "Please go on. You were describing the Copts and the Muslims."

"*Iwa.* I lose my train of thought easily these days. We Copts now make up only about 10 percent of the population of Egypt. On the surface, we get along relatively well, but I'm afraid the friction is growing once again. Copts are rarely elected to local offices or Parliament, even when we see fit to run. Our women do not cover themselves, so we stand out more than ever. We keep too much to ourselves. We're the Jews of the twenty-first century." He sighed.

"But you do have some common ground, don't you? Muslims believe that Jesus was a great prophet, and Mary is honored."

"Jesus is considered a prophet—but not a son of God. And, curiously, Mary is spoken of quite often in the Koran. You might say that the Virgin Mary is a bridge between our two religions, especially in Egypt," said Father Zein. "The Muslims accept almost no Christian miracles, but the Virgin birth is one of them."

"Are there others?" Justine slid forward on the velvet chair. "I love a good story."

"Just one. The story of St. Samaan, the Tanner." Father Zein turned to Ibrahim. "Do we have time to tell this story?"

"I think we should take the time," said Ibrahim. "It's an important story for her to hear."

Justine looked quizzically at Ibrahim. "I'd like to hear it."

Father Zein tipped his head in acquiescence. "In the late tenth century, Caliph Al-Mu'iz Li Din Illah was the first Fatimid ruler of Egypt. Copts were still in great number then and led by Pope Abram, a Syrian. Samaan was a devoted Christian tanner living in the village below Muqattum." The priest pointed northwest with his shaky left hand. "Samaan knew his scriptures well. One day, a beautiful woman came in to be measured for some shoes. Although he prided himself on his self-discipline, that morning Samaan felt lust for this woman. Knowing the wishes of Jesus from the Sermon on the Mount, Samaan took his tanning tool and plunged it into his right eye. His right eye had offended God, he reasoned. He would pluck it out."

Justine inhaled sharply, her mind racing back to the note pushed under her door. *If your right eye offends you, pluck it out.* She glanced at Ibrahim, who nodded as though to say, "This is why I brought you here."

"But this is not the point of the story," declared Father Zein, bringing their attention back to him. "Sometime after this incident with Samaan, the caliph called together the Coptic pope and a Jewish scholar. The caliph was a man of learning who liked to listen to fierce debates. The Jewish scholar quoted from Jesus: 'If you have faith as small as a mustard seed, you can say to this mountain, "Move from here to there," and it will move. Nothing will be impossible for you.' Surely the pope could not move mountains, challenged the scholar."

"And this was taken literally?" Justine asked in amazement.

"Quite literally, my dear. The caliph's advisor said to him: 'Ask the pope to move the mountain, my lord. If their faith is the true one, the mountain will move. If it is not a true faith, it will not.' The caliph thought this a fine idea and demanded it so. As you can imagine, Pope Abram was perplexed. What could he do? He asked his people to fast and pray, fast and pray, but no solution appeared to them. Finally, the solution appeared in the image of the Virgin Mary, who said to the pope: 'Go out through the iron gate and into the market. Find the one-eyed tanner, the one called Samaan, for he is pure. He will show you the way.' And he did. Samaan told the pope to take his leaders and his people to the mountaintop with bibles and candles and pray four hundred times, one hundred times in each direction. They prayed all night. By dawn, the pope told the caliph they were ready to perform the miracle. While the caliph and his men watched from a distance, a great quake came and moved the mountain, dividing it into three parts. For some moments, the caliph could even see under the mountain to the sunrise beyond. The caliph and his people became frightened and soon cried out: 'God is great; may his name be blessed. You have proven that your faith is the true one!'"

"What happened then?" interjected Justine. "Were the Christians more accepted?"

"Many, many things happened, my eager young friend. Many churches were restored, and Christians were protected for some time to come. Peace replaced upheaval and war. Pope Shenouda III kept the miracle in our hearts by adding three days to the Christmas fast and building a great church in the name of St. Samaan at Muqattum." Father Zein paused, sipped his tea, and shifted into a more comfortable position.

"Why 'Muqattum'? What does it mean?"

"To 'cut up.'" God cut up the mountain that morning into three pieces."

"Is there any physical evidence of an earthquake occurring at that time?" ventured Justine, immediately regretting her infidel impulses.

"You Westerners," said Father Zein with a tolerant smile. "You want to get to the bottom of things, to dissect, to study. Orientals can simply appreciate an icon behind glass; Westerners want to know how old it is, what it is made of, how much it's worth. You want to take it out from behind the glass and hold it. We accept God's gifts on faith. We're more spiritual. You Westerners, you take away the mystery."

Justine offered her most engaging smile. "This is so. Even though I am only part American, I confess to the sin of reason."

Father Zein laughed heartily, holding his stomach. Ibrahim followed suit, the mood lightening as the pink and lavender glow of early evening filled the room. Finally Father Zein asked, "Do you have more questions?"

"My head and heart are quite full, Father," Justine said with appreciation. "Any other questions can wait for another day."

It was nearly dark by the time the taxi carrying Ibrahim and Justine began to weave through the traffic on Qasr al-Ainy. "Zein is a dear friend, but he lives in a boxed-in faith. He knows nothing of Nag Hammadi, or anything else that would challenge his beliefs in the slightest. He's not curious in the usual sense, but he's a happy man."

"I was raised to think that educated people are by nature curious."

"That's not always true in Egypt, my dear. Of course there are those who escaped the curses of colonization. They're intensely curious. But remember, before 1952, we hadn't ruled ourselves since before the Ptolemys, and even then it was a theocracy."

"I do have another question. For you." Justine hesitated. "I know Andrea talked to you about the missing pages. What do you suspect? What could have happened to them?"

Ibrahim watched the traffic as though he were the driver, then turned to her. "I don't know. I'm sure the codex was secure in my little safe . . . I have no idea. That's what I told Andrea. No idea. No idea." His hands trembled; his voice was raspy.

"I don't like to press you on this, professor, but those pages disappeared within the space of two days. Someone is responsible. You're sure you didn't leave the codex lying on your desk? For just a moment? I could understand that happening." She didn't say, *Where Amir could find it*, or ask, *Are you protecting Amir?*

"Where's Zachariah?" Ibrahim's eyes looked panicked; he began to rub his knee vigorously. "Watch out, my boy! Those bullies . . ." His eyes refocused on Justine. "My knee hurts, my dear. The stairs, you know . . ."

Justine's eyes moistened as she watched Ibrahim become disoriented. Images surfaced of her grandfather Jenner moving in and out of clarity on his farm in Nebraska. She hadn't understood it then, and it had scared her. An hour later he would be fine again, playing checkers with her on the kitchen table. It wasn't long before his senility turned to Alzheimer's. "Let's get you home," she said, resting her hand on the professor's trembling arm. "I'm grateful that you brought me to hear Samaan's story."

Chapter 15

⸻

THE RED SEA COULD BE ASTONISHINGLY BEAUTIFUL, especially in the evening. As Nasser and Justine turned into El Ain Bay, the sea and the sky were at their most stunning. Shades of warm pink and cool lavender enveloped the sky and reflected in the watery mirror. Flickering lights on the horizon reminded the world that Moses' path now hosted immense ships and tankers from every trading country in the world. These moving islands of steel had emerged from the locks of the Suez Canal into the Gulf of Suez and were finally freed into the Red Sea. To the southeast, amethyst peaks reached into the hovering sky, at the center of which sat Mt. Sinai.

Justine's nerves had been stretched further than she liked to admit by all of the unknowns surrounding the codex and the dangers that had plagued her since she'd arrived in Cairo. So when Nasser invited her to accompany him to a family villa on the Red Sea, east of the city, she'd quickly accepted.

The villa was one of a cluster of three-story stucco holiday homes with ocher tile roofs. About half of the homes were being warmed by the presence of weekenders, while the other half lay darkened and silent. Justine found the contrast with Cairo striking. The resort was spacious, clean and quiet, with broad gardens growing down to the beach. Scattered shadows told of trees, flowers, and shrubs, the identity of which would only become apparent in the morning light.

Nasser parked in the driveway and unloaded their bags at the bottom of a stairwell leading to the house above. The villas were built on two levels: the lower level opened onto a patio and garden, the upper level held a more commanding view from two terraces. "Let me show you around," he offered as he opened the door at the top of the stairs. A small entryway led to a kitchen, living room, two bedrooms, and a covered terrace; on the floor above were two more bedrooms and a stairwell to an open terrace on the roof.

Nasser placed Justine's two small bags in the southern bedroom on the second floor. "This room has the long view," he noted, "through the gardens, miles of white beach, the sea, and the mountains of the Sinai beyond." Justine stood by the window as the last remains of dark blue and purple gave way to a star-filled night. She was grateful to have the privacy of the second floor to herself.

"Thank you. I think I'd like to change clothes and freshen up a bit," she said. After the drive, she would relish a few moments alone. The villa was only an hour and a half from the outskirts of Cairo, but it had taken an hour just to get through the city.

"I'll meet you on the terrace," he replied, partially shutting her door.

She sat on the side of the bed facing the window. Why had she felt awkward during the drive? She hated secrets, yet had to be careful not to cross any more boundaries about the codex. Deliberately leaving information out of a casual conversation was difficult.

Ornate Muslim prayer beads hung on the wall above the bed; antiques from Nasser's family shop gave the room a twentieth-century aura. Justine opened the larger of the two bags, hung up a few outfits, and placed the rest of her clothes in the large walnut dresser. Changing into a light green silk blouse and cotton skirt, she set her dark green shawl on the end of the bed and slipped into buckskin sandals. As she brushed her hair and touched up her lipstick in the ornate mirror above the dresser, she asked herself again: *Why didn't I tell Nasser about the incident at Wadi Natrun? I've already told him about the codex.*

She took a long, deep breath, examining herself. Sometimes her image surprised her, as though it was someone else she was viewing in the mirror. After all, her mother was the striking beauty in the family. She resembled neither her mother nor father; some said she had a likeness to her Italian grandmother. Having chestnut hair and amber eyes, rather than the classic dark coloring of her mother's country, made it more difficult for her to call herself Egyptian. She turned away from her reflection and climbed another set of stairs to the third-floor terrace.

Nasser sat gazing toward the southeast, an opened bottle of Grand Marquis cabernet and two filled glasses beside him on the wrought iron table. "I always find it difficult to believe that I'm looking at Asia from here." He had changed into a lightweight pale blue sweater and tan slacks. "Wine?"

"Love it," Justine said, choosing a chair facing the lights on the southern horizon. "I find it amazing that we're actually sitting in Africa. Somehow, Egypt seems a continent unto itself." She paused. "How long has your family been coming to this villa?"

"About a year. This is a new development. As you may have noticed, the project is still being built, and many of the houses are not yet occupied. Since my father and his colleague work with the government, we got in on the ground floor. We bought it in partnership with the El Bakrs."

"It's so quiet here—as though the continent were pausing before handing over its power to Asia," she said.

"Mm . . . personifying these continents helps us to understand their uneasy relationship. As you suggest, Egypt doesn't really identify with either one." He lit two candles as a nearly full moon crawled up from behind the mountains of the Sinai. "We might not need these candles."

"Not with that moon," she said and sipped her wine.

They fell silent for a few moments, then Nasser said, "What?"

"I didn't say anything," she replied, intoxicated by the wine and the evening air. The moonlight.

"I thought you said something. You often wiggle your nose when you're starting to speak." The night's soft glow highlighted his even, rugged features and crooked smile.

Justine laughed softly.

"Do you have secrets? Childhood secrets? Tell me two that no one else knows."

"Ah, a social pact," Justine whispered flirtatiously. "I'll tell you secrets if you tell me some of yours."

He grinned. "It's a deal. When I was in high school I read one of my sister's diaries."

"You read your sister's diary? What a terrible thing to do! A capital offense," Justine exclaimed with feigned seriousness. "Was it interesting?"

He chuckled. "It was not, although it seemed scandalous at the time. She was crazy about a boy in her class. It was filled with pages of how terribly in love she was."

"Did she go out with him? Marry him?"

"No. It turned out to be just a fantasy. He didn't even know she existed. And you?" He lifted a picnic basket from the floor to one of the chairs. Justine reached in and began to set out the feast that she had brought along. Cold chicken, labna, baladi bread, stuffed zucchini, and fruit.

"I cheated at cards," Justine admitted, opening each container.

"Do you still cheat at cards?" When she nodded, he added, "I'm not sure that anyone who cheats at cards can be trusted," then winked.

She laughed. "You're probably right. You can't trust me." The wink sent a warm pulse through her body. "Your turn." She passed the chicken and zucchini.

"When I was a child, small enough to fit under a table or behind a stuffed chair, I used to listen in when my parents and their friends would talk politics. I think many of my ideas were formed then," he said, filling his plate.

"What did they talk about? What ideas stayed with you?" She spread labna on her baladi bread.

"Remember, that was twenty-five years ago. New countries were forming in Africa, colonization was finally dissolving, the Cold War gave everything an ominous feel. My father said when the U.S. didn't need us anymore, they'd discard us like yesterday's fish."

"My parents talked the same way. As you know, my father is American and my mother Egyptian. Even during intense discussions, my father remained optimistic, as you would know." She cut the mangos and papayas into small slices.

Nasser nodded, swallowed a slice of mango, then grinned. "What other wicked behavior are you guilty of?"

"I read *Lady Chatterley's Lover* when I was fifteen. My grandmother had quite a collection of D.H. Lawrence's works. I hid under the blanket with a flashlight—just in case Dad wandered in. Is that what you mean by 'wicked'?"

"Charming . . . very risqué."

She was enthralled with his lips as they sensuously encircled the mango. "I read it again a few years ago."

"And?" Nasser tilted his head, a spark in his dark blue eyes.

"I think I understand it now," she said, relishing her own fruit, its sumptuous flavors and texture.

"Perhaps you're not as innocent as you seem."

"Innocent?" She was disappointed. *Does that make me unapproachable?*

"You're always elegant and uncreased, a little untouchable. You remind me of a beautiful doll on my sister's bed with flaxen hair and a delicate, creamy complexion. So healthy looking."

"What would it take to get you to see me otherwise?" she challenged. "Dirt on my face? Arm wrestling? A sweaty competition?"

"I could go for the arm wrestling," Nasser replied with a broadening grin. "But right now I would settle for a walk on the beach. You'll need a shawl."

Justine stopped by her room and picked up the green shawl. *Am I so inexperienced, unsophisticated? Do others see me this way?* She realized that she was still standing in the middle of the room.

"Are you ready?" Nasser called from the landing.

"I'm coming."

They walked side by side down the earthen path leading east. As the path turned to sand, Nasser took her hand and held on, moving them closer to the silvery black sea. The sand was still warm from the sun, but the air held a chill. She welcomed the coziness of the shawl and Nasser's touch.

"Tell me," she said softly, "what do you think is up there?" Vibrant stars blanketed the sky as though they were inside a planetarium.

"Up there? You mean like another civilization, or heaven?"

"Like that. Another universe, another existence . . . or something after death. I mean both, I guess." It was easy to talk in the dark, walking so close they could feel each other's breath.

"I guess I believe in both. Another civilization on another planet far away. I don't think I could be a good scientist if I didn't. And I believe there is something more after death. I'm not so sure of its geography."

Justine sensed his amusement. "And what's it like, this afterlife of yours?"

"I wouldn't call it mine," he emphasized, "but I believe the hereafter is made up of countless heavenly realms and countless hellish realms. If we create a heavenly consciousness within ourselves here on earth, we will later experience a heavenly outer realm. And it follows that if we create hell within, we will later experience an outer realm of hell as well."

"You've thought a great deal about this, haven't you? It sounds very Buddhist . . . or Gnostic. But who are *we*?" She steered him to a bench near the path, where they could sit facing each other.

His gaze fixed on her face, sending a warm pulse of desire through her. "At one time I told you I was a Christian of sorts. I am a Nazarene Essene. We think of ourselves as a Buddhist branch of the original Christianity. Our sect existed before Christianity, grew up in the area around Mt. Carmel, and has long considered Jesus Christ the true manifestation of both the Divine Father and the Only Begotten Son."

She was surprised. "I thought the Essenes disappeared hundreds of years ago, or at least fused into Christianity."

"We're very much a living sect. And we've fused more deliberately with the Buddhists and Sufis in recent centuries." He took her hand in his. "Are you warm enough?"

She nodded, drawing an ankh in the sand with the tip of her sandal.

"What do you believe is beyond?" Nasser asked.

"If there is something else, I don't think it's a place. Perhaps it's a state of mind. I think we can find bliss while we're still on earth. I'd like to find such a state of mind here that would carry me on through the hereafter."

He nodded. "You once told me there were two great terrors to overcome— one was the fear of punishment after death. Does your notion of the hereafter conquer that fear?"

"Somewhat. But the responsibility to create your own Heaven through your consciousness is a bit overwhelming. A burden of sorts."

"Those are ambitious thoughts," he said. "Perhaps we want it all. Nazarene Essenes believe that the entire universe is a cosmic school system for the education of souls. This is how I think about my life."

"I like that," she said. "Very much." She fell silent, listening to the sea. *Do I want it all? Am I a part of this cosmic school system?* "I probably do want it all," she finally said, "but I hadn't thought of it in that way." She looked up at him. "It's starting to get chilly. Shall we head back?"

Strolling back toward the villa, Justine noticed a particularly huge star emitting large spokes of light that made it appear to be a child's drawing of the star of Bethlehem. "What's that?" she asked, pointing toward the southern horizon.

"Some say it is a space station, others say the North Star, some say it's Mars or Venus, others say it's something even more mysterious, like an alien ship."

"Others?" she teased. "How many women have you brought here?"

"Just you," he said.

∾

Justine slipped out of the quiet house the next morning for a run. Back in her room, she stepped into a one-piece black swimsuit and a put on a white cotton shirt. Placing sunscreen, glasses, and a sarong into her canvas bag, she recalled the day when she'd pulled the codex out of a duplicate of this very bag. Little had she known that the small book would pry open her need for adventure even as she attended to her new job and attempted to define her life. She had a devil of a time pulling those three things apart. *You probably can't have all,* she realized, even though she'd told Nasser last night that she could.

Nasser was waiting with a cup of tea. "Milk? Lemon? Sugar?" he asked, eyeing her appreciatively as she descended the stairs. "Did you sleep well?"

"Just a little milk, thank you. The best sleep I've had in a long time. I was quite energized this morning. And you?"

"I slept long and well. Just woke up. I thought I heard you leave the house this morning."

"My morning run. I'm quite addicted," she said, somewhat guiltily. She hadn't invited him. "Join me tomorrow?"

"Absolutely. I'd love to. I see you're already dressed for the beach—I'll be ready in a few moments."

"I'll just drink my tea on the terrace while you change." She smiled. In the morning light she could distinguish flowers planted in orderly rows around the paths, leading toward the sparkling water: blazing yellow acacia, a few flamboyant royal palms and fan palms, hibiscus, birds of paradise, oleander, crepe myrtle, and generous bougainvillea climbing up onto several terraces. Two hoopoes drew her attention—beautiful birds, starkly black and white, like little penguins.

Walking with Nasser toward the sea, Justine pointed to small rattan umbrellas scattered like Chinese hats along the southern beach. The atmosphere was buoyant, invigorating, as if the air had more oxygen here. None of it seemed real.

Nasser spread two large towels under an umbrella and set a small chest of water to the side. "Do you swim? What a silly question. Would you like to swim?"

"There are some things I can't do!" she insisted.

"Such as?"

"I'll think of something," she laughed, and ran toward the water.

They swam for almost an hour before emerging exhausted from the warm sea and throwing themselves onto the waiting towels. Nasser brushed the sand from Justine's feet while she dried her hair with the edge of the towel. "Do you know how to play siga?"

"Siga? Never heard of it," she said, turning onto her elbows.

Nasser rolled onto his stomach and drew four parallel lines in the sand, then crossed them with four perpendicular lines. "It is an ancient Egyptian game." It looked like tic-tac-toe. He gathered a small handful of shells for Justine and kept an assortment of pebbles for himself. "The objective of the game is somewhat like chess; each player aims to take the pieces of the opponent. Let's play a practice game." After Nasser had won three games and Justine the fourth, she called a truce.

Leaning on one elbow, they faced each other. "I've been thinking about our discussion last night about the Nazarene Essenes. Will you tell me more?"

"Let's see ... what would be of most interest? We believe in what we call an Order of One, meaning that the Godhead is One, yet made up of a sort of trinity: the Godhead, or source, who is neither male nor female; the father, or only begotten son; and the mother, or only begotten daughter. The cosmic union between the Father God and the Mother God brought forth Creation."

"Only begotten daughter? A woman goddess in the trinity? Has she arrived on the scene yet?"

"I don't think so. We have something to look forward to." Nasser smiled at her excitement. "We believe in the equality of women. And, clearly, some women are more equal than others." He threw a handful of sand across her legs. "We also believe that people with special powers can channel knowledge from the ancients."

"Such as?"

"Ever heard of Edgar Cayce?"

"A famous channeler, wasn't he? In the early part of the last century, I think."

"Correct. He was a Nazarene Essene. Much of our recent knowledge about the time of Jesus Christ was channeled though Cayce. For instance, what Jesus was doing during the 'silent years.'"

"'Silent years'?" The ones before he started his ministry?"

"Exactly. Except for the story of his chasing the Rabbis out of the Temple at age twelve, we knew little about him."

"But you do now?"

"More or less. Cayce revealed that Jesus was not raised as a Jew, but lived among the Essenes, perhaps at Mt. Carmel. That would account for many of his teachings, which seem in sharp contrast to Jewish law at the time. In one of the last years of Cayce's life—1922, I believe—he gave a speech in Alabama where he noted that DaVinci had understood that Mary Magdalene was an important disciple and painted her to the right of Jesus in his work *The Last Supper.*"

"So that's where Dan Brown got the idea for *The DaVinci Code!*"

"No doubt. Even more interesting, I think, is what the findings at Nag Hammadi revealed. Those scrolls contained many of the Essene scriptures,

such as notions about the Godhead, women, and the symbolism of the resurrection."

"Those finds are more familiar to me. We learned in Alexandria that some
of them are still being translated."

"Now it's my turn to be amazed. I had no idea that there might be more
scriptures to come." Nasser smoothed sunscreen on Justine's back and arms.
"These straw umbrellas are deceptive: the sun's rays come right through
them."

A wave of desire moved though her thighs as Nasser massaged her. "For
Lucretius, the poet my mother was named for, truth was the cornerstone of
moral behavior and free will allowed us to choose truthfulness. Without
choice, we cannot take responsibility for our actions." As she relaxed under his
touch, she wondered where her choices would take her before the weekend
was over. "This massage feels awfully good. And that is the absolute truth." She
laughed, turning to brush a curl out of Nasser's eye.

Tilting his head, he caught her hand as it dropped from his forehead. He
pressed it to his lips, gazing at her intently.

A white wooden boat with unfurled, billowing sails appeared on the horizon, drawing their attention away from each other. It moved steadily toward
the shallow waters near the shore. Four bare-chested men busied themselves
in gathering and folding large fishing nets with aging floats. The fading blue
letters on the side said *Isis*.

"The water is shallow here," Nasser said, raising his hand to his forehead to
get a better look. "They're bound to get stuck." At the last moment, the boat
turned slightly, dropped its sails, and came to a stop as the bow plunged
through the watery sand, tilting the vessel in a southerly direction. One of the
young men jumped into the water while another handed him a heavy basket
that he carried toward the beach.

Justine tensed. She was surprised to notice her own mounting fear at the
stranger's appearance. The incidents in the market and on the desert road had
left her quite shaky.

"He has fish to sell," declared Nasser with delight. "Let's go see."

They met the young man at the edge of the water and examined the fish:

drug, tahela, blue crab, calamari, shrimp. "What would you like, Justine? We can grill these tonight." She selected a drug and six giant shrimp. Nasser bargained with the young man, settled on a price, and placed the fish into the small ice chest he'd brought with him. He had been prepared.

The youthful fish purveyor made his way back to the boat, clinging to the side as it moved down the shore toward other sunbathers. Justine's face was ashen.

"Are you okay?" Nasser asked, frowning with concern.

"I'm fine. I seem to be getting a little paranoid." She told him about the incident on the desert road.

Nasser was indignant. "This episode sheds a new light on the previous incident. I had almost dismissed those as pranks or misunderstandings. What has been done to catch the thugs?"

"Amir called the police. Although we filed a report, we didn't feel like we could share the whole story about the codex. Consequently, they're without a motive. Amir is not hopeful that they'll take any action. As to why I didn't tell you—I've tried to figure this out myself. I guess I have an aversion to being protected. Probably a holdover from my father's excessive protectiveness." She shrugged apologetically. "I do apologize for keeping you in the dark." She was beginning to lose track of the secrets that she hadn't told Nasser. Ever since the discussion with Andrea at San Giovanni, she'd been more wary, more cautious.

Nasser reached out and touched her hair. "Do I make you feel overprotected?" His voice seemed far away.

"You make me feel protected." She smiled, color returning to her face.

Nasser was quiet for a several moments. "Have you had enough sun for today? Perhaps you could rest and read while I clean the fish and finish my novel." Justine nodded. Nasser brushed the remaining sand off their feet, shook out the towels and threw them over his shoulder, then grabbed the ice chest. Justine put on her shirt and sarong, feeling the warm sand rise between her toes.

༄

"Do you know about fish rice?" Nasser asked as they prepared dinner.

"Fish rice? You mean rice that only goes with fish? Teach me," said Justine. The shower and nap had relaxed her immensely. She now wore her favorite white linen dress with a flowing skirt, one that she considered exceedingly romantic in an Ingrid Bergman sort of way.

Nasser handed her an apron. He chopped up a red onion and sautéed it in butter until it was golden brown. Justine cut the tomatoes and stacked them on a plate with white cheese, pickles, and marinated eggplant. Sliced lemons were arranged on a separate plate.

"Now, we just put in the rice and add enough water to cook it. Lid on, heat down, and wallah!" announced Nasser, swinging a large wooden spoon in the air.

He seems to have recovered from the earlier slight, she thought, not at all sure he could forgive her for keeping the desert road incident from him. "Love it," she said. "Are we ready to grill the fish?"

"Almost. You know, if I were a devout Essene I wouldn't eat fish or chicken. We're vegetarians. But I am weak," he said with a hint of irony.

"I'm sorry. I didn't know—about this weakness, I mean—I wouldn't have brought chicken last night." She wrapped her arms around his waist and set her chin on his shoulder.

"Not to worry. Eating living things is not my only transgression."

Later, Nasser poured another glass of champagne as they enjoyed the last of their delicate morsels of Red Sea drug. Candles and moonlight illuminated the terrace, sparkled the champagne, and lent a radiant glow to Justine's white dress. She retrieved her matching sweater to guard against the moist chill moving in from the sea.

"It's been a wonderful day, Nasser. A perfect day, in fact. You're a terrific cook. I either burn fish or serve it too raw. I told you there were some things I couldn't do."

He placed his hand on hers and held it there.

"What was the novel you were finishing this afternoon?" she asked, slipping her sandals off and tucking her legs into the folds of her dress.

"Hemingway's *Farewell to Arms*," he said, running two fingers along the inside of her wrist. "Have you read it?"

"Many years ago. Are you fond of him?"

"He has a way of creating conditions that test men. In *Farewell*, he recreated the chaos of war in Italy and showed how men respond to a world where they have no control. Hemingway gets at the depth of character, I think. Make sense?" The bougainvillea curled around the roof and flowed onto the terrace floor. Nasser picked one of the delicate fuchsia petals off her sweater and placed it behind her ear.

"In a way," she said, fingering the petal. "It seems to me that Hemingway never understood women, though. The women in his books are so one-dimensional, so superficial. I remember that Catherine used silly words like 'grand,' 'sweet,' and 'lovely,' even as their life became frightening and she was about to die."

Nasser began to tickle her toes with a hoopoe feather.

"You're making me lose my train of thought," she said, folding her skirt over her toes again and pulling back from his touch. ". . . And women have fewer choices than men."

"You overestimate us," he said, raising an eyebrow. "Men have much less control than you'd think. Certainly as the only man in a household of women, I rarely felt in control."

"Mm . . . Perhaps I do overestimate men," she said with exaggerated seriousness. "Since you've been in charge, the world doesn't seem very rational. We might be better off without men entirely."

"I don't want to be thrown out like yesterday's fish. Besides, I'm perfectly harmless. I'm not in charge of much. Certainly not you!"

"No one is in charge of me," she said, cocking her head to one side in a defiant gesture she'd used since the 8th grade. "But men could make different choices."

"I'll concede that point. But men and women share some of the same desires, don't we?" He stretched out his words like a rubber band, inviting her to fill in the sentence. After a long pause, he continued, "To be in control, to have choices, to make sense of their lives, to be in love."

"Does your life make sense?" she asked, extending her legs and arms, avoiding the 'be in love' comment.

"Make sense? Perhaps not. But right now it makes a great deal of sense." He stepped back inside and put on a CD that Justine had brought along. Madeleine Peyroux's voice broke through the night air with "Dance Me to the End of Love." "Would you like to dance?" he asked, taking her hand and pulling her toward him.

Justine moved unhesitatingly toward him, laying her head on his shoulder as they swayed to the rhythm of the French melody. She felt her heart quicken as Nasser steered her toward the terrace wall and pressed her against a long branch of a white bougainvillea. Petals showered down on her hair and sweater. They gazed at each other through the dark silver of the moonlight, she fully aware that a person who feels music in every muscle is sensuous, somehow more abundantly alive.

"So you have put me in a veil," she teased. Nasser didn't respond, but gently blew the petals from her face and hair, and brushed his mouth against her slightly opened lips. As she leaned into his chest, the kisses became more desperate, the longing more intense.

Nasser picked her up in both arms and carried her into his bedroom, laying her on top of his bedspread.

"This is not a good idea," she said breathlessly, making a disingenuous effort to push him away.

"Actually, I think it's a very good idea," said Nasser, with the desire of someone who hadn't satisfied a thirst for a long time.

She unbuttoned her own sweater and loosened her belt.

Every inch of her skin felt magnetic as they explored each other's bodies. Nasser rolled her on top of him and smiled up at her. A stream of moonlight fell across his blondish hair, rendering it white as snow. A cool breeze drifted in through the terrace door, ruffling the gauze curtains above her head.

She gazed down at him, then slowly closed her eyes as passion melted any remaining doubts. When she opened her eyes, he was still staring at her with exhilarating wildness. They gently exchanged positions, she now on her back. He massaged her thighs and entered her, moving with a gentle rhythm that reminded her of their dancing, igniting nerves throughout her body. She shuddered first, and he moaned in deep satisfaction as she drew him to that fulfilling release.

"I hope the neighbors don't think I'm murdering you," Nasser laughed.

"You are . . . you are . . ." she murmured as they lay trembling, surprised by their easy sense of abandon in each other's arms.

∽

As Justine opened her eyes, she saw Nasser gazing at her once more. They both smiled, enjoying their newly shared secret. He touched her nose, wiggled it from side to side and trailed the touch down to her full lips. Then he winked.

Raising herself onto one elbow, she lifted her hair and let it fall fully around her shoulders. "Porcelain doll?" she asked impishly.

"Hardly." He grinned. "More like Odysseus' siren."

"I'll settle for that," she said generously. As he reached for her, she slid her legs out of bed, exposing the long scar on her right leg that had refused to tan. "Do you drink coffee?"

"I could," he conceded, "just so it isn't that weak American stuff."

"I make only Egyptian mud," she said, grabbing a towel from the bathroom to form into a sarong.

"Sugar, I assume?" she called from the hallway.

"Of course. Then come back to bed."

Charged memories poured out across the terrace later that morning. "You're so beguiling," Nasser said. "Enticing, alluring, tempting . . ."

"Are you practicing your English?" Justine laughed. "Or trying to seduce me again?"

"Both, my darling, both." He pulled out the chair next to hers and sat down, legs apart, his hands folded between them. "What's for breakfast?"

"Ah, you would also have me as your slave."

"That I would," he admitted with the grin she yearned for.

Justine set out a breakfast of sliced mango, yogurt, toast, hibiscus juice, and more coffee. Nasser looked around the table, walked back into the kitchen, and returned with the peanut butter. He spread it lavishly on his buttered toast, sculpting the edges with a knife.

She watched, fascinated by his methodical moves. "Peanut butter on toast is uncivil!" she declared. "And you carve like an engineer."

"You don't like peanut butter? What kind of American are you anyway? Except for your weird tastes, this could have been the beginning of a beautiful friendship," he said, sculpting the sides of his peanut butter toast like piecrust.

"*Casablanca.* My favorite movie." *What is he doing? Creating distance between us so soon?*

"My second favorite," he said. "My first has to be *Lawrence of Arabia.* Nice guy unwittingly betrays Middle East. Familiar theme."

"It was a great film," she said, stirring her mango into the yogurt.

"All too familiar," he repeated absently as he spread a mound of peanut butter on a second piece of toast. He didn't look up, as though to do so would break the spell.

"Do we have time for a swim before we need to head back?" she asked.

"I think so. I hope so," he said, but they didn't make it past the bedroom.

CHAPTER 16

━━⟨∞⟩━━

*I*S *THIS LOVE?* JUSTINE WONDERED. SHE WAS walking east toward Qasr al-Ainy, on her way to catch the underground to Old Cairo in order to meet Amir at the crypt beneath St. Sergius. She felt hesitant to work with him now, suspicious of his motives, not at all sure that he hadn't stolen the missing pages. But she was also eager to learn whether the codex had fallen from a niche in the wall of the crypt. And there was something else, she admitted. The thought of reentering the crypt alone frightened her.

Is this love? She'd asked herself this question over and over during the two days since returning with Nasser from the Red Sea. What was it her mother had said about love? Something like having the flu, a slight fever and joyful ache. The piece of that advice that bothered her was the likelihood that she could lose all perspective . . . that the object of her love would grow perfect before her very eyes. *Has he already become perfect?*

She stepped into the boulevard just as the light turned red. Blaring horns warned of collisions ahead, while the nearest car veered to the right and came to a screeching stop. Two cars traveling too close to each other collided into the left bumper of the first car, whose driver was now stepping into the jammed street. A stranger's hand took hold of her arm and firmly steered her back to the curb. "In Cairo, my lady, red lights are for decoration."

I knew that, she said to herself with no small amount of embarrassment, glancing over her shoulder at the disaster she had caused. "I know that," she said defensively. "I guess I was deep in thought." *How much more perspective can I lose?* Then, to apologize for the defensive edge to her voice, she smiled faintly and said, "Thank you," to her unfamiliar young savior. "I think I'll be fine now." Her breath came rapidly and her hands were shaking. She wasn't fine at all.

"We want to make sure, my lady," said the man. As she looked up, she saw that he was quite young and clean-shaven, wearing a smart wool jacket and starched shirt. "Let me ask you to step right over here to my friend's car." He steered her toward a familiar black sedan. Two men sat in the front seat.

"No—no thank you. I'm fine now," she said anxiously. Try as she might, she couldn't unlock his grip. Just as she started to scream, her escort's left hand covered her mouth and he pushed her into the backseat. He slid in beside her and the sedan pulled out into traffic with as much speed as conditions would allow.

"Hello, my lady," said one of the men from the front seat. "Please be calm." The man who had forced her into the car tied a damp handkerchief over her eyes. In the moment before the blindfold was tied, she glanced at the driver in the rearview mirror and saw the misshapen lip.

"What do you want from me?" she demanded. "Stop this car immediately!"

"We have some friends who want to talk with you. Don't worry, you're perfectly safe. You wouldn't want to make a fuss and cause us to hurt you," said the driver. The sedan moved east through the morning traffic, its occupants quiet. Justine concentrated on the route. Now turning north, the noises of Tahrir Square were unmistakable. A right turn would take them through downtown and out by the Khan El Khalili bazaar and Al Azhar University. The next couple of miles were slow going, a cacophony of market sounds, screeches, and shouts.

Justine attempted to chatter in Arabic above the noise. "I'm an American, you know. The police will come after me. I am due at an appointment. Stop this car!"

Eventually, the driver turned right onto what felt to Justine like the ring road encircling Cairo and the Citadel. *My god, they're going to throw me off the wall of the Citadel like Mamluk infidels.* She shuddered, perspiring at the same time.

"No need to be afraid," the man next to her said, then repeated the statement, as if he was trying to convince himself. "No need to be afraid."

Someone inserted a CD into the car player. Allison Mosley began to sing "Cry Me a River." If this was protest music, it suited Justine just fine. What was it her dad had told her about fear? All she could remember now was, avoid it when you can. Not so much the things that cause you fear, but your reaction to it. She had avoided many things that made her fearful: climbing high ledges, going over Niagara in a barrel, running with the bulls that summer in Spain. She didn't have a choice this time, but trying to figure things out preoccupied her mind, warding off panic. By now they had passed the Citadel and were curving left onto what felt like a poorly maintained dirt road.

"We must drive slowly through this community, my lady," the driver said, then told the man in the backseat to remove her blindfold. "It's a small, friendly village, and we wouldn't want anyone to get suspicious. To think anything is wrong."

"Oh, no," she said defiantly, "we wouldn't want anyone to think anything was wrong." *Since they've removed my blindfold, they know I can remember where they're taking me. I'd be able to find this place again. Unless they don't intend to let me go. If I'm dead, it doesn't matter what I know, does it? When we slow down, I'll jump . . .*

The stench invaded her lungs, nose, and eyes. Garbage was everywhere, piled into heavy, dirty white plastic bags and piled into Chevy diesels, Jeeps, Isuzu pickups, and donkey carts. She found perverse pleasure in cataloging the variety of vehicles. Trucks without garbage toted equally high piles of cauliflower, oranges, and crates of chickens and pigeons. Schoolchildren, properly dressed in Walmart-like clothes or wearing dark blue and white uniforms, proudly marched through the narrow streets. Younger brothers and sisters, dressed in rags, peered out from shadowed doorways. *Not so unlike the City of the Dead.* Children ran and jumped onto the backs of the trucks and carts, makeshift school buses.

"The Copts have been the garbage collectors of Cairo for over fifty years," the young man in the front passenger seat said with marked disgust. "They use pigs to eat the unusable garbage. The women—we call them the *zabbalin*—use recycled paper and cloth to produce all sorts of things . . . you know, like clothes and carpets . . . they recycle nearly 85 percent of what they collect. Wouldn't buy the stuff myself. Can't get the smell out, if you ask me." The chatty guide was delivering a travelogue while Justine was dying of fright in the backseat. Fear both chilled and heated her skin, making it difficult to focus.

Life along this marred passageway was much like that in any other Egyptian community, except for the horrible smell and narrowness of the street. Men drank their morning tea around small tables in crowded coffee houses in the midst of hovels made of crumbling clay brick huddled together like the homeless on a cold night. From their expressions of dignity and contented concentration, they might just as well have been sipping a latte at a Kansas City Starbucks. Dumbwaiter baskets were lowered from second-story windows, and small children filled them with cauliflower and baladi bread and oranges.

Justine's thoughts of jumping out of the car in this village dissipated. Her left wrist was held firmly by her backseat companion, making it impossible. She assumed that this was the community of Muqattum and they were driving toward the Church of St. Samaan.

The man in the passenger seat continued talking: "More than 20,000 people live here. They have water now, and electricity, medical services, schools—you name it. At the top of the mountain there"—he pointed up beyond the eastern buildings—"two great churches and grand scenes of the devout are carved into the sandstone walls and caves. If you can believe it, the sandstone for the pyramids came from these caves, yet they were only discovered in 1974. Just 1974. I . . ."

"Shut up," said the driver, "just shut up." The man grew quiet.

Justine's thoughts scattered, fragmented by fear. Her eyes and throat burned from the stench and the pressing heat; she fought back tears that threatened to blur her vision. *Who is this man who speaks excellent English with both pride and contempt? Is he Christian? Muslim?*

Suddenly, small hands covered the windows, smudging dozens of fingerprints across the glass. Beautiful faces with pug noses pressed against the windowpanes. With her right hand, Justine slowly lowered the pane a few inches.

"Hello, lady, welcome to Egypt. Where you from? Pencils!" The children chanted their few English phrases. Small fingers hooked over the edge of the window as they held on and began to run sideways to keep up. "Hello," she said quietly. "How old are you? I like your dress." Then she leaned closer to the window and whispered, "Tell your fathers I need help."

"Roll up that window!" the man in the front passenger's seat demanded. As he turned, she could see that he wore a priest's collar. She blinked in bewilderment. Muslims and Christians? Together? The driver rolled up the window with the electric lever, almost catching the children's fingers. "If you try anything like that again, Dr. Jenner, you will find yourself greatly inconvenienced," the priest warned, no longer the chatty guide.

She glanced back at the children, who stared in confusion.

The sedan turned to the right and sharply ascended, passing through a massive arch. The world opened up into a clean, park-like setting. Once again, Justine was amazed by larger-than-life biblical scenes carved into the sandstone cliffs. The car pulled up to the side of the Church of St. Samaan. Her "protector" in the backseat released her wrist. She fiercely reclaimed her hand and rubbed the deadened nerves.

The priest opened Justine's door and took firm hold of her right hand, while her backseat companion took hold of her left wrist once again. *I feel like I'm five years old.* "You can let go of my hands now," she said.

"We wouldn't want you to fall, my lady," said her backseat companion. "These steps can be treacherous. It's much safer if we hold on to you until we get to the office," he said with oozing sarcasm.

The office? The office? "A job interview?" she asked, mocking his tone. Her captors ignored her.

The driver of the sedan slowly backed the car into the far side of the parking lot as Justine was led down an inclining walk to the side entrance of the huge church dug out of the mountain. Hundreds of stadium seats ascended upward and descended downward toward a stage far below. An overhanging natural sandstone ceiling covered the entire stadium. Justine stopped in her tracks, forcing her companions to stop as well, as she took in the gaping vastness before her. Thousands could fit into this church. A massive painting of

The Last Supper, so primitive that it bore little resemblance to DaVinci's, stretched across the top of the stage, which was encircled by lights, speakers, and scenes of the crucifixion. The soft sandstone walls surrounding the stage were carved with more biblical scenes, nearly as large as the ones on the cliffs. Doves flew in and out of the enormous space while women cleaned the stairs by brushing wood chips across the shiny stones. The two men jerked Justine forward, down into the well of the church, across the wooden stage, and into the small room beyond.

A youthful man, thin and bearded, casually smoked a cigarette and drank tea while he sat erect in a fragile wooden chair in the back of the office. He rose when Justine and her escorts entered the room. She was led to a chair facing an inner wall of the office. The carved wall above her announced: "If your right eye offends you, pluck it out. Matthew 29:19." She began to tremble uncontrollably, grasping her own shoulders in an unsuccessful attempt to steady herself. After a few moments, she managed to say: "Fine theater."

The man at the table walked toward her. In spite of his youth, he projected an air of refined, well-bred authority. "Let me introduce myself and the others," he said graciously. "My name is Hussein, and this is Anwar"—he motioned to the travel guide, whom Justine now recognized as one of the novitiates at the Church of Saint Barbara.

"Your driver is Fathi. I believe you met in the Khan and on the desert road." He bowed slightly as though acknowledging an old friend, revealing the gun protruding from his jacket pocket. "And your other companion, who I understand rescued you from the busy street this morning, you may call Youssra. We only want to talk with you. If you cooperate, understand our views, you need not worry about your safety."

Justine stopped listening as she stared at the man who had introduced himself as Hussein. He looked familiar, yet she was sure she hadn't seen him before. "What do you mean, you only want to talk to me? Your friends here ran us off the desert road. We could have been killed. And what about the note? And the kidnapping? Are you members of Al Qaeda?"

"Serious charges, Dr. Jenner. I must admit, some of my colleagues have a flair for the dramatic. Too many American movies. Please accept my apologies," said Hussein, speaking in the classical Arabic used only by more educated Egyptians. Moving his chair to face Justine, he cautiously set his burning cigarette on the end of the small table.

"Your apologies are not accepted! What do you want to talk with me about?" she demanded defiantly, although her chest was tight with fear.

"There is a case of a certain book—a codex, I believe," began Hussein. "We have concerns."

"Concerns? Concerns about what? I don't even know what book you're talking about," she insisted, employing the most righteous and confident tone she could muster.

"Questions . . . questions, Dr. Jenner. If you'll be patient, I'll explain. I believe you met a young man named Michael in the Church of St. Sergius on the day of the earthquake. A colleague of Father Anwar, here." The priest bowed slightly. "When Michael aimed his flashlight into the crypt to find you, he saw you pick up something. Now, we didn't know what it was, of course, but further information suggests it may be a leather codex having some relationship to the Holy Family."

"Your information?" she demanded, now thoroughly disconcerted.

"I choose not to reveal all of our sources, Dr. Jenner," Hussein said dryly.

"My father works in the small kitchen in the Rare Books Library," said Youssra proudly. "Small, but adequate for making tea and biscuits."

Hussein frowned at Youssra's indiscretion.

Justine stared at the eager young man as her memory captured the small, bent elderly man who regularly delivered tea to Ibrahim's office. She turned back to Hussein. "What questions would concern both Muslims and Christians? Some of you are Muslim and some Christian, I presume."

"You observe correctly. We are of both faiths. I find that highly gratifying, don't you? We have so little common ground, but this issue is one upon which we find some agreement."

"What common ground are you referring to?" she pressed.

"The importance of Mary's purity, for one." Hussein stared at Father Anwar, then back to Justine, changing course. "We share a belief in the vital role played by the prophet Jesus. If this book belonged to someone who may have known him, we want to make sure its contents would not threaten those be-liefs. You might think of this as a preemptive strike, as you Americans like to say." He grinned for the first time. Perfect teeth, flashing black eyes. "While we don't know what's in the codex, we also don't wish to take chances."

Mary's purity? "What makes you think the contents would challenge those beliefs?" she asked. A wave of panic thundered through her. *Mary's purity? What is he talking about, and why did he change course in the middle of his ex-planation? How could he have discovered that the codex had anything to do with Mary? Even I don't know that. The missing pages . . . but why would he take a few pages and not the whole codex?*

"Don't be naïve, Dr. Jenner. Faith is based on shared beliefs that cannot be shaken without upsetting the balance of society. That's why we vigilantly guard against apostasy, and against the Western obsession with grasping, touching, analyzing. The Nag Hammadi find was a crushing blow to both faiths. Sayings by Jesus that contradict the New Testament. Very disruptive."

Father Anwar appeared shocked; apparently he wasn't familiar with Nag Hammadi.

Justine stared at the priest, then back at Hussein.

"The Holy Family is an important link between our religions," continued Hussein, bowing ever so slightly toward Father Anwar. "You undoubtedly know that churches are being burned in Alexandria. Well-meaning terrorists are striking at our tourist lifeline on the Sinai. Economic unrest has led to religious strife and violence. It has always been so."

"Well-meaning terrorists?" she asked with a strained laugh.

"'Terrorist' is a Western word, quickly adopted by the Jews to condemn Palestinians," said Hussein. "Those who commit acts of violence in the name of Islam are defenders of the faith, as well as defenders of our lands from Western occupation. Yet such acts are a heavy blow to our economy. It's a dilemma."

"To you, perhaps. But why are you talking to me? What do you want of me? I'm not in possession of any such book."

"Our experience tells us that foreign scholars who discover our treasures hold a great deal of the power over their fate. Take your father, for instance.

He has managed to keep certain discoveries out of the public eye, as have other archaeologists. We suspect you will have much to say about bringing the contents of the book to light—or not. There will be choices." He grabbed his cigarette, threw it on the floor and stamped it out.

"I'm not an archeologist," insisted Justine. Deeply shaken by the reference to her father, her voice trembled. "I'll have little to say in the matter."

"Helplessness does not become you, Justine," Hussein said coldly. "You *will* have a great deal to say. We want to make sure you consider the consequences."

"And they are?" *Damn. I wish I hadn't asked.*

"I prefer to speak in generalities here, since the full ramifications in this situation are not as yet known. Let me just say that religious violence, once it starts, is difficult to contain. You may want to consider your career in the Middle East, and that of your father."

"You seem to know a great deal about my father. So you should know that his work now takes him in other directions."

"Roads may lead him elsewhere, but he always returns to Egypt. In the future, you may find the name 'Jenner' *persona non grata* in this part of the world. Lives are at stake, including the lives of your friends. Professor Andrea . . ."

"Andrea?" Justine's mouth went dry. "Why are you threatening her?"

"Nadia . . . Let's just say we keep track of the people who are important in your life, including a certain young man named Nasser."

She began to scream. "You terrorists! You have no right, no authority to demand anything!"

Hussein calmly lit another cigarette, placed it in his left hand, stepped forward, and slapped her hard across the face, with such force that her chair spun out from under her and she fell backward onto the stone floor. Tears rushed to her eyes as blood surged down the side of her swelling mouth.

Gently, she touched her face and felt her jaw. She managed to slowly rise on both elbows, hair sticking to the blood on her face. She had difficulty focusing, the world spinning out of control. Closing her eyes, she forced her mind back into the conversation, yet didn't speak. *Who is this man?*

Hussein left her on the floor and blocked the young priest from helping her. He drew up a chair and faced her. "This is what I want," he began.

There was noise outside—footsteps on the wooden stage. Fathi and Youssra moved to block the door. Fathi drew his gun just as two men pushed past them and entered the office. The two guards looked to Hussein for instructions. He waved them off.

Amir stared at Justine, then at Hussein. "Zachariah! What have you done?" He grabbed hold of Hussein by the neck, lifted him off the chair and threw him against the wall, then rushed toward Justine and put an arm around her to help her stand.

"Zachariah?" she mumbled through her swelling mouth, pushing Amir away, plopping back down on the slab floor. "Who's Zachariah?"

"That would be me, Dr. Jenner." The man who'd called himself Hussein straightened his body and adjusted his collar.

"Amir," she shrieked, nearly hysterical, making no effort to get up by herself. "I knew you were in on this when I saw you in the Khan! You and your brother! *You* took the missing pages."

Zachariah grinned and took a long draw on his cigarette. Having his brother accused amused him.

"In on what, Justine? What are you talking about?" demanded Amir. He made no further move to help her.

"I've been kidnapped and threatened by your brother—and these other men." As she waved a hand toward the others, the second new arrival caught her attention. "Mohammed," she gasped. "What are you doing with these criminals?"

"Amir requested my help," Mohammed said seriously. He came over and helped Justine to stand, then set her fallen chair upright and sat her down. "You can trust him," he said quietly.

"A Muslim doing bidding for the Copts," Zachariah sneered. "The Prophet would not be pleased."

Mohammed moved aggressively toward Zachariah, but Amir stepped into his path. "Not now, Mohammed," he warned with a glance.

Amir looked at Justine, then his brother. "When Justine didn't show up at St. Sergius this morning and the boab assured me she had gone out, I feared that something had happened. Grandfather told us the tale of St. Samaan when we were boys, but it's taken me a couple of days to make the connection between the story and the warning you slipped under her door. I suspected you, but at first I couldn't understand why a newly converted Muslim would be in a Christian church." He glared at Father Anwar, who lowered his eyes. "What tricks does the Brotherhood have you performing now, Zach?"

Zachariah snorted. "And as you know, Anwar and I were friends before I converted, and he understands that we still share a few common goals. We've merely been having a pleasant conversation with Dr. Jenner. I believe she understands the gravity of the situation."

"You've gone too far this time," said Amir sadly. "She's hurt, and I can't help you any longer."

Justine interrupted. "Zachariah and his friends seem to think that I am in possession of a book that may be important in understanding the Holy Family. They said it would not be 'healthy' for me, my father, or Andrea if information came to light that would contradict beliefs shared by both Christians and Muslims." *Best to leave Nasser out of this.* "How do they know about the codex, Amir?"

Amir's eyes narrowed as he glared at his brother. Bending down on his haunches, he gazed up into Justine's eyes and spoke to her as though there was no one else in the room. "Justine," he said softly. "I know I've been distracted, secretive. When you found me in the Khan I was looking for my brother. My parents and grandfather have been panicked and I've been following up on leads, trying to find him. Certainly before he did anything like this." He glanced at his brother with bitterness. "My brother and I went our different ways when he joined the Brotherhood. Please reconsider, Justine, I am not the person you're accusing me of being . . ."

Justine watched him closely, her eyes filling with tears. She was silent. Confused.

Amir's eyes softened, a pleading expression washing through them.

She took a deep breath and let it flow slowly through her aching body. "I'm so sorry, Amir. I do believe you."

"As a recent convert, it would seem you may be overstepping your bounds," observed Mohammed, speaking directly to Zachariah.

"Not at all. I've been asked by MBI and certain leaders in the Coptic Church to help stabilize religious strife in Egypt. The Western world must be our target, not each other," Zachariah said with the pride of someone who is chosen.

"MBI?" asked Justine, dabbing her lip with Amir's handkerchief.

"Muslim Brotherhood International," responded Mohammed darkly. "An expanded version of the MB working throughout the Islamic world to teach fundamentalists how to win sympathy and elections. Hezbollah. Hamas. Even the Syrians."

"Very astute, Mohammed. Surely you must find the effort admirable," suggested Zachariah.

"Not at all," replied Mohammed. "Islamic countries like Egypt can't enter modern history under Shariah Law. A society based upon such law only dredges up our historical failures and cripples our chances of economic development. Throughout history the real catalyst for religious change has been the rejection of violence."

"Well said, my friend," said Amir admiringly, giving Zachariah and his colleagues a sweeping look of contempt. Zachariah returned his glare.

"A naïve worldview. Undoubtedly that is why you and Amir are friends. Two of a kind." Zachariah turned toward Justine. "Just keep in mind what we've talked about, Dr. Jenner. This is a dangerous world."

"It is you who are now in danger, my brother," Amir said. "I assume that Dr. Jenner is free to go." He took Justine by the hand and led her toward the door. Mohammed followed. Fathi drew his gun and stepped forth to block their escape, but Zachariah scoffed and nodded to his companion to let them pass.

On the slow drive out of Muqattum, the three discussed Amir's intention to work with the police to arrest Zachariah. "You would have your brother arrested?" Justine asked, incredulous. "Are you sure?"

"I can't protect him any longer. He's dangerous. Do you agree, Mohammed?"

Mohammed concurred, so they stopped at the police station near the Citadel. Amir's eyes were moist as he, rather than Justine, signed the report. They both knew that a report signed by a woman held less weight. "This is the most difficult thing I've had to do, but not as difficult as telling my parents and grandfather. Grandfather will be especially distressed. But I have no other choice."

Two hours later, Justine and Amir sat in the emergency room at Ain Shams University hospital, she holding an ice pack to her jaw. As soon as they'd left the police station, Amir had insisted she have her jaw X-rayed. They'd let Mohammed off at the Heliopolis bus stop as they crossed town.

"I swear, Amir, emergency rooms are alike the world over. Crowded and sterile." She noticed that he'd rolled up the sleeves of his soiled cotton shirt. "It looks as if you were doing some digging in St. Sergius," she said, curiosity overcoming the pain.

"I'd just gotten started on the east wall of the crypt when I realized something was very wrong. You were too late, even for a woman." He grinned. "The next time I enter the crypt, you'll be with me. Now, no more talking," he said, gently placing his warm hand over her mouth.

She kept drifting off, twice nearly falling out of the chair.

"It could be a concussion," said Amir, gently squeezing her shoulders. "You need to stay awake."

She knew she needed to talk in order to stay conscious. "Zachariah knows more about the codex than we do, Amir. How is that possible? He kept saying something about Mary's purity—what did he mean?"

The startled look that crossed Amir's face was genuine. "It means that he has seen the missing pages of the codex. Let me show you a photo I took after you first brought the codex to my grandfather." He turned on his mobile phone, pulled up the photo, and handed the phone to her. It was the cover page of the codex, written in Aramaic. "The first word, 'KTWbH,' is Aramaic for 'book,' meaning 'little book'—something like a diary or journal. Andrea and grandfather knew what this meant right away. Even without the benefit of our experts, it wouldn't have been difficult for Zachariah to find someone to translate this page."

Justine blinked and stared as Amir spoke the title of the codex: "Diary of Mary of Nazareth."

CHAPTER 17

———✦———

I F YOUR LIFE CAN PASS BEFORE YOUR EYES IN the moments before you are assured of dying, surely your life can pass by measurably well in just a few weeks. For Justine, the following weeks raced by as though time was pushing up against itself. It was curious how waiting became its own form of time . . . waiting for her face to heal . . . waiting for the carbon dating on the codex . . . waiting, if she could call it that, for the next stage of her affair with Nasser . . . waiting for the police to find Zachariah or for the Muslim Brotherhood to make another move . . . waiting for the school at Birqash to be reopened. The missing pages had not been found, and Mostafa was pressing for the storage of the codex in the museum safe.

Yet waiting was much too passive a notion. *Perhaps "unfolding" is a more accurate word*, she thought, her feet pounding the pavement in rhythm with her heart. "My time is improving," declared Nasser, keeping pace with her during their morning run on the Corniche. "At least I have become a 'contenda.' And I can also talk while I'm running. Well, almost," he affirmed breathlessly.

"You certainly have improved!" They shared a morning run perhaps three days a week now. The Nile's breath was steaming in the summer morning.

"You've been deep in thought for about a mile now. What's on your mind?" he asked.

"I've been thinking about these last weeks and all that has happened. So many things. Yet . . ." Justine stopped running and stood still.

"You're nervous about the presentation." Nasser reached over and pulled her ponytail gently, a gesture she found both endearing and disconcerting.

"I shouldn't be," she said. "Nadia will be with me, but I haven't met the Minister before. His background is law, so my challenge is to not to use 'educationese.'"

"You'll do fine. You really come alive when you talk about the young girls. He'll be enchanted."

"I know," she grinned, "I know." They were almost perpendicular to the Roman aqueduct and the south end of Roda Island now; Justine motioned for them to turn back toward Aisha El Taimuriyya.

"I may have to get another car one of these days," Nadia said as Justine struggled with the door on the old Renault. "What do you think?"

"I wouldn't rush into things," she laughed, turning to place her buckskin briefcase in the backseat. "After all, you've only had this car for eighteen years and"—she leaned across the seat—"175,000 miles."

"You cut me to the quick." Nadia pulled onto Qasr al-Ainy, artfully weaving into traffic. "See how nicely she handles? An old friend."

"Never sacrifice an old friend on the altar of modernity, I say," Justine said with exaggerated seriousness.

"By the way, any news on the codex? "

"Everything's a little on hold while we wait for the carbon dating from the Arizona lab. But speculations run high! I have my own."

"Oh, tell me."

"Nope. Keeping them to myself right now." Ever since Zachariah used the phrase 'Mary's purity,' Justine had been trying to discover whether it might have been possible that Jesus' mother could write. But then, she didn't want to be embarrassed, either. After all, history holds a million Marys.

Nadia rolled her eyes. "You don't want to be wrong—right?"

Justine grinned. "What can I expect today? Will the Minister have read the report?"

"Probably not. He's a very busy man." Nadia pulled into the narrow concrete garage under the Centre.

The National Education Centre was on the eleventh and twelfth floors of an office building bought by the Ministry of Education from the Americans seventeen years earlier. The dirty tan façade possessed no redeeming features. It might have stood in Alexandria or Detroit or the outskirts of Milan. The usually cluttered roofs of surrounding buildings, crowned with satellite dishes, had recently been swept and adorned with large potted plants for an impending visit by President Mubarak.

A research center, several small companies, and the Bank of Egypt shared the Centre's sharply vertical space, which was held together by two poorly functioning elevators hardly large enough to accommodate the growing number of occupants. Fortunately the air-conditioning worked better than the elevators.

The Minister's secretary invited the two women into the waiting room. A regal woman of around fifty, she projected an air of authority, as was expected in the offices of Cabinet members.

"Isn't it a bit unusual for a Minister to receive an interim report on a UNESCO project?" asked Justine as she and Nadia stood by the window, observing as bean pots and steaming corn ovens were rolled into the street fourteen stories below.

"Actually, it is. The Minister has taken a personal interest, which I think he'll explain himself."

"You may go in now," said the secretary. "Dr. Ghalib is expecting you."

"Morgan Jenner's daughter, I presume," said the Minister as he extended his hand to Justine and kissed Nadia on both cheeks.

"You presume correctly, Dr. Ghalib. Do you know my father?"

"No, but Ibrahim El Shabry is an old friend. I've heard of your father's adventures. Tell me, Nadia, how did we have the good fortunate to hire this beautiful part-American, part-Egyptian anthropologist?" he asked. Turning to Justine, he added, "I know of your mother's family also."

Justine hoped he hadn't noticed the goose bumps that had risen on her arms. She had come to expect conflicting views on her parents' adventures.

". . . so I told Dr. Jenner that we needed a fresh pair of eyes," Nadia was saying. "For a person to look at her own culture is like a fish studying water."

The Minister laughed whole-heartedly, warmly, setting Justine at ease. "I've taken a personal interest in this project, Dr. Jenner, since in the Middle East the adult literacy rate among women is only half that found in other countries.

Further, the United Nations' studies indicate a direct positive correlation between the education of young women and a thriving economy, environment,
and health of the citizens of that country." The rotund Dr. Ghalib wore a beige
Armani suit and tie adorned with miniature golden Sphinxes. His creamy
complexion and hazel eyes belied his Egyptian heritage.

"I am thoroughly convinced that your proactivity in partnering with
UNESCO to establish Community Schools for Girls will play a major role in
Egypt's development," Justine said with confidence.

He was genuinely pleased. "*Absolument.* Thank you. Let's hear what you
have for us. Tea?"

"I'd love some tea," she said. The interim report sat in front of her, several
post-its marking key pages. For nearly a half hour, she reviewed key features.
"As you know, sir, the mission of the schools is 'to provide quality, sustainable
education for all with an immediate emphasis on girls' education.' I have
found the focus on literacy, thinking skills, and leadership to show noteworthy
success. I've had a chance to observe students and teachers in the schools in
The City of the Dead, Asyut, Sohag, and Qena. Soon in the reconstructed
school in Birqash, I hope," she concluded.

The Minister was pensive. "What do you think of Asyut?" He addressed the
question to both women.

"A hotbed of radical Islam," Nadia said without hesitation. "We were lucky
to even get a school there, yet haven't found quite the same success."

"Nadia is right, I didn't find the same results at the Asyut school," admitted
Justine. "Neither in literacy nor leadership. Much more submissiveness—or,
conversely, authoritarian behavior. As you know, submissiveness can look like
cooperation. And vice versa. For instance, girls who are brought up to please,
to serve, to relinquish their own needs and desires for others may appear to be
cooperating, yet . . ."

"We've noticed strongly submissive behaviors in girls new to the schools,
regardless of age," offered Nadia. "For instance, three twelve-year-olds at Qena.
They learned to read in less than three months, but my, they were submissive."

"How do we tell the difference between submissiveness and cooperation,
Dr. Jenner?" asked the Minister pointedly.

"I struggle with that issue, sir. I am alert for girls who find their voices, speak out without undue attention to the opinions of others," she said. "Co-operation, and leadership, means that each girl has developed a point of view, and that she speaks from that point of view rather than waiting for others to tell her what to think."

The Minister nodded. "Distinguishing submissiveness from cooperation and then teaching assertiveness without bossiness—tall orders," he observed. "This is what I'm hoping for in my own daughters. Just make sure the parents are with you each step of the way. But right now, I have a Cabinet meeting." He rose and walked around the desk. "Thank you, ladies, I'll look forward to your next report. Good work."

As they walked out, Justine turned to Nadia and grinned; she felt valued and listened to. Nadia patted her on the arm and tried to call for an elevator, but the man in possession of the key was nowhere to be found, so they sauntered down the seventeen flights into the dark garage.

"Better down than up," said Nadia, breathless. "I've done that a few times!"

I hope the rest of the day goes as well, thought Justine, shifting her thoughts to her rendezvous with Amir at St. Sergius.

In spite of a successful morning, approaching the crypt in St. Sergius filled Justine with dread. But she was prepared this time; she wore heavy jeans and a T-shirt that announced the "Napa Triathlon," and her ponytail spilled out of a Giants baseball cap. She met Amir at the entrance to Old Cairo. Although engineers had propped up the ceiling and braced the walls of the crypt, he carried a bulging backpack full of flashlights, a small camera, and two microscopes.

Amir and his museum colleagues had rigged up lighting and carried in heavy equipment the morning Justine was kidnapped. He leaned and flipped a switch, filling the cavity with a glow like the Blue Grotto of Capri, although not quite so blue. Justine shivered. Amir noted her trepidation, took her by the arm, and escorted her down the now-infamous thirteen steps. "I have a gift for you," he said, pulling her camera out of his backpack.

"Amir! That's great! Where did you find it?"

"Right over here," he said. "Just sitting there. No one had been back in here since the quake."

"Thank you," she said, hugging the camera to her chest and glancing around the crypt with surprise. It wasn't as completely devastated as she'd imagined. "It's like daylight down here!" she exclaimed, grateful to find no shadows, dark corners, or lurking, imaginary menaces.

"The better to see you with," he said playfully. "Now, show me where you were standing when the earthquake hit."

Justine stood near the middle of the crypt to orient herself. She stared back at the steps, the ceiling, and the walls, this time noticing that the once-cave was deeper than it was wide. She walked to the northwest corner and stood for a moment. "Just before it began," she said, "I was running my hands across the wall, imagining what it would be like to live here. I actually said to myself, 'What stories these walls could tell!'"

"Almost psychic," he grinned.

"I think this is where I was standing and that's the pillar that forced me to the floor." The pillar had been raised and stabilized by two-by-fours. She patted it like an old friend. *After all, it kept me from being crushed.*

"That makes sense. It's almost exactly where the camera was. Your position is only three feet or so from the northwest wall, which has several areas of cracked plaster. Let's take them one at a time." Amir pulled a small flashlight and tweezer-like tool from his backpack and a magnifying glass from his leather belt—a required accessory for a proper archeologist.

Both of them explored the surface with delicate movements and open palms.

"What are your expectations?" Justine asked. "How will we know if we've found the right space, the space from which the codex may have fallen?"

"The most curious aspect of cave patina is that it forms in the shape of a cauliflower," said Amir. "On the inner face of the correct niche, we may find a cauliflower pattern that will be nearly identical to the patina on the codex."

"That's astounding! Yet it's information we don't have as yet."

"Exactly, but the designs are like fingerprints. If the two images are a fit, we'll know we've found the right spot. And it will go a long way toward solving the provenance issue." An unabashed smile flickered across his face; Amir was in his element. "I don't anticipate a second treasure, although ancient peoples kept many of their smaller possessions in cave niches—cups, shoes, pans, jewels, you'd be surprised what can be found. A team from the museum was excavating in the western desert where layered rock is stuffed with sea shells from the ice age and came across an ice pick of sharpened iron and gold fili-gree earrings wrapped in Chinese silk."

"Cauliflowers and Chinese silk! Sounds incredible," Justine exclaimed, con-tinuing to explore with her palms, her earlier fears assuaged. "Here," she said, "this niche is a few inches wide."

Amir focused the flashlight and examined the crevasse with the magnifying glass. "I see something," he said. Reaching in, he pulled a wooden spoon from the opening and held it in the air.

Justine flushed with excitement. *Who might have held that spoon? What were they eating? Warm soup on a cool November day?* She held open a large plastic Ziploc bag as Amir lowered the spoon in, then made notes on a map of the wall.

"Terrific," he exclaimed. "Now let's look for more signs of life . . ."

Hours passed, and they lost all sense of time. As they examined wall cre-vasses, they found two more small discoveries: shards from broken clay cups and four partially burnt candles.

"I see something!" Justine nearly yelled, her heart quickening. Amir stepped to her side to examine the niche, this one a little wider than the others.

"I don't see it . . . what are you seeing?"

"Something small and flat, with a pearl-like substance." She was breathless.

With the light, magnifying glass, and tweezers, Amir located and gently extracted the object from its resting place.

"What is it? It's definitely man-made. I can't quite make them out, but it looks like there are some kind of carvings around the edges!"

"Possible. This niche looks large enough to be the location of the codex as well." He grinned, masking his own excitement in exchange for hers. "We'll get an imprint of the niche and see what we have."

They turned to one another. Justine threw her arms around his neck. He smelled like musk in her arms, his warmth blending with her own for the full length of their bodies. They held on for several moments.

∾

"Where have you been?" asked Nasser, extending a glass of wine. "You look as though you've crawled through the sewer."

While Nasser had a key to her apartment, Justine resisted living with him. It was inappropriate behavior in Egypt, but that wasn't her only reservation. She also needed her own time and independence, something that she couldn't find in the continual presence of another. "Not exactly," she said, removing her T-shirt in exchange for another, changing from her filthy jeans into yoga pants, and throwing her ball cap to the floor. "We were in the crypt, searching for a niche." Barefoot, she sat down and swung her legs over the arm of her favorite overstuffed chair.

"We?" he asked.

"Amir and I. You'll remember, the day I was kidnapped we'd made plans to return to the crypt so that I could point out where I found the codex," she said, still flushed with excitement.

Nasser kissed her lightly on the lips. "I hope you found it." He paused. "Have you talked with Amir about the hunt for his brother?"

"No. No, I haven't," she admitted. "I trust he'll tell me when they learn something."

"Perhaps . . ." he said, turning toward the kitchen. "I've prepared some lunch for us. It'll be ready shortly." They both heard the light knock on the door.

"I'll get it," offered Nasser, starting to get up.

"No," said Justine. "I'll get it." She set her glass down on the coffee table and walked toward the door. Amir stood outside. "I didn't hear the elevator," she said, waving him in.

"I came up the stairs," he said, turning into the living room. "You left this in the car." He handed over her denim jacket. At the sight of Nasser, his face and voice tensed. "I need to go, but just one more thing."

"Please join us," offered Nasser, with the casual assurance of a man who knows he has already won the trophy, if not the crown. "I'm Nasser," he said, extending his hand. Justine flushed. She hadn't thought about how the two men would meet.

"I don't want to interrupt," said Amir, ignoring the outstretched hand, then proceeding with exaggerated formality. "I just received notice that a preliminary meeting has been set up with our team for tomorrow afternoon in the Rare Books Library conference room. The Jewish scholar Isaac Yardeni will be joining us to prepare for the meeting with Mostafa and Al Rasul."

"I'll be there," she assured him with equal formality. "What time?"

"Four o'clock. Shall I pick you up?"

"I'll be coming straight from The Fayoum," she said, feeling as though she was involved in a clandestine affair—which, of course, she was.

"I'll be going, then." Amir walked toward the door unescorted.

Nasser called after him in an even tone, "How did you manage to get your brother out of the country, Amir?"

Amir slammed the door behind him. He didn't wait for the elevator.

CHAPTER 18

———⟨∞⟩———

"How could you say that?" Justine demanded of Nasser as Amir's footsteps faded down the stairwell. "You've humiliated him."

"Do you have any doubt that Amir got Zachariah out of the country to avoid his being imprisoned?" Nasser questioned, poised to walk into the kitchen to finish lunch.

"Perhaps, but keep in mind that he was the person who went to the police. Signed the police report."

"A good cover."

"I'm not sure I wouldn't have done the same thing if he were my brother. He'd rescued him from a number of scrapes before. Regardless, Amir is a valued colleague. That's more important to me right now."

"More important than your safety?" Nasser was incredulous.

"More important than my safety." *Must all men see it as their duty to protect me?*

"Are you attracted to him?" pressed Nasser.

"Attracted to Amir? Absolutely not. But he has become a friend." Still, she couldn't meet Nasser's gaze. In her head, she saw Amir's penetrating black eyes. "Besides, the man I'm attracted to is sitting right here, right now." She smiled.

Nasser visibly relaxed and gave her one of his crooked grins. "You're going to The Fayoum tomorrow? May I drive you?"

"I'm going with Nadia," she said, leaning over to kiss him. "Lunch ready?"

Nasser caught her around the waist with both hands and pulled her toward him.

∽

By late May, the summer heat was stifling—especially in the Rare Books Library conference room, where outdated fans stirred the heat like a convection oven. Lines of wooden tables and chairs surrounded by blackboards gave the room the impression of a junior high classroom. Justine, having arrived back in town from a school in The Fayoum less an hour before the meeting, joined the investigative team in conversation.

Seated near the end of the oblong cedar table, Andrea swept her ebony hair off her neck and addressed her colleagues: "We are fairly certain now that the title page says: 'The KTWbH of Mary of Nazareth.' I'll remind you all that KTWbH is Aramaic for 'little book,' something personal, like a journal. And while 'Mary of Nazareth' is not an unusual name, when we consider where it was found . . . well . . ." She smiled and paused. "The title page was one of the missing pages, though, as you know, Amir had smartly photographed it before the pages disappeared. Now that we have the missing pages back in our possession, however, we can proceed with the translation."

As surprised exclamations erupted around her, it was clear that Andrea relished controlling this news.

"The pages were returned? How? Why didn't you call us?" demanded Justine, glancing at Amir, who glared at Andrea. Ibrahim fiddled with his teacup. The man sitting to Ibrahim's right, a stranger to Justine, appeared confused by the fuss.

"Easy, Justine," said Andrea. "The pages simply appeared in a manila envelope on my desk at AUC this morning. I didn't have time to call you before we arrived here. And I don't know the answers to those questions. Does it matter?"

"Of course it matters. If someone would remove and steal pages from such a valuable artifact, what else might they steal? Who can we trust?" Justine glanced around the room. *Am I the only one upset here?*

Amir appeared agitated. He cleared his throat, attracting Ibrahim's attention. The professor stared at his grandson and blinked, his face brightening as though he were emerging from a cloud of confusion. "Amir! Did you find anything in the crypt yesterday? You and Justine?"

"We did," Amir nodded. "We're not sure what it is, but it has pearl-like qualities and possible carvings around the edges. The object is in the lab being X-rayed and cleaned, and the photos of the niche are being developed." His pride in the discovery was evident in spite of the awkward tension in the air regarding the returned pages.

"The item is about as big as the palm of my hand, sir," added Justine, holding up her hand, allowing herself to be momentarily distracted by this conversation about their new find.

Ibrahim swallowed, his Adam's apple bobbing up and down. He turned and patted the shoulder of the man next to him. "This is my good friend and colleague, Dr. Isaac Yardeni. He's an expert on Semitic languages and Jewish life in the Diaspora. Isaac has met with Andrea and me a couple of times. It's an honor to have him with us."

Dr. Yardeni bowed slightly.

Both Justine and Amir leaned across the table to shake hands and express their welcome.

When Andrea spoke again, all eyes turned to her. "Quite thrilling, Amir. Justine. I can hardly wait to learn more about this object. In the meantime, I'm confident we'll be able to translate these newly found pages before our meeting with Mostafa the day after tomorrow." Her palm rested on the manila folder.

Justine rolled her eyes. It was not lost on her that Andrea no longer referred to the pages as "missing" but as "newly found."

"Omar Mostafa informed us that the technical data is nearly ready. We may be able to see the carbon dating information by tomorrow morning," added Isaac. "I'm very impressed that so much of the diary had been translated by the time I arrived." A short, scholarly man with a goatee and a wiry head of hair that reminded Justine of Nadia, he wore a black bowtie and suit jacket worn shiny at the elbows. A friend of Ibrahim's for generations, Yardeni was staying with him in his refurbished apartment under the Roman aqueduct.

"I am most eager to see the physical results," said Ibrahim. "If it confirms our hunches and translations, we have an amazing discovery on our hands."

Justine watched Ibrahim closely, then addressed all three translators, her voice edgy. "From your translations so far, can we really assume that this is the journal or diary of the Virgin Mary, Jesus' mother? This just seems beyond belief!"

Slow grins widened on Amir's and Andrea's faces. The excitement in the room was palpable.

"Careful, careful," begged Isaac. "Until we have the physical evidence . . ."

But anticipation pushed Justine forward. "What kind of a woman was she? How did she learn to read and write?" *Was she the smart, insightful woman that my mother assumed she was?*

"These are—were—challenging questions," said Andrea, pulling a warm bottle of Evian from her briefcase. "We ran into difficulties with sequencing and time because of some difficulty in understanding her maturation. Then, it occurred to us that she would have added pages to the diary. As you know, in a codex, the flat sheets of papyrus are added in the middle of the book, and then fastened to the center by untying the original pages and retying the codex back together. We came to a place where her son was about two or three years old, but from there the codex skips to his seventh year, and then returns to his fourth year. But I think we've figured it out." She took a long swig of water.

"You refer to 'her son.' Jesus?" Impatient with Andrea's technical description of the pages, Justine didn't wait for a response. "I didn't think women were literate then . . . are we sure this was written by a woman? Not about a woman?"

"The author mentions that her grandmother Faustina from Mt. Carmel taught her to read and write," Andrea said, teasingly postponing a response about Jesus.

"And 'sure' is like 'proof,' my dear," answered Ibrahim, more animated than earlier. "We infer from what we have."

"You spoke of several different years. Do we know how long the family lived in Egypt?" Amir shifted in his chair. His eyes sparkled with amusement as he watched Justine. She could hardly sit still.

"There are entries into her son's eighth year," said Isaac. "But the author didn't write every day. Sometimes she would go for long periods without

writing. We can partially understand her by noting what she chose as important enough to record. For instance, there are many entries in which she and
her son—she and Jesus—are together and she is teaching him. I'm relatively
sure that she was both literate and very smart."

"Then you do think it is the diary of the Virgin Mary and that she is writing
about Jesus!"

"That's correct. Wouldn't you agree?" Andrea turned toward Ibrahim and
Isaac. Both men nodded cautiously, eyes wary, as though full agreement would
be a violation of some kind.

"She was his teacher, Jesus' teacher," Andrea said without hesitation. "Certainly not his only one, but perhaps his most important. The author of the
codex was quite insightful about nature and her own emotions."

"It seems to me you are inferring a great deal," said Amir, rapidly making
his own notes. "That can be dangerous."

Dangerous? What does dangerous mean in this context?

"Remember, until we receive the physical data, we're on shaky ground,"
cautioned Ibrahim. Justine watched a current of pain fill his eyes—but why,
she wasn't sure.

"But for our purposes here today, we are assuming that the author is the
mother of Jesus." Justine required clarification on this. "It does give texture
and meaning to what we know about the Holy Family. The experience of Jews
at that time."

"You're right, *chérie*. For instance, sometimes in the diary she is sad, reflecting on losses she's experienced." Andrea read from her notes: "'I hold Rachel.
Praise God. My heart hurts with memories of holding my own little girl.'"

"She had another child? A girl?" Justine was nearly shouting. "How could
that be? What happened to her?"

"She died," said Ibrahim with far-away sadness, as though he was experiencing Mary's loss. "She died."

"Surely, if God was with her, He wouldn't have taken her child away," insisted Amir. "Could you be mistaken?"

"I'm afraid he's not mistaken," said Isaac, his voice soft, raspy. He looked
from Amir to Justine, then to Andrea. "She writes often of the child."

"It would appear that she died on the journey from Palestine and was buried at Mataria," added Andrea.

"Mataria? Just north of downtown Cairo?" Justine felt lightheaded with this news. There was no doubt that it would shake the world.

"There must be a reason, one we can't understand," said Amir politely, his pen frozen in mid-air. Justine could almost see his Coptic upbringing forcing itself into his professional mind.

"God always has His reasons," echoed Isaac.

"Does he?" challenged Andrea with more than a little bitterness.

"I've found it so," said Isaac, alternating hands as he smoothed his wiry goatee.

"And the Holocaust, Isaac?" snapped Andrea. "You've found a reason?" As soon as the words left her mouth, regret washed over her face.

"No," said Isaac, turning away.

"I'm sorry," said Andrea, catching Ibrahim's glare. "I'm sorry," she repeated. Her voice trembled.

What just happened here? I've never seen Andrea diminish herself, even when her own words stung or discounted others. There is so much here I don't yet understand.

Ibrahim moved slowly across the room, parting the painful divide between history and self. "I will order tea from my new man," he said, "and then we will have another story." He lifted the phone, requested tea. The others shifted as well; their moods were grave, and a theatre cast change was needed to alter the tempo of the dialogue.

"So," began Ibrahim after a short break, cups of tea scattered across the table. He lowered himself into a rickety chair at the end of the table and reached into his pile of notes. "This large bird is an eagle, to be sure," he said, holding up a poorly sketched drawing of a bird with extended wings. The bird was perched on top of an ornate gate. "According to the author—and her drawing is better than mine—this is the gate to the temple in Jerusalem. Apparently, when Herod rebuilt the temple area, he had this image of an eagle placed on top of the gate. The Jewish population was inflamed, as you can imagine," he said, glancing at Isaac, who had regained his composure.

"The Jews seethed with anger at the audacity of a craven idol," continued Isaac. "A group of young Israelites climbed the gate and James pulled down the offending bird. Herod's men sought out the offenders, torturing and crucifying them all. But Joseph's son, James, was only nine at the time. He was released in deference to his youth."

"So this is why they left Palestine?" asked Amir, somewhat impatiently. "This makes more sense than the biblical story assuming a chase by Herod, who, judging from historical records, died before Jesus was born."

Ibrahim nodded agreement. "One of the reasons, to be sure, my boy. Along with a collapsing economy and oppressive Roman rule. The author expressed her fear of James' impulsiveness and Joseph's yearning to travel to the land of Moses. To Egypt. Listen: 'My Joseph says the land of Moses will embrace us. We prepare to go to Egypt, a long journey, difficult . . .' the following segment is blurred, then: 'Rachel will be at my side.' We believe Rachel was the midwife who delivered Jesus."

"No command by Herod to kill all baby boys under the age of two? No angel Gabriel telling them when to leave and when to return?" asked Justine, pacing the conference room in agitation. She paused occasionally to grip a chair as though she intended to sit down, which she did not. "As it is written in Matthew?"

"So it would seem," confirmed Isaac. "I'm acquainted with the incident of the eagle and the Temple gate, but of course I didn't know that James was involved." When he spoke, he often stood as well, drawing himself up to his full height, which, beside Justine and Andrea, accomplished little.

"As we know, James became one of the key leaders of the Christian movement after his brother's death, but as a young man he appears to have been impulsive, impatient," said Ibrahim, leaning forward and rubbing his knees to relieve their stiffness. "Now I must ask: How will our people, even our colleagues, handle this information? This diary shakes the foundations of both Christian and Muslim faiths. It undermines the credibility of the New Testament and the Koran: it changes why and how the Holy Family left Palestine and how long they remained in Egypt, and it presents Mary as the mother of more than one child." His tired eyes drifted toward the tall, open window, fixing his stare on a hoopoe bird perched in one of the garden's majestic date palms.

Amir motioned to the others that the time had come to adjourn the meeting. None of these questions would be answered quickly.

As they prepared to leave, conversations sparked and passions varied. For Isaac, unearthing the Messiah mythology and confirming a portrait of Jesus as a practicing Jew was not a displeasing idea. Andrea was captivated by the myth-shattering significance of this find—and its implications for her career. She, and Justine as well, gladly embraced Mary's independence and strength. Ibrahim and Amir, on the other hand, were experiencing a more difficult struggle: the pull of professionalism against a lifetime of Coptic indoctrination. Amir seemed more open to evidence than his grandfather and more able to reconstruct some of his most basic assumptions. Ibrahim now seemed fatigued and reticent, growing more silent, yet Justine knew how deeply moved he must be by touching a book that had been handled by the Mother of God.

Justine rose and moved closer to Andrea. "What was that business with Isaac?" she asked. "Your remorse? Your apology?"

Andrea swallowed and looked down. "Certain topics are beyond the pale, Justine. Too painful to broach. Isaac's parents and two sisters were exterminated at Dachau. But he was caught in a protective bubble of air between the bodies of his parents and rescued by a girl of nine—a girl who would eventually become his wife. A woman he loved, but whose face reminded him daily of his slain family."

Andrea left quickly to teach a class across campus; Isaac moved more slowly, taking each step in turn as he aimed for a bench in the garden where he would await his friend. Justine stopped at the garden's edge and stood still for several moments. Amir waited. Justine pivoted and asked him to return to the conference room with her. "I want to talk with your grandfather."

Amir's eyes narrowed, but he turned around without comment and followed her back upstairs.

They found Ibrahim still sitting at the table. Head down. Justine pulled up a chair beside him. She spoke gently. "You took the pages, didn't you, Ibrahim?" Such a confrontation of an elder was not in her nature; in fact, she could not remember ever having done it before. None of her grandparents had ever witnessed an indignant granddaughter.

Amir cringed, but remained quietly standing.

Ibrahim glanced up with watery eyes and nodded. "I've disappointed you. My grandson. Myself." His eyes implored her. "When I read those first few pages, the gravity, the burden of my beliefs, weighed down on me with such force that I felt alone in the desert. Perhaps I thought I had misinterpreted them, that further examination would change their meaning, I'm not sure . . . but in that moment, I couldn't let those pages out of my possession."

"What gravity? What burden? What information startled you so much that it caused you to act irrationally?" Justine demanded, if softly, her voice falling. "What do those pages say to you, sir?"

Ibrahim stalled, rubbing his knees yet again, staring at the bulging floorboards.

She turned to Amir. "You knew all along."

Shadows filled the room, dimly lit by a single hanging bulb. She could feel his avoidance. "I didn't know who else could have taken the pages, since it had to be someone who could read Aramaic and had access to the codex. The choices were limited." His voice trailed off, as if in disappointment.

She turned back to Ibrahim. "It doesn't seem like the behavior of a man who pursues the Tao, who understands that there are many truths."

Ibrahim flinched. "I know, my child. It sounds more like the young boy who was a true believer, who became frightened by so great a challenge to his beliefs . . ." The evening glow against harsh artificial light carved his wrinkles into a macabre mask. "That young boy has come back to visit me recently. He deeply believed the story about the Mother of God being a virgin—Jesus' avoidance of the human struggle for breath, of the birthing process. I found myself confronting the lingering question, the haunting question: Does the revelation that Mary was not a virgin mean that Jesus was not the Son of

God?" Ibrahim paused breathlessly, sagging further into himself, into the small upright chair.

Justine gasped. "So that's what's in those few pages—that Mary was not a virgin?" *That's what Zachariah meant by Mary's purity.*

Ibrahim nodded. "I know the legend of the ancients about immaculate conception isn't essential. God works His wonders in many ways, and yet . . ." He murmured this almost inaudibly.

"Who sits here before us now?" Justine asked more gently.

He grinned weakly. "Professor Ibrahim El Shabry, a man in his eighties who has put away his younger self." He paused, and his next words surprised her. "It may help to talk to your mother."

"To my mother? Why?" Justine was taken aback.

"Lucrezia's a wise woman. I've watched her negotiate difficult situations over the years. She may have some helpful insights about the codex."

The codex? What does she know about the codex? As she watched the resignation in Ibrahim's eyes, Justine felt something that she'd hoped never to feel for someone she admired: pity. With this realization, her anger began to dissipate. Without further comment, she patted Ibrahim on the hand, picked up her belongings, and headed for the door.

Amir walked her to the top of the stairs. "Justine, wait . . . I'm the one who placed the missing pages on Andrea's desk this morning." Without saying more, he turned back toward the conference room and his grandfather.

CHAPTER 19

⸺⸙⸺

"**D**AD? IS THAT YOU? WHERE ARE YOU?" Justine asked into her mobile phone. Curled up in her bed since 5 a.m., she'd been sporadically watching the early edition of BBC news and thinking about the team meeting set for this morning. How would they react to the findings in Mary's diary? She was apprehensive.

"I'm in Cuzco," Morgan Jenner said. "First time in months I've been near a reliable phone. I've taken a warm shower, poured a scotch over real ice, and settled in for a talk with my favorite daughter."

Her father's warmth and good humor inevitably made her laugh. "Your only daughter, I assume." She could imagine her ruggedly handsome father slung carelessly into a large armchair, staring at the Cuzco lights framing the night skyline. *How much I've missed him.*

"Still sassy, I see."

"Learned it from the best of teachers. Any earth-shaking news from the Peruvian front?"

"Too early to tell, but some interesting clues. We're digging near Chinchero, an important population center during Inca times. What at first looked like large niches for holding bodies, much like a crypt, may turn out to be scroll niches, an essential feature of a library." Whenever Morgan Jenner was desperately trying to be casual, his voice revealed an unmistakable, suppressed excitement.

"That's what you were hoping to find, isn't it?"

"I don't want to jump to conclusions. You know I like to be careful."

Justine's mind raced back to comments made by Nadia, Ibrahim, and even Zachariah about her father and his finds here in Egypt. Had he concealed something for political or religious reasons, or refused to bring it to light due to lack of evidence? "Dad, there are a few persistent rumors here about a possible find made by you and Ibrahim years ago. At Darshur. About the Passover and whether it happened at all."

A long pause. "That old dog? I'm amazed the rumors are still alive. Nothing to it, honey. We found something of interest suggesting a bargain of sorts."

"I'm surprised that you weren't more careful. Didn't take any photos . . ."

His voice was edgy now. "Didn't think of it at the time. Just made a few notes. *Why* is this so important to you?"

That question was hard to handle. *Why is it so important?* "It seems to go to credibility. My credibility now. I don't like defending you without all the facts."

"*Defending me?* Forget about it—it was a long time ago. I made some mistakes . . ."

She could tell by his voice that the topic had come to a close, but she had little doubt that he had been careless, perhaps even complicit. Justine felt a gripping pain in her chest. "How long will you be there?" she decided to ask.

"I'll need to stay in the area for quite awhile, but may try to meet you somewhere in Europe for a short visit around Christmas."

"I would like that. How soon will you know?" she asked, attempting to sound enthusiastic. She needed time to process what she now knew: the rumors held a lot of truth.

"Within the month. As soon as our team firms up the work schedule. But enough about me. Tell me about yourself."

"There's so much to tell. A few days ago I presented my first UNESCO report to the Minister of Education. The young women in the schools are doing amazing work, and I think my report was well accepted."

"Congratulations, honey! Your first work product on your first professional job since graduation. Presented to the Minister, no less. I'm so proud of you."

Justine felt that her father's admiration was real. "Thanks, Dad. And something else is happening that Mom may have told you about."

"The codex? Your mother told me something about it. But she was rather vague." Although separated, Morgan and Lucrezia spoke when they could. Mostly about Justine. She called it long-distance chaperoning.

"Yes. The codex. I think you already know that it fell in front of me during the earthquake. During these past several weeks, a team of specialists has been working with Ibrahim and Andrea LeMartin to date and analyze the findings. Later this morning, we're meeting to review the test results. Everyone will be there." She decided not to tell him that Ibrahim had tried to suppress some of the pages. She wasn't sure why.

"A competent man, Ibrahim. I've heard about Andrea from your mother, but never met her. I assume Omar Mostafa is involved," he said evenly, though she could sense reservations.

"Uh huh. As you know, in Egypt, nothing happens without Mostafa's involvement."

"An understatement, honey," he said wryly. "And you're aware that he will take credit for any find of importance? How important is this?"

"Oh my god, it could just be the most important find in a century. Perhaps even among religious discoveries of all time. We now think it's the diary of Mary, mother of Jesus. But we won't have confirming physical data until later today." Several moments passed. "Dad? Are you still there?" Justine tapped the phone.

"I'm here, Justine. Are you safe?"

"There've been a few incidents, but don't worry; they're resolved now. Ibrahim's grandson, Amir, a friend of mine, Nasser, and the local police have been especially protective." *Perhaps too protective.* "We have reason to believe that the men who were trying to prevent the codex from coming to light have fled the country. Or at least gone underground."

"That's good to hear! As we know from the Nag Hammadi finds and the lost Gospel of Judas, once such information goes public, you will be safe. I know Amir—Ibrahim's grandson, I believe—but who is this Nasser?"

"You know him, Dad. Nasser Khalid. He was a student of yours at Berkeley. We've been seeing each other for a couple of months."

"When was he at Berkeley?"

"He was there from 2001 to 2003. Majored in archaeology. Handsome, medium height, crooked grin. You must remember him."

"No . . . no, I'm certain I don't. Justine, you may have forgotten, but I wasn't at Berkeley during most of that time—the Borneo dig was going on. I don't know a Nasser Khalid."

"Are you sure, Dad? He's got a smile that's hard to forget. He's Egyptian, but with sandy hair."

His voice turned sharp. "Justine, you know I remember the names of all of my students."

She froze, the phone turning cold in her hand. Her lungs failed to exhale. She felt lightheaded.

"Justine . . . Justine, are you all right? This relationship is serious, isn't it? Justine, answer me."

"I guess it is serious, Dad. Look, I have to think. I need a little time. Let's talk again tomorrow. Okay?" Without waiting for a response, she hung up.

Justine sat paralyzed, one foot hanging off the bed. Her mind was incoherent. Slowly she reached for her baggy running pants and big T-shirt, mechanically getting dressed. No socks. No mirrors. No thinking. No feeling. Oblivious to her frantically vibrating phone, she opened her door and ran down the six flights of stairs and onto the street below.

Blind to her surroundings, she ran. A mile north on the Corniche, the tension in her body released and she began to cry uncontrollably. As the sobs came, Justine lowered herself onto a nearby bench sheltered by the bulging roots of a giant banyan tree. Her mind loosened and fragments oozed out in staccato hysteria . . . *My father is wrong . . . his memory is going . . . he was right, Nasser lied to me . . . I'm wrong about the dates and his claims—but still, he didn't know Nasser's name. I'm not in love with Nasser, so it doesn't really matter . . .*

As the sobs subsided, a new kind of tension, one with which she was more familiar, grasped her body: the tension of growing anger. Was Nasser's mendacity more than a misleading introduction? *Did he have anything to do with running our car off the desert road? With the kidnapping?* With anger came energy. She placed both feet firmly on the cement walkway with a hand on each thigh, stretched her back, and shook her head to clear it.

Turning left across the July 23rd Bridge, she ran onto the island of Zamalek, circled the Gheriza Club, turned again onto Azziz Osman Street, and headed to the old Mayflower Hotel, now an apartment building near Sunshine market. She ran up the four flights of stairs and pounded on the door.

"Justine! You look like hell!" said Andrea, opening the door.

"What in the hell happened to my intuition?" demanded Justine. "How could he expect to get away with it? Surely he knew I would talk with Dad sooner or later. What happened to the self I trusted so well? How could I have been so wrong?" Justine was incredulous. She paced back and forth in Andrea's kitchen.

Andrea hadn't said a word since her opening greeting. She busied herself making strong coffee. At 7:30 in the morning, with tousled hair and a cleanly scrubbed face, she looked younger than her age.

"You're talking about Nasser, I assume. There is only one way to find the answers to those questions," interrupted Andrea, placing her hands on Justine's trembling shoulders. "You have to ask him."

"I never want to see him again as long as I live!"

"A reasonable response," said Andrea. "That is exactly what you should do."

"Don't be ridiculous!" Justine snapped.

"Excuse me," Andrea said as she walked toward the ringing phone in her bedroom.

"Who was on the phone?" Justine asked when she returned to the kitchen with a hairbrush in hand.

"Your mother. I told her you were on your way home."

"Thank you. I assume that Dad called her." Andrea nodded. With a deep sigh, Justine relaxed her shoulders and folded them in toward her sunken chest. "I'll call her from my apartment."

Thirty minutes later, Justine was on the phone to Italy. "Hi, Mom. Sorry to have missed your call. I didn't realize you'd kept track of Andrea all these years." She paused. "Dad called you?"

"He did. And I've kept in touch with Andrea ever since our scintillating salons in Florence." Justine could hear her mother take a deep breath. "Honey, are you in love with Nasser?"

"I think I am—I was—in love with him. I don't think I knew that before I talked with Dad. It felt like I'd been kicked in the stomach. Nasser lied to me, Mom, although I'm sure he'll explain it away. 'Just a small lie in service of a smooth introduction.' Something like that. My heart wants to believe him, but something just doesn't feel right."

"You don't trust him," her mother said frankly.

"How can I?"

"Truth has always been enormously important to you, even as a child. Remember when you told Susan there was no Santa Claus? She didn't talk with you for a year."

"Oh, Mom! That was so silly." Justine paused, surprised by the statement. "Isn't truth important to you?"

"There are many kinds of truths. Sometimes I have edited out faults in those I love. I'm not sure how I actually do that, but I do know that if we expect others to change very much, we are chasing rainbows and unicorns. Only adolescents think they can change another person, that any of us have that much power."

"Were you an adolescent when you married Dad?" She snuggled the phone between her chin and shoulder while she laid out her clothes for the upcoming meeting, casually selecting chunky silver earrings that looked very much like something her mother would wear.

"Of course I was!" Lucrezia laughed aloud. It was a delightful laugh . . . full and rolling, infectious. *The laugh of someone who accepts herself. Right now I envy her so.* "But *you're* not an adolescent."

"Then how could I have been so deceived? I thought he was genuine, or at least truthful." She felt her eyes well with tears. *Does he mean this much to me?*

"You're too hard on yourself. You're a remarkably open women who can give your heart fully. At the same time, you're an anthropologist who picks up sophisticated signals. This internal tension will probably always frame who you are."

"Why aren't you haunted by the same dilemmas? You live such a buoyant, exotic life and seem to expect that things will turn out all right."

"I've made many mistakes in my life—plenty—as has your father. I'm not afraid to make them, is all. Terribly liberating. I try to find virtue in charity rather than moral certitude. And that means charity toward myself as well. But you know . . ."

"Moral certitude? Is that how you see me?" Justine felt an unpleasant warmth rise up her chest.

"I'm talking about myself, Justine, and when I was young. I was so sure then. So sure of what was right and wrong. The search for charity has been a desperate one, and it's taken me decades," said Lucrezia.

"I know I sometimes hold back for fear of making mistakes," Justine admitted quietly. "I want—I need—to learn from your sense of abandon."

"Abandon may not be quite the right word, Justine. I still do exercise self-restraint, mostly, but I live with many tensions, too." There was a silence, both women thinking, pondering their responses. "What are you going to do about Nasser?"

"I don't know, Mom, I just really don't know."

Once she'd hung up, Justine realized she'd forgotten to ask why Ibrahim had insisted, "Talk to your mother."

OLD CAIRO 2 CE

"Easterners for dinner!" cries Noha as we prepare the meal with the cherished saffron. "Why invite Easterners for dinner? They will steal our goats and dirty our home. You can't trust them farther than you can throw a donkey!"

I place my arm around her shoulders and feel her body relax. She smiles faintly as though to say, "I know, Mary, I'm trying to harness my tongue."

"Mary, I am pleased," asserts Joseph, who is washing his hands nearby. "The invitation was a generous offer. We will welcome them to our home. Who are these new friends from the East?" Always eager to hear the stories of travelers and life in other lands, Joseph yearns to know where the world is changing, where the world is at peace, where a man could raise his family in safety.

"*The father and his son have traveled from India, Joseph,*" I tell him. "*The father is named Pravar and the son is Ravi. Jesus is quite fond of the boy already.*"

"*It is good for Jesus to have a friend his own age,*" says Joseph. "*But it is unfortunate that traders who come for market day do not stay long.*"

"*But they often return,*" I remind him.

Joseph smiles and nods, drying his hands on the tails of his rough cotton shirt.

A handsome man of perhaps forty summers, Pravar dresses much like his son and emanates a quiet confidence and curiosity. As Joseph introduces our guests to the family, they bow in the elaborate way Jesus noticed in the market. Ravi hands me gifts of saffron and tea, for which I am grateful.

James impatiently carries two small benches from outside to accommodate our visitors. Tired by the long day of working at the canal, he has little energy for a formal dinner with strangers.

As the family members and visitors seat themselves, Joseph politely turns to Pravar to explain: "*We begin the meal with a prayer from our holy books, Master Pravar. If you will bear with us.*"

"*We are honored to be a part of the ceremony of your family, my lord,*" responds Pravar with great sincerity. Pravar and Ravi bow their heads as well.

Their God is generous with His followers. Would our God allow such reverence for another? Isaiah says ours is a jealous God. Yet Joseph tells us that our God wants us to pursue knowledge. Who is this God we worship so?

While we begin to share the meal of bread, cheese, olives, and stew, Joseph says: "*Tell us about your journey, my friends. We are interested to know about your world.*" All eyes turn expectantly toward our guests.

"*The journey is a long one,*" begins Pravar. "*We left our home in the province of Cheros in the Kingdom of Tamil in India four months ago and came by ship most of the way, through the Indian Ocean and the Arabian Sea and up to the Red Sea. We will not return for six more months.*"

"*That is a long time, and I've heard the crossing is difficult,*" says Samir, tearing off a piece of bread and soaking it in the stew.

"*The passage from India is rough. Ravi, why don't you tell our hosts of our problems?*" suggests his father.

Ravi's eyes sparkle as he takes in each person around the table, drawing the collective attention to him as though by some hidden force. "The longest part of the trip, from India to the Arabian land, is trying and scary," Ravi begins in whispered tones. "A storm nearly swallowed us like a giant whale, and the sky stole the stars. Our navigator, who was very clever, became terribly sick. A high fever didn't leave him for many days. Without our navigator and the stars to guide us, we were lost."

"What happened?" presses James, drawn into the story in spite of himself.

"He died," says Ravi sadly, turning to James. "We buried him at sea."

"Do you always bury your dead at sea?" asks James. Our older son is suspicious of these foreign ways.

"That is our custom, James," says Ravi simply.

"We have no way to properly keep our dead with us at sea," explains Pravar. "It makes their passing even more difficult for their families at home."

James nods and falls silent.

"Easterners," grumbles Noha with nearly inaudible contempt.

Joseph raises his voice, hoping the visitors haven't heard Noha. "Did you find land soon thereafter, Ravi?"

"The day after that," Ravi says with a swell in his now unsteady voice, "a gigantic wave took our cabin boy out to sea." No one speaks; they wait for him to regain his composure. "We tried to find him, but could not. On the fourth day, another ship appeared nearby. We thought it might be a pirate ship, one of the Sea Peoples." He pauses to draw out the tension. Jesus holds his breath; James leans forward encouragingly.

"We were almost out of water and others were falling ill, so we signaled the other ship. I thought we would be sliced to pieces by pirate scimitars! But finally, the other ship gave us a welcoming sign and we went alongside. They were returning to India, and still had water to share. That night, the stars returned and we made our way to Arabia. From Arabia, we journeyed up the Red Sea."

Two deaths, and one only a child. How tragic. Death does not always respect age, but why is it necessary to take our children? What does our God have in mind? When I was a child, my mother told me to listen. I have listened, but I hear only part of the answer. The fault is mine, no doubt. I feel a pain move through my chest; I take a deep breath and a sip of water.

"Why did your family choose such dangerous work that takes you far from home?" Jesus asks.

I notice that Joseph seems uneasy with this question. He may feel that Jesus is challenging the good judgment of our visitors.

Unruffled, Ravi replies, "Our fathers and grandfathers before us were traders. It is what we do."

Jesus seems satisfied with this answer. Noha less so. Holding her dripping bread in mid-air, she opens her mouth to speak. I catch her eye, halting the words before they can rush out.

Pravar continues, "On the shore of the eastern desert of Egypt, we moored our ship and bought four camels from Nubia for the two-day trip to Babylon, where we sold them—to the same men we bought them from, I think." He grins. "From here, we will journey on the Great River and Sea." He says to Joseph, "We noticed a canal being built across the eastern desert. Its completion will make our trip easier."

"The canal is being built by the Romans, Pravar. James works there a few days a week. While we are pleased that the canal will be helpful to you, we are becoming weary of the Roman presence. Each day more men are forced into labor or conscripted into their growing armies," he says.

James nods slightly to Pravar, whose eyes narrow at the news of Roman aggression.

Pravar explains that he has encountered these forces before—that he was beaten and robbed by two drunken Roman soldiers in Crete. "I am always on guard."

Not eager to pursue a conversation about forced work, a condition that embarrasses him, James changes the subject, "How did you learn to speak Aramaic, my friends?"

"Language is a skill of our trade. An exchange of ideas is essential if we are to work in other lands. Each land has a different tongue. We set about to learn the languages as we would learn a trade," replies Pravar.

"Father, may I take Ravi above?" Jesus asks. He has finished his stew and now squirms in his chair.

"As you wish, my son. Our new friends graciously brought us some tea that we will now enjoy."

James asks to be excused as well, leaving the table quietly and walking toward the east.

I watch my son lead Ravi outside and up the stone stairs to the top of the cave. A ribbon of warm crimson lies on the western horizon. The soft blue blanketing the crimson turns dark, revealing a few stars. The Great River's black mantel is interrupted by light reflected from a full moon of muted orange rising out of the east. Later, my son tells me of their conversation.

"You have brought the full moon with you from the East," observes Jesus as both young men sit down on top of the cave. Ravi crosses his legs, folding each foot underneath him. Jesus shifts his position to mirror that of his new friend.

"It is said," Ravi responds, "that the full moon comes to remind us of the great circle of life. When our hearts are full, everything and everyone joins hands and encircles the earth. You are fortunate to have your family and home with you each day. I miss my mother and sisters."

"How many sisters do you have?" asks Jesus.

"Three," Ravi replies, "Apala, Charu, and Kala. Sometimes I tease them and they become angry with me, but I miss them when I am gone. I hope they miss me."

"Mother says that sisters are a treasure, God's special gift to the world. Women understand much and can give and forgive."

Ravi laughs softly. "I will let my sisters know that they are appreciated," he says with a mischievous smile, as though he is not sure he wants to reveal his soft heart to women of any age.

"What knowledge do you bring from the East, Ravi? What do you know that I may know?" Jesus leans forward.

"A difficult question, my friend. For what I know is who I am." After a pause, Ravi says: "My father has said that if you can train your mind to flow like the river, you will forever be calm. In my home we follow the teachings of the Buddha, and we meditate."

"Who is the Buddha? Is he a god?"

"No, not a god, but a great man, a wise one, who lived long ago in my homeland."

"I see. Do you worship and make sacrifices to this wise one?"

"No," Ravi smiles. "He is to be followed, not worshiped. He is our teacher."

"And it is he, the Buddha, who has taught you to meditate?" presses Jesus. "What is it to 'meditate'?"

"There are many ways to meditate. It is how we reflect and contemplate about the world and ourselves."

"Will you show me your way? I would learn what it is to meditate." He edges closer, facing Ravi with open palms.

Without a word, Ravi sits up straight and closes his eyes. Jesus follows.

"Now," Ravi says, "listen to your breath as it moves in and out. If your mind runs away, gently bring it back to your breathing."

"My mind has a mind of its own," Jesus laughs, "it bounces around like a nervous grasshopper. I will try to catch it."

The boys meditate in silence for several minutes. The sounds of the Great River speak loudly through the stillness. The golden glow turns to dark pink and purple. Two kingfishers dive through the moonlit path into the water beyond.

Ravi interrupts the stillness. "Now, beginning at the top of your head and moving throughout your body, pay attention to how you feel. Do not name the feelings, just pay attention."

Without opening his eyes, Jesus follows Ravi's words. He feels his breath move through his body like a small bird fluttering about.

After several long moments, Ravi says: "Do you see how the sensations rise and fall like the river? Always changing. This is a law of nature, of life. It is the lesson of impermanence. Everything is temporary. One who understands—who is awake—lights up the world like the moon when it is freed from a cloud."

"Ravi, my friend," asks Jesus, "what does it mean to be awake? Are we not awake when we open our eyes?"

Ravi smiles. "My father says the awakened one does no wrong, only good. He does not want, nor feel fear. He lives in love and in peace. He purifies his mind through meditation. The awakened call patience the highest sacrifice."

Jesus does not reply. He only smiles in return. They continue to sit in silence, watching and listening to the sounds within and without. A feeling of peaceful joy comes upon Jesus' young mind and attaches itself to his soul. The night replaces *the deep flaxen hue of the horizon. The stars grow brighter. In the cavern below them, their fathers talk into the night.*

Later, as Jesus prepares for sleep, he sits on his bed pallet with his legs folded beneath him. "I found a connection between my mind and my body and the river, Mother," he tells me. "I have found new and mysterious ways. Yet their teacher is not here with them. He has been gone a long time, and he is not a god."

"We have many teachers such as this, Jesus. Remember the lessons we have learned from Abraham, David, and Moses. God has given us teachers in countless ways. Life has many mysteries. Learn from them."

"And my new friend, mother," asks Jesus with the desperation of someone who realizes a sudden loss. "Do you think he'll ever return?"

"I am sure that he will return, Jesus. Have faith."

CHAPTER 20

———⦿———

"W ESTERNERS, ESPECIALLY AMERICANS, have a disgraceful lack of historical consciousness. Not having a history of their own, they think our antiquities are for decoration. For show. National identity measured by abundance." Omar Mostafa, Director of the Supreme Ministry of Egyptian Antiquities, held forth to the members of the investigation team as he described his recent travels and impressions. The informal gathering clustered in a corner of the mammoth conference room in the Egyptian Museum. Mostafa's spirited pontifications were well known; many sought out his company, and almost as many wished they hadn't.

"St. Louis and Chicago were most trying. Each museum and its generous sponsors take great pride in what is not theirs. St. Louis missed the deadline I gave them for returning the mask to Egypt. It will amuse me to give them trouble. A press conference or press release, perhaps."

Amal Al Rasul had driven in alone from Alexandria this morning, and stood with the others, his expression carefully blank. Everyone in his field had had to work with the pompous director at one time or another.

"What mask is that, Dr. Mostafa?" asked Amir, seeming impressed by his flamboyant supervisor in spite of himself. It wasn't often that younger employees were in the presence of the Great Mostafa. "I'm determined to reclaim many of the Ptolemaic artifacts scattered around the world." Ibrahim stood near his grandson paying little attention, seemingly lost in thought, pondering the meeting ahead.

"A funerary mask from around 1550 BCE, my boy," replied Omar, "A relatively small item, but the only one of its kind in the known world. I suspect there are many walls in American game rooms lavishly decorated with such masks, surrounded by polar bears and our African gorillas. Come see me, Amir, and I'll give you a few pointers on how to get our treasures back."

"I'll definitely drop by," said Amir with an appreciative tone. "Thanks." Ibrahim now glanced up at his grandson, brows rising, as if to say, *Ah, the excitement of the young.*

"How do you manage to lose these artifacts in the first place?" asked Al Rasul. "If Petra and Abu Simbel weren't carved into mountains, they would have disappeared a long time ago."

"Glad you asked," said Omar, bowing slightly and overlooking the subtle criticism. With a willing audience, his chest extended like that of a preening bird, his eyes glowing. "The colonists exchanged antiquities like dice or outright stole them from each other. In the past half-century, the antiquities markets have become the official, albeit illegal, source of precious goods. Museums procure great treasures this way. I find it even more scandalous when curators turn a blind eye to the covetous actions of private collectors who also happen to be large donors. At their worst, museums are erected and run by the collectors themselves. Such is the case of Peggy Guggenheim and the Gettys."

"I understand the U.S. Cultural Property Advisory Committee is seeking to stop much of this illegal trafficking—" began Isaac Yardeni.

Mostafa glared at him, his implication clear: a Jewish defense of the U.S. was not particularly welcome in the Arab world.

"I see that Mostafa is holding court this morning," observed Andrea as she and Justine arrived and took their seats at the ornate mahogany table. "Since he was named one of the fifty most influential people in the world by *Fortune* magazine, there's no stopping him. Be prepared."

"Ah, Doctors Jenner and LeMartin. Please join us," suggested the director. "Dr. Jenner, please enlighten us. What is your father's view of the antiquities market?"

The two women rose and joined the group. "Dr. Mostafa. How good to see you again. Gentlemen," said Justine, lowering her head respectfully. "Please tell me more about your question. You were asking for my father's view?"

"*Bizobt*! Exactly. Does he think such markets have a legitimate role to play in the transfer of antiquities today?"

What a strange question. No one supports these markets—unless they're black marketers themselves. "My father has strong views on this subject, as you do, Dr. Mostafa. He thinks 'antiquities market' is an oxymoron. The only rightful owners of antiquities are the countries in which they were created, even though these countries have a professional obligation to retain the artifacts in the public domain and loan them to foreign museums. We all want to share knowledge with the rest of the world, don't we?"

Ibrahim smiled proudly at Justine.

Mostafa's laugh was wholehearted. His stomach and jowls shook; his eyes danced as his hands met each other with a gleeful clap. "My dear, you have won my heart! Of course the country of origin must control the loan of such treasures—and require adequate compensation."

Justine gave the director her most disarming smile. From what she'd heard, "adequate compensation" from Mostafa's perspective was nothing short of extortion. "I am deeply honored, sir. Your heart could not be in safer keeping."

As the Great Mostafa moved to the head of the table, he briefly placed his hand on Andrea's shoulder and murmured something in her ear about the honor of her presence. The others seated themselves.

"Let us begin," Mostafa said. "We're here today to learn about the dating and translation of a codex found several weeks ago by Dr. Jenner." He introduced those around the table, then paused briefly. "Dr. Jenner, I understand this find is unprovenanced, precisely because you picked it up and carried it out of the crypt under St. Sergius. Is that correct?" His tone was now one of exacting professionalism. Any warmth earned earlier was pushed to the margins.

"That's correct, Dr. Mostafa," Justine said. "As you know, the conditions of the find were rather harrowing. I didn't realize the object that had fallen to my feet during the earthquake wasn't mine. The crypt was dark, smothered in sandstone dust and falling debris, so I just picked up whatever was close by." Warned by her colleagues that Mostafa would pull no punches in spite of his charming welcome, she was prepared to be equally straightforward, as well as contrite, if necessary. In spite of feeling fragile from this morning's heartbreaking revelation about Nasser, she allowed no hint of defensiveness to enter her voice.

"The water has flowed under the bridge, Dr. Jenner," said Mostafa. "It can't be helped now." He smiled and held her gaze. "But it does add a complication, doesn't it?" Not waiting for a reaction, he turned to Ibrahim. "Professor, would you tell us what we have in front of us this morning?"

Ibrahim gave a small nod, although his glare communicated his displeasure with the director's treatment of Justine. "The report you have before you is a summary of the interim findings regarding a codex discovered in the crypt under St. Sergius Church in Old Cairo during the earthquake of April 12th, 2006," he began. "We are in possession of a leather-bound codex of papyrus approximately sixty-five pages in length, which came into my possession, courtesy of Dr. Jenner, on April 14th. I subsequently placed it in my safe at the Rare Books Library."

"Where was the codex between April 12th and 14th?" Mostafa asked sharply.

"The codex was in a canvas bag in my room at the Shepheard," answered Justine, annoyed that she found herself apologizing for a second time. "I didn't realize I had it until two days after the earthquake."

"I see," said Mostafa, with an intonation designed to tell everyone in the room that he didn't. "Please continue, Professor." Tea arrived on a large, circular brass tray. Seven fourteenth-century Chinese ceramic cups, clearly a prized possession of the museum, steamed with the fragrance of Arabian tea from the Sinai. The teapot matched the cups, as did the large, mounded container of sugar and miniature plate of lemons.

"On May 2nd through 4th, Drs. LeMartin and Jenner took the codex to the Centre for Calligraphy and Writing at the Bibliotheca Alexandria. To the office of the director, Dr. Al Rasul, for his opinion, as well as that of his Jordanian colleague, Mahmood Hassen. After their return, the codex was again placed into my safe, from which it was periodically removed to obtain leather, including patina, and papyrus samples." Ibrahim closely followed his notes. "During the period May 10th through 15th, the codex was separated, placed under glass, and photographed by a specialist from Geneva, who noted that having the pages and margins so intact is a rare occurrence."

"*Absolument*," interrupted Andrea, passing a plate of small vanilla cakes to the director. "The exacting photographs have allowed Ibrahim, Isaac, and myself to translate key portions of the codex, although there are still many fragments. Dr. Al Rasul has also made occasional visits to Cairo to assist with some of the more difficult passages. It's written primarily in Aramaic, though several Greek and Hebrew phrases are used as well. In that regard, as well as in style of letter formation, it's a close facsimile to the Dead Sea Scrolls."

"Thank you, Dr. LeMartin," said Mostafa, attempting to swallow one of the cakes nearly whole. He paused, then spoke again, "Once the pages were photographed, we moved the original under glass to my safe here in the Ministry. The photographed copy was kept with Ibrahim and his team. I saw to it that twelve small pieces of the papyrus and four pieces of the leather were sent to the University of Arizona radio carbon dating lab in Tucson. The very same lab, as you may know, where the Dead Sea Scrolls and the Nag Hammadi codices were dated. I also asked for an analysis of the ink on the papyrus using their state-of-the-art transmission electron microscopy equipment."

"It sounds as though you have considerable familiarity with the Arizona lab," observed Al Rasul, leaning forward somewhat impatiently.

"I visited last year, Dr. Al Rasul. It is my hope that within five years our own Ministry of Antiquities will be as well equipped." The director ran his hand carefully across the report. "It is only fitting that the best lab for analyzing Egyptian antiquities be right here in Egypt, don't you think?" He didn't wait for an answer. "But let us get on with the findings.

"The AMS—Accelerated Mass Spectrometry—carbon-14 dating on the leather and the papyrus dated the codex in the period 20 BCE to 40 CE. That's what I expected to find," declared Mostafa, partially reading from the report. "The ink is made of the usual soot and gum adhesive, somewhat different in each sample, but coherent."

"You say 'expected to find,' Dr. Mostafa, but I find such early dating remarkable. Don't you?" asked Amir, glancing at Justine, who avoided his eyes. It was the first time they had seen each other since she'd walked away from him and his grandfather at the Rare Books Library, and she was struggling to work through her feelings about a number of men in her life at the moment. *What am I going to do about Nasser?*

"You're right, my boy, it is remarkable. But as you know, most of our recoveries are much older. Pharaonic Egypt. Your own Ptolemy period. Those are our specialties."

"Point well taken, sir," said Amir, staring directly at the director. "Yet we have almost no finds from the period designated here."

"How do you account for the differences in ink samples?" interjected Al Rasul.

"This would appear to be a codex written over a period of time," noted Isaac. "Changes in locale, time, and climate could account for a variety of ink ingredients as well as the reaction of the inks to the environment. No surprise there."

"No surprise there," repeated the director. "One of the more significant findings is the delicacy of the fibers of the papyrus."

"The dryness of the sandstone cave appears to have held the sap together and kept the pigment evenly distributed," offered Justine. "A rare find."

"An astounding find indeed," said Al Rasul. "For a two-thousand-year-old codex to be so well preserved . . . It's almost unbelievable. But too many rarities can spell trouble. How sure are we that the codex came from that cave? Amir, I understand that you and your team from the Museum studied the cave patina."

Did he just call me a liar? Justine glanced across the table at Al Rasul, who stared down at his notes with feigned attention. She had come to learn that he coveted his role as cynic and accuser; she decided not to take it personally.

"With *Dr. Jenner's* help," Amir said with emphasis, "we were able to examine the patina in several likely niches in the crypt under St. Sergius. As you are all aware, the patina is formed by chemicals that seep out of or drip onto the surface of an artifact over hundreds of years as it lies in its secure environment. In this case, a cave. We transported the newly acquired binocular scanning electron microscope—thanks to Dr. Mostafa—into the cave and photographed the patina *in situ*."

Although seated, the director bowed royally from the waist to acknowledge his cleverness in securing the essential equipment from National Geographic.

"The most curious aspect of cave patina is that it forms in the shape of a cauliflower," continued Amir. He flashed a conspiratorial smile at Justine. "On the inner face of the third niche, we found a cauliflower pattern nearly identical to the remains on the codex." He rose, handed out photographs of the pattern and walked to the blackboard to draw an image of two interlocking cauliflower buds. "The two images are a fit. Like fingerprints." An unabashed grin flickered across his face.

He's pleased with himself, Justine recognized, warming to Amir once again in spite of herself. "And we found something else of exceptional interest," she added.

Amir nodded, then slowly pulled on a pair of sheer plastic gloves, reached into his briefcase, and removed a pint-sized Ziploc bag. He waited until the attention in the room was undivided before reaching into the bag and extracting an object that, now cleaned, looked very much like a small yellow bone.

"What is it?" demanded Al Rasul.

"A comb," Justine said evenly. "A little comb." The outline of the comb now became apparent: small, fine teeth, probably made of ivory, and crowned with a cluster of carved lotuses.

Omar's arms swung open in a grand gesture of excitement, knocking one of the priceless Chinese cups and a saucer to the floor. Turning his back to the breakage to avoid embarrassment, he intently stared at the comb. Isaac and Andrea pushed their cups back from the edge of the table.

"Is there . . . is there any hair in the comb?" asked Andrea. It was her turn to be surprised.

"Hair with follicles? Testable?" interjected the excited director. "For DNA?"

Amir could hardly get a word in edgewise. "Hair, yes. Enough follicles for DNA testing? I'm not sure. Could we actually have the author's DNA? We don't know yet."

"But we may well have some hair from the author of the codex," said Ibrahim quietly. "That is valuable in and of itself."

"I'd bet my career on that much," said Amir. "We can now date the comb and see if it corresponds to the dates of the codex." A lock of his curly black hair fell onto his forehead.

He looks like a mischievous child. Justine grinned. After their experience with the missing pages, she found his new excitement most pleasing. She realized she'd forgiven him for the intrigue about those pages. After all, Ibrahim was his grandfather, and she could respect his need to protect him. To an extent.

"I would suggest that we take a break so that we can all get a closer look at this amazing find," suggested the director. "Amir, do you have any more gloves?"

OLD CAIRO 2 CE

"I have something for you, Mary. Today is a day for remembrances and small gifts." My husband hands me a small package wrapped in papyrus. On this first day of Passover, we are preparing for the Seder dinner, each of us deep in thoughts of the future. I open the package carefully, revealing a beautiful ivory comb about as wide and as tall as my hand. The teeth are delicately carved and across the top, graceful lotuses cling to each other. The ivory glistens like pearls.

"Joseph, it is truly beautiful. You gladden my spirit." I hug him and kiss him on both cheeks. *"Where did you find such a beautiful object?"*

"You know the Roman, Flavius, who has been working with me on the gates? He found the comb near their building site and brought it to me. Flavius believes he will never see his wife again. I feel great pity for this man who longs so for his family and his homeland. I gratefully accepted his offering. Noha found fine reeds with which to clean it."

"I must thank her also. And this Flavius, he is a good man?"

"He is a good man, Mary. He has been helpful to me in my work and our sons have learned from him. Men can be different, even when they are of the same people."

"That is so, my husband." I embrace him again and hold on, finding reassurance in his arms. For a long time he returns my embrace, and then he steps back, places his hands on my shoulders, and says quietly, *"We must ready ourselves for a change. We will speak of it after the Seder."*

"Rachel is with child," I tell him, deciding he needs to know of this news before the evenfall, as it will surely influence his planning. He does not respond at first, but stares around the room with an expression difficult to grasp. *"This is good news,"* he declares at last, *"but it does complicate the decisions ahead."*

CHAPTER 21

———⊗∞⊗———

"**N**OW THAT WE'VE ALL HAD A LOOK AT THIS new evidence, I would suggest that we summarize the verifiable physical evidence we have so far, then move on to context clues. If I may . . ." Mostafa said, an even more commanding figure now that he was on his feet. After the brief break and several side conversations, the group was now reseated. More tea had been set on the table, and the director's cup and saucer had been replaced. "So far, we have heard the following information." He summarized point by point:

"First, the carbon-14 dating of the calf leather and papyrus pages places the codex between approximately 20 BCE and 40 CE.

"Second, patina patterns from the crypt niche match the patterns on the leather cover. Since the pattern was undisturbed, it is most likely that the codex remained in the niche for the full time, or most, of these two thousand years. Fair to say, Amir?"

Amir nodded.

"Third, the paleography examination suggests that the patterns and forms of the letters place the codex during the approximate period of the c-14 dating. Is this correct, Al Rasul?" He didn't wait for a response.

"Therefore, we are representing this find thus far as an authentic codex created during the period 20 BCE to 40 CE and hidden in a wall niche in the crypt below the St. Sergius Church. We've heard nothing as yet about authorship." All eyes turned to Ibrahim as he placed his shaking right hand on the report and pulled himself toward the table.

"Before we begin to talk about context clues and possible authorship," Ibrahim said, "let me remind everyone that there are many different points of view regarding the presence and traveling of the Holy Family in Egypt. The 'Holy Family' is generally thought of as Mary, Joseph, and Jesus. Many Protestants think that Joseph's son James was among them. Some believe that other children followed. Many religious traditions outside of the Middle East, perhaps even within the Catholic faith, don't believe that the Holy Family came to Egypt at all. But of course the Copts think they came here and traveled around a great deal—since they were being chased by Herod's soldiers—and then returned to Palestine after about two and a half years. Muslims believe the family stayed in Egypt for as many as seven years. My point in reminding everyone of these variations is to clarify some established theories for the conversation."

"It sounds as though you've already made a decision on authorship," said Al Rasul. "I thought we were reserving judgment until all the data was in." He cushioned his sarcasm only slightly in regard for Ibrahim's antiquity.

"Fair enough, but I will add this caveat: if, and only if, a member of the Holy Family wrote the codex, there are many different assumptions about where and when that could have occurred," said Ibrahim, mildly embarrassed at the suggestion of rashness. Andrea, Isaac, Amir, Justine, and himself had decided to take this expanded gathering through the process step by step rather than rapidly revealing their conclusions about authorship.

"I will admit that most of our initial impressions have been borne out," acknowledged Al Rasul. "While we recognize that alphabets change over time, these linguistic formations are consistent with the patterns found in the period in question. It's also important to note that we have no samples of female writing during this period of history with which to compare the codex."

"Do you think that would make a difference?" asked Amir, glancing at Justine.

"I do," said Al Rasul. "My Jordanian colleague, Mahmood Hassen—who couldn't be with us today—pointed out that the formations and patterns in this codex, although highly congruent with the Dead Sea Scrolls, are more delicate, have more flourish. The lines are also thinner, meaning the stylus may have been smaller or held by a hand with less strength than a man's.

These subtleties, this elegance, may—just may—suggest that the author was a woman." He glanced at Andrea and nodded. "We can also say that the inscriptions are written by the same person, but over a period of time. The style and form became more sophisticated over a period of perhaps eight years."

"Thank you. That's helpful," said Andrea, nodding slightly. "As we've worked to translate the photographed pages, we've been guardedly impressed by the coherence of historical context clues. As Dr. Al Rasul just noted, the linguistic patterns are in nearly the same style as the Dead Sea Scrolls of Qumran. We believe that the diary—and from now on I will refer to this codex as a diary—explains many of these mysteries." She paused, slowly sipped her tea, and gazed from person to person. "The author would appear to be Mary, mother of Jesus."

Sharp intakes of breath could be heard from Omar Mostafa and Al Rasul, both of whom must have had his suspicions but had not heard the information directly. "The cover page says simply: 'Diary of Mary of Nazareth'—inverted, of course, since ancient Aramaic was written from right to left. Granted, that statement alone would not establish authorship, but taken together with the content, we believe it does."

Even though the original team members had engaged in earlier discussions about this probability, saying it aloud had a profound affect on them all. Their faces projected a unique spiritual stillness, as though each was consulting some inner oracle. No one spoke.

Mostafa interrupted the stillness. "We've had little reason to think that women of this period were literate, Andrea. Why don't we start there?" He watched Andrea with unshielded admiration. "What explanation does this so-called 'diary' provide?"

"Mary tells Jesus she was taught to read and write by her grandmother, Faustina of Mt. Carmel. Mt. Carmel was an Essene community, and we've found entries suggesting an Essene influence on Mary's family. This would not only explain her literacy but also the similarity to the Dead Sea Scrolls, which were unmistakably written by the Essenes."

Justine's mind unwillingly turned to the Red Sea and her discussion of the Essenes with Nasser. He was undoubtedly right about the Holy Family and the

Essenes. The warm memory was quickly clouded by the freshness of the early morning call from her father. She shivered, placed both hands on her arms.

"Names used throughout the diary are consistent with the life of Mary: Jesus, Joseph, James, Rachel, cousin Elizabeth, nephew John," Andrea continued, leafing through her notes. "Mentions of places such as Palestine, Nazareth, Mt. Carmel, and Babylon situate the family in the expected locales. Discussions about the Romans, including conscription, the building of the canal and fortifications, and the growing tension with the Israelites are consistent with what we know about Roman-Egyptian life at that time."

"No mention of Bethlehem?" asked Mostafa.

"No mention of Bethlehem," replied Ibrahim. "The diary begins shortly before Mary's marriage to Joseph and continues until Jesus is almost nine years of age. James is seventeen or eighteen by that time. Any visit to Bethlehem would have been mentioned."

Al Rasul stared at his notes intently, marking out and adding words and phrases.

"Other clues are also consistent with Jewish life at the time," offered Isaac. "For instance, the family held discussions about the Law and ethics and quoted from the Book of Psalms. A lengthy passage describes their celebration of Passover, which tells us that this was a diary written by a member of a Jewish family and not a local Egyptian."

"And are we to think they lived in the same place all that time? In the cave below St. Sergius?" asked Mostafa, incredulous.

"We have no reason to believe otherwise," replied Isaac, stroking his wiry goatee.

"Before we continue," Andrea suggested, "I'd like to ask Justine to tell us more about Mary as a woman, mother, and wife."

Justine, alerted earlier that this invitation would be made, had studied the meticulous notes she had compiled as she'd listened to the conversations and translations of her colleagues closely in preparation for this moment.

All eyes turned toward her. "I am grateful to my colleagues for inviting me to join in these conversations, and I'm representing our team as I summarize our findings and inferences about Mary." She was immersed in the moment now, a moment she had been waiting for. *What a pleasure, an honor, to bring new understandings to light about a woman I admire so much.*

"We believe Mary, often referred to as the Virgin Mary, to have written this diary from the age of thirteen to perhaps twenty-two years of age, at which point she completed these pages or discontinued her writing for some reason. She was a confident, independent, even sensuous woman who cherished her freedoms in Egypt and took full advantage of her liberties, such as going to the market alone or with her son Jesus, traveling across the river to purchase household necessities, and extending invitations to her home. Although she found pleasure in her freedoms, however, there is an unmistakable tone of melancholy that pervades her writing. Yet she was far more than a survivor; she was a purposeful teacher of her sons, and a caring wife."

"Sensuous? That seems an odd word to use in reference to the Virgin Mary," exclaimed Al Rasul. "Disrespectful."

"Mary revealed a deep and poetic appreciation of the beauty of nature," said Justine. "In her writings, we can almost hear the sounds, sense the touch, and inhale the fragrances of her world—the way she describes the birds and her beloved sycamore tree that she brought from Palestine. She is also affectionate toward Joseph and her sons."

"She was a teacher to her sons, you say? Give us an example," ordered Mostafa.

"Mary reports several conversations with her sons, especially Jesus. She spoke to them of inequities and imbalances, the disenfranchisement of the powerless—not in so many words, of course. Her Aramaic is often intermingled with Greek and Hebrew phrases such as '*ger*,' meaning 'other,' with admonitions to care about the other, watch out for the other, put the other before self. Stories that take place in the marketplace when she is with Jesus speak of compassion and charity and forgiveness. These were her words to him."

"My god," exclaimed Al Rasul, "you're telling us that Mary was Jesus' primary teacher?"

"In important ways. *Iwa*," acknowledged Ibrahim.

"Perhaps your interpretations are being influenced by your own . . . what do you call it in America? 'Feminism?'" charged Mostafa, glaring at Justine and Andrea.

Justine smiled and remained composed. Confident of her knowledge and choice of words, she stood her ground. "I'm sure every researcher brings to the task his or her own experiences and biases. Don't you think, Dr. Mostafa?" Justine then turned toward Ibrahim and Isaac. "I have every reason to believe that our team shares the opinion that these interpretations of Mary are valid. Lest you think that we ignored other influences, we can say that the wisdom of Joseph was influential in teaching the Law, but also in promoting openness to other points of view. Jesus sat routinely with a local Rabbi and was influenced by friends, particularly a young man from India."

"India? What young man from India?" demanded Mostafa. "What did he have to teach Jesus?"

"May I?" interjected Andrea. Justine nodded graciously and slid back in her chair. "This boy, called Ravi, meaning the 'Sun,' taught Jesus to meditate, to reflect, to know what it is to be conscious. Jesus retold these conversations to Mary. Ravi and his merchant father followed a trade route from India to Crete that stopped at the marketplaces along the Nile." She paused. "Imagine a boy of just eight and another of perhaps ten. How introspective and smart they were. We can no longer deny the influence of Eastern thought on Jesus."

"While we know Jesus was a Jew, his philosophy has often been seen as more Eastern than would be expected from Jewish Law at that period in history," added Isaac. "His belief in equality, especially for women, forgiveness, and compassion often transcended the letter of the Law. Dr. LeMartin is correct, for the most part. Jesus' ministry was a departure from most traditional Judaism at the time, especially as practiced by the temple rabbis. However, there were many smaller clusters of Jews, such as those living in the outreaches of the Diaspora, who also diverged from tradition. These groups could have influenced Jesus' thinking as well. Now that we understand more about his childhood, we can begin to sort out those influences."

"What was he like? Jesus, I mean," asked Al Rasul with uncharacteristic gentility.

Ibrahim excitedly spilled out his words. "Jesus was precocious and curious, thoughtful and confident, playful and persistent, particularly in pursuit of answers to his many questions."

"What makes you think he was persistent?" Al Rasul's eyes narrowed. This time he was demanding. After all, Ibrahim was a Copt expressing adoration for his own Messiah.

"His mother recounted conversations at the dinner table in which Jesus would insistently question his father. If I'm remembering it correctly"—Ibrahim glanced at Andrea for assurance—"in one such instance he interrogated his father on whether it was right to learn about other gods. This was during a discussion of Isis."

Andrea smiled and nodded.

"It's as though the Virgin was prescient," concluded Ibrahim, "expecting the diary to be read someday."

"Don't get carried away, Professor," Mostafa said. "Answer this for me: Why did the family come to Egypt? Why take such a big risk? Was King Herod chasing them, as the Gospels of Matthew and John tell us? Somehow I'm beginning to think nothing is quite as it once seemed."

"There was a single defining occurrence involving James that made Joseph decide to go to Egypt," offered Isaac. "Although there were many cultural and political reasons causing their readiness, the tension between the Jews and the Romans was at a new high. It was like waiting for another sandal to fall away. Joseph had stopped taking James into Jerusalem to find work because it was no longer safe. Then something happened that served as a turning point." Isaac explained the incident of the eagle Herod had built above the gate entering the Temple and its consequences for the young men involved.

"What did this have to do with James?" Mostafa asked.

"James was the one who pulled down the eagle. But he was only about nine years old, so they released him," explained Isaac.

"Joseph found this to be a major sign." Amir joined the dialogue. "Telling the family to leave Palestine. It made sense to Joseph that the land of Moses, the place where Moses was found as a child and from which he led the Exodus, was the best place for his family. Mary was hesitant because of having just given birth. But with Rachel, the midwife, along, Mary tells us she was assured of a safe journey."

"So you're telling us that the story about Herod killing all newborn sons in order to eliminate the Messiah might not be a true story? Damn! Are any of

the stories surrounding the Holy Family true? Or are they all just metaphors?"
Mostafa was thoroughly exasperated.

"We have no evidence to tell us this story is true," said Ibrahim, stroking his
beard mercilessly. "Keep in mind, the killing of newborns appears in the Bible
more than once . . . but that doesn't mean it isn't true . . ."

"How are we to make sense of all of this?" lamented Mostafa. "The Christian narrative is being changed and we hold it delicately in our hands. Allah,
help us." After an uninterrupted pause, he continued: "Let me complicate our
work with the most fundamental of questions. Was Mary a virgin? And, further, was she a perpetual virgin, as the Copts believe?"

Justine assumed that, like many Muslims, Mostafa believed Mary to have
been a virgin when she gave birth to the prophet Jesus. It said so in the Koran,
which followers of Mohammed understood unwaveringly as the word of Allah. However, unlike Ibrahim and Amir, the Muslims in the room separated
virginity from divinity. Mary's virginity didn't necessarily establish Jesus as the
Son of God.

Before the question could be answered, Mostafa's assistant waved urgently
from the hallway. "If you'll excuse me," he said, and stepped out into the hall.
Within moments he returned, his complexion pale. "I'm afraid I have to deal
with an urgent matter. I'd suggest we reconvene at ten in the morning. Professor, can we be ready to proceed at that time?"

"Ten will be fine," responded Ibrahim. "We've made copies of several translated pages responding to the question of Mary's relationship with Joseph."

Everyone nodded. Until this question was answered, no one could return
to business as usual.

"As you like, Professor. Now, if you'll excuse me." Mostafa rushed from the
room.

OLD CAIRO 2 CE

*On the morning of Passover, a fierce pounding on the side of the cave startles me.
Although our family members are awake and sitting at the table, the eastern sun
has not yet flooded the rough sandstone floor, so they remain in the shadows.*

"Down there! Show yourselves!" commands an unfamiliar voice. The pounding continues. Shards of an earthen jug—shattered by a soldier's careless boot—scatter around the work area and tumble into the cave's walkway.

Earlier, I started the charcoal fire, replaced the grate, and set on a pot of water for tea. Joseph, James, and Jesus remain below, finishing their tea and getting ready for the festive day ahead. I see the uniformed soldiers enter the kitchen area above. Now my hand tightens on my husband's shoulder.

The soldiers shuffle from foot to foot, their boots kicking at the fire. Sparks fly into the air and dance on the hard surface near the exterior worktable.

"I'll go—the rest of you stay here," directs Joseph as he steps out into the open.

"What do you want?" he demands of the soldiers.

"We want your sons, old man," one of the Roman soldiers commands. "Emperor Augustus has decreed that more soldiers are to be conscripted into his army. The prefect Julius Alexander will be here in a few days, and we must give him a full accounting of all of the young men in the village. How old are your sons?" Two of the soldiers rummage through nearby family belongings.

Joseph hesitates. Our oldest works on the canal, so they know of him. "James is of seventeen years and Jesus is but eight," he replies as James steps outside and takes his place beside his father. I realize that I must keep Jesus from joining his father and brother. I hold on to his arm tightly. He nods as though to say, "I know what you require."

The soldier in charge stares at James with contempt: "So, this must be the canal worker."

"I am," James says with the irritability of a firstborn son who has not been allowed to eat during the first days of Passover.

Stay calm, my son. My own anger, mixed with fear, tightens my chest. Don't let your temper get you hurt again.

"When the prefect arrives in a few days, you will report to the canal zone ready for travel." The spokesman among the soldiers towers above Joseph and James, his stature enhanced by the hulking uniform and polished weaponry of the Roman military. He directs his comments to James, ignoring Joseph.

"Where will I be going?" James inquires forcefully.

"*That is not for your ears. Just do as you are told.*" *The soldier turns sharply on his heels, ready to walk east into the village.*

Before the soldiers can take their leave, Joseph cries out, "We had an agreement with Rome. The Israelites in Egypt do not participate in the benefits of the empire. We pay more taxes and keep to ourselves. We are to be left alone."

"*Things change, old man.*" *The soldier laughs, turning to the others, who join in his ridicule. "The Emperor is not bound by agreements with the Israelites. If you do not report," he warns James, "the consequences will be swift . . . for you and your family." His expression leaves little doubt that he relishes whatever vengeance might lie ahead.*

Four oil lamps glow with a golden aura, replacing the sunlight receding to the west. I spread the finely mended linen cloth from Grandmother Faustina over the table before adorning it with clay dishes and single-stemmed jasmine and oleander. Our family members take their places for the Seder, each holding his or her own secret. They are pensive, subdued. Rachel, with an air of giddiness, is the exception. Even Samir looks somber.

I wonder why he is so quiet. Samir is often the most talkative among us—the first to greet, the first to tell of good news. So many mysteries today . . . I feel the tension in James, his pent-up rage. Tears form in my eyes.

Joseph reaches out and pats my arm, then breaks the silence over the first cup of wine. "God be with us on this day of Passover. We bring our hearts to you and seek your counsel. Let us begin." Relieved to begin, the others look to Jesus expectantly.

Jesus does not need encouragement; he is ready to ask the question reserved for the youngest: "Why is this day different from all others?" Glancing at James, he says this in a tone revealing the significance of the question he has asked each year since he was two. Now he understands it.

Joseph begins the familiar story of the suffering of the Jews in Egypt. Each word holds tenderness, fragility.

"*Finally,*" *concludes Isaiah, who customarily shares in the storytelling, "the Lord decreed the death of all first-born Egyptian sons. But He passed over the* houses of the Children of Israel. The Pharaoh sent his soldiers after the fleeing Israelites, who crossed the Red Sea just before them. Moses lifted his rod and the sea closed in over the soldiers, drowning them in deep waters. Moses and the Children of Israel wandered in the Sinai for forty years and camped at the base of Mt. Sinai, where God gave Moses the Ten Commandments. Sadly, Moses died before the Children of Israel reached the Promised Land." Isaiah pauses breathlessly as though he has climbed the mountain himself.

Forty years. Forty years. Such patience, such endurance. Would that my sons had such qualities. Now our oldest will be challenged again by the Romans—he may not be able to survive it this time.

As though James has read my thoughts, he lowers his head just moments before his father's invitation.

"Let us pray," Joseph says.

We drink the remains of our second cup of wine, wash our hands, and share a small amount of matzah passed around the table. We are silent once again as the rituals of this important evening are observed. Even more than usual, our actions are deliberate, as though our very salvation depends upon them.

Rachel chooses a small piece of lettuce and dips it in the charoset of apples, cinnamon, nuts, and wine. "Bitterness dipped in mortar," she says. I, too, place charoset on a tiny piece of matzah and take a bite. The others follow.

"Thank you, Lord, for the delivery of our people from the hands of the Pharaoh and for these eight years in your presence here in Egypt," says Joseph.

Thank you, Lord, for these eight years, and the many gifts of this sacred land. Are they coming to a close? Will God take Egypt away from me too?

After our family has consumed all the lamb we can hold, a small piece of the remaining matzah is eaten with a sip from the third cup of wine. Earlier, I poured some wine for the Prophet Elijah and set it at one end of the table. It was Elijah, my husband reminds us, who told of the coming of the Messiah. "And this coming will be soon, very soon," he says. We are silent and wait.

Opening the Book of Psalms, Joseph says, "I have a blessing fitting for us today.

"By the streams of Babylon, there we sat and

Wept at the thought of Sion!

There on the poplars we hung up our harps, when

Our tyrants asked for a song;

Those who had harried us bade us be merry, 'Sing us a song of Sion,'

they said.

But how can we sing the Eternal's songs, here, in a foreign land?

Jerusalem, if ever I forget thee, withered be this hand! May my tongue cleave

to my mouth, if ever I think

not of thee, if ever I prize not Jerusalem above all joys!

"Next year," he continues, "may we celebrate Passover in Jerusalem." Each of us turns to stare at him. Even though this is a traditional closing for the Seder, it's the first time in seven celebrations in Egypt that he has suggested we will find ourselves at home next year. The family elders coddle their cups with both hands and examine them like crystal balls.

"Jerusalem? Jerusalem?" starts Noha. "When have you spoken of Jerusalem?"

"All these years in the land of Moses and you have not spoken of a return to Jerusalem," says Isaiah. The two boys nod in agreement. Samir puts his arm tightly around Rachel's shoulder.

Expressions of gratitude and regret, anticipation and sadness appear on our family's faces. I gaze at them one at a time. "Let us listen to Joseph." My voice is strengthened by the inevitability of his resolve. "He has something important to tell us."

"That is so," he says, "that is so." He explains the morning's visit from the Roman soldiers and the conscription of our oldest son.

The rage that has been simmering in James all though the Passover dinner now explodes. He blurts out, "I won't report to the Roman army! We need the monies I earn at the canal. Father needs my help!" His face reddens as he speaks, and he grips the wooden spoke as though it is a weapon.

Samir adds sympathetically, "They came to our home too. I am to be taken into the Roman army within the week."

Startled, Rachel says, "I didn't know. Why did you not tell me, Samir?"

"Being with child is a great joy for both of us, I didn't want to spoil these moments with unhappy news." Rachel begins to cry.

Samir glances at our oldest son. "Might we move to Alexandria?" he asks. "There is a large Jewish community there, and I have many family members who would welcome us. We would be invisible to the Romans there . . . it's a big city."

"And I hear of a great lighthouse and library," Jesus says, eyes wide with the wonders of this remarkable vision. He claps his hands, and then quickly places them into his lap when he notices that his brother's rage hasn't abated. More softly, he says, "The Rabbi told me our Holy Scriptures are being translated into Greek there." He looks around the table, expecting others to rally to Samir's idea.

James seems even more troubled. "I heard a story at the canal this week." He seeks everyone's attention before continuing. "At the Alexandria theater there is a play with music. As part of the entertainment, actors dressed as Jews are brought on stage, and they pretend to be hung up, bound to a wheel. Mauled. They are marched through the orchestra. All the while, the dancers, flute players, and mimes continue to perform, to the delight of the audience." He takes a deep breath and sits back in his chair, smoothing the fine linen tablecloth.

We are horrified to hear that persecution of our people is beginning again, this time in a community with such a large number of Israelites, many of whom are well-respected scholars.

"Why is that, Father?" asks Jesus. "Why would our people be treated like that? Why would people find it funny?"

Innocence is a wonderful gift. It asks explanations of us we might not other-wise want to consider. Are we trapped by both the Romans and the Alexandrians? I wonder. Will our people ever be at peace?

Joseph hesitates for a moment, then replies, "We are a special people, my son. We keep our own laws and do not participate in many of the pagan and Roman celebrations. By separating ourselves, we raise suspicions and distrust. We make people uncomfortable. It is the price we pay for keeping to ourselves." Isaiah and Noha nod in agreement.

"These pagans want us to pollute ourselves," Noha says, smirking. "They want us to prostrate ourselves to strange, animal-like gods. Better that we keep to our-selves."

Joseph flinches at the raw truth of Noha's comment. "We must return to Pal-estine soon. I have heard that Herod Antipas is much like his father, capricious and unpredictable, so we can expect the Romans to cause their armies to swell with Palestinians as well. Yet the Romans have been in Palestine much longer than in Egypt, and there are certain agreements there."

"Our Rabbis have more authority over our people in Palestine, it is true," adds Isaiah. "Egypt is being treated as a land subject to the whims and desires of the Romans. We may be safer among our own people." Isaiah yearns for the support of the larger family and familiar customs in his advancing years. He thinks that Noha might be happier there as well, although he is doubtful.

I have known this moment was near. I will miss Egypt so. In Palestine, women are often thought unclean and unable to do many things men do. In Egypt, I have seen women sell in the market, work in the fields, make beer, pilot boats . . . and when they die, their property is granted to their children as they will it. My grandmother and mother would have been pleased with this land. Perhaps the goddess Isis created such freedom. Yet even in a land of freedom, my duty is to my family. I will not make my own thoughts known. Not now.

"There is a further reason," begins Joseph, his tired eyes glowing with new-found energy. "I was visited by a dream."

I am shaken out of my private thoughts. Grasping my chair tightly with both hands, I rest my eyes on this man I have learned to love. His declaration draws rapt attention from everyone, for we all know well that a dream is a revelation from God.

"There are wolves, many wolves," he begins, his brows furrowing. "They are chasing a group of young men and biting at their legs, trying to kill them. Our sons and their cousin John are among them. The fangs of one of the wolves takes hold of John's leg, cutting deeply into his flesh, but James pulls him away. Suddenly a figure, a guide, in a long white tunic and golden girdle appears, holding a lantern to show them the way out. He comes out from among the hills, and I can see the skyline of Jerusalem in the background. As the young men follow the guide, the wolves fall away. I look closely at the guide." He turns his gaze on our youngest son. "His face is that of Jesus."

I hear a gasp and realize it is my own.

"I've had this dream three times. We must return to Palestine," Joseph concludes. "This is what God wants, Jesus." My youngest son nods, already at peace with this revelation.

The knock at the entrance to the cave comes suddenly, violently. No one moves.

CHAPTER 22

FORTUNATELY, NASSER WASN'T IN JUSTINE'S apartment when she arrived home. She'd forgotten that he was involved in a Nazarene conference in Port Suez today and tomorrow. Just in case he might show up early, she sent him a text message saying she would be very busy, tied up with meetings for a couple of days. She had no intention of running into him before she had sorted out what she would say to him about his deception.

Waking up the next morning, Justine stretched, but failed to get out of bed. Through the tall Victorian windows, she methodically counted the television satellites on the building facing the street behind her as she reflected back on the dream she'd had on her first day in Cairo. *What will be my impossible choice? Choices? Nasser? The codex?*

It was early, and she had time for a run before the 10 a.m. meeting at the Museum. It would clear her head.

As her feet pounded the earthen path on Roda Island, her heart was a miniature pendulum setting the rhythm of her run. The morning was clammy, a warm and humid harbinger of June. Above her, the rising sun, made deep orange by Cairo's omnipresent smog, cast a distinctive glow. Her chest tightened and her heart sped up as she sank into her hips with each footfall. The more she thought, the more her pace became uneven, erratic.

The Red Sea. Mornings on the Corniche. Nights in her apartment. Nasser. She halted her run at the crest of the hill, breathed deeply, and shook her head to clear it of decisions ahead. *This morning, I'm with Mary of Nazareth.* She pivoted on the balls of her feet and ran back to her apartment to shower and dress for the challenging day ahead.

∽

"I have an announcement," began Mostafa, standing before the group with uncharacteristic diffidence. It was nearly 10:00 a.m. and everyone had shown up early, a historical event in Egypt. He was sweating profusely; his tight voice struggled to sound casual. "The codex has been stolen. It was taken from our safe yesterday morning, or the night before."

Al Rasul grunted like an annoyed camel. Andrea and Justine, wide-eyed, stared at each other, while Amir's pencil broke under the pressure of his shaking hand. Only Ibrahim and Isaac gazed hazily at the front of the report, as though they didn't quite understand what was being said.

"Not quite sure when it was taken?" challenged Andrea. "How could you not be sure? What kind of security do you have in your office, Mostafa?" Her tone dripped contempt.

"Excellent security, I assure you, Dr. LeMartin. But the guards don't open the safe during every shift to examine its contents," he said defensively. "Laser beams surround the safe, but the electricity had been turned off, and the generator failed to kick in." The Great Man twisted the large gold ring on his right hand. "The codex will show up on the black market."

"Great comfort," said Al Rasul acidly. The two men had known each other since their days at Cairo University. This would not be the first time, nor the last, that Al Rasul had found reason to admonish the famed Omar Mostafa. "It may or may not show up in the market, but someone will buy it at a trumped up price. You should be more careful, my friend."

Amir couldn't contain himself; he lashed out at his boss. "This isn't the first time, Mostafa! Why did it take years to translate Nag Hammadi fragments? You kept 'losing track' of them."

Obviously stung by Amir's embarrassing comments, the director continued: "This isn't my greatest problem at the moment. I—we—have more at stake here."

"You have a greater problem than the theft of the codex?" Justine was incredulous. "I think we would like to know what it is."

"How am I going to explain this to National Geographic? We have, let me say, a financial agreement." Mostafa said this with the reluctance of a boy caught with his hand in the cookie jar.

"A financial agreement? With National Geographic? Are you telling us you sold the rights to the codex without consultation?" asked Ibrahim, finally provoked to respond. The tone in the room grew increasingly hostile. The Supreme Minister of Antiquities cringed.

"Such an arrangement is not unusual," Mostafa protested, allowing himself to be briefly distracted by the arrival of the Chinese tea service. "I didn't sell the codex. It belongs to Egypt, only to Egypt. The arrangements concern publication and co-hosting the entry of the codex into the world of religious history. Not ownership."

And controlling its release. "These are major arrangements, Dr. Mostafa," insisted Justine, emboldened. "Ones that should have been made in consultation with those of us involved in the discovery and translation of the codex!" She held his stare, refusing to relinquish further authority over the codex. "Fortunately, we have the photographed images of the pages made last month, which clear the way for continued translation. At least, I assume the copy has not been stolen as well."

"The copy is still in our possession," affirmed Ibrahim, his classic Semitic features moving in on themselves, extending the nose, narrowing the eyes. "It will have to do for now. But this is such a blow to credibility, I don't know if the results will mean anything. First we have an unprovenanced find, then no find at all."

"This may be merely an academic exercise," said Amir, thoroughly disgusted, "without any validity in the field of archeology."

"I'd suggest we proceed with our agenda," said Mostafa, although charges continued to fly, the group dividing into side conversations. "Ibrahim?"

"I think it would be wise to take a break before we continue," said Ibrahim. The other team members were already pushing back their chairs from the table as though to unbridle themselves from the debacle and speculate on the theft.

∾

"Professor Ibrahim. I believe you have something for us." The group had settled down, patience bought with tea and chocolate. It was anticipation that now tensed the air as the elder man sorted through a pile of xeroxed pages, cradling them gently, and handed four to each person at the table. Careful hands received the pages as though they were touching a divine tunic.

"I believe they're in order," said Ibrahim, pulling at his nose. "We've selected four entries from the period immediately following Mary's marriage to Joseph. History tells us that her parents were older and that they chose to entrust her to a good man, an older man, someone who was trustworthy and could be counted on to take care of Mary and a family. In the diary, Mary verifies these assumptions herself. The pages you have before you are meant to answer your questions about Mary's relationship with Joseph." He was surprisingly matter-of-fact.

Justine wondered whether Ibrahim was numbed by the events of these two days or resigned to the revelations he was presenting, the very pages he had stolen and returned. Her anger toward him had diminished; she now redirected a part of it toward herself. *Two men, two deceits. Just a coincidence? Or am I losing myself in the chaos around me?*

An air of rapt attention pervaded the room. Each person, even those familiar with the pages Ibrahim had just handed out, quietly devoured the sacred words before them.

Al Rasul appeared pleased, even as he struggled to keep his features noncommittal. The muscles on either side of Mostafa's mouth quivered. Andrea and Isaac were quietly engrossed in a side conversation. Amir closely observed his grandfather.

Justine looked down at the pages, still amazed by what she held. She read again the four entries translated from the opening pages of Mary's diary:

Three nights have passed since Joseph and I became husband and wife. Each day he sits with me, talking, telling me his stories. He speaks of his wife Zeinab, who is with God, and his dreams for son James. He speaks with me as a wife, but with the voice of a loving father. Joseph is a kind man. I am learning to trust him.

∽

It is now four nights since we made our vows. Joseph touches my hair and holds my hand. He tells me stories of the House of David. I fear he does not want me, but thinks of me as a child to be cared for. At first I feared his touch, now I fear he does not look at me with desire, that he does not want me as his wife.

✍

Five days since we were married. Joseph comes to me dressed in beautiful new clothes with small golden buttons on the girdle. Will you travel? I ask. Perhaps he came to tell me goodbye, that he would leave me. Joseph laughs and cradles my face in his rough hands. He says, today I come to make you my wife. I am not afraid, for my heart is glad. He kisses me on my face, neck, and hand with tenderness. I feel a stirring inside . . . a desire for something with no name. He lies beside me and unties my tunic. He does not hurry. On this day, we know each other. I am a married woman. Thanks be to God.

After his colleagues had read the entries several times, Ibrahim said: "Although there are no dates in the diary, we believe the fourth entry that you have in front of you was written about three months later."

I am with child. Joseph and I thank God that a child is given to us. I am well and able to take care of Joseph and James. I pray each day that my mother will be well again so I may stay with her. If she is not well, when I grow larger, I will find help from cousin Elizabeth. Joseph wants me to think of Elizabeth as my mother. I say to Joseph: If the child is a girl, I will call her Elizabeth.

"There's no mention of an Annunciation? No diary pages between entries three and four?" demanded Al Rasul.

"There are a few pages of daily life, preparing a household, discussions of the life ahead together, but no mention of an Annunciation," affirmed Ibrahim, patting the report softly, pain flashing through his watery eyes. "She didn't write every day, but it seems unlikely she would leave out a visit by the Angel Gabriel."

"The entries leave little reason to doubt a sexual relationship between Mary and Joseph," observed Isaac. "After the initial consummation, they continued to grow closer. Keep in mind that being 'older' then was different. Joseph may have only been in his forties."

"We seem to have little basis to doubt her word if we're confident that the codex authorship and content are authentic. Is that how the rest of you see it?" asked Mostafa, attempting a blustery and commanding performance once again.

Everyone began speaking at once. Mostafa held up his hand and turned to Ibrahim. "Coming to know each other, knowledge of a man and a woman, this is code language for sexual congress," admitted Ibrahim. "Based on the validity of these entries, we have no reason to assume a virgin birth."

"It could still be a fraud, written by a cult of heretics like the Gnostics. Not many of the devout accept the Gospel of Thomas," said Al Rasul mockingly. By the third century of the current era, the Church had soundly rejected Gnosticism, a doctrine asserting that divinity could be found within each person and claiming a Teacher of Righteousness who spoke like Jesus Christ.

"You'll find a range of opinions in this room about the Gnostics, but I'm convinced we have the genuine diary of Mary of Nazareth before us," said Andrea. "As you know, a number of ancient religions, including Greek polytheism and Christianity, have packaged virginity and divinity together. Breaking that bond doesn't necessarily mean Jesus wasn't divine. But, of course, we are all free to explore different theories of origin."

"I appreciate what you're trying to do, Andrea, but we Muslims have never found it necessary for Jesus to be understood as the son of God in order to worship him," Mostafa reminded her.

"I understand that. My objective is to draw our attention to the idea that nothing about this information need undermine basic beliefs about Jesus Christ," said Andrea, tilting her head so that a golden earring lay on her cheek.

"It's presumptuous of you to protect our tender beliefs, Andrea," Mostafa exclaimed with an air of condescension. "No one in this room is fragile. We're scientists."

"Your criticism is heard." Andrea ignored the insulting tone. "I trust you will all forgive my 'protectionism'?"

Amir glanced at Andrea and grinned before returning to his persistent doodling.

"Just forget about us," said Mostafa, impatient. "This information is going to be earthshaking beyond this room, particularly in the Coptic, Catholic, and

Anglican communities. I can't even predict how the Muslim community will react. But I am fearful."

"We have to discuss how this information is to be released—under what circumstances, and through what medium," said Ibrahim. "Shouldn't we alert the leaders of churches and mosques before it is released to the press? And do we have any right to release such provocative information without the original codex?"

"Good questions, Dr. Ibrahim." Mostafa paused and stared above Ibrahim's head into the ceiling-high bookcases. "If we're not cautious, or at least responsible, we'll ignite the dry tinder around us. Then we'll have to deal with the consequences." He drew out a handkerchief from his back pocket and wiped his brow.

With the keen eye of an anthropologist, Justine observed the layers of volatile feelings in the room. *We're all wallowing in our own fears. I wonder how long our restraint will hold?*

"Religious temperaments are explosive, and I don't want to feed these hostilities unnecessarily," Mostafa concluded as though answering Justine's unasked question. "Are we through here?"

"Wait. There's something else, isn't there?" asked Al Rasul, glancing around the room. "Yesterday, Justine, I think you used the phrase 'an unmistakable tone of melancholy' to refer to Mary's mood. What would cause that sense of melancholy? She had a loving husband and sons and was enjoying Egypt."

Not one of the translators spoke. Each of them looked down at the report as though they were scanning for information that already resided vividly in their own minds, information even more explosive than Mary's loss of virginity, and which, by unspoken agreement, they all hesitated to report. But what was the point in exposing the truth if they didn't expose all of it? Justine chose to respond: "There had been a loss—the loss of a daughter." She calmly picked up her teacup and waited for the expected response. It was not long in coming.

"The loss of a daughter? How? When? What daughter?" demanded Mostafa.

"A daughter named Elizabeth. Let me read two entries from the diary." Justine picked up a single page that she had set aside in anticipation of this moment.

"*Elizabeth is so ill. Her small body has been hot for many days. I am scared. We wash her body in cool waters. Rachel says a palate of balsam leaves will cool her, and when we come to Mataria the holy waters will heal her. Joseph walks her all night. I tend to Jesus. God, please save our Elizabeth, we beg of you . . .*

"*Elizabeth died this morning . . . Why, why, God? Why must you take our Elizabeth so soon? She did not have time to please you. What did I do to lose your protection?*"

"She died at Mataria? On the way from Palestine? How old was she?" demanded Mostafa, shivering in spite of himself. Even though Al Rasul had been called in for technical assistance, this information was new to him as well.

Ibrahim turned to Andrea, then Justine and Isaac. They had hoped to postpone this revelation until the information about Mary's virginity had settled. "She died on the trip to Egypt and was buried at Mataria," said Andrea gently.

"Then she must be a stepchild, like James," said Mostafa. "An older daughter born to Joseph and Zeinab before Mary's marriage to Joseph."

"We think she was about three months old when she died," said Justine.

"The same age as Jesus," affirmed Andrea.

"The same age . . . the same age . . . Elizabeth was a twin?" cried Mostafa.

"Elizabeth was Jesus' twin," said Ibrahim, dropping both hands in his lap. The word "twin" ricocheted around the room as people clawed desperately for its meaning. After several minutes of stunned silence in which no one spoke, the meeting adjourned with little fanfare and few words.

Justine and Amir scurried down the museum stairs, splitting up to round the fountain on opposing sides before exiting through the well-guarded gate and onto the frontage road bordering Tahrir Square. They walked rapidly; neither spoke. Ibrahim remained behind with his notes, Andrea with her last chocolate cookie, each of the others searching for someone to blame. Isaac had quickly stuffed his notes into a worn satchel and taken a taxi to the airport.

Deep in thought, the two crossed the Square and turned into a side street leading to the Corniche overlooking the Nile. It was dusk, a pale pink glow blanketing the Great River. Feluccas were everywhere. When they encountered the railing overlooking the Nile, they stopped, turned simultaneously and stared into one another's eyes.

"Do you still think I did it?" asked Amir with amusement.

"Do you want to confess? That would simplify everything." Justine was moving south now, past the Four Seasons to cross into Aisha al-Taimuriyya. *I seem to be headed home*, she said to herself.

"I make a mean spaghetti," Amir offered, uninvited. "If you have the ingredients."

"Okay. I also have plenty of Cleopatra cabernet."

He feigned an expression of repulsion. "It'll have to do."

Justine fished into her purse for the key to 10 Aisha al-Taimuriyya, unlocked the heavy wrought iron door, and started for the elevator. Amir passed her and began to climb the seven flights of stairs. Driven by the energy that accompanies tension, he took two steps at a time. Justine followed close behind.

"Make yourself at home," she said as they walked into the apartment. Before changing clothes, she stacked the kitchen counter with fresh tomatoes and garlic, a can of tomato paste, pasta noodles, oregano, and Italian seasoning. Two bottles of cabernet. Parmesan. Matches for the gas burners. She placed fresh lettuce into a bowl of vinegar water to clean.

"No sausage?" Amir asked, searching through the refrigerator and freezer.

"Nope. I'm getting out of these warm clothes. I'll be right back."

In the bedroom, she removed her work clothes—deciding again to give up clingy silk blouses—and stepped into the shower, washing her hair. As the suds flowed down her back, she considered the possibility of Nasser showing up uninvited. After all, he still had a key. *It won't happen. My texts were crystal clear. Busy for a couple of days, I told him. After work tomorrow is soon enough! By then, I'll surely know what to do.* But for now, she and Amir had bigger fish to fry: figuring out the theft of the diary.

Ten minutes later, she returned to the kitchen in her favorite Napa Triathlon T-shirt and shorts. No shoes. "Can I help?" She watched his intense black eyes studying the sauce as though it were a witches' brew and grinned to herself. *Mm . . . he is disconcertingly handsome.*

"It needs to simmer for a while. Get us a couple of wine glasses, will you, and set the table. I've opened the wine to let it breathe."

"Breathing doesn't seem to help Cleopatra," she laughed, pleased with her cleverness.

Amir winked at her and poured two glasses of the vinegary ruby liquid. His sports jacket hung on a kitchen chair, his short-sleeved dress shirt was opened at the neck. No undershirt. Justine smiled, recalling her dad's reason for always wearing an undershirt, even in hot and humid weather. "Less laundry," he'd insisted.

"What's so funny?"

She told him and then led him into the living room, where the overhead fan stirred the warm air. He sat on the couch, but Justine preferred the floor, cushioned only by an aging Berber carpet. "Amir. Did you tell Zachariah what was in those missing pages?"

He stiffened and set his glass on a peeling side table. "I hadn't talked with Zachariah since he disappeared—several months before the kidnapping—until that day in Muqattum." He stared at her as though waiting for an apology.

"I believe you, Amir. It's just that it was you who returned the pages, who placed them on Andrea's desk . . ."

"I thought we were past suspicions. Weren't we?"

She paused, dropped back on both elbows and watched the fan rotate for several moments. "Okay. What's your theory?"

Amir grinned in relief. "Who stole the diary? Actually . . ." he paused and picked up his glass. "I think you did."

Justine managed a poker face. "You're onto me. And what is my motive, may I ask?"

"You're ambitious. Possession of a world-shattering artifact could bring you fame and fortune."

"Mm. What I've always wanted. I'd have no problems getting it out of the country. My mother is involved in the black market in Italy."

"And you could show up your dad, the famous archeologist."

"And publish the findings, shocking the old boys in the Vatican." Her eyes twinkled with amusement as she sipped her wine. "This stuff really is terrible, isn't it?"

"It is, but the second bottle will taste much better," he assured her.

She agreed. "As for the theft, remind me again why you're not guilty?"

"I don't want to lose my job at the Museum? It's just too much fun working with the Great Mostafa?"

She laughed. "What a blowhard! How do you do it?"

"He's rarely around, so I hardly ever see him. But I wouldn't put anything past him."

"That's certainly my take on Omar Mostafa," she said. "But I watched him closely today—why would he endure such criticism? Such humiliation? No one would deliberately bring that down on himself, would he? And, then there's his secret contract with National Geographic."

"It depends on the stakes. And they're very high."

"Explain it to me. Pretend that I'm a babe in the woods, unacquainted with Egyptian culture, religion, whatever . . ." She curled her legs underneath herself and sat under the rotating fan.

"Okay. Here's what's at stake. Politically, Mubarak has kept the Muslims and the Coptic Christians at arm's length from each other. They're like two roosters aching for a fight. If he lets go, they could be at each other's throats. Churches are burned for very little reason. Last year, a priest in Alex tried to keep a young girl from converting to Islam, even though her boyfriend insisted, by holding her hostage in the priory for a couple of days and trying to convince her not to do it. A demonstration ensued and the church was burned. Any major challenge to beliefs on either side is grabbed onto as an excuse for violence. Suggesting that Mary wasn't a virgin and Jesus was a twin, a twin of a female, would be more than enough reason to upset the mango cart. Remember the Danish cartoon that sparked demonstrations throughout the Muslim world? Several deaths? That is child's play compared to a serious challenge to the Koran."

Amir got up and went to check on the spaghetti sauce. He stirred it, tasted it, and dumped the noodles into boiling water. "It's almost ready," he called from the kitchen.

Justine stretched out, rubbing the long scar on her right leg, and poured herself another half glass of the wine. "You're right about this wine. It's getting better." She grinned as he returned to the couch. "But those are not the real reasons for the tensions, are they?"

"Ah, you are so perceptive—and correct. Those reasons have little to do with religious strife throughout the Muslim world. The Copts are like the Jews were at the time of the revolution. In the '50s, the Jews were made quite unwelcome by President Nasser. Like the Jews, the Copts now own more than their share of the businesses, their women don't cover their heads, and they go about their lives freely while Muslims are praying five times a day. It has a great deal to do with economics. It always does. Perhaps even more important, Christianity is identified with the West. Infidels. Heathens. Imperialists."

"That's me. An infidel and heathen." She paused and grew serious. "Is that why Zachariah converted? Because Christianity is too identified with the West?"

Amir's face registered anguish. "That's part of it. It's also an act of rebellion—rejecting his family—and, of course, disgust with a society that can't solve its most miasmic problems of poverty and unemployment and extremism."

She watched him closely. "I'm so sorry, Amir. It must be painful to watch your family being pulled apart like this." She asked the next question gently, hesitantly. "Could he have taken the diary? He certainly talked that way in Muqattum."

"He has his reasons for suppressing the codex, but steal it? I don't think that's his nature . . . but then, I don't know him well anymore, either . . ." His eyes moistened as he forced himself to confront the fact that his brother was now a stranger to him. Justine scooted closer to the couch and laid a comforting hand on his arm. "If he is involved, it would be at the behest of the Brotherhood. But they have a larger agenda now. To take over the country."

"They've been suppressed for so long—are they capable of such grandiose plans?"

"They're very well organized. Efficient. And they don't like chaos, unless it serves a larger purpose," he said, eyes steely.

"And the codex could bring chaos. Even violence. What kind of a larger purpose?"

"If the chaos could allow them to fill a vacuum, secure power while others were distracted . . ." He paused, staring at the candle Justine had lit after the sun set.

"How fragile is Egypt? What's ahead?"

"Here's what I fear . . . if Egypt can't liberalize soon, it could be too late."

"Liberalize? What exactly do you mean?"

"If the Mubarak government falls apart before we have democratized our institutions—the courts, the rule of law, a constitution that protects individual rights. Before we've narrowed the chasm between rich and poor and grown more of a middle class. If that happens and we move to elections too soon, like in Gaza and Iraq, we could lose our country to the Brotherhood."

She shook her head. "Without a democratic foundation, the Brotherhood would win."

"I'm sure of it." He gazed at her with an intensity that set her heart racing, then changed course. "It's startling how many bit players had a part to play in our little drama. How their pieces of knowledge came together like a perfect storm."

"You mean like the docent Michael at St. Sergius, Youssra's father at the Rare Books Library. But what's your point?"

"As you know, Youssra's father disappeared. Replaced by another anonymous man. There are eyes and ears everywhere. Invisible men and women slithering through life unnoticed. They can do things that others can't." He stared at the ceiling fan, as though burrowing into a wounding memory from long ago.

"A sad commentary," Justine said, grabbing her knees to her chest. She was beginning to feel intoxicated.

Amir watched her, a deep sadness flickering through his eyes. "Ready to eat?" he asked, getting to his feet.

She nodded gratefully.

❧

"Not bad," she grinned, having found the spaghetti amazingly good. "The sauce has a Moroccan flavor."

"I put a little sugar and nutmeg in it," he explained. "Old family recipe." He poured another glass of wine for the two of them.

"Leave the dishes, I'll do them later." She paused. "When considering the thief, we always say 'he.' What about she?" Justine stretched out on the floor, closing her eyes for a moment.

"Andrea? Not likely. True, she's mysterious, complex. I never know what she's thinking . . . but that isn't cause for an accusation."

"She would have nothing to gain, as far as I can figure. Like me, she needs to be involved in translating the original, not a copy."

"But it's the copy that is used during translation, Justine. Not so?"

"As long as you have the real codex—it's like having gold in Fort Knox to back up the paper."

"I thought you were no longer on the gold standard?" His shoes now off, Amir propped his legs up on the couch.

"Cute—but it's a good analogy." She lit two more candles and spread out again on the floor. She gave Amir a silly grin as she watched the easy breeze from the French doors join the air movement of the fan and flicker the flames. She realized they were thinking too simply. *How is everyone, everything connected? There are several moving parts here.* "We can't go at this one person at a time," she said.

Amir stared at her, slightly glassy-eyed, at first not comprehending. Then a slow grin crept around his face as comprehension moved in like a leisurely train to Luxor. "Everyone has a motive," he said.

CHAPTER 23

———⟨∞∞⟩———

NASSER SPORTED HIS TEMPTING GRIN as he sat down opposite Justine at their usual table in the Shepheard's Caravan Café the next evening. Friends and lovers, almost soul mates, his eyes spoke with soft seduction. *But how well does he know me? At times, his face reflects such familiarity, and I think he understands me well. At others . . .*

When she offered only a perfunctory greeting, Nasser stared at her across the wide table. She watched as his expression revealed clarity, then darkness. "You've talked with your father," he finally said.

"He doesn't know you, Nasser." Her tone was even—her eyes didn't leave his uneasy face. "You lied to me." The smiling waiter approaching the table quickly turned on his heel and left.

She'd deliberately chosen a public setting for this conversation, although she was keenly aware that this was the very table where she and Nasser had met more than three months before. After the dinner with Amir, she'd made up her mind—the disappearance of the codex required her attention, and she needed to get this discussion with Nasser over with.

"I didn't exactly *lie*," Nasser said defensively.

"You said you were a student of my father's. Did you ever meet him?"

"No."

"You gave me the impression that you had met him . . . that you knew him . . . correct? When you say you're a student of my father's, we both know what that means. It implies a mentor-like relationship, more than even a student-teacher connection. It means get-togethers at our house and wine in the afternoon. It means sharing books and family stories . . ."

"I'm not sure I would have understood a teacher-student relationship in such intimate terms. Don't make cultural assumptions so blithely, Justine. Such familiarity with an eminent professor would not be acceptable here. I did sit in the back of the room during one of his lectures before he left Berkeley again in '03. I didn't say we were close," declared Nasser, his eyes now steely and determined.

"But you let me jump to those conclusions. During our times together, I made several references to your experiences with my father. You knew what I thought . . . I thought you knew him well. Early on, you talked about his habits and expectations. There were many opportunities to define the relationship as it was—or was not." When her voice tightened and her breath came rapidly and shallow, she knew that tears were not far behind. She was determined not to cry.

"You don't know how many times I wanted to correct your assumptions, especially at the Red Sea. A few times I started to, but just couldn't carry it off."

"What amazes me, Nasser, is that you had to have known I would talk with my father eventually. How did you plan to handle it then?" She tilted her head, aware that her whole face must be a landscape of puzzlement and anguish.

"I ran through several scenarios, including the one where he tells you that he can never remember all of his students and that I might have been a student of his. That was my most hopeful fantasy. I kept telling myself I would tell you before you talked with him and you would forgive me. The worst of all scenarios is the one before us now." His voice revealed his resignation and hopelessness.

"I'm afraid you're right. This scenario is complicated. But *why*, Nasser?" She knew she was wearing her heart on her sleeve, making herself vulnerable, but she needed to know there'd been something there that she hadn't imagined.

"Perhaps to meet a beautiful woman," he began weakly. "I'd heard you were at the hotel, and as I walked toward you it popped into my mind as the easiest introduction. I didn't think it through."

"Even though it wasn't true?"

He flinched and corrected her. "Not entirely true."

"Do you often lie so casually? " Her voice was firm once again, determined, sure.

"If you're asking how I negotiate my way through life, how often I tell small lies to ease my path, I'm not sure I know. Does anyone? The position you're taking, Justine, is a hard one. I thought you valued flexibility and forgiveness."

"I seem to value the truth even more." She found her own voice strangely theatrical. *Am I being childish?*

"I hope in the long run you can live up to your own standards." His eyes, as well as his words, challenged her now.

She was momentarily taken aback. *Mother suggested as much.* Was there ever a situation in which she would lie? Of course there was. She could think of several. "I know I'm sounding moralistic, but I have to think about other aspects of our relationship—what is true, what isn't."

"In the service of full disclosure, I have something else to tell you. Your beauty wasn't the only seduction, at least after the first several days." He was difficult to read now—his renewed strength was not defensive, but something else.

Justine was physically jolted by the realization that she had almost bought the "easy introduction to a beautiful woman" line. Before he could continue, she saw the story laid before her mind's eye. Her eyes narrowed. "It has something to do with the Nazareth Essenes, doesn't it? And the codex."

"It does." He turned toward the waiter, encouraging him to return to the table. "We'll have two cups of tea. *Shukran.*" The waiter jotted a few words on his pad and headed for the kitchen.

"The Essenes have everything to gain and nothing to lose by the revelations in this codex, Nasser. Why couldn't you tell me?" *Did he steal it?*

"After you told me about the codex, my task was to protect you and to make sure the codex came to light. I followed you out of Alexandria on your way back to Cairo, but drove on when the monks appeared and the men in the Mercedes rushed off. I was prepared to stop."

"You were there? And you didn't stop?" She paused, the past days churning in her mind. "When I told you about the incident at the Red Sea, you already knew. Nasser, you already knew . . ."

"I didn't want to tell you," he confessed. "In retrospect, I was embarrassed that I didn't stop. Justine, the codex is so important. We hope to learn something about Mary's origins as an Essene, perhaps more about Jesus himself. If Jesus is the Essene Teacher of Righteousness, that knowledge would validate our long struggle for legitimacy." Nasser was now himself again, assured, articulate. Redirected by his own mission.

"You didn't do all that well in protecting me, did you? I find it disturbing that you were not far behind us and yet waited until we were run off the road. We might have been killed. But perhaps we have both failed in our mission," she said with disdain. "The codex has been stolen."

"Stolen? How could that happen?" he demanded, his expression outraged. "Do you have a copy?"

She watched him closely. *Is he really surprised?* "We have a photographed copy. And frankly, I don't know how it could have been stolen. It was in Mostafa's safe and the Ministry claimed security was top-notch." *Well, almost.*

"Whatever that means," Nasser said sarcastically. "But you have a copy and have been able to translate most of it?" As if he realized he sounded overeager, he cleared his throat. "And you're safe, Justine. That is more important to me than the fate of the codex." The tea arrived and Nasser busied himself attending to their preferences: three spoons of sugar for himself, lemon for her.

Justine thought back over the preceding months. On the sidewalk below the large picture window, young women wearing headscarves walked in both directions, holding hands and talking rapidly. She paid close attention to the nonsensical ensembles . . . tight jeans and spike heels. Matching colors, designer sunglasses. She turned back to Nasser. "Who are you, Nasser? What has our relationship been to you?" Her voice felt hollow.

"If I may, Justine . . . I'm a man who found an easy, but granted, untruthful, entrée into a relationship with a beautiful, smart woman. I'm also a committed man of beliefs who later found that by protecting you, I was furthering my own mission. Ultimately, I'm the man who fell in love with Dr. Justine Jenner. That's who I am." For the first time since his arrival this afternoon, that crooked grin slowly emerged.

Justine could feel herself dissolving; an unexpected ripple of desire ran down her back and into her thighs. She lowered her hands below the table and clenched her fists to fight against the surrender her body was more than willing to make.

As he sensed what was happening to her, his grin widened into a smile. "Can you ever forgive me, Justine? Please."

His timing is artful. Some men seem to think that 'love' is the magic word that erases everything else. She knew she had to wrest herself away from this conversation. To think. She didn't trust her own capacity to resist his charms. "I may be able to forgive you as a person, as a human being . . . perhaps. But forgive you as a lover?" She shook her head. "You were on the desert road that night when my life was in danger. That's a greater indiscretion than any other lie."

"Let me get this straight." Nasser allowed disbelief to crawl into his voice. "You're telling me our relationship is over? That taking more time isn't going to make you change your mind? Does it make any difference that I love you?" Dark gray crept into his blue eyes.

"Of course it does. And I'm not sure that I don't love you. But this relationship could never work now."

CHAPTER 24

─oᴔᴔo─

T HE FOLLOWING DAY, JUSTINE AND Andrea were summoned to a meeting of
religious leaders to be held in the conference room of the Sultan Hassan
Mosque. It was a Friday, an unusual day for any meeting, business or otherwise.

The streets of Cairo were quiet on Friday mornings, as though an evacua-
tion notice had emptied the city. One or two cars moved with lonely self-
consciousness. Friday was the Muslim holy day, and businesses, government
offices, and schools were closed. As a rule, Christians did not work on these
days either, but congregated as families in havens like the Church of Our
Blessed Virgin on the Nile in Maadi, where benches and fountains adorned a
circular terrace above stairs that descended to the Nile below. Legend had it
that the Holy Family had left for Upper Egypt from the bottom of those very
stairs. Or so Michael had told Justine on the day of the earthquake.

Mosques, of course, were open on Fridays. Throughout Cairo, men gathered well before noon for the most important prayer day of the week. Row
upon row of Muslim men knelt on green and red mats in long alleyways, facing east toward Mecca. Throughout Cairo, believers listened to the rhythmic
calls of Imams chanting Koran surahs over strategically placed loudspeakers.
Other men and women, seemingly oblivious to the aura of worship nearby,
went about their daily lives, selling newspapers, flowers, roasted corn, and
foul, thinly sliced lamb. Parallel worlds, parallel lives; neither embarrassed by
the other.

The Sultan Hassan Mosque was the most exotic of them all. The towering granite walls of the entry hall led upward into the cool inner chambers of fourteenth-century Mamluk life, turning twice again before entering a secluded courtyard of worn marble. A three-tiered, white marble fountain formed the circular centerpiece of this sheltered chamber, its waters flowing from the top into a pool that served as a bath for visiting worshipers. A giant chandelier of blue glass towered over the fountain. Minutes before the midday call to prayer, men knelt at the fountain to purify themselves, washing their hands, forearms, and faces. This intimate courtyard led into the main hall of the mosque.

Justine parked her newly acquired Suzuki on a curb usually cluttered with tour buses, and she and Andrea headed toward the side door of the mosque. They arrived to find Ibrahim already sitting near the window, the afternoon sun accentuating his weathered face and untamed eyebrows. Omar Mostafa sat at a long table near six cups and saucers.

Within moments, Father Zein Hakeem entered with a shorter man with a long beard and flowing black robe. When Father Zein spotted Justine, he broke into a broad smile and steered the shorter man toward her, stopping to acknowledge his old friend Ibrahim.

"Dr. Jenner, I'd like for you to meet the Imam Mohammad El Awady from Al Azhar University." It was more of a pronouncement than an introduction.

Justine bowed slightly, extending her hand to the Imam, who reluctantly touched, but did not grasp or take hold of, the offering. Mostafa suggested they take their seats.

"Where is Isaac? And Amir?" Justine whispered to Andrea.

"I don't know," Andrea whispered in return as she turned her attention toward Mostafa. "I don't even know why we're here."

"Let me clarify the purpose of our meeting," began Mostafa. "We've invited the honorable Imam El Awady here as the leading representative of Islam in Egypt. Pope Shenoba is out of the country and asked Father Zein to represent the Coptic Church. After our last meeting concerning the codex, I felt it necessary to confer with religious leaders about the revelations that may soon be made public. I gave them my personal assurances—as has the professor—that we believe the codex may be authentic."

May be. Justine noted the sharp contrast to the conclusions they'd made in the Museum. She glanced at Andrea.

"They have many doubts," Mostafa continued, "which we may have to live with for now. However, they share my concern that the primary revelations about Mary's virginity, her Essene upbringing, and the reasons for the family leaving Palestine are shocking and may cause tremendous reverberations throughout the religious world. The 'twinness' issue presents even more serious problems."

"We are delighted, however," said Father Zein, "with the revelation that the Holy Family fled to Egypt and lived here during Jesus' formative years. This pleases us enormously. We knew the apostle Mark had begun the church in Alexandria, but now Egypt has an even greater role to play in the development of the teachings of the Church. I'm assured by the Imam that Muslims will also find comfort in a more prominent role for Egypt in the history of their faith." Father Zein turned to the Imam, who nodded solemnly.

Where is this going? I doubt we're here to hear glowing reports from these religious leaders. Mostafa could have handled that himself.

"However," said the Supreme Director.

Here it comes.

"We agree that further shocks to the religious community would be unwise at this time. Relationships among the religions are fragile at best. Acts of religious violence are everywhere."

Of course, that is why Isaac isn't here, because he's a Jew. Justine could feel herself stiffening as she began to anticipate an agenda that she would find hard to accept.

"Let me explain what these gentlemen have shared with me," said Ibrahim, glancing toward Andrea and Justine without making eye contact. "They— we—feel that the presence of a female twin of Jesus' would be unacceptable news at this time."

"Unacceptable? What do you mean unacceptable?" demanded Andrea.

"Please explain," said Justine evenly.

Ibrahim flinched and rose haltingly from his seat by the window. He slowly picked up his cane and made his way to the table. "The existence of a twin sister is difficult to interpret," he said. "While there may be several interpretations, none of them are, shall I say, suitable. Does this mean that the female child was also a child of God? If she was a child of God in the sense that Jesus was, why did He allow her to die?"

"And if Allah didn't intend for her to die," interjected Mostafa, "was it a mistake? Allah doesn't make mistakes."

"Perhaps He changed his mind," suggested Andrea with a hint of irony. "Perhaps he decided that the world wasn't ready for a woman prophet."

The Imam shifted in his seat, clearly impatient. "There are too many women trying to expand their influence in our faiths—to the detriment of all." He made an exaggerated, encompassing motion with his arm. "Those of you who are interpreting this codex would have us think that Mary was a primary teacher of Jesus, when it is clear in our faiths that Jesus was the teacher from infancy. I would draw your attention to the obscenities the Catholic Church is struggling with regarding Mary of Magdalene. The role of women in the lives of prophets must be minimized." The Imam's stubby hand reached for his tea. Peering out over his cup, his round face made him look more like an obstinate child than a man with the authority to dismiss more than half the human race.

"But why?" asked Justine impulsively. "Why minimize the role of women?" She instantly knew she didn't want to hear the response. In an effort to draw attention away from her own question, she continued: "She might have been the Daughter of God as envisioned by the Essenes."

Visibly startled by this irreverent interpretation, Mostafa, Father Zein, and the Imam looked at each other as though a tribal secret had been unleashed before them. The Imam was compelled to react again. "Why, you ask, young woman," he said with unveiled contempt. "Let me tell you why. God—Allah—created women to please and to serve men. So it is written. The Prophets are the source of the Priesthoods. The sex of the prophets is no accident, nor is their masculinity incidental. This is a divine choice!"

Speechless, Justine and Andrea turned to each other. Ibrahim and Father Zein were embarrassed, Mostafa impatient to complete his agenda. For the moment, no one challenged the Imam.

To challenge him would be pushing the stone uphill. She took a long sip of her tea. *Be calm, Justine, be calm.*

"If I may continue," Mostafa said sternly. "We are here this afternoon to ask—no, to direct—that the information about the alleged female twin in the codex be kept confidential. It is not to be released under any circumstances."

"Elizabeth," corrected Justine, "her name was Elizabeth." She felt personally offended by such depersonalization.

"What?" he asked impatiently. "Oh, yes. Elizabeth. If I may continue—if this information is made public, I will deny its credibility. Since the original codex is no longer present to challenge or confirm the validity of the released information, I can assure you that anyone bringing the information to light will be discredited. Do I have your assurances?"

"I will have to take that command under advisement," said Andrea with cool detachment. "I am a scholar first and a politician second. You must know, Dr. Mostafa, such directives are not well received by self-respecting scholars." Andrea directed her comment to Omar Mostafa, but stared at Ibrahim, who sat gazing down at his own twisted hands.

"While you are 'advising' yourself, Dr. LeMartin, do not forget that you are a guest in Egypt," Mostafa said cryptically.

"It doesn't surprise me," said the Imam, "that a woman would take that position. It is only further testimony of the need to diminish the role of women in decision circles. I made it clear today that I would not attend a meeting with a Jew. I should have included women as well." Everyone in the room looked surprised that the Imam would allow himself to be moved to such impolitic words.

Simultaneously, Andrea and Justine picked up their belongings and headed for the door. "I believe our meeting is over, gentlemen," said Justine.

"Maybe they're right," said Andrea as they moved rapidly down the stairs and into the sun-strewn courtyard.

"What? What are you talking about?" asked Justine, stopping abruptly.

"About the danger of a twin, a female twin." Andrea watched small children playing around the marble fountain, daringly dunking their toes or fingers. Alabaster sculptures of bygone heroes stood proudly on the emerald carpet of well-tended grass. "That reality could break apart the male mythology of faith."

"I don't understand."

"I had a twin, Justine. A fraternal twin. There are things about being a twin that others can't grasp." She collapsed onto the smooth edge of the fountain.

"I had no idea." Justine's voice softened, and she joined her. "Did he die?"

"Christopher died on our fifth birthday," Andrea said, her moist eyes catching the shimmer of the fountain. "Oddly, I remember it vividly. Or perhaps my memories are formed by stories I've heard."

Justine moved closer, placing her hand on Andrea's forearm.

"Even though we were in different placentas, we shared the same sounds, the same sights, the same nutrients in the womb. When our mother was upset or tired, we felt the same stress. We tussled back and forth in there."

"How do you know all that?" Justine was incredulous.

"I don't remember, I guess, but I feel it—I've always felt it. I miss him as though part of me has been amputated. Bereaved twins are half-souls you know. Twins develop in relation to each other. When a twin is lost, a part of ourselves is lost. You have to recalibrate your heart."

"You're talking about Jesus and Elizabeth also?"

"Two thousand years ago, a multiple birth was a miracle in itself. So many things could go wrong. They were a great gift from God. And people were wiser about binding them together. They would have slept in the same bed, been held to Mary's breasts at the same time."

"What does this tell us about Jesus? About who he became?"

"Jesus would have defined himself in relation to Elizabeth, taking on many of the female qualities she represented—just as he would have done if she'd lived. He may have absorbed sensitivity, empathy, connectedness, an aversion to injustice . . . the qualities women hold dear."

"And if he defined himself in relation to Elizabeth . . ."

Andrea finished her thought: ". . . then Mary would have helped him develop the essential qualities of both genders, to become remarkably balanced and perceptive."

✍

"Yes, yes, Mom, thanks . . . I'm doing well. All mended . . . or almost." Justine had dialed Italy as soon as she got back to her apartment, wanting to hear her mother's voice. *Tell her about the meeting.* Given the rising level of threat, she really needed to know why Ibrahim had told her to call her mother.

"And your heart? It's mending too?"

Justine hadn't told her mother about the decision to break up with Nasser. *How does she know these things?*

"Well, let's say my mind is working better than my heart, but you know me: I keep it beating regularly by jogging on Roda Island."

"Ah, Roda. My closest friend lives behind the Manial Palace. Beautiful gardens . . ."

Lucrezia sounded ready to be interrupted, so Justine changed the topic. "I have an issue concerning the codex . . . and Ibrahim . . . and you, Mom."

"Ibrahim? And me?" Stillness now on the other end of the phone. Justine could hear the squabbling shrieks of jays in her mother's garden. *She must be standing on the terrace.*

"Andrea and I had a difficult meeting today with Ibrahim. There was some conflict over his reluctance to let parts of the codex come to light—sections that would challenge strongly held religious beliefs, both Christian and Muslim. Earlier, he said: 'Talk to your mother.'"

"Talk to your mother? Ibrahim asked you to talk with me about the codex?" There was a tone of incredulousness in her mother's voice, and Justine could almost feel her thinking. "Ah . . . Ibrahim is being cautious again and he thinks that I might support him. Is that it?"

"I would say that's pretty close." Justine grinned into the phone. "He, along with Omar Mostafa, the Imam, and a Coptic priest named Father Zein. They want to keep it secret that Jesus had a twin sister. And, of course, they would like to suppress that Mary wasn't a virgin. And the Holy Family's reason for coming to Egypt. Pretty much the whole thing, really."

Lucrezia laughed. "The Church—Rome and Alexandria and Constantinople—has thousands of years of practice in deception and burying new revelations. They'll not give up easily. Consider what happened to the finds of the past sixty years and the recent Gospel of Judas. Have they really changed anything?"

Justine was quiet, considering. "I see what you mean. Information that could, would, alter the meaning of Christianity is cleverly deflected. But tell me, why did Ibrahim ask me to talk with you? What is your connection to him? Other than as a family friend, I mean."

"Okay . . . well . . . this is going to be a long story. Do you have time?"

Justine's stomach tightened. "Go ahead. I have time."

"From my home here in Fiesole I overlook the Duomo—it's my constant reminder of the collusion of the Church with what seems to be a universal male need for a virgin mother. But I'm getting ahead of myself. You first should know that Ibrahim watched me grow up, and when he deemed me old enough, he seduced me."

"An affair, Mom? With Ibrahim? Mother! How could that happen? Did Father know?" Her shocked voice gained momentum as she spoke.

"Slow down, Justine. One question at a time! No, your father never knew. And I'd like to keep it that way. Please. After all, Ibrahim was his mentor and colleague."

"Okay . . . but Ibrahim is so much older. How . . . why?"

"Twenty-seven years older. But remember, my anthropologist daughter, that in many parts of the world a difference in age is not considered relevant."

"Now I remember the mischievous sparkle in his eyes when he talks about you," Justine said wryly. "But I never suspected. That scoundrel! My god . . . what happened?"

"Ibrahim was a friend of the family. We attended the same church and we all belonged to the Ghezira Club. I had a teenage crush on him, I suppose. In those days, he was dashing and thoroughly mysterious. When he began to make advances, I was flattered. Enthralled, actually. It was a seduction, yes,

Justine, but I went along with it. My parents never knew." Justine was trying to take all this in when her mother continued with, "Thank god I never got pregnant." Lucrezia said this calmly, as though she were reporting a routine event.

"How old were you?" asked Justine, bracing herself to be shocked again.

"Seventeen . . . or maybe a little younger."

"In America we would put him in jail!" Justine said with an air of self-righteousness. She felt angry, righteously angry, with Ibrahim.

"The rest of the world is not as puritanical as America," reminded her mother.

"I know . . . I know that . . . But why is Ibrahim so sure you would support him?"

"Ibrahim thinks he knows me. He thinks I'm still that devout young girl, loyal to Coptic Christianity. Unwavering in my beliefs. But he hasn't known me for a long time. I'm quite a different person now. You might even say I'm a devout agnostic."

Justine nearly dropped the mascara she was holding, but she couldn't help laughing. "A devout agnostic? I knew you were an agnostic. But devout? Isn't that an oxymoron?"

"No . . . I'm just passionate about knowledge. And since God is unprovable, at least in my mind, he or she is unknowable. I'm more drawn to explanations of the universe that are Epicurean or Kabbalistic in nature. In those traditions, the world is explained as atoms and personal experience. An energy source in the universe. But then you and I have explored these ideas before. Let me just assure you, daughter, that it is not in my nature to withhold knowledge in the interest of faith."

"I'd never thought otherwise, Mom. And just so you know, I think Ibrahim is edging into senility and that his distant memory is probably more vivid than his memory of yesterday. I'm sure he remembers the young, compliant Lucrezia."

Lucrezia only sighed, and Justine said, "Thanks Mom. I think that tells me what I needed to know."

"But wait a minute, Justine. You know that your dad and I talk . . . right? We are both worried there are dangers there you're not telling us about. You said the meeting with the Minister of Education went well. So why don't you just get out of there . . . come home?"

Justine wasn't prepared for this. "Mom . . . thank you. I always feel your support. Yours and Dad's. But I don't think I'm ready yet. I've still got work to do in the schools . . . with the girls. And Mom, about the codex . . . somehow I feel I was just meant to find it." *If they knew the full story, they'd send the National Guard after me.*

"Justine! That's sounds a bit too mystical. I . . ."

"Love you, Mom. Gotta go. Bye."

CHAPTER 25

⸨⸩

"I S THERE ANYTHING TO THE RUMOR, Dr. Mostafa, that the diary of the Virgin Mother has been found?" asked the interviewer on Al Ahram television. Having explored new finds in the western desert and a tomb that could possibly belong to Hatshepsut, the half-hour program was nearing its end.

"Little at this point. But of course, speculations run wild," replied Mostafa, with exaggerated nonchalance. "What I can tell you is that an ancient book has been found, somehow appearing in the bag of a young American woman who is not an archaeologist." He struck a dismissive air. "As you know, artifacts found out of context—taken from their place of origin—are highly suspicious. We validated the time period during which the document was written, but the contents raise many questions." Mostafa filled the chair and the studio with his sense of regal presence, exuding authority and charm like some people exude fear.

"Questions? Such as . . ." asked the eager interviewer.

"Many writings have been discovered in the past several decades that appear to have been written by members of a radical and discredited cult known as Gnostics. A godless bunch. Findings such as the Gospel of Thomas and the Gospel of Judas are good examples. Their claims are in direct contradiction to centuries of religious teachings and more solid evidence. These documents have been largely discredited by the world's religious scholars. What we have here may be another such example."

"Your comments whet my appetite, Dr. Mostafa. Can you reveal any of the contents? I'm sure that our audience would be most interested. One of the wildest speculations around is that the book may have been written by the Mother of God herself. What can you tell our listeners about that?"

"A foolish conjecture, I assure you. I can promise your audience that they can continue to count on my office for breaking news as soon as the information becomes authenticated."

"At this point, then, you would warn listeners not to be taken in by the rumors?"

"Exactly," said Mostafa, flashing his infamous smile.

"My visa's been revoked," Andrea said with characteristic calm as she curled up on Justine's couch. "I'll even have to get coverage for the balance of my classes."

Justine kicked off her shoes and released her body into the embroidered armchair across from the couch. "Revoked? What happened?" She was chilled by the news, though not entirely surprised.

"It's begun, Justine. No telling what will happen next," Andrea said, her black eyelashes fluttering like small velvet fans holding back the tears. "Mostafa . . . the Imam . . . the Copts . . . the plan is being set in place to discredit us. Me, at least,. You may not have seen Mostafa's interview last night."

"I didn't. I was on the phone much of the evening. And working on a school report."

Andrea summarized the Great Man's claims in the Al Ahram interview.

Justine was stunned; she was speechless for several moments. "My god! I had no idea he would lie so directly! Can't the University do anything? At least get your visa extended for the rest of the semester? This is so abrupt."

"The AUC President asked Minister Ghalib to intervene. We'll see. But you need to prepare yourself for what's ahead," said Andrea, twisting the golden ankh on the long chain around her neck.

Justine could feel her chest tightening. "Mom pointed out what we already knew: the churches—and mosques—are very practiced at deflecting truth."

She grabbed two bottles of Evian from the fridge, handed one to Andrea, and began to pace back and forth across the room. When she turned around, Andrea was crying. *Why am I surprised? Did I think Andrea was too mature, too strong . . . beyond crying? Is anyone beyond crying?* She sat down beside her friend, taking her hand as tears welled up in her own eyes.

"Don't be shocked by anything that happens now," said Andrea, so softly it was difficult for Justine to hear her. "The gears have been put into place to erase the evidence of apostasy, faithlessness."

"Evidence? You mean the codex?" Justine was startled once again.

"A small item appeared in the paper this morning. It's titled, 'What is this we hear about a diary?' Or some approximation in Arabic."

"Such a small town! It continues to amaze me how rumors can go viral—it's as though the city were an engorged Internet!"

"You're so right. Rumors move faster than a dust storm in this damned desert," affirmed Andrea. "Speaking of secrets, did your mother understand why Ibrahim asked you to talk to her?"

Justine walked into the kitchen and grabbed two glasses and a bottle of Antinori cabernet she'd been saving for a special occasion. *This occasion warrants indulgence,* she reasoned. Returning to Andrea, she replied: "Ibrahim first knew my mother when she was a devout young woman. Apparently, he thought she'd want to preserve the beliefs of the church. At one time he knew her very well . . . but he doesn't know her now."

"What do you mean 'very well'? Were they involved?" Andrea asked with an air of amusement.

"A young woman, twenty-seven years his junior, seduced by the charming professor, a friend of the family," Justine said. "My father never knew. At least that's what she claims."

"I never suspected, but I should have. Ibrahim was quite a womanizer in his day." Andrea tilted her head and winked.

Justine stared at Andrea. "You, too?" She allowed herself to be astonished once again. "Will surprises never cease?" She grinned. "And I thought Ibrahim's flirtatious manner with you was just an unrequited fantasy; really, it was fond memories."

Andrea waved her hand as though such old news was not worth pursuing. "I'm surprised that Ibrahim would still think of Lucrezia as the innocent he knew years ago. He's losing touch."

"A victim of those finely edited memories, I suppose. And age." Justine grew pensive, calm. "I'm sure to be asked to leave Egypt. But I have no intention of going quietly. We must write about what we've found. Can you agree to that?" She tightened her grip on her friend's hand. Andrea flashed an enigmatic smile. "Where is the copy right now?"

"It's still with Ibrahim, as far as I know," said Andrea, staring into the ruby liquid. She glanced up. "You're taking this better than I expected."

"I'm fearful—fearful of abandoning my work with the girls, fearful of leaving friends, fearful of the effects of all of this on my career, even fearful of what is still unknown. Embarrassed, too, since I was warned about extracurricular involvements. It makes sense that they would need to discredit us. Me as the unqualified discoverer of an unprovenanced find, and you as the major translator. Isaac, being Jewish, can be easily discredited. That just leaves Ibrahim. Do you think the codex copy is safe with him?"

"I'm not sure . . . I'm not at all sure. He violated our trust once before. But there are others on the team; can they get to all of them? How about Al Rasul? Amir?"

"Many of these men have known each other for a long time, so nothing would surprise me. As for the copy of the codex, we need to find out if it's safe, how to get access to it. The sooner the better. When do you have to leave Egypt?"

"I have a week to find a replacement for my classes and conclude other obligations to the university. At least, that's where it stands right now."

Justine's cell rang. "Yes, okay, I understand," she said, ending the call. "Nadia's picking me up," she told Andrea. "We have an appointment with the Minister. She sounded ominous."

CHAPTER 26

━━⟨∞⟩━━

JUSTINE'S MORNING RUN ON RODA ISLAND was fierce, fast, a failed effort to clear her head of the disturbing meeting with the Minister of Education. Dr. Ghalib had been the carrier of bad news: her expulsion from Egypt. Embarrassed, humiliated, Justine had fought back tears of anger and sadness as she apologized for depriving the schools of her services, for using poor judgment, for permitting her passions to pull her into uncharted territory.

She stepped out of the shower as her phone rang. It would be Nadia again, arranging for a meeting this morning at the Marriott. She grabbed the phone as though it were an offending appendage. "Okay, Nadia. More bad news? Am I going to prison?" she nearly yelled into the phone. Calming herself, she asked, "What time are we picking Andrea up?"

"I don't think prison is likely," said Amir.

"Oh! Amir. Hi," she said, discombobulated. She could almost feel his amusement over the phone. "Please forgive me. I'm feeling a little touchy this morning." She sat on the bed and dried her wet hair.

"No kidding. I think you've answered my question. I called to find out how the meeting with the Minister went."

She told him. Then paused. "Any other theories on the theft?" Throwing the towel on the floor, she hugged the phone between her chin and shoulder and walked to her dresser, picking out lingerie and a deep green silk blouse—*a mistake in this heat*, she reminded herself, but everything else was dirty or needed ironing.

"A few thoughts—not much more. As we agreed, everyone has a motive, and it probably involves a number of co-conspirators. And there are actors on- and off-stage."

"What do you mean?"

"The invisible crowd. Thousands of options. But I'm persuaded that Mostafa and his cabal are involved somehow, although he appears to also be the victim. A clever ruse, I suspect. Then there's the Alex crowd. Perhaps even Grandfather."

"How does the Brotherhood figure in?" She buttoned her blouse and grabbed gold hoop earrings from a side table. They were warm in her hand.

"Anything is possible with the Brotherhood, although most of these folks would find working with them offensive. On the other hand, there are many professionals in the organization and it's often difficult to know who's a member."

"The young priest from Santa Barbara was at Muqattum. Strange bedfellows," she reminded him. "Amir," she paused, giving full consideration to what she was about to say. "Do you think Nasser is involved? The Nazarene Essenes have a great deal at stake here. They're searching for a female god."

"Nothing I'd like better, but I don't think so. If you'll forgive my saying so, they're disorganized and have few contacts with the Supreme Director's office or the Museum. But anything is possible."

And Nasser was genuinely surprised when I told him about the theft. "Amir. I've broken off my relationship with Nasser." She let her words hang in the air. He said nothing. Embarrassed, she continued: "There's a missing piece of this puzzle. What are we not seeing?"

"Aisha would never have allowed it!" Nadia exclaimed. "Fourteen hundred years, and sometimes I think women are no better off." Her face was flushed, eyes wide, hair more wild than usual. Embarrassment and anger consumed her as she faced Justine and Andrea over lunch in the Palace Garden in Zamalek. Once the palace that Sheikh Pasha built in honor of Eugenia Napoleon during the construction of the Suez Canal, it was now owned and operated by the Marriott Corporation. The women sat around a classic rattan table in the mostly deserted garden restaurant.

"Aisha?" Andrea asked, interrupting Nadia's rant.

"Aisha. *Iwa*," Nadia said. "The beloved wife of the Prophet. It was Aisha who wrote down most of the teachings of Mohammed, from Mecca at least. When tribal clerics insisted on the submission of women, she alone resisted. We like to call her the first Muslim feminist."

"Do you consider her spirit still alive?" asked Justine.

"You bet it is," insisted Nadia. "Muslim feminism is spreading throughout the Islamic world. She'd have been angry as hell at the expulsion of two accomplished women from Egypt. On the other hand, it's unfortunate that you involved yourself with this controversial business about Mary and her daughter. The community schools will now be deprived of your insights . . ."

Justine felt defensive. The meeting with the Minister had been painful enough. "The codex fell in my lap—or at my feet. It's not as though I went in search of trouble. But, I'll admit, after the incident on the desert road, you did warn me. I was just too deeply involved by then."

"I'm not accusing you. Have I given you any reason to think I wasn't supportive? Yet . . ."

"Go on," Justine interrupted, feeling the sting of regret redden her cheeks. She knew exactly what she was guilty of. Even if Nadia hadn't warned her, becoming involved in the political and religious conflicts of a host culture was considered unethical for an anthropologist, regardless of how intriguing the situation.

"If you hadn't let yourself be drawn in, you wouldn't be leaving now. This unfortunate business is threatening the whole notion of community schools for girls as well. Many in power would relish an opportunity to close us down." Nadia fanned herself rapidly with her spiral notebook.

Tears formed in Justine's eyes. "You're right," she said. She rose and walked to the wall overlooking the pool, remembering her parents, together then, dancing to the music of a small orchestra perched under towering date palms. Her mother had worn a gauzy gown of flowing white, her father had looked eternally handsome in his best black Egyptian suit. The memory returned with the scent of jasmine floating in the air that night. *How simple life seemed then. I thought it would always be that way. But now my parents are divorced and I've failed in my first professional assignment.*

"Enough," Andrea said from the table. "That's just enough. We know the protocol in our fields, yet there isn't one of us who could have resisted getting drawn in by the diary of the Virgin Mary. Not you, Nadia. Not me. Not Justine. Curiosity drives what we do. Besides, accusations can't help us now."

"When you leave here, Dr. LeMartin, you'll be back in your comfortable world where women are equals. We have to be ever-vigilant about women's rights here, rights to work, to discovery. While we do have new laws protecting women's rights, they are fragile. No-fault divorce. Improved child custody rights. Yet extremists are calling them "Suzanne's Laws" since Suzanne Mubarak—a professional and activist—challenges their archaic notions of how a decent woman should behave. If Mubarak ever falls, women may also." Nadia addressed Andrea with heavy sarcasm. "It's easy to expel non-Egyptians, but there may be repercussions for the rest of us as well. The Muslim Brotherhood is alert for opportunities to sidetrack our advancement, and whenever they have a chance to suppress an issue regarding women, it strengthens their hand."

"I see. I'm sure you're right," Andrea said demurely. "We're all edgy today. Leaving Egypt is a personal tragedy for me as well, and I want to leave without losing the friends I've made."

A softer expression washed across Nadia's face. She reached out and held both of Andrea's hands. "I'm sorry, Andrea." Twisting toward Justine, she said, "Justine. I'm so sorry I couldn't prevent your expulsion. I feel that I've failed you."

"You haven't failed anyone," said Justine, returning to the table, recalling Nadia's comments about her hungry guilt, her need to feed it. "I got myself into this mess. I knew early on that the situation could get rough. I should have just kept my eyes on the schools. Now it looks as though Omar Mostafa and his consorts—whoever they are—will have the last word."

"There's one more chance," offered Andrea, biting into a delicately frosted cookie. "We'll see Ibrahim tomorrow. I'm not confident that he can help, but we have to give it a try. And we have to obtain the copy of the codex."

"Why wouldn't he help?" asked Nadia. "If he could."

"He will if he can," said Andrea. A piece of frosting fell into her coffee. She looked shocked.

"We're just not sure how deep the cover-up goes," offered Justine. "But one thing is sure: It involves both Copts and Muslims, perhaps everyone from Pope Shenoba to the Imam. And the Ministry of Interior." The opposition was overwhelming.

Nadia spoke, softly this time, realizing that any interventions at their disposal lacked power, authority. After all, NGOs like UNESCO had only informal power to bring to bear against patriarchal bureaucracies, mosques, and churches. "I'm afraid we have little direct recourse. The future of Egypt's girls rests in education and in women working with other women. Confronting power directly has little chance of success."

Justine fidgeted with her plate, slowly turning it round and round.

Nadia stared into the distance as though reminiscing. "I'm still encouraged by the courage of Egyptian women—and by the new policies allowing women to be more self-sufficient. I still meet with a group of women from Shoubra in the basement of the Anglican Church. They want to know how to talk about their wants and desires directly. How to involve men in raising their own children, how to say 'no' to giving birth to more children, the importance of education for their daughters, even letting those daughters choose their own husbands," she said. "And the birth rate *has* fallen in the past few years. Nearly in half. But if the Brotherhood has its way, we'll lose the momentum we have." She grew quiet, sipping her second Diet Coke, an addiction she'd picked up from Justine.

Justine harbored her own thoughts as Nadia spoke. *What does freedom mean to Arab women? What did it mean to Mary? For her, Egypt was freedom— yet two thousand years later, Egypt denies me freedom.*

"When do you leave, Andrea?" Nadia asked.

"A week from today," said Andrea, tears trickling down her cheeks and staining her lavender linen blouse with drops of black mascara.

Justine glanced at her, then Nadia. Her chest contracted with the pain of loss, the consternation of regret. *I'm leaving the girls, those who have learned to trust me, rely on me. Who believed that somehow I could help them create a promising future. Ibrahim is our final chance, but I don't see what he can do. Yet, as Dylan Thomas would say, I don't intend to go gentle into the good night.*

CHAPTER 27

TWO YOUNG MEN DRESSED IN WESTERN attire entered the square near St. Mark's Church in Heliopolis. The first man, stocky and muscular, driver of the dilapidated vehicle they traveled in, stepped from the car and reached into his trunk for a long, sturdy two-by-four. Holding the board in both hands, he walked toward the massive church door and wedged the long plank into the iron rings dangling from ancient knockers. The second man, thin and wiry by contrast, walked around the five-hundred-year-old structure, spreading gasoline from red cans with aluminum nozzles. Neither man spoke or paid attention to the children playing nearby. They had their orders: burn one Coptic Church in northern Cairo, one in the south. Almost simultaneously.

Removing a small black cigarette lighter from his jean pocket, the second man set fire to the puddles of gasoline surrounding the church. Flames exploded into the night sky.

A third young man, younger than the others, expected but late, parked thirty meters south of the car with the open trunk. Screams could be heard from the church. Horrified, he rushed to the barred door, wrestled the plank loose, flung open the door, took the arms of two terrified, elderly men, and helped them down the steps. By now, flames licked the darkened sky, reaching high above the profiles of adjoining apartments. To the south, a blazing echo radiated from the direction of Old Cairo. Two Coptic churches, torched in the night, burned uncontrollably. Fire engine and police sirens pierced the distant air. Terrified children, reporting to equally terrified parents, had sounded the distress alarm.

The younger man ran toward the other two. "*Kafiya, kafiya,* stop!" he yelled, knocking a gasoline can from the hands of one of the men, causing the stream of fuel to run rapidly toward the waiting car with the open trunk. The car exploded into flames.

The stocky man cried out to the late arrival: "Are you crazy? In the name of Allah, stop! We have our orders." Infuriated by his burning car, the desire for revenge welled up in his chest. He drew a knife from his peeling leather belt; the steel glowed with reflected flames.

"You are here to put fear in the hearts of Copts. Undermine their security under the regime. Not take lives," screamed the younger man.

With a screech of rage, the stocky man lunged toward the younger man, grabbing him by the back of his neck with his left hand and thrusting the knife toward his throat. The younger man grabbed hold of his attacker's arm and threw them both forward, rolling them onto the burning ground. The blaze caught hold of flapping fabric and rapidly engulfed the two men as they struggled.

Distracted by the searing pain of the flames and unable to hold his attacker at bay, the younger man felt the knife slide across his throat. The blade tumbled into the burning gasoline. Soon, the inferno swallowed the two men and the church.

The thinner man, confused and horrified by the ghastly bodies of his two associates, fled into the darkened alleyway.

To the south, St. Sergius, already severely damaged by the quake, burned to the ground. The holy crypt now opened directly into the night air. The results were exactly as the Muslim Brotherhood wished: caught in the crosshairs of sectarian strife, Egypt reverberated with scattered acts of violence. Chaos. President Mubarak had always protected Christians, but his reign was weakening. What would happen if the Brotherhood had their way?

OLD CAIRO 2 CE

On the last evening of Passover, Joseph draws the reed curtain across the mouth of the cave. When the abrupt knock comes, no one knows whose fist has sounded the alarm.

"The Romans!" yells Jesus. "They're here. They've come for us!"

"Shhh," I caution, grabbing my son's arm to keep him from flying out of his chair.

"Not yet," says Samir, "we were told we had a few more days."

"You expect the Romans to keep their word?" snarls Noha.

Both Isaiah and Joseph rise and move toward the door. The others remain at the table. Joseph glances around the room for a weapon of some sort, though he knows it will do no good.

Isaiah slowly draws back the curtain of fine reeds. The light from the full moon rushes in, carving out the dark silhouettes of two visitors.

I stare at James, who looks as though he is being called to atone for pulling Herod's graven eagle down from the temple gate. For it was James who, more than eight summers ago, stood on the shoulders of the older boys, boys who were caught and brutally slaughtered by Herod's soldiers while James went free. I know that guilt has followed him like a stalking lion ever since, eating away at his mind during the night and in the quiet moments when he works on the canal.

"Pravar!" I exclaim, rising from my chair, surprised and relieved to see friends instead of soldiers.

"Ravi," echoes Jesus, escaping from my grasp and running to his young friend.

"Why have you returned?" asks Joseph. "Surely you could have been to Alexandria by now. Was your boat not allowed to pass into the delta?"

"As we loaded supplies in Heliopolis, we overheard Roman soldiers talking," replies Pravar, out of breath from rowing up the Great River. "They will raid your homes tonight. Joseph, Mary, they will not wait for the prefect to arrive. Take only what you can carry and come with us. But hurry."

"The animals!" cries Rachel.

"Zechariah's bible stand?" asks Joseph, his voice falling off in resignation.

"Only what we can carry," I repeat, rolling up the bedding and grandmother's linen tablecloth, wrapping it carefully around eight wooden spoons. I reach into a niche near the dishes to find the earthen jar that contains our few dinars, and I allow my hand to linger inside the niche, grasping my precious calfskin book. Forcing my fingers to separate, I withdraw my hand, holding only the jar. "Only what we can carry," I repeat.

Before we flee the cave, our home for these many years, I draw my hand over the mouth of the cave. Eight summers, and now we must leave behind so much of ourselves. Will I ever know freedom again?

Hooves on the dry earth sound a crackling alarm as Roman riders drive their horses across the rise from the east. Moonlight witnesses the release of our donkeys and sheep from our corrals. Raised Roman swords glow like torches in the night.

I am the last family member to step onto the waiting ark. "My comb, Joseph . . . I've forgotten my comb!" I cry, pulling away from my husband's grip just as Pravar places his heavy boot on the shore and pushes the boat into the rapidly moving current.

CHAPTER 28

———∞∞———

"CAN YOU HELP US, IBRAHIM?" Justine and Andrea sat anxiously across from the aging professor in his cramped library office. Their stories of impending expulsion had evoked no response from him. *Did he already know?* The two women glanced at each other, wondering if he were listening at all.

Ibrahim El Shabry sat lost in another world. "I think it was a Tuesday after-noon . . . *iwa*, a Tuesday," he began, his voice disembodied, his eyes concentrating on the warping floorboards. "I'd just finished cataloging the new Rameses exhibit. My grandson, Zachariah—he was about eight—had gone with his father to work in the British Embassy. But then he came storming into my office in the Museum. I was in the Museum then. He must have run all the way. His face was red; he was out of breath. 'What's wrong?' I asked. The boy stood there and trembled as he described what he had seen at the embassy. To a less sensitive boy, it might not have meant much . . . but to Zachariah . . ."

"What's happened?" asked Andrea, realizing that he did not hear her.

Ibrahim continued talking, as though to himself. "His father, my son-in-law, had been called to account by the British for some slip in protocol. One of the bureaucrats, strutting like a colonial master, dressed down Gamel in the most wretched terms . . . called him a damned savage . . . Gamel was darker-skinned, you see, like Sadat . . . a noose around the neck of the British, an embarrassment to the office. From what my grandson heard, his father had forgotten to invite the Jordanian consul to a meeting on Israel. He didn't understand the importance of this slip in protocol, but his father's devastating humiliation was obvious. His father didn't say anything. He just stood there and took the verbal whipping while his son watched. After that day, the boy was more distant, more sullen. Humiliated for his father. Such a sensitive boy . . ."

"Ibrahim . . . Ibrahim . . ." tried Justine, placing her hand on his trembling arm. "Something has happened. What is it?"

"Zachariah was never quite the same, you know," he said, glancing briefly at Justine, eyes glassy, flat. "He could not tolerate injustice. He was fiery, passionate. When he got into high school, he volunteered at St. Mark's, helping the elderly, those unable to walk on their own. Taking them home, he would stop to buy groceries from his allowance. I understand he converted to Islam—a generous religion, but I'm afraid his motives were not religious." Ibrahim's face contorted in agony. "And now he is dead. Dead. Left to burn with the church he tried to save, the church where he grew up . . ."

Andrea held him while he sobbed. Neither woman had heard about Zachariah's death. They had both thought he had left the country.

Grief washed over Justine's face. *But what was he doing at the Christian church? He was in a Christian church the day of the kidnapping, and he explained his mission then. But burning churches?* "I'm so sorry, Ibrahim," she said. "I know it must be so terribly painful for you, the family." She thought of Amir, his loyalty to his brother, and then his accusations. *Will he feel responsible?* She clasped her hands, digging her fingernails into her palms and burying them in her full khaki skirt.

"Is there anything we can do, Ibrahim, anything at all?" Only silence greeted Andrea's offer of help. "We will go then," she said quietly, nodding to Justine, who rose, hugged Ibrahim, and kissed him on the forehead before stepping toward the door. The question about access to the copy of the diary would have to wait.

Ibrahim sat slumped in his chair, broken by the death of his favorite grandson. With head still down, he called after them. "No . . . No, don't go yet. I've more to tell you."

"*Iwa,*" Andrea said, relieved and surprised. She held Justine's moist eyes as they sat back down.

"When you brought me the codex, Justine, I knew it was important," he began. "My excitement grew when we were able to get Andrea, and then Isaac, to assist with the translation. I soon regretted bringing you in, my dear," he said to Andrea. "With your expertise and courage—and Isaac's—I knew I would have little chance of keeping the findings secret, for by then I had managed to read several words on the opening pages. I was stunned by what I learned, but it was too late to simply make the codex disappear. So I took the first few pages until I could figure out what to do. You understand that religion is a tinderbox in our part of the world. Old myths are the glue that keeps life in delicate balance." He sat up more erect and blinked several times, his heavy brows nearly touching.

"That's when Zachariah came to me. Told me of his mission. It was worthy: To keep the two religions from destroying each other. Aim their rage toward the West, not each other. He told me this was his charge from the Brotherhood." He drew in a deep breath. "I couldn't believe it at first, but he insisted, told me things had changed. But he was being used, Justine, manipulated, tested. There wasn't any real intention to bring the religions together. The burning churches and his death confirm that."

The mission Zachariah had described to her in Muqattum was false, a cover. She shook her head, still experiencing a little vertigo when she did so. *I knew he had seen the pages, or heard about them . . . and I blamed Amir. Ibrahim let me blame Amir.*

As though reading her thoughts, Ibrahim said, "Amir is a good boy, and he is strong. He can take care of himself. I let him think that Zachariah was out of the country; I told you they were close."

"But why? What difference did it make?"

"Zachariah meant the world to me. Since he was a child. So vulnerable. I couldn't have him blamed for whatever he was about to do. Then Mostafa came to me. When he realized what we had, what the codex represented, he consulted the Imam. I conferred with Father Zein. We all agreed."

Justine could feel her hands grow clammy, chilled, in spite of the heat. She glanced at Andrea who was stiff, clearly anticipating the worst. "Agreed?"

"Everyone's needs seemed to converge. Zachariah's mission to reduce religious conflict. The Imam's denial of a female twin. The Coptic Church's concern for Mary's virginity. Even the Pope agreed. These aims are noble, can't you see? So Mostafa planned for the original codex to disappear. That's why he transferred it to his private safe . . ."

"Mostafa stole the codex from the museum safe?" Justine interrupted in astonishment.

"Something like that," said Ibrahim in flat tones. Emotion, feelings, no longer seemed parts of his being. He appeared numb.

"Then why was Mostafa so startled by the theft?" asked Andrea. "That doesn't make sense."

"Because the codex was stolen from him, taken from his private safe. It will surface somewhere in the antiquities market, probably in Milan, but we've lost control. That is, unless he actually has it and plans to sell it himself."

"You mean no one knows where the original codex is?" demanded Justine.

"No, my dear. So Mostafa has to discredit the team, especially you two, so that when the codex shows up, the scholarly world will give it scant attention. Did you hear his interview last night? He is just getting started. The find will be dismissed as unprovenanced, the translation faulty, performed by an unqualified French woman and a Jew. And . . ."

"Unqualified? Unqualified!" exclaimed Andrea, any tenderness she had earlier exercised toward her old lover disappearing. Her reputation, her very identity, was now at issue. "How could that case be made?"

Ibrahim turned to Andrea, tight muscles causing him exaggerated pain. "By suggesting that your work on the Nag Hammadi codex was influenced by your Gnostic beliefs, my dear, that the Gospel of Thomas was a sham, misinterpreted by a French humanist." Ibrahim's voice remained severed from emotion, as though Andrea had never been an important part of his life.

Andrea turned pale. As one of the foremost linguists in the world, it had never occurred to her that her own credentials would or could be challenged. Being forced to leave Egypt for political reasons was one thing, but having her qualifications dismissed was quite another.

"And Justine has no qualifications to justify her involvement," Ibrahim continued stoically. "The codex can be considered a plant by a godless American, made to further her own interests."

Justine flinched. "These charges can be fought. The dating processes have verified its authenticity," she insisted, keeping her hand on Andrea's, partly to offer support and partly to restrain her. "Or have the data reports disappeared as well?"

"You are still in possession of copies of the data reports, but they represent only dates, not authorship. And to whom would you make your appeal, my dear?" asked Ibrahim, tears forming in his eyes. As he gazed at Justine, emotion began to surge above his numbness. "Let it go, Justine. Please," he begged.

Let it go. Like my father might have? Is that the choice I must make? Justine swallowed hard at the truth of this statement: *To whom would we appeal?* "But why make us leave Egypt?"

"Because the copy is here and you are sure to pursue its further revelation. Are you not? Someone has to take the fall. You're young, Justine, you'll recover." He paused and stared out the window for several moments. "I'm so sorry. Lucrezia's daughter . . . Morgan's daughter . . ." His voice softened, trailing off.

Justine stared at Ibrahim, hoping that his vulnerability might provide an opening. "The copy is with you, then? Here in your office safe? What will happen to it, Ibrahim?"

"It may be destroyed," Ibrahim said laconically, not confirming its whereabouts.

"But surely you can't help Zachariah now. Why destroy the copy?" asked Andrea.

"My grandson is dead. True. But other churches will be burnt. If Christianity suffers any more blows, it may not survive in Egypt, the land of its birth. I'm afraid I can't help you." He dropped his eyes and massaged his right knee.

Disoriented by Ibrahim's rejection, Justine glanced up to find Amir leaning in the doorframe as though it would support his weakened limbs. Their eyes met and held; he made no move to wipe away his tears. "Grandfather, Grandfather," he uttered with the forlorn voice of a child.

CHAPTER 29

T HE DUSTY DRIVE THROUGH DOWNTOWN Cairo and into the suburb of Shoubra was more crowded than usual. It was 10 a.m. Justine still felt stunned
by the conversation with Ibrahim the day before, the unraveling of the story
of the codex, Zachariah's death, and her expulsion from Egypt. She hadn't
been able to reach Amir since she'd seen him in Ibrahim's office.

Now, horns were blaring and a bus driver was hammering his fist on the
roof of her car; she was not moving as expediently through the red light as he
would like. She passively observed that her roof had been dented once again.
A metaphor for my life: repeatedly dented. To what extent have I let this happen?

She stepped out of her Suzuki across from the walled garden of Mataria,
grabbing up once-fresh roses from the worn passenger seat. Guards motioned
her through an alley of towering, decrepit apartment buildings and into a side
entrance. Inside the enclosure, natural spring water bubbled through an ancient stone fountain and down into the collection pool below. An elderly
woman dressed in a green kaftan and white hijab held out her gnarled hand,
catching and sipping the holy waters.

Justine rested her exhausted body on a stone ledge facing the vista and the
ancient sycamore alongside it, its tired, twisted branches held stable by hefty
wooden props. Bare limbs with giant clusters of leaves were smothered at the
top by the unrelenting smog. Jasmine and honeysuckle sprang boldly in irregu-
lar patches from the sacred ground. Mataria, the Holy Family's resting place just
north of downtown Cairo, was well preserved, at least by Egyptian standards.

The site drew a small but steady stream of eager worshipers who knelt at the fountain to solicit favors from the Virgin Mary and Jesus, known as either the Christ or Prophet.

It was said that the Virgin Mary planted the legendary sycamore that had died here only a hundred years ago. But others claimed it was already there when she and the family arrived. Justine judged it highly unlikely that this tree had survived nineteen hundred years. She also knew that Elizabeth's bones would have been disturbed when the old tree fell. Perhaps there had been several trees planted and replanted on this spot, disturbing the bones of the sacred child. Crooked roots, like giant fingers, spreading out to protect the sacred resting place. She rose, stepped forward, and kneeled at the base of the imposter to place her drooping roses on Elizabeth's unmarked grave. She bowed her head and surprised herself by whispering,

"Small and precious Elizabeth,

Left alone in this ancient land made holy by your presence,

Daughter of God, how might you have changed the world? We will never know . . .

Rejoined with your loving family, you can

Rest in peace, little one."

MATARIA, 6 BCE

I cup my unsteady hand and dip it into the healing waters flowing from the grotto spring into the pool below and release the cool liquid onto Elizabeth's burning forehead, dampening her curly black hair. I tremble in panic, for she is so ill, so quiet and still in my arms. Rachel has promised that the waters and sacred leaves of the balsam will heal her.

For three nights and days Elizabeth has been ill, and now she has stopped crying. She refuses my milk, moving in and out of fitful sleep. I walk with her, rocking her gently from side to side, singing the ancient song I learned as a child. Noha watches over the sleeping Jesus in a tent nearby.

This giant sycamore tree provides shade we did not know for many days as we walked southwest across the eastern desert to here, to Mataria, stopping at Tanta

and Zagazig. Warm by day, freezing at night. Here we find flourishing trees, stones moist with moss, lilies and bougainvillea, and meandering meadows alive with green grasses and purple lilacs. Surely this is Eve's garden, although the joy I might have known drowns in my fears for Elizabeth.

I kneel under the canopy of the tree to pray. Joseph and the others join me. "Please God, let us keep our Elizabeth," I plead. "She will serve You with love and charity."

Tears form in Joseph's eyes, as he softly repeats my desperate appeal to our God. I stare at him. Does Joseph know something I am not ready to accept? He is close to God and often knows His will before others.

In the early hours of the morning, Elizabeth dies in my arms. Joseph tries to take her from me, but I won't let go until I wrap her frail body in a blanket of white lace and lay her in the small coffin of balsam wood made by Isaiah and James. The sycamore makes way among its sprawling roots for the small grave. We mark her grave with a mound of stones and a tablet engraved with the name Elizabeth of Nazareth, daughter of Joseph and Mary of Nazareth, Galilee.

Clasping my hands to my chest to control my sobs, I kneel and gaze upward once more. Why? I implore Him. What do You want of me?

Justine's eyes were still closed when a small hand touched her shoulder. She gazed into the face of a little girl in a once-pink dress. Her shining black eyes reflected wisdom beyond her few years. *How old is she? Four? Five?*

The girl touched Justine's cheek, her small thumb gently wiping away a tear.

"What's your name?" Justine asked.

The girl smiled. "Aisha," she said.

"Aisha," repeated Justine. "What a beautiful name. Do you live nearby?"

The girl pointed to the apartment building across the alley. "Would you like to see Mary's home?" she asked, taking Justine by the hand.

Aisha led her north from the fountain toward a small structure, a miniature museum, and a terrace covered with sycamore branches.

"See. See," said Aisha, pointing toward a mural painted on the internal wall. It depicted Mataria as it was envisioned two thousand years ago: lush greenery, a flowing stream, a fertile valley with the divided mountain of Muqattum in the distant background.

"How perfect," Justine said. "How perfect." This was Mary's resting place, but also where she lost her daughter.

Aisha smiled up at her with a sense of ownership, as though she, too, had lived in that ancient valley. "*Shukran*," she said when Justine handed her a cookie from her canvas bag and lifted her into a chair near the terrace wall. Her short legs dangled free as she gave her undivided attention to the cookie.

"*Afwan*," returned Justine, taking the chair beside Aisha. *What was it that called to Aisha from this holy garden? Does she have a mother who guided her?* "What is your mother's name?"

"Miriam," the child said proudly. "She is pretty like you." Aisha slipped off the chair and laid her hand on Justine's knee. "I must go now," she announced, drawing Justine's face toward her so she could plant a kiss on both cheeks.

Justine watched Aisha run toward the side gate of Mataria. The guards paid her no mind.

"I thought I would find you here," said a familiar voice from the lower step of the terrace. Justine tore her gaze from the gate. Amir stood holding tight to a cluster of white lilies.

"Did you see her? The little girl?" Justine asked. She looked into the eyes of the handsome man standing before her. *How is it that he always knows where I am?*

"Who?" Amir asked gently. "I walked straight through the garden and all I saw was you. I didn't see any girl."

"Her name was Aisha," said Justine. *Am I seeing visions? Was she here at all?*

"Like the Prophet Mohammed's wife?"

"Exactly," Justine said with waning confidence. She shook her head once and turned her full attention to Amir. She loved the way his black hair curled over his forehead, how earnest his eyes were. After witnessing his pain at his grandfather's betrayal, she felt an even greater tenderness toward him. His vulnerability was both jarring and reassuring. "You didn't return my calls."

"I'm sorry. I've been busy with my family. Funeral arrangements. How are you?"

"I'll be okay. How are *you*, my friend?" she asked, still distracted by the child's presence. "I'm so sorry about your brother, and your grandfather. If there is anything that I can do . . ."

"Thank you. The service for Zachariah is this afternoon. And my grandfather is his own jury."

She was still for several moments, observing the pain moving through his eyes, deciding whether to ask the next question. "Will you take any action regarding the theft of the codex? Now that you know the story."

His eyes became steely. "I don't think so. To make the full confession public would endanger my grandfather. And assure my dismissal from the Museum. Mostafa is very well connected, and there is little actual evidence, so I don't think Grandfather should carry the responsibility for exposing the thieves, testifying in court." He sat down in the chair beside her and placed a package on the ground at his feet.

"I see," she said, with a tone of mild accusation. "It sounds as though you have doubts, reservations, about bringing the truth to light."

He flinched. "It's not that simple, Justine. I have to consider the consequences of making the whole sordid affair public. My brother's role, my grandfather's. Mostafa's and Father Zein's. For now, I've decided to press for the investigation of Zachariah's murder."

"I understand, Amir. I really do." *What is it that Mom said? "Truth has always been so important to you, Justine." But this . . . Perhaps I've finally encountered a dilemma too complicated for truth.*

Amir was still. "When do you leave?" he finally asked.

"In three days. I'll send my final report back electronically." Her voice was weary. Both of them felt the word "final" to be jarring.

"I'm so sorry. And I'm surprised the UNESCO intervention didn't work, although the forces in charge here are coming from high up in the government." He paused. "You're tired." He reached over and laid his hand on her forearm, leaving it there.

"I've lost faith in myself, Amir. My mother is Egyptian and my father worked here during much of his life, and now their daughter is kicked out at the age of twenty-six."

"You know it's not your fault. You were pursuing truth in a codex you accidentally found."

"But the fact remains that after only a few months in Egypt, I'm being told to leave. And the church our families attended has been burned. Your brother is dead . . ."

Amir sighed. "My deepest regret is that Zachariah and I didn't work through our problems before he died. Now he'll never know that I loved him." His voice grew hoarse as he fought back tears.

Justine reached out and touched his cheek. "You've had so many losses, Amir. Even your faith has been challenged. Do you sometimes feel that Christianity was a fraud all along, teetering on the thin mythology of a virgin and a son of God? Maybe your grandfather was right; some truths are better left undiscovered, unsaid."

"Surely you don't believe that. The pain seems overwhelming right now for both of us, but we need to give ourselves time. The message of Christianity is not propped up like that old tree there. It's a living message of love and forgiveness. I still believe."

She stared at him for several moments. "In these past months, my life has been propped up by miscalculations. What good is an anthropologist without self-trust? My own crisis of faith in myself—let alone whatever god is out there—has really shaken me. I trusted my senses, my intuition, my powers of observation. And I was wrong. I was wrong about your grandfather. About Nasser. Perhaps about everything." She spoke rapidly, almost hysterically, starting to cry. Amir pulled his chair closer and she let her head sink against his shoulder. She shivered.

Amir held her until the sobs subsided, then wiped her wet cheeks with the palm of his hand. "Consider this," he said tenderly. "Your quickness to trust both my grandfather and Nasser came from your father."

"My father? Ah, yes, my father," she whispered, taking a tissue from her canvas bag and blowing her nose. Embarrassed, she sat up straight and smoothed her hair.

"Your father knew and trusted both men—at least you thought he did, so you suspended your own judgments. You accepted both men at face value. I suspect that if your father hadn't known them, or at least you believed he hadn't, you would have assessed both men with circumspection."

"Even your grandfather?"

"Even my grandfather."

Justine's thoughts wove themselves through a tangled emotional terrain. Her features reconfigured themselves into a faint smile. "Thank you," she said, relief rippling through her. Although disappointed that she hadn't made up her own mind, it was better than thinking of herself as a failed anthropologist. *Whatever my professional future holds, my decisions will be different from my father's. I could never withhold information—truth—in the name of religion or politics. Or anything else. The contents of the codex must come to light.*

"What now?" he asked, handing her another tissue.

"Reconnect with my family. Look for a job. Search for the codex."

Without explanation, he handed her the package that sat on the ground beside him. "From Grandfather," he said simply, taking a deep breath, holding her gaze. They both knew what the package contained. "After a while, you'll be allowed to come back to Egypt. I don't want to lose you, Justine." His face was that of an adolescent asking for his first dance, anxious about whether the girl would smile and take his hand—or not.

"Thank you, Amir, thank you." Several moments passed as she hugged the package to her chest and studied his serious face. *It would be so tempting to surrender myself to this attractive man.* "I've so much to figure out, and I'm just beginning to experience what freedom is going to require of me." Justine realized how vague she sounded. "Does that make sense?"

"I think so," he said slowly. His black velvet eyes were damp, holding her gaze. "Where will you go?"

"To Italy. For a while, anyway." She smiled at him as they rose, and let him hold her in his arms for what seemed a very long time before, together, they walked through the garden, past the fountain, toward the entrance. Justine turned one last time, her eyes tenderly embracing the crumbling sycamore. *Goodbye, Elizabeth.*

She had come to Egypt alone and now she was leaving alone, without the exultation she had felt only a few months before. She blinked back tears as she clasped the package from Ibrahim. Wrapped in plain brown paper and tied simply with string, it represented her best hope for a future. She patted the small bundle and smiled.

EPILOGUE

───※───

The Spirit of the Lord is upon me, because He has anointed me to preach the gospel to the poor; he has sent me to heal the brokenhearted, to proclaim liberty to the captives and recovery of sight to the blind, to set at liberty those who are oppressed; to proclaim the acceptable year of the Lord.
—Jesus of Nazareth, The Gospel of Luke, 16:19-31

JERUSALEM, 26 CE

How long has it been? I ask myself as I stand on the rise above Jerusalem facing the disappearing sun on the western horizon that will always be Egypt. Those misty mornings by the Great River, the air that taught me to breathe . . . fragrances floating like sea birds . . . my toes warmed by the golden sand. How long has it been? A lavender haze paints the hills surrounding scattered tents on the rise above the great city. Pilgrims busy themselves preparing for the Passover dinner.

"Mother."

"Jesus? I did not know you would come." I look upon the face of my grown son, whom I have not seen for more than a year. Has he changed? He seems calmer, quieter.

"I am here, Mother. Where are your thoughts?" he asks, standing beside me.

"By the Great River, my son, with your father and his dream. It was on the night of Passover when he said we would return to Jerusalem. Do you remember?"

"I remember. I was frightened."

"Are you frightened now, my son?" I take his arm and lead him into the tent. We sit face to face on my worn carpet, the light from the oil lamp casting our two shadows on a wall of sewn sheepskin.

"God has taken away all fears and I glory in His presence. He has shown me the way." I notice an inner light radiating from his dark eyes.

"The way is glorious, my son. What have you learned?"

"You were my first teacher, Mother. From you I learned patience and love. I learned to open my heart to everything around me. You taught me that birds have a story to tell, as do all who walk God's earth. I found a still place within where I could hear the voice of God and listen for His meaning."

"My deepest desires for you, Jesus." I smile in the presence of a grown man made humble by the gifts he has received.

"And father . . . and Ravi, and the others, they were my teachers too. Father taught me to ask the difficult questions, to endure in the face of hardship. Sometimes I've been my own teacher, taking counsel in silence."

"At times you turned away from me, Jesus," I say without condemnation. "I did not understand."

"Forgive me, Mother. I gave my attention to the ministry and felt that if I let my feelings of duty fill my mind I might not be able to hear God."

"God does not limit His grace, Jesus."

"I did not fear for God, but for my own ability to hear what He wanted."

"Do you still doubt?"

"My doubts traveled with my fears, Mother. I am at peace."

"That is good. I've harbored many doubts in my life, but have found what God wants. I, too, am at peace."

"I am sorry I was not with you when Father died. I am grateful that James and the others could be by your side," he says, his face shadowed by the shifting light.

"It was painful, Jesus. I suffered until God assured me I was not alone. Ravi . . . he is with you?"

"Ravi is a loyal witness. Three summers ago he moved from India to share in my calling. He wanted to become a Jew and a Palestinian, so he changed his name. He is now Judas Iscariot. We are brothers, Mother. Our minds are one." He tilts his head to better bring his features into my sight.

"Your twin soul, Jesus?"

"At times, I think he is the only one, other than my two Marys, who understands me. I must ask you, whatever happens, that you trust God and trust me."

"I came to trust you many years ago, my son. You have grown into a man of whom I am most proud. Your father would be proud too."

Jesus smiles, reaching out to hold my hand.

A third shadow flickers across the tent. We turn to find Mary of Magdalene stepping inside.

"We are waiting for you, Jesus," she says.

HISTORICAL NOTE

———∞∞∞———

THE COPTIC CHRISTIANS OF EGYPT, as well as the Muslims, believe that the Virgin Mary, her son Jesus, her husband Joseph, and their friends took flight into Egypt immediately after the birth of Jesus. Many believe that James and perhaps other children belonging to Joseph were with them. The Gospel of Matthew tells us that the Angel Gabriel appeared to Joseph and said: "Rise, take the child and his mother, and flee to Egypt." According to the gospel, King Herod, having heard that the Messiah, King of the Jews, had been born, ordered the slaughter of all infant boys under the age of two. Herod wanted to make sure that no divine king would challenge his own son's succession or the preeminence of Rome. According to history, however, the senior Herod died just before the birth of Jesus, so it would have been his son, Herod Antipas, who carried out the horrendous deed.

Arriving in Egypt with the baby Jesus in their arms, the travelers crisscrossed the Nile, stopping at twenty-eight towns—now home to grand churches and monasteries that welcome thousands of pilgrims each year—as they went. The family kept moving, worried that Herod's soldiers were pursuing them. The Holy Family is believed by Coptic Christians to have resided for a short while—perhaps six months—in a cave that is now a crypt beneath St. Sergius Church in Babylon, the ancient name for Old Cairo.

Matthew also tells us that the Angel Gabriel appeared once more to Joseph and said: "Arise and take the young child and his mother, and go into the land of Israel; for they are dead which sought the young child's life." By that time,

Coptic Christians believe, the family had lived in Egypt for less than three years; Muslims, however, believe the Holy Family remained in the land for as long as seven years. *The Cairo Codex* proposes that the family lived in the cave in Babylon well into Jesus' eighth year.

ACKNOWLEDGEMENTS

—◦◦◦◦—

IN WRITING *THE CAIRO CODEX*, I HAD THE privilege to witness the evolving history of Egypt through my own eyes, as well as through the eyes of many Egyptian friends and colleagues. These are some of the Egyptians who made this novel possible: Ambassador Hussein and Nevine Hassouna; Dr. Kawsar Kouchok; Madam Ansaf Azziz; Hanna Ibrahim and Laurence Amin; Dr. Waguida El Bakary; Nadia El Araby and her daughters; Dr. Magda Laurence; Mary Megalli; Dr. Pam El Shayeb; Dr. Mohammed Rabei; Vice-President of Egypt Fathi Sorour; Mohammed Khattab; Hassan Osman; Supreme Director of Antiquities, Zahi Hawass; Dr. Malek Zaalouk; Baher El Awady; the staff of the Centre for Curriculum and Instructional Materials Development, the UNESCO staff, and the staff of the Alexandria Library. I especially want to thank Dr. Samira Hradsky, who served as the Director of North African Affairs for the Education Development Center when I was employed as an educational consultant in Egypt. The voices of hundreds of generous Egyptians resonate in my mind: taxi drivers and shopkeepers, teachers and boabs, priests and imams, tour guides and housemaids, professors and grocers, diplomats and artists. I thank them all.

American friends and family members graciously volunteered to read early drafts of this novel and to provide invaluable insights and feedback. I wish to thank Mary Gardner, who helped with the research as well; Bob and Barbara Blackburn; my son, Tod Green; Zane and Janet Todd, my brother and sister-in-law; Delmo Della Dora; Ellen Johnson, our daughter; Rita King; and Judy Vandergrift.

I especially want to thank my writing coaches, Susan Efros and Ida Egli. Caitlin Alexander, editor, brought *The Cairo Codex* to fruition.

Most deeply, I want to thank my husband, Morgan Lambert, whose love, patience, editorial talents, and wisdom made the writing of this work a pleasure that we shared as we spent our incredible years together in Egypt and in California.

Linda Lambert, Ed.D.
The Sea Ranch, California
www.lindalambert.com

ABOUT THE AUTHOR

LINDA LAMBERT, ED.D. IS PROFESSOR Emeritus from California State University, East Bay, and a full time author of novels and texts on leadership. During Linda's career she has served as social worker, teacher, principal, district and county directors of adult learning programs, as well as university professor, state department envoy to Egypt, and international consultant. Her international consultancies in leadership have taken her to the Middle East, England, Thailand, Mexico, Canada, and Malaysia. Linda is the author of dozens of articles and lead author of *The Constructivist Leader* (1995, 2002), *Who Will Save Our Schools* (1997), and *Women's Ways of Leading* (2009); she is the author of *Building Leadership Capacity in Schools* (1998) and *Leadership Capacity for Lasting School Improvement* (2003). *The Cairo Codex* is the first novel in a trilogy. She lives with her husband, Morgan, a retired school superintendent, on the Sea Ranch, California.